THE

Complete Tales

OF

Nikolai Gogol

Volume 2

THE

Complete Tales

OF

Nikolai Gogol

Volume 2

*Edited, with an introduction
and notes, by*

LEONARD J. KENT

❖❖❖❖❖❖❖❖❖

*The Constance Garnett translation has been
revised throughout by the editor*

THE UNIVERSITY OF CHICAGO PRESS
Chicago and London

Published by arrangement with Chatto & Windus Ltd. — The Hogarth
Press Ltd., London and A. P. Watt Ltd.

Portions of this book are adapted from the following translations of
Nikolai Gogol by Constance Garnett: *Evenings on a Farm near Dikanka*
© 1926 by Constance Garnett, renewed 1954: *The Overcoat and Other
Stories* © 1923 by Constance Garnett, renewed 1950.

The University of Chicago Press, Chicago 60637
The University of Chicago Press, Ltd. London

© 1964 by Random House
© 1985 by The University of Chicago
University of Chicago Press edition 1985
All rights reserved. Published 1985
Printed in the United States of America

14 13 12 11 10 09 08 07 06   8 9 10 11 12

Library of Congress Cataloging-in-Publication Data

Gogol', Nikolaĭ Vasil'evich, 1809–1852.
    The complete tales of Nikolai Gogol.

    "The Constance Garnett translation has been revised throughout by the
editor."
    Bibliography: p.
    I. Kent, Leonard J., 1930–   II. Title.
PG3333.A15   1985   891.73'3   84-16221
ISBN 0-226-30068-4 (vol. 1)
        0-226-30069-2 (vol. 2)

⊗ The paper used in this publication meets the minimum requirements
of the American National Standard for Information Sciences—Permanence
of Paper for Printed Library Materials, ANSI Z39.48-1992.

For VALERIE

CONTENTS of Volume I

CONTENTS

ABOUT THE TRANSLATION

The decision made twenty years ago to use the Constance Garnett translation as the basic text for a collected edition seems now even more obvious and correct than it did then. Despite an infrequent mis-reading or Victorianism, her work remains remarkable; indeed, in the context of almost all subsequent efforts, her grace, eloquence, and verve now seem even closer to the tone and letter, the very spirit of Gogol. Then, too, did she not have the marvelous good sense and rare taste to preserve the interrelated thematic cycles without which others "make mincemeat of the author's intentions"?

The thousands of revisions made earlier have been augmented by a far more modest number of new ones. The effort to keep faith with the soul of the original continues. To this end, among other things, Cossacks have still not learned to say "Hi!" All the Agafyas and Matveys have refused to become Agathas and Matthews. The medium of exchange remains kopeks and rubles. (Indeed, could one ever again sleep the sleep of the truly innocent if Akaky Akakyevich—in a Penguin edition, almost certainly—was but once to shriek, "Sixteen quid for an overcoat!"?)

L. J. K.

THE

Complete Tales

OF

Nikolai Gogol

Volume 2

MIRGOROD

OLD-WORLD LANDOWNERS

I am very fond of the modest manner of life of those solitary owners of remote villages, who in Little Russia are commonly called "old-fashioned," who are like tumbledown picturesque little houses, delightful in their simplicity and complete unlikeness to the new smooth buildings whose walls have not yet been discolored by the rain, whose roof is not yet covered with green lichen, and whose porch does not display its red bricks through the peeling stucco. I like sometimes to descend for a moment into that extraordinarily secluded life in which not one desire flits beyond the palisade surrounding the little courtyard, beyond the hurdle of the orchard filled with plum and apple trees, beyond the village huts surrounding it, lying all aslant under the shade of willows, elders, and pear trees. The life of their modest owners is so quiet, so quiet, that for a moment one is lost in forgetfulness and imagines that those passions, desires, and restless promptings of the evil spirit that trouble the world have no real existence, and that you have only beheld them in some lurid dazzling dream. I can see now the low-pitched little house with the gallery of little blackened wooden posts running right around it, so that in hail or storm they could close the shutters without being wetted by the rain. Behind it a fragrant bird-cherry, rows of dwarf fruit trees, drowned in a sea of red cherries and amethyst plums, covered with lead-colored bloom; a spreading maple in the shade of which a rug is laid to rest on; in front of the house a spacious courtyard of short fresh grass with a little pathway trodden from the store-house to the kitchen and from the kitchen to the master's apartments; a long-necked goose drinking water with young goslings soft as down around her; a palisade hung with strings of dried pears and apples and rugs put out to air; a cartful of melons standing by the storehouse; an unharnessed ox lying lazily beside it— they all have an inexpressible charm for me, perhaps because I no longer see them and because everything from which we are parted is dear to us.

Be that as it may, at the very moment when my chaise was driving up to the steps of that little house, my soul passed into a wonderfully sweet and serene mood; the horses galloped merrily up to the steps; the coachman very tranquilly clambered down from the box and filled his pipe as though he had reached home; even the barking set up by the phlegmatic Rovers, Pontos, and Neros was pleasant to my ears. But best of all I liked the owners of these modest little nooks—the little old men and women who came out solicitously to meet me. I can see their faces sometimes even now among fashionable dress coats in the noise and crowd, and then I sink into a half-dreaming state, and the past rises up before me. Their faces always betray such kindness, such hospitality and singleheartedness, that unconsciously one renounces, for a brief spell at least, all ambitious dreams, and imperceptibly passes with all one's heart into this lowly bucolic existence.

To this day, I cannot forget two old people of a past age, now, alas! no more. To this day I am full of regret, and it sends a strange pang to my heart when I imagine myself going sometime again to their old, now deserted dwelling, and seeing the heap of ruined huts, the pond choked with weeds, an overgrown ditch on the spot where the little house stood—and nothing more. It is sad! I am sad at the thought ! But let me turn to my story.

Afanasy Ivanovich Tovstogub and his wife Pulkheria Ivanovna, as the neighboring peasants called her, were the old people of whom I was beginning to tell you. If I were a painter and wanted to portray Philemon and Baucis[1] on canvas, I could choose no other models. Afanasy Ivanovich was sixty. Pulkheria Ivanovna was fifty-five. Afanasy Ivanovich was tall, always wore a camlet-covered sheepskin, used to sit bent over, and was invariably almost smiling, even though he was telling a story or simply listening. Pulkheria Ivanovna was rather grave and scarcely ever laughed; but in her face and eyes there was so much kindness, so much readiness to regale you with the best of all they had, that you would certainly have found a smile superfluously sweet for her kind face. The faint wrinkles on their faces were drawn so charmingly that an artist would surely have stolen them; it seemed as though one could read in them their whole life, clear and serene—the life led by the old, typically Little Russian, simplehearted and at the same time wealthy families, always such a contrast to the meaner sort of Little Russians who, struggling up from making tar and petty trading, swarm like locusts in the law courts and public offices, fleece their fellow villagers of their last kopek, inundate Petersburg with pettifogging attorneys, make their pile at last, and solemnly add V to surnames ending in O.[2] No, they, like all the old-fashioned, primitive Little Russian families, were utterly different from such paltry contemptible creatures.

One could not look without sympathy at their mutual love. They never addressed each other familiarly, but always with formality. "Was it you who broke the chair, Afanasy Ivanovich?" "Never mind, don't be cross, Pulkheria Ivanovna, it was I." They had had no children, and so all their affection was concentrated on each other. At one time in his youth Afanasy Ivanovich was in the service and had been a lieutenant major; but that was very long ago, that was all over, Afanasy Ivanovich himself scarcely ever recalled it. Afanasy Ivanovich was married at thirty when he was a fine fellow and wore an embroidered coat; he even eloped rather neatly with Pulkheria Ivanovna, whose relations opposed their

---

[1] The devoted couple, in Greek legend, who graciously supplied food and shelter to Zeus and Hermes after they had been turned away by others, and, as a result of their kindness, survived the flood Zeus unleashed to destroy their neighbors. (ed.)

[2] In an effort to be considered a Great Russian. Ukrainian surnames usually end in "o," Russian names in "v." (ed.)

marriage, but he thought very little about that now—at any rate, he never spoke of it.

All these faraway extraordinary adventures had been followed by a peaceful and secluded life, by the soothing and harmonious dreams that you enjoy when you sit on a wooden balcony over-looking the garden while a delicious rain keeps up a luxurious sound pattering on the leaves, flowing in gurgling streams, and in-ducing a drowsiness in your limbs, while a rainbow hides behind the trees and in the form of a half-broken arch gleams in the sky with seven soft colors—or when you are swayed in a carriage that drives between green bushes while the quail of the steppes calls and the fragrant grass mingled with ears of wheat and wild flow-ers thrusts itself in at the carriage doors, flicking you pleasantly on the hands and face.

Afanasy Ivanovich always listened with a pleasant smile to the guests who visited him; sometimes he talked himself, but more often he asked questions. He was not one of those old people who bore one with everlasting praise of old days or denunciation of the new: on the contrary, as he questioned you, he showed great inter-est and curiosity about the circumstances of your own life, your failures and successes, in which all kindhearted old people show an interest, though it is a little like the curiosity of a child who ex-amines the seal on your watch at the same time as he talks to you. Then his face, one may say, was breathing with kindliness.

The rooms of the little house in which our old people lived were small and low-pitched, as they usually are in the houses of old-world people. In each room there was an immense stove which covered nearly a third of the floor space. These rooms were terribly hot, for both Afanasy Ivanovich and Pulkheria Ivanovna liked warmth. The stoves were all heated from the outer room, which was always filled almost up to the ceiling with straw, commonly used in Little Russia instead of firewood.[3] The crackle and flare of this burning straw made the outer room exceedingly pleasant on a winter's evening when ardent young men, chilled with the pursuit of some dark charmer, ran in, rubbing their hands. The walls of the room were adorned with a few pictures in old-fashioned nar-row frames. I am convinced that their owners had themselves long ago forgotten what they represented, and if some of them had been

---

[3] *Kiziak*, pressed brick of manure and straw, was the common fuel. (ed.)

taken away, they would probably not have noticed it. There were two big portraits painted in oils. One depicted a bishop, the other Peter III; a flyblown Duchesse de La Vallière[4] looked out from a narrow frame. Around the windows and above the doors there were numbers of little pictures which one grew used to looking upon as spots on the wall and so never examined them. In almost all the rooms the floor was of clay but cleanly painted and kept with a neatness with which probably no parquet floor in a wealthy house, lazily swept by sleepy gentlemen in livery, has ever been kept.

Pulkheria Ivanovna's room was all surrounded with chests and boxes, big and little. Numbers of little bags and sacks of flower seeds, vegetable seeds, and melon seeds hung on the walls. Numbers of balls of different-colored wools and rags of old-fashioned gowns made half a century ago were stored in the little chests and between the little chests in the corners. Pulkheria Ivanovna was a notable housewife and saved everything, though sometimes she could not herself have said to what use it could be put afterwards.

But the most remarkable thing in the house was the singing of the doors. As soon as morning came, the singing of the doors could be heard all over the house. I cannot say why it was they sang—whether the rusty hinges were to blame for it or whether the mechanic who made them had concealed some secret in them—but it was remarkable that each door had its own voice. The door leading to the bedroom sang in the thinnest falsetto, and the door into the dining room in a husky bass; but the one on the outer room gave out a strange cracked and at the same time moaning sound, so that as one listened to it one heard distinctly: "Holy Saints! I am freezing!" I know that many people very much dislike this sound; but I am very fond of it, and if here I sometimes happen to hear a door creak, it seems at once to bring me a whiff of the country: the low-pitched little room lighted by a candle in an old-fashioned candlestick; supper already on the table; a dark May night peeping in from the garden through the open window at the table laid with knives and forks; the nightingale flooding garden, house, and far-away river with its trilling song; the tremor and rustle of branches, and, my God! what a long string of memories stretches before me then! . . .

The chairs in the room were massive wooden ones such as were

---

[4] (1644-1710), mistress of Louis XIV. (ed.)

common in the old days; they all had high carved backs and were without any kind of varnish or stain; they were not even upholstered, and were rather like the chairs on which bishops sit to this day. Little triangular tables in the corners and square ones before the sofa, and the mirror in its thin gold frame carved with leaves which the flies had covered with black spots; in front of the sofa a rug with birds on it that looked like flowers and flowers that looked like birds: that was almost all the furnishing of the unpretentious little house in which my old people lived. The maids' room was packed full of young girls, and girls who were not young, in striped petticoats; Pulkheria Ivanovna sometimes gave them some trifling sewing or set them to prepare the fruit, but for the most part they ran off to the kitchen and slept. Pulkheria Ivanovna thought it necessary to keep them in the house and looked strictly after their morals; but, to her great surprise, many months never passed without the waist of some girl or other growing much larger than usual. This seemed the more surprising as there was scarcely a bachelor in the house with the exception of the houseboy, who used to go about barefoot in a gray tail coat, and, if he were not eating, was sure to be asleep. Pulkheria Ivanovna usually scolded the erring damsel and punished her severely so that it might not happen again.

A terrible number of flies were always buzzing on the windowpanes, above whose notes rose the deep bass of a bumblebee, sometimes accompanied by the shrill plaint of a wasp; then, as soon as candles were brought, the swarm went to bed and covered the whole ceiling with a black cloud.

Afanasy Ivanovich took very little interest in farming his land, though he did drive out sometimes to the mowers and reapers and watched their labors rather attentively; the whole burden of management rested upon Pulkheria Ivanovna. Pulkheria Ivanovna's housekeeping consisted in continually locking up and unlocking the storeroom, and in salting, drying, and preserving countless masses of fruits and vegetables. Her house was very much like a chemical laboratory. There was always a fire built under an apple tree; and a cauldron or a copper pan of jam, jelly, or fruit cheese made with honey, sugar, and I don't remember what else, was scarcely ever taken off the iron tripod on which it stood. Under another tree the coachman was forever distilling in a copper retort vodka with peach leaves, or bird-cherry flowers or centaury or cherry stones, and at the end of the process was utterly unable to control his tongue, jabbered such nonsense that Pulkheria Ivanovna could make nothing of it, and had to go away to sleep it off in the kitchen. Such a quantity of all this stuff was boiled, salted, and dried that the whole courtyard would probably have been drowned in it at last (for Pulkheria Ivanovna always liked to prepare a store for the future in addition to all that was thought necessary for use) if the larger half of it had not been eaten up by the serf girls, who, stealing into the storeroom, would overeat themselves so frightfully that they were moaning and complaining of stomach-ache all day. Pulkheria Ivanovna had little chance of looking after the tilling of the fields or other branches of husbandry. The steward, in conjunction with the village elder, robbed them in a merciless fashion. They had adopted the habit of treating their master's forest land as though it were their own; they made numbers of sleds and sold them at the nearest fair; moreover, all the thick oaks they sold to the neighboring Cossacks to be cut down for building mills. On only one occasion did Pulkheria Ivanovna desire to inspect her forests. For this purpose a chaise was brought out with immense leather aprons which, as soon as the coachman shook the reins, and the horses, who had served in the militia, set off, filled the air with strange sounds, so that a flute and a tambourine and a drum all seemed suddenly audible; every nail and iron bolt clanked so loudly that even at the mill it could be heard that the mistress was driving out of the yard, though the distance was fully a mile and a half. Pulkheria Ivanovna could not help noticing the terrible devastation in the forest and the loss of the oaks, which even in childhood she had known to be a hundred years old.

"Why is it, Nichipor," she said, addressing her steward who was present, "that the oaks have been so thinned? Mind that the hair on your head does not grow so thin."

"Why is it?" the steward said. "They have fallen down! They have simply fallen: struck by lightning, gnawed by maggots—they have fallen, lady." Pulkheria Ivanovna was completely satisfied with this answer, and on arriving home merely gave orders that the watch should be doubled in the garden near the Spanish cherry trees and the big winter pears.

These worthy rulers, the steward and the elder, considered it quite superfluous to take all the flour to their master's granaries; they thought that the latter would have quite enough with half, and what is more they took to the granaries the half that had begun to grow moldy or had got wet and been rejected at the fair. But however much the steward and the elder stole; however gluttonously everyone on the place ate, from the housekeeper to the pigs, who guzzled an immense number of plums and apples and often pushed the tree with their snouts to shake a perfect rain of fruit down from it; however much the sparrows and crows pecked; however many presents all the servants carried to their friends in other villages, even hauling off old linen and yarn from the storerooms, all of which went into the everflowing stream, that is, to the tavern; however much was stolen by visitors, phlegmatic coachmen, and flunkeys, yet the blessed earth produced everything in such abundance, and Afanasy Ivanovich and Pulkheria Ivanovna wanted so little, that this terrible robbery made no perceptible impression on their prosperity.

Both the old people were very fond of good food, as was the old-fashioned tradition of old-world landowners. As soon as the sun had risen (they always got up early) and as soon as the doors began their varied concert, they were sitting down to a little table, drinking coffee. When he had finished his coffee Afanasy Ivanovich would go out into the porch and, shaking his handkerchief, say: "Kish, kish! Get off the steps, geese!" In the yard he usually came across the steward. As a rule he entered into conversation with him, questioned him about the field labors with the greatest minuteness, made observations, and gave orders which would have impressed anyone with his extraordinary knowledge of farming; and no novice would have dared to dream that he could steal from such a sharp-eyed master. But the steward was a wily old bird: he knew how he must answer, and, what is more, he knew how to manage the land.

After this Afanasy Ivanovich would go back indoors, and going up to his wife would say: "Well, Pulkheria Ivanovna, isn't it time perhaps for a snack of something?"

"What would you like to have now, Afanasy Ivanovich? Would you like biscuits with lard or poppy-seed pies, or perhaps salted mushrooms?"

"Perhaps mushrooms or pies," answered Afanasy Ivanovich; and the table would at once be laid with a cloth, pies, and mushrooms.

An hour before dinner Afanasy Ivanovich would have another snack, would empty an old-fashioned silver goblet of vodka, would eat mushrooms, various sorts of dried fish, and so on. They sat down to dinner at twelve o'clock. Besides the dishes and sauce bowl there stood on the table numbers of pots with closely covered lids so that no appetizing masterpiece of old-fashioned cookery might be spoiled. At dinner the conversation usually turned on subjects closely related to the dinner. "I think this porridge," Afanasy Ivanovich would say, "is a little bit burned. Don't you think so, Pulkheria Ivanovna?" "No, Afanasy Ivanovich. You put a little more butter in it, then it won't taste burned, or have some of this mushroom sauce; pour that over it!" "Perhaps," said Afanasy Ivanovich, passing his plate. "Let us try how it would be."

After dinner Afanasy Ivanovich went to lie down for an hour, after which Pulkheria Ivanovna would take a sliced watermelon and say: "Taste what a nice melon, Afanasy Ivanovich."

"Don't you be so sure of it, Pulkheria Ivanovna, because it is red in the middle," Afanasy Ivanovich would say, taking a good slice. "There are some that are red and are not nice."

But the melon quickly disappeared. After that Afanasy Ivanovich would eat a few pears and go for a walk in the garden with Pulkheria Ivanovna. On returning home Pulkheria Ivanovna would go to look after household affairs, while he sat under an awning turned toward the courtyard and watched the storeroom continually displaying and concealing its interior and the serf girls pushing one another as they brought in or carried out heaps of trifles of all sorts in wooden boxes, sieves, trays, and other receptacles for holding fruit. A little afterward he sent for Pulkheria Ivanovna, or went himself to her and said: "What shall I have to eat, Pulkheria Ivanovna?"

"What would you like?" Pulkheria Ivanovna would say. "Shall I go and tell them to bring you the fruit dumpling I ordered them to keep especially for you?"

"That would be nice," Afanasy Ivanovich would answer.

"Or perhaps you would like some jelly?"

"That would be good too," Afanasy Ivanovich would answer. Then all this was promptly brought him and duly eaten.

Before supper Afanasy Ivanovich would have another snack of something. At half past nine they sat down to supper. After supper they at once went to bed, and complete stillness reigned in this active and at the same time tranquil home.

The room in which Afanasy Ivanovich and Pulkheria Ivanovna

slept was so hot that not many people could have stayed in it for
several hours; but Afanasy Ivanovich, in order to be even hotter,
used to sleep on the platform of the stove, though the intense heat
made him get up several times in the night and walk about the room.
Sometimes Afanasy Ivanovich would moan as he walked about the
room. Then Pulkheria Ivanovna would ask: "What are you groaning for, Afanasy Ivanovich?"

"Goodness only knows, Pulkheria Ivanovna; I feel as though I
have a little stomach-ache," said Afanasy Ivanovich.

"Hadn't you better eat something, Afanasy Ivanovich?"

"I don't know whether it would be good, Pulkheria Ivanovna!
What should I eat, though?"

"Sour milk or some dried stewed pears."

"Perhaps I might try it, anyway," said Afanasy Ivanovich.

A sleepy serf girl went off to rummage in the cupboards, and
Afanasy Ivanovich would eat a plateful, after which he usually said:
"Now it does seem to be better."

Sometimes, if it was fine weather and rather warm indoors,
Afanasy Ivanovich, being in good spirits, liked to make fun of Pulkheria Ivanovna and talk of something.

"Pulkheria Ivanovna," he would say, "what if our house were
suddenly burned down, where should we go?"

"Heaven forbid!" Pulkheria Ivanovna would say, crossing herself.

"But suppose our house were burned down, where should we
go then?"

"God knows what you are saying, Afanasy Ivanovich! How is it
possible that our house could be burned down? God will not permit it."

"Well, but if it were burned down?"

"Oh, then we would move into the kitchen. You should have for
the time the little room that the housekeeper has now."

"But if the kitchen were burned too?"

"What next! God will preserve us from such a calamity as having
both house and kitchen burned down at the same time! Well, then
we would move into the storeroom while a new house was being
built."

"And if the storeroom were burned?"

"God knows what you are saying! I don't want to listen to you!
It's a sin to say it, and God will punish you for saying such things!"

And Afanasy Ivanovich, pleased at having made fun of Pulkheria Ivanovna, sat smiling in his chair.

But the old couple seemed most of all interesting to me on the occasions when they had guests. Then everything in their house assumed a different aspect. These good-natured people lived, one may say, for visitors. The best of everything they had was all brought out. They vied with each other in trying to regale you with everything their husbandry produced. But what pleased me most of all was that in their solicitude there was no trace of unctuousness. This hospitality and readiness to please was so gently expressed in their faces, was so in keeping with them, that the guests could not help falling in with their wishes, which were the expression of the pure serene simplicity of their kindly guileless souls. This hospitality was something quite different from the way in which a clerk of some government office who has been helped in his career by your efforts entertains you, calling you his benefactor and cringing at your feet. The visitor was on no account to leave on the same day: he absolutely had to stay the night. "How could you set off on such a long journey at so late an hour!" Pulkheria Ivanovna always said. (The guest usually lived two or three miles away.)

"Of course not," Afanasy Ivanovich said. "You never know what may happen: robbers or other evil-minded men may attack you."

"God preserve us from robbers!" said Pulkheria Ivanovna. "And why talk of such things at night? It's not a question of robbers, but it's dark, it's not fit for driving at all. Besides, your coachman . . . I know your coachman, he is so frail, and such a little man, any horse would be too much for him; and besides he has probably had a drop by now and is asleep somewhere." And the guest was forced to remain; but the evening spent in the low-pitched hot room, the kindly, warming and soporific talk, the steam rising from the food on the table, always nourishing and cooked in first-rate fashion, was compensation for him. I can see as though it were today Afanasy Ivanovich sitting bent in his chair with his invariable smile, listening to his visitor with attention and even delight! Often the talk touched on politics. The guest, who also very rarely left his village, would often with a significant air and a mysterious expression trot out his conjectures, telling them that the French had a secret agreement with the English to let Bonaparte out again in order to attack Russia, or would simply prophesy war in the near future; and then Afanasy Ivanovich, pretending not to look at

Pulkheria Ivanovna, would often say: "I think I shall go to the war myself; why shouldn't I go to the war?"

"There he goes again!" Pulkheria Ivanovna interrupted. "Don't you believe him," she said, turning to the guest. "How could an old man like him go to the war! The first soldier would shoot him. Yes, he would! He'd simply take aim and shoot him."

"Well," said Afanasy Ivanovich, "and I'll shoot him."

"Just hear how he talks!" Pulkheria Ivanovna interrupted. "How could he go to the war! And his pistols have been rusty for years and are lying in the cupboard. You should just see them: why, they'd explode from the gunpowder before they'd fire a shot. And he'd blow off his hands and disfigure his face and be miserable for the rest of his days!"

"Well," said Afanasy Ivanovich, "I'd buy myself new weapons; I'll take my saber or a Cossack lance."

"That's all nonsense. An idea comes into his head and he begins talking!" Pulkheria Ivanovna interrupted with some annoyance. "I know he is only joking, but yet I don't like to hear it. That's the way he always talks; sometimes one listens and listens till it frightens one."

But Afanasy Ivanovich, pleased at having scared Pulkheria Ivanovna a little, laughed sitting bent in his chair. Pulkheria Ivanovna was most attractive to me when she was taking a guest in to lunch. "This," she would say, taking a cork out of a bottle, "is vodka distilled with milfoil and sage—if anyone has a pain in the shoulder blades or loins, it is very good; now this is distilled with centaury— if anyone has a ringing in the ears or a rash on the face, it is very good; and this now is distilled with peach stones—take a glass, isn't it a delicious smell? If anyone getting up in the morning knocks his head against a corner of the cupboard or a table and a bump comes up on his forehead, he has only to drink one glass of it before dinner and it takes it away entirely; it all passes off that very minute, as though it had never been there at all." Then followed a similar account of the other bottles, which all had some healing properties. After burdening the guest with all these remedies she would lead him up to a number of dishes. "These are mushrooms with wild thyme! These are with cloves and hazelnuts! A Turkish woman taught me to salt them in the days when we still had Turkish prisoners here. She was such a nice woman, and it was not noticeable at all that she professed the Turkish religion: she went about almost exactly as we do; only she wouldn't eat pork; she said it was forbidden somewhere in their law. And these are mushrooms prepared with black-currant leaves and nutmeg! And these are big pumpkins: it's the first time I have pickled them in vinegar; I don't know what they'll be like! I learned the secret from Father Ivan; first of all you must lay some oak leaves in a tub and then sprinkle with pepper and saltpeter and then put in the flower of the hawk-weed, take the flowers and strew them in with stalks uppermost. And here are the little pies; these are cheese pies. And those are the ones Afanasy Ivanovich is very fond of, made with cabbage and buckwheat."

"Yes," Afanasy Ivanovich would add, "I am very fond of them; they are soft and a little sourish."

As a rule Pulkheria Ivanovna was in the best of spirits when she had guests. Dear old woman! She was entirely devoted to her visitors. I liked staying with them, and although I overate fearfully, as indeed all their visitors did, and though that was very bad for me, I was always glad to go and see them. But I wonder whether the very air of Little Russia has not some peculiar property that promotes digestion; for if anyone were to venture to eat in that way here,[5] there is no doubt he would find himself lying in his coffin instead of his bed.

Good old people! But my account of them is approaching a very melancholy incident which transformed forever the life of that peaceful nook. This incident is the more impressive because it arose from such an insignificant cause. But such is the strange order of things; trifling causes have always given rise to great events, and on the other hand great undertakings frequently end in insignificant results. Some military leader rallies all the forces of his state, carries on a war for several years, his generals cover themselves with glory; and in the end it all results in gaining a bit of land in which there is not room to plant a potato; while sometimes two sausage makers of two towns quarrel over some nonsense, and in the end the towns are drawn into the quarrel, then villages, and then the whole kingdom. But let us abandon these reflections: they are out of keeping here; besides I am not fond of reflections, so long as they get no further than being reflections.

Pulkheria Ivanovna had a little gray cat, which almost always lay

---

[5] I.e., St. Petersburg. (ed.)

curled up at her feet. Pulkheria Ivanovna sometimes stroked her and with one finger scratched her neck, which the spoiled cat stretched as high as she could. I cannot say that Pulkheria Ivanovna was excessively fond of her; she was simply attached to her from being used to seeing her about. Afanasy Ivanovich, however, often teased her about her affection for it.

"I don't know, Pulkheria Ivanovna, what you find in the cat: what use is she? If you had a dog, then it would be a different matter: one can take a dog out shooting, but what use is a cat?"

"Oh, be quiet, Afanasy Ivanovich," said Pulkheria Ivanovna. "You are simply fond of talking and nothing else. A dog is not clean, a dog makes a mess, a dog breaks everything, while a cat is a quiet creature: she does no harm to anyone."

Cats and dogs were all the same to Afanasy Ivanovich, however; he only said it to tease Pulkheria Ivanovna a little.

Beyond their garden they had a big forest which had been completely spared by the enterprising steward, perhaps because the sound of the ax would have reached the ears of Pulkheria Ivanovna. It was wild and neglected, the old tree stumps were covered with overgrown nut bushes and looked like the feathered legs of trumpeter pigeons. Wild cats lived in this forest. Wild forest cats must not be confused with the bold rascals who run about on the roofs of houses; in spite of their fierce disposition the latter, being in cities, are far more civilized than the inhabitants of the forest. Unlike the town cats, the latter are for the most part shy and gloomy creatures; they are always gaunt and lean; they mew in a coarse, uncultured voice. They sometimes scratch their way underground into the very storehouses and steal bacon; they even penetrate into the kitchen, springing suddenly in at the open window when they see that the cook has gone off into the high grass.

In fact, they are unacquainted with any noble sentiments; they live by plunder, and murder little sparrows in their nests. These cats had for a long time past sniffed through a hole under the storehouse at Pulkheria Ivanovna's gentle little cat and at last they enticed her away, as a company of soldiers entices a silly peasant girl. Pulkheria Ivanovna noticed the disappearance of the cat and sent to look for her; but the cat was not found. Three days passed; Pulkheria Ivanovna was sorry to lose her, but at last forgot her. One day when she was inspecting her vegetable garden and was returning with fresh green cucumbers plucked by her own hand for

Afanasy Ivanovich, her ear was caught by a most pitiful mew. As though by instinct she called: "Puss, puss!" and all at once her gray cat, lean and skinny, came out from the high grass; it was evident that she had not tasted food for several days. Pulkheria Ivanovna went on calling her, but the cat stood mewing and did not venture to come close; it was clear that she had grown very wild during her absence. Pulkheria Ivanovna still went on calling the cat, who timidly followed her right up to the fence. At last, seeing the old familiar places, she even went indoors. Pulkheria Ivanovna at once ordered milk and meat to be brought her and, sitting before her, enjoyed the greediness with which her poor little favorite swallowed piece after piece and lapped up the milk. The little gray fugitive grew fatter almost before her eyes and soon did not eat so greedily. Pulkheria Ivanovna stretched out her hand to stroke her, but the ungrateful creature had evidently grown too much accustomed to the ways of wild cats, or had adopted the romantic principle that poverty with love is better than life in a palace (and, indeed, the wild cats were as poor as church mice); anyway, she sprang out of a window and not one of the house serfs could catch her.

The old lady sank into thought. "It was my death coming for me!" she said to herself, and nothing could distract her mind. All day she was sad. In vain Afanasy Ivanovich joked and tried to find out why she was so melancholy all of a sudden. Pulkheria Ivanovna made no answer, or answered in a way that could not possibly satisfy Afanasy Ivanovich. Next day she was perceptibly thinner.

"What is the matter with you, Pulkheria Ivanovna? You must be ill."

"No, I am not ill, Afanasy Ivanovich! I want to tell you something strange; I know that I shall die this summer: my death has already come to fetch me!"

Afanasy Ivanovich's lips twitched painfully. He tried, however, to overcome his gloomy feeling and with a smile said: "God knows what you are saying, Pulkheria Ivanovna! You must have drunk some peach vodka instead of the concoction you usually drink."

"No, Afanasy Ivanovich, I have not drunk peach vodka," said Pulkheria Ivanovna. And Afanasy Ivanovich was sorry that he had so teased her; he looked at her and a tear hung on his eyelash.

"I beg you, Afanasy Ivanovich, to carry out my wishes," said Pulkheria Ivanovna; "when I die, bury me by the church fence.

Put my gray dress on me, the one with the little flowers on a brown background. Don't put on me my satin dress with the crimson stripes; a dead woman has no need of such a dress—what use is it to her?—while it will be of use to you: have a fine dressing gown made of it, so that when visitors are here you can show yourself and welcome them, looking decent."

"God knows what you are saying, Pulkheria Ivanovna!" said Afanasy Ivanovich. "Death may be a long way off, but you are frightening me already with such sayings."

"No, Afanasy Ivanovich, I know now when my death will come. Don't grieve for me, though: I am an old woman and have lived long enough, and you are old, too; we shall soon meet in the other world."

But Afanasy Ivanovich was sobbing like a child.

"It's a sin to weep, Afanasy Ivanovich! Do not be sinful and anger God by your sorrow. I am not sorry that I am dying; there is only one thing I am sorry about"—a heavy sigh interrupted her words for a minute—"I am sorry that I do not know in whose care to leave you, who will look after you when I am dead. You are like a little child. You need somebody who loves you to look after you."

At these words there was an expression of such deep, such distressed heartfelt pity on her face that I doubt whether anyone could have looked at her at that moment unmoved.

"Be careful, Yavdokha," she said, turning to the housekeeper for whom she had purposely sent, "that when I die you look after your master; watch over him like the apple of your eye, like your own child. Make certain that what he likes is always cooked for him in the kitchen; that you always give him clean linen and clothes; that when visitors come you dress him in his best, or else maybe he will sometimes come out in his old dressing gown, because even now he often forgets when it's a holiday and when it's a working day. Don't take your eyes off him, Yavdokha; I will pray for you in the next world and God will reward you. Do not forget, Yavdokha, you are old, you have not long to live—do not take a sin upon your soul. If you do not look after him you will have no happiness in life. I myself will beseech God not to give you a happy end. And you will be unhappy yourself and your children will be unhappy, and all your family will not have the blessing of God in anything."

Poor old woman! At that minute she was not thinking of the great moment awaiting her, nor of her soul, nor of her own future life; she was thinking only of her poor companion with whom she had spent her life and whom she was leaving helpless and forlorn. With extraordinary efficiency she arranged everything, so that Afanasy Ivanovich should not notice her absence when she was gone. Her conviction that her end was at hand was so strong, and her state of mind was so attuned to it, that she did in fact take to her bed a few days later and could eat nothing. Afanasy Ivanovich never left her bedside and was all solicitude. "Perhaps you would eat a little of something, Pulkheria Ivanovna," he said, looking with anxiety into her eyes. But Pulkheria Ivanovna said nothing. At last, after a long silence, she seemed trying to say something, her lips stirred—and her breathing ceased.

Afanasy Ivanovich was absolutely overwhelmed. It seemed to him so uncanny that he did not even weep; he looked at her with dull eyes as though not grasping the significance of the corpse.

The dead woman was laid out on the table in the dress she had herself decided upon, her arms were crossed and a wax candle put in her hand—he looked at all this impassively. Numbers of people of all kinds filled the courtyard; numbers of guests came to the funeral; long tables were laid out in the courtyard; they were covered with masses of funeral rice, of homemade beverages and pies. The guests talked and wept, gazed at the dead woman, discussed her qualities, and looked at him; but he himself looked peculiarly at it all. The coffin was carried out at last, the people crowded after it, and he followed it. The priests were in full vestments, the sun was shining, babies were crying in their mothers' arms, larks were singing, and children raced and skipped about the road. At last the coffin was put down above the grave; he was asked to approach and kiss the dead woman for the last time. He went up and kissed her; there were tears in his eyes, but they were somehow apathetic tears. The coffin was lowered, the priest took the spade and first threw in a handful of earth; the deep rich voices of the deacon and the two sextons sang "Eternal Memory" under the pure cloudless sky; the laborers took their spades, and soon the earth covered the grave and made it level. At that moment he pressed forward; everyone stepped aside and made way for him, anxious to know what he meant to do. He raised his eyes, looked at them vacantly, and said: "So you have buried her already! What for?" He broke off and said no more.

But when he was home again, when he saw that his room was

empty, that even the chair Pulkheria Ivanovna used to sit on had been taken away—he sobbed, sobbed violently, inconsolably, and tears flowed from his lusterless eyes like a river.

Five years have passed since then. What grief does not time bear away? What passion survives in the unequal combat with it? I knew a man in the flower of his youth and strength, full of true nobility of character. I knew him in love, tenderly, passionately, madly, fiercely, humbly; and before me, and before my eyes almost, the object of his passion, a tender creature, lovely as an angel, was struck down by merciless death. I have never seen such awful depths of spiritual suffering, such frenzied poignant grief, such devouring despair as overwhelmed the luckless lover. I had never imagined that a man could create for himself such a hell with no shadow, no shape, no semblance of hope. . . . People tried not to leave him alone; all weapons with which he might have killed himself were hidden from him. Two weeks later he suddenly mastered himself, and began laughing and jesting; he was given his freedom, and the first use he made of it was to buy a pistol. One day his family were terrified by the sudden sound of a shot; they ran into the room and saw him stretched on the floor with a shattered skull. A doctor, who happened to be there at the time and whose skill was famous, saw signs of life in him, found that the wound was not absolutely fatal; and, to the amazement of everyone, the young man recovered. The watch kept on him was stricter than ever. Even at dinner a knife was not laid for him and everything was removed with which he could have hurt himself; but in a short time he found another opportunity and threw himself under the wheels of a passing carriage. An arm and a leg were broken; but again he recovered. A year after that I saw him in a roomful of people: he was sitting at a table saying, gaily, "*Petite ouverte*," [6] as he covered a card, and behind him, with her elbows on the back of his chair, was standing his young wife, turning over his chips.

At the end of the five years after Pulkheria Ivanovna's death I was in those parts and drove to Afanasy Ivanovich's little farm to visit my old neighbor, in whose house I used at one time to spend the day pleasantly and always to overeat myself with the choicest masterpieces of its hospitable mistress.

As I approached the courtyard the house seemed to me twice as

---

[6] "Small bid." (ed.)

old as it had been: the peasants' huts were lying completely on one side, as no doubt their owners were too; the fence and the hurdle around the yard were completely broken down, and I myself saw the cook pull sticks out of it to heat the stove, though she need have only taken two steps further to reach the fagot stack. Sadly I drove up to the steps; the same old Neros and Trustys, by now blind or lame, barked, wagging their fluffy tails covered with burdocks. An old man came out to greet me. Yes, it was he! I knew him at once; but he stooped twice as much as before. He knew me and greeted me with the old familiar smile. I followed him indoors. It seemed as though everything was as before. But I noticed a strange disorder in everything, an unmistakable absence of something. In fact I experienced the strange feelings which come upon us when for the first time we enter the house of a widower whom we have known in old days inseparable from the wife who has shared his life. The feeling is the same when we see a man crippled whom we have always known in health. In everything the absence of careful Pulkheria Ivanovna was visible: on the table a knife was laid without a handle; the dishes were not cooked with the same skill. I did not want to ask about the farm; I was afraid even to look at the farm buildings. When we sat down to dinner, a maid tied a napkin around Afanasy Ivanovich, and it was good that she did so, as without it he would have spilled sauce all over his dressing gown. I tried to entertain him and told him various items of news; he listened with the same smile, but from time to time his eyes were completely vacant, and his thoughts did not stray, they vanished. Often he lifted a spoonful of porridge and instead of putting it to his mouth put it to his nose; instead of sticking his fork into a piece of chicken, he prodded the decanter, and then the maid, taking his hand, directed it back to the chicken. We sometimes waited several minutes for the next course.

Afanasy Ivanovich himself noticed it and said: "Why is it they are so long bringing the food?" But I saw through the crack of the door that the boy who carried away our plates was asleep and nodding on a bench, not thinking of his duties at all.

"This is the dish," said Afanasy Ivanovich, when we were handed curd cakes with sour cream; "this is the dish," he went on, and I noticed that his voice began quivering and a tear was ready to drop from his leaden eyes, but he did his utmost to restrain it: "This is the dish which my . . . my . . . dear . . . my dear . . ." And all at once he burst into tears; his hand fell on the plate, the plate turned upside down, slipped, and was smashed, and the sauce was spilled all over him. He sat vacantly, vacantly held the spoon; and tears like a stream, like a ceaselessly flowing fountain, flowed and flowed on the napkin that covered him.

"My God!" I thought, looking at him, "five years of all-destroying time—an old man already apathetic, an old man whose life one would have thought had never once been stirred by a strong feeling, whose whole life seemed to consist in sitting on a high chair, in eating dried fish and pears, in telling good-natured stories—and such long, such bitter grief! What is stronger in us—passion or habit? Or are all the violent impulses, all the whirl of our desires and turbulent passions, only the consequence of our ardent age, and is it only through youth that they seem deep and shattering?"

Be that as it may, at that moment all our passions seemed like child's play beside this effect of long, slow, almost insensible habit. Several times he struggled to utter his wife's name, but, halfway through the word, his quiet and ordinary face worked convulsively and his childish weeping cut me to the very heart. No, those were not the tears with which old men are usually so lavish, as they complain of their pitiful position and their troubles; they were not the tears which they drop over a glass of punch either. No! They were tears which brimmed over uninvited, from the accumulated rankling pain of a heart already turning cold.

He did not live long after that. I heard lately of his death. It is strange, though, that the circumstances of his end had some resemblance to those of Pulkheria Ivanovna's death. One day Afanasy Ivanovich ventured to take a little walk in the garden. As he was pacing slowly along a path with his usual absent-mindedness, without a thought of any kind in his head, he had a strange adventure. He suddenly heard someone behind him pronounce in a fairly distinct voice: "Afanasy Ivanovich!" He turned around but there was absolutely nobody there; he looked in all directions, he peered into the bushes—no one anywhere. It was a still day and the sun was shining. He pondered for a minute; his face seemed to brighten and he brought out at last: "It's Pulkheria Ivanovna calling me!"

It has, no doubt, happened to you, some time or other, to hear a voice calling you by name, which simple people explain as a soul grieving for a human being and calling him; and after that, they say, death follows inevitably. I must admit I was always frightened by that mysterious call. I remember that in childhood I often heard it. Sometimes suddenly someone behind me distinctly uttered my name. Usually on such occasions it was a very bright and sunny day; not one leaf in the garden was stirring; the stillness was death-like; even the grasshopper left off churring for the moment; there was not a soul in the garden. But I confess that if the wildest and most tempestuous night had lashed me with all the fury of the elements, alone in the middle of an impenetrable forest, I should not have been so terrified as by that awful stillness in the midst of a cloudless day. I usually ran out of the garden in a great panic, hardly able to breathe, and was only reassured when I met some person, the sight of whom dispelled the terrible spiritual loneliness.

Afanasy Ivanovich surrendered completely to his inner conviction that Pulkheria Ivanovna was calling him; he submitted with the readiness of an obedient child, wasted away, coughed, melted like a candle, and at last flickered out, as a candle does when there is nothing left to sustain its feeble flame. "Lay me beside Pulkheria Ivanovna" was all he said before his end.

His desire was carried out and he was buried near the church beside Pulkheria Ivanovna's grave. The guests were fewer at the funeral, but there were just as many beggars and peasants. The little house was now completely emptied. The enterprising steward and the elder hauled away to their huts all that were left of the old-fashioned goods and furniture, which the housekeeper had not been able to carry off. Soon there arrived, I cannot say from where, a distant kinsman, the heir to the estate, who had been a lieutenant, I don't know in what regiment, and was a terrible reformer. He saw at once the great slackness and disorganization in the management of the land; he made up his mind to change all that radically, to improve things and bring everything into order. He bought six splendid English sickles, pinned a special number on each hut, and managed so well that within six months his estate was put under the supervision of a board of trustees.

The sage trustees (consisting of an ex-assessor and a lieutenant in a faded uniform) had within a very short time left no fowls and eggs. The huts, which were almost lying on the earth, fell down completely; the peasants gave themselves up to drunkenness and most of them ran away. The real owner, who got on, however, pretty comfortably with his trustees and used to drink punch with them, very rarely visited his estate and never stayed long. To this day he drives about to all the fairs in Little Russia, carefully inquiring the prices of all sorts of produce sold wholesale, such as flour, hemp, honey, and so on; but he only buys small trifles such as flints, a nail to clean out his pipe, in fact nothing which exceeds at the utmost a ruble in price.

❧❧❧❧❧❧❧❧❧❧❧❧❧❧❧❧❧❧❧❧❧❧❧❧

TARAS BULBA¹

I

"Turn around, son! What a sight you are! Are those priests' cassocks you are wearing? And do they all go about like that at the seminary?"

With these words old Bulba greeted his two sons, who had been studying at the Kiev seminary and had come home to their father.

His sons had just dismounted from their horses. They were two sturdy young men who still looked sullenly from under their brows, as befits seminarists fresh from school. Their strong, healthy faces were covered with the first down of beard not yet touched by

---

¹ This highly romantic story is not to be confused with history. It is essentially an imaginative recreation of the tone and quality of an historical period written in the epic tradition. To add to its verisimilitude, Gogol uses several names and situations that existed in fact, yet the story contains anachronisms (e.g., Bulba, we are told, could only have lived in the fifteenth century, yet his sons return home from a seminary which did not exist until the beginning of the seventeenth century). But Gogol's description of Cossacks and their affairs seems, from all accounts, remarkably accurate, if romanticized. A community of Cossacks was established, in the location described by Gogol, as early as the first half of the fifteenth century, apparently to defend the Ukraine against Tartar raiding parties and, after 1659, to defend Ukrainian sovereignty against the Poles. (ed.)

the razor. They were much disconcerted at this reception from their father and stood motionless with their eyes on the ground.

"Stand still, stand still! Let me have a good look at you," he went on, turning them around: "what long frocks you have on! Strange frocks! Such frocks have never been seen before. One of you take a little run! I'd like to see whether he won't fall flat on the ground, entangled in his skirts."

"Don't taunt, don't taunt, Father!" the elder of them said at last.

"My, what a precious fellow! And why not taunt?"

"You may be my father, but by God I'll beat you if you go on taunting us!"

"What! You're a nice sort of son! Your father?" said Taras Bulba, retreating a few paces in surprise.

"Yes, though you are my father. If I am insulted it makes no difference to me who does the insulting."

"How do you want to fight with me? With fists?"

"Any way you like."

"Well, let it be with fists!" said Bulba, rolling up his sleeves: "I'll see what you are worth with your fists!"

And, instead of a welcome after their long separation, father and son began punching each other in the ribs and the back and the chest, stepping apart and looking about them and then beginning again.

"Look, good people! The old man is crazy! He's gone off his head!" said their pale, thin, and kindly mother, who stood in the doorway and had not yet succeeded in embracing her precious children. "The boys have come home, we've not seen them for over a year; and a peculiar whim takes him: a fist fight!"

"But he fights very well!" said Bulba, stopping. "I swear he does!" he went on, rearranging his disheveled clothing. "One doesn't want too much of it! He will make a good Cossack! Well, how are you, son? Give us a kiss!" And father and son kissed each other. "Bravo, son! You whack everyone as you thumped me; don't let anyone off! But it is an absurd outfit, though. What's that cord hanging? And you, you fool, why do you stand doing nothing?" he said, turning to the younger. "Why don't you try me, you son of a bitch?"

"What will he think of next!" said the mother, who was meanwhile embracing the younger boy. "Has anyone heard of such a thing as a child hitting his own father! And as though he were fit for that now: the child is young, he has had such a journey, he is tired out . . ." (the child was over twenty and more than six foot) "he needs to rest now and have something to eat, and here you are forcing him to fight."

"Well, you are a dainty fellow, I see!" said Bulba. "Don't heed your mother, son: she is a woman, she knows nothing. What do you want with spoiling? What you want is the open plain and a good horse: that's the best treat for you! And you see this saber here? That's the mother for you! It's all nonsense—what they have been stuffing your heads with: and the seminaries and all the books and vocabularies and philosophies, and all that rubbish. I'd spit on it all!" Here Bulba finished up with a word which is positively inadmissible in print. "I'll tell you what, I'd better send you this very week to the camp of the Dnieper Cossacks. That's the place for learning! That's the school for you; it's only there you'll pick up sense."

"And are they to be only one week at home?" said the thin old mother piteously, with tears in her eyes: "and they won't have time to enjoy themselves, poor dears; they won't have time to get to know their own home, and I won't have time to look at them!"

"Stop whining, stop whining, old woman! A Cossack's not for hanging about with women. You'd hide them both under your petticoat and sit on them as though they were hen's eggs. Go along, go along, quickly, and set all you have on the table for us. We don't want doughnuts, honey buns, poppy cakes, and other dainties; bring us a whole sheep, serve a goat and forty-year-old mead! And plenty of vodka, not vodka with all sorts of fancies, not with raisins and flavorings, but pure foaming vodka, that hisses and bubbles like mad."

Bulba led his sons into the parlor where two pretty serf girls in necklaces made of coins were busy. They scurried out, apparently alarmed at the entrance of young masters who were not in the habit of leaving people alone, or perhaps they simply wanted to observe feminine tradition by shrieking and rushing headlong at the sight of a man, and then hiding their faces in their sleeves from bashfulness. The room was decorated in the taste of that time—of which hints have survived only in the songs and popular ballads, no longer sung in the Ukraine by old bearded blind men to the gently tinkling bandore, while a crowd stood around to listen—in the taste of those turbulent troubled times when the struggles and battles for the union of Russia and the Ukraine were beginning. Everything was clean and covered with colored clay. On the walls were sabers, whips, bird nets, fishing tackle, and guns, an elaborately worked horn for powder, a golden bridle for a horse, and a harness with silver disks. The windows in the parlor were small, with dingy round panes such as are only seen nowadays in old-fashioned churches, so that one could only look out by raising the movable pane. Around the windows and doors were red sills and lintels. On the shelves in the corners stood jugs, bottles, and flasks of green or of dark blue glass, ornamental silver mugs, gilt goblets of various patterns—Venetian, Turkish, and Circassian—that had come into Bulba's parlor by devious routes after passing through several hands, as such things often did in those lawless days. Birchbark benches ran all around the room; an immense table stood in the center under the icons; a wide stove with cozy projections and nooks covered with bright-colored tiles. All this was very familiar to our two young men who walked home for the summer holidays every year—walked because they had then no horses and because it was not customary to allow students to ride on horseback. They wore long forelocks which any Cossack carrying a weapon had the right to pull. Only just before they had left the seminary for good had Bulba sent them a pair of young stallions from his herd of horses.

In honor of his sons' arrival, Bulba had bidden all the officers of the regiment who were on the spot to be summoned; and when two of them and his old comrade, Captain Dmitro Tovkach, arrived, he presented his sons to them at once, saying: "Here, look what fine lads! I shall soon send them to the Cossack camp." The guests congratulated both Bulba and the two young men, and told them they were doing the right thing and that there was no better training for a young man than the Zaporozhsky camp.

"Well, friends, sit down each where he likes best at the table. Come, sons! First of all, a drink of vodka!" said Bulba. "God bless you! To your health, sons: yours, Ostap, and yours, Andrei! God grant that you may always be successful in war! That you may beat everyone—pagans, Turks, Tartars, and that when the Poles begin attacking our Church, you may beat the Poles. Come, pass up your goblet; well, is the vodka good? And what's vodka in Latin? They were morons, you know, the Latins, son; they did not even know there was such a thing as vodka in the world. What is his name, who wrote Latin verses? I am not strong in literature, and so I don't know; Horace, was it?"

"What a fellow Father is!" the elder son Ostap thought to himself. "The old man knows it all, the dog, and feigns ignorance, too."

"I expect the archimandrite didn't let you have a sniff of vodka," Taras went on. "Confess, sons, they whipped you soundly with birch rods and a fresh cherry switch on the back and everything else a Cossack has? And perhaps since you became too intelligent, you were lashed with whips, too? Not only on Saturdays, I bet, but on Wednesdays and Thursdays too, you caught it?"

"No need to recall the past, Father," Ostap answered coolly, "the past is over!"

"Let him try it now!" said Andrei: "let anybody dare touch me now. If only some Tartar gang would turn up now, they would learn what a Cossack saber is like!"

"Good, son! I swear that's good! And since it's come to that, I'll go with you! Yes, I will. Why the devil should I stay here? To sow buckwheat and mind the house, to look after the sheep and the swine, and to drag about with my wife? Plague take her; I am a Cossack, I won't allow it! What if there is no war? I'll go with you anyway to the Cossack camp for a little junketing. I swear, I will!" And little by little old Bulba grew hotter and hotter till at last he worked himself into a fury, got up from the table, and drawing himself up to his full height, stamped on the floor.

"We'll go tomorrow! Why put it off? What enemy can we hatch out here? What do we want with this house? What use is it all to us? What are these pots for?" Saying this he began flinging down and smashing the pots and bottles.

The poor old woman, accustomed to such outbursts from her husband, sat on the bench mournfully looking on. She dared say nothing; but hearing of this terrible decision she could not refrain from tears; she looked at her children from whom she was threatened to be parted so soon—and no one could describe the mute bitterness of the sadness which seemed quivering in her eyes and her tightly compressed lips.

Bulba was terribly stubborn. He was one of those characters which could only appear in that half-nomadic corner of Europe, in the cruel fifteenth century when all primitive South Russia, abandoned by its princes, had been laid waste and burned to ashes by the ruthless onslaughts of the Mongol hordes; when, deprived of home and shelter, men here grew bold and daring; when they settled on the ashes of their burned villages, in sight of menacing neighbors and perpetual danger, and grew accustomed to looking them straight in the face, forgetting that there was such a thing as fear in the world; when the inherently peaceful Slav character was tempered in the flames of warfare, and the Cossack organization arose—the expression of the broad dashing recklessness of Russian nature. By every ferry, at every fording place, every strip by a riverbank, every convenient spot, there were countless Cossacks, whose bold comrades properly answered the Sultan when he wanted to know how many there were: "Who knows! They are spread all over the steppe: wherever there's a hillock there's a Cossack!" It was truly a marvelous manifestation of Russian strength: it was struck out of the heart of the people by the flint and steel of calamity. In place of the old districts and little towns filled with huntsmen, in place of the unimportant princes who were always fighting and selling their towns, there sprang up strong Cossack villages and districts, settlements bound together by a common danger and a common hatred of the heathen savages. Everyone knows from history how their turbulent life and perpetual struggle saved Europe from the ruthless onslaughts which threatened to destroy it. The Polish kings who found themselves, in place of the district princes, sovereigns of these wide though remote and weak lands, saw the importance of the Cossacks and their value as soldiers and guards. They encouraged them and flattered their warlike disposition. Under their remote authority the Hetmans, elected from the Cossacks themselves, transformed the villages and districts into regiments and divisions. It was not a regular standing army; no one would have noticed it; but in case of war and general uprising, within a week or less, every man appeared on his horse, fully equipped, receiving only one gold coin of pay from the King, and within a fortnight an army was assembled, such as no drafting of recruits could have raised. When the campaign was over the warrior went back to his meadows and his plowlands, to his ferry over the Dnieper, caught fish, traded, brewed beer, and was a free Cossack. Foreign contemporaries rightly marveled at his wonderful capacities. There was no craft which the Cossack did not know: distilling spirits, building carts, making gunpowder, doing blacksmith's and carpenter's work, and in addition doing all that carousing with reckless gaiety, drinking, and merrymaking that only a Russian can—it all came easy to him. Besides the registered Cossacks who considered it their duty to appear in wartime, it was possible at any time of urgent necessity to collect whole crowds of volunteer cavalry: the esauls (or captains) had only to go about the fairs and markets of all the villages and hamlets and standing in a cart shout at the top of their voices: "Hey, you beer swillers and brewers! Drop your brewing and lolling about the stove, feeding the flies with your fat bodies! Come and win knightly glory and honor! You plowmen sowing buckwheat, minding your flocks, and running after the wenches! Enough of following the plow, muddying your yellow boots on the land, running after women, and losing your knightly valor! It is high time to win a Cossack's fame!" And those words were like sparks falling on dry wood. The brewers and distillers threw down their casks and broke their barrels, the craftsmen and the tradesmen sent craft and shop to the devil, broke the pots in the hut—and everyone mounted his horse. In fact, here the Russian character found the full outlet for its expression.

Taras was one of the original old colonels: he was created for the excitement of battle and was distinguished by the coarse directness of his character. In those days the influence of Poland was already beginning to be apparent in the Russian nobility. Many of them were already adopting Polish manners, introducing luxurious habits, keeping a magnificent retinue of servants, hawks, and hunting dogs, giving banquets, laying out courtyards. All that was not to Taras' taste. He liked the simple life of the Cossacks and quarreled with those of his comrades who were disposed to follow the Warsaw fashion, calling them the servingmen of the Polish lords. Always tireless, he regarded himself as the authorized champion of the Russian Orthodox Church. At his own initiative he would go into villages where there were complaints by people against their landlords or of new taxes being laid on each chimney. He would with his Cossacks deal with the oppressors, and made it a rule always to have recourse to the sword in three cases: namely, when the commissars showed any lack of respect for the elders and did not take off their caps while standing before them; when the Orthodox faith was insulted and the traditions of their forefathers were disregarded; and lastly, when the enemies were Turks or pagans, against whom he always thought it permissible to lift his sword to the glory of Christianity.

Now he was already gloating over the thought of arriving with his two sons at the Zaporozhye camp and saying: "Here, look what fine fellows I have brought you!" He thought how he would present them to all his old battle-seasoned comrades; how he would watch their first feats of arms and their carousing, which he regarded as also one of the chief distinctions of a warrior. He had meant at first to send them off alone; but at the sight of their youth and vigor, their sturdy handsomeness, his warlike spirit flared up and he resolved to go with them next day himself, though the only necessity for doing so was his own stubborn desire. He was already busily engaged giving orders, selecting horses and their trappings for his young sons, superintending preparations in the stables and the storehouses, and picking out the servants who were to go with them the next day. He handed over his authority to Captain Tovkach along with a stern injunction to come at once with the whole regiment if he should send a summons from the camp. Though he had been drinking heavily and the fumes were still in his head, yet he forgot nothing; he even remembered to order that the horses should be given drink and that the best wheat should be put in their mangers. He came in tired from his exertions. "Well, children, now you must sleep and tomorrow we shall do as God wills. But don't make up a bed for us! We need no bed; we will sleep in the open air."

Night was only just embracing the heavens, but Bulba always lay down to sleep early. He stretched himself on a rug, and covered himself with a sheepskin, because the night air was rather fresh and because he liked to be wrapped up warmly when he was at home. He soon began snoring, and the whole courtyard followed his example; everywhere in the different corners there was snoring and whistling. The watchman was the first to fall asleep, for he had drunk more than any in honor of the young masters' arrival.

Only the poor mother did not sleep. She stooped down to the pillow of her precious sons who were lying side by side; she combed out their carelessly matted youthful locks and wetted them with her tears. She gazed at them, and her whole being, every feeling was in that gaze, she was entirely absorbed in it and could not gaze enough. She had nursed them at her own breast; she had petted and tended them as they grew—and now only for one minute could she see them. "My sons, my darling sons! What will happen to you? What awaits you?" she said, and tears lingered in the wrinkles that

transformed her once lovely face. She was indeed to be pitied, like
every woman of that fierce age. For only a moment had she lived in
love, in the first fever of passion, in the first fever of youth, and
then her harsh lover forsook her for his sword, for his comrades,
for carousing. She would see her husband for two or three days in
a year and then hear nothing of him for years. And, indeed, when
she did see him, when they did live together, what was her life?
She endured insults, even blows; the only caresses she knew were
given as a favor; she was an alien creature in this crowd of wifeless
warriors, on whom the reckless life of the Dnieper Cossack had
put its harsh stamp. Her youth had flashed by without joy, and
her lovely fresh cheeks and bosom had withered without kisses
and were covered with premature wrinkles. All love, every emotion, all that is tender and passionate in woman had in her turned
into the one feeling of motherhood. With fervor, with passion, with
tears, she hovered like a gull of the steppes over her children. Her
sons, her darling sons were being taken from her—she might never
see them again! Who knows, perhaps in their first battle the Tartars
would hack off their heads and she would not know where lay their
forsaken bodies, pecked by the wild birds on the roadside; and for
each drop of their blood she would have given all of hers. Sobbing,
she looked into their eyes, as an overpowering drowsiness was beginning to close them, and thought: "Maybe when Bulba wakes he
may put off their going for a day or two; perhaps he thought of
going so soon only because he had drunk so much."

For hours the moon high up in the heavens had flooded with
light the yard filled with sleepers, the thick bush of willows, and the
tall weeds in which the fence that surrounded the yard was lost.
Still she sat by the pillow of her darling sons and never for a moment took her eyes from them nor thought of sleep. Already the
horses, scenting the dawn, lay down on the grass and stopped
grazing; the top leaves of the willows began whispering, and little
by little the whisper ran eddying down them to the lowest branches.
She sat till daylight, feeling no weariness and inwardly longing for
the night to last on and on. The ringing neigh of a foal floated from
the steppe; red streaks gleamed brightly in the sky.

Bulba suddenly woke and leaped up. He remembered very well
the orders he had given the day before. "Come, boys, wake up! It's
time, high time! Water the horses! And where's the old woman?"

(This was his usual name for his wife.) "Look alive, old woman, prepare food for us; a great journey lies before us!"

The poor old mother, deprived of her last hope, dragged herself dejectedly into the hut. While she was tearfully preparing what was wanted for breakfast, Bulba was giving orders, looking after things in the stables, and picking out his best equipment for his sons.

The seminary students were transformed; instead of their muddy boots, they had boots of red morocco with silver taps; trousers as wide as the Black Sea, with thousands of folds and pleats, were drawn in with a golden cord; to the cord were attached long straps with tassels and various trifles for a pipe. A Cossack coat of crimson cloth bright as fire was girt with a gaily patterned sash; embossed Turkish pistols were thrust into this sash and a saber clanked about their legs. Their faces, still scarcely sunburned, looked handsomer and fairer; their young black mustaches seemed to emphasize the whiteness of their skins and the healthy vigorous hue of youth; they were handsome under their black, gold-topped astrakhan caps. Poor mother! As she looked at them she could not utter a word; tears stood in her eyes.

"Well, sons, everything is ready! There's no need to linger!" Bulba pronounced at last. "Now, as is the Christian custom, we must all sit down before the journey."

All sat down, even the young men who had been standing respectfully at the doors.

"Now, mother, bless your children!" said Bulba; "pray that they may fight bravely, that they may ever defend the honor of knighthood; that they may ever champion the Christian faith, and that if they don't—that they be dead and leave no trace behind them. Go up to your mother, children: a mother's prayer brings safety on land and on sea!"

The mother, weak as a mother, embraced them and, bringing out two small icons, put them on their necks, sobbing as she did so. "May the Mother of God . . . keep you . . . don't forget your mother . . . send me just a word of news . . ." She could say no more.

"Well, come along, children!" said Bulba.

Saddled horses were standing at the steps. Bulba leaped on his Devil, which reared wildly, feeling a terrific weight on the saddle, for Taras was exceedingly thickset and heavy.

When the mother saw that her sons were mounted on their horses, she flew up to the younger one, whose features betrayed more of something like tenderness; she clutched his stirrup, she clung to his saddle, and with despair in her eyes held him tight in her arms. Two strong Cossacks took her carefully and bore her away into the hut. But when they rode out at the gate, she ran out with the nimbleness of a wild goat, hardly believable at her years, and with startling force stopped the horse and embraced one of her sons with blind frenzied fervor. She was taken away again.

The young Cossacks rode on in embarrassment, restraining their tears for fear of their father, who for his part was a little troubled, too, though he tried not to show it. It was a gray day; the green leaves and grass glittered brightly; the birds chirped discordantly. After riding on they looked back; their home seemed to have sunk into the earth; nothing was to be seen above ground but two chimneys of their modest little hut and the tops of the trees, on the branches of which they had climbed in old days like squirrels. There still lay stretched before them the meadow which might have recalled to them the whole story of their lives, from the age when they used to roll on its dewy grass to the age when they waited in it for the black-browed Cossack girl who timidly fluttered across it on her swift young feet. And now only the post over the well with a cart wheel fastened to the top stood out forlornly against the sky; by now the plain which they were riding through looked in the distance like a mountain and hid everything from sight. Farewell to childhood, to play, and to everything, everything!

II

All three rode in silence. Old Taras was thinking of long ago: before his mind passed his youth, those years, those bygone years, always regretted by the Cossack, who would like this whole life to be youth. He wondered whom he would meet of his old comrades at the camp. He tried to recall which were dead, which were still living. Tears slowly gathered in his eyes and his gray head drooped mournfully.

His sons were occupied with other thoughts. But we must say a little more about those sons. They had been sent in their twelfth year to the seminary in Kiev, for all persons of consequence in those days thought it necessary to give their sons an education even if they were only to forget it completely afterwards. They were then, like all who came to the seminary, wild creatures reared in freedom, and in the seminary the boys commonly acquired a certain polish and gained a common quality which made them resemble each other. The elder boy, Ostap, began his career by running away in his first year. He was brought back, severely flogged, and sent back to his books. Four times he buried his reading text in the earth and four times after beating him inhumanly they bought him a new one. And he would undoubtedly have done the same again for the fifth time, if his father had not solemnly given his word that he would keep him for twenty full years as a lay brother in a monastery, and sworn that he should never see the Cossack camp in his life if he did not learn all his lessons at the seminary. It is curious that this was said by Taras Bulba, who abused all learning and, as we have seen already, advised his sons to pay no attention to it at all. From that time Ostap began studying the tedious book with extraordinary diligence and was soon on a level with the best of the scholars. The kind of education in vogue in those days was terribly divorced from the manner of life: these scholastic, grammatical, rhetorical, and logical subtleties had absolutely no relation with the times, and were never applied or repeated in life. Those who studied them could not connect their acquirements, even the least pedantic, with anything in their lives. The most learned men in those days were more ignorant than the rest, because they were entirely removed from experience. Moreover, the democratic organization of the seminary, the immense numbers of young, sturdy, healthy fellows, were bound to impress upon them a reality absolutely remote from their studies. Sometimes their poor fare, sometimes their frequent punishments by hunger, sometimes the many cravings that spring up in a fresh, strong, healthy lad, and all these in conjunction, aroused in them that spirit of enterprise which was afterward developed in the Cossack camp. The hungry students lounged about the streets of Kiev and forced everyone to be on his guard. The market women always covered their pies, their pretzels, and their pumpkin seeds with their hands, as eagles cover their young, as soon as they saw a student coming. The monitor, bound by his duty to watch over the colleagues committed to his charge, had such enormous pockets in his trousers that he could have stuffed them with the entire shop of an unwary market woman. These seminary students made up a separate world; they were not admitted into the higher circles consisting of Polish and Russian noblemen. Even the military governor, Adam Kisel, in spite of his patronage of the seminary, did not admit them into society, and gave orders that they should be disciplined as strictly as possible. This injunction was quite superfluous, however, for the rector and the monk-professors did not spare the rod and the whip, and often the lictors, by their orders, thrashed the monitors so cruelly that the latter were rubbing their trousers for weeks afterward. To many of them this was a matter of little importance, hardly more stinging than good vodka with pepper in it; others became fearfully sick at last of these incessant drubbings, and they ran away to the Cossack camp, if they could find the road and were not caught on the way. Though Ostap Bulba began with great diligence studying logic and even theology, he did not escape the merciless rod. It was natural that all this should in a way toughen the character and give it the hardness that has always characterized the Cossacks. Ostap was always considered one of the best of the comrades. He did not often take the lead in rash enterprises, such as plundering an orchard or a vegetable garden, but he was always one of the first to follow the lead of an enterprising student, and never under any circumstances betrayed his comrades; no rods nor lashes could make him do that. He suppressed any interests other than fighting and carousing; anyway he scarcely ever thought of anything else. He was frank with his equals. He was kindhearted as far as that was possible with such a character and in those times. He was genuinely touched by the tears of his poor mother, and her grief was the only thing that troubled him and made his head lower pensively.

His younger brother Andrei had rather refined and as it were more sensitive feelings. He studied more eagerly and without the effort with which a man of plodding mind usually sets to work. He was more inventive than his brother, more frequently took the lead in rather a dangerous enterprise, and sometimes, thanks to his resourceful wit, managed to escape punishment, while his brother Ostap, without a second thought, slipped off his jacket and lay down on the floor, not dreaming of asking for mercy. Andrei, too, was boiling with the desire for adventure, but at the same time his soul was open to other feelings also. A yearning for love flamed hotly in him after he had reached his eighteenth year; woman was more often the subject of his ardent dreams; as he listened to philosophic arguments he saw her every minute, fresh, black-eyed, ten-

der. Her firm breasts, her lovely, delicate naked arms were continually flitting before his eyes; the very dress that clung to her
maidenly and yet strong limbs had in his dreams a fragrance of inexpressible sensuousness. He carefully concealed from his comrades these emotions of his passionate youthful soul, for in those
days it was a shame and a dishonor for a Cossack to think of woman
and love before he had seen any fighting. Of late years he had less
often been leader of a rowdy gang; more often he sauntered alone
in some solitary Kiev lane drowned in a sea of cherry trees between
narrow little houses that looked appealingly into the road. Sometimes he also wandered into the street of the aristocrats in what is
now Old Kiev, where the Little Russian and Polish nobles lived,
and where the houses were built with a certain pretentious taste.

One day when he was not looking, the coach of some Polish
nobleman almost drove over him, and the coachman, with terrific
mustaches, lashed at him from the box with good aim. The young
student flew into a rage: recklessly he clutched the hind wheel in
his powerful hands and stopped the coach. But the coachman,
dreading retaliation, whipped up the horses, they dashed forward—
and Andrei, who luckily just had time to snatch away his hands, fell
face downward in the mud. A most musical and melodious laugh
rang out above him. He raised his eyes and saw standing at a window the loveliest creature he had seen in his life, with black eyes
and a skin white as snow when it is lighted up by the flush of the
dawning sun. She was laughing heartily, and her laughter gave a
sparkling brilliance to her dazzling beauty. He was disconcerted.
He gazed at her, completely overwhelmed, while he absent-
mindedly rubbed the mud off his face, smearing it the more as he
did so. Who could this beauty be? He tried to find out from the
servants who stood in expensive livery at the gate listening to a
young bandore player. But the servants laughed when they saw his
muddy face and did not choose to answer. At last he found out that
she was the daughter of the Kovno military governor who had come
on a visit to Kiev. The very next night, with the audacity of which
only seminary students are capable, he climbed over the fence
into the garden, and climbed up a tree, the branches of which
reached the very roof of the house; from the tree he jumped up on
the roof and climbing down through the chimney of the open
fireplace, made his way straight into the bedroom of the beauty
who was at the moment sitting in front of a candle and removing

her expensive earrings. The lovely Polish girl was so frightened at seeing an unknown man suddenly confronting her that she could not utter a word; but when she noticed that the student was standing with downcast eyes, too shy to move a hand, when she recognized in him the youth who had tumbled into the mud before her eyes, she was overcome with laughter again. Moreover, there was nothing alarming in Andrei's face: he was very handsome. She laughed with genuine mirth and for a long time amused herself at his expense. The beauty was as lighthearted as Polish girls are; but her eyes, her wonderful, piercingly bright eyes looked at him steadily. The seminary student could not stir a limb, but stood stiffly as though tied in a sack, while the military governor's daughter went boldly up to him, put her glittering diadem on his head, hung earrings on his lips, and threw over him a transparent muslin chemisette with ruffles embroidered in gold. She dressed him up, and, with the naughty childlike ease characteristic of frivolous Polish girls, played a thousand silly pranks with him, and this put the poor student into even greater confusion. He was a ridiculous sight standing with his mouth open, staring into her dazzling eyes. A knock at the door at this moment alarmed her. She told him to hide under the bed, and as soon as the interruption was over, called her maid, a Tartar captive, and gave her orders to guide him cautiously to the garden and from there to help him over the fence. But this time our student did not climb over the fence so successfully: the watchman, waking up, caught him firmly by the legs and the assembled servants gave him a good beating, pursuing him even after he was in the street, where only his swift legs saved him. After this it was very dangerous to go near the house, for there were a great many servants in the governor's household. He met the daughter once more at church; she saw him and smiled to him very graciously, as to an old friend. He caught a passing glimpse of her once again; but soon after that the Kovno general went away, and, instead of the lovely black-eyed Polish girl, an unknown fat face looked out of the window. This was what Andrei was thinking of as he rode on with hanging head and eyes fixed on his horse's mane.

Meanwhile the steppe had long since wrapped them in its green embraces, the high grass hid them from sight, and only glimpses of their black Cossack caps showed from time to time among its flowering spikes.

"Aie, aie, aie! Why are you so quiet, lads?" said Bulba at last, rousing himself from his reverie. "As though you were monks! Come, to the devil with all brooding! Take your pipes between your teeth, let us light up and spur on our horses and fly so that no bird can overtake us!"

And the Cossacks, bending forward on their horses, disappeared in the grass. Now even their black caps could not be seen; only the lines of crushed grass showed the track of their swift course.

The sun had long since risen in the clear sky and was flooding the steppe with its warm, life-giving light. Every trace of trouble and drowsiness in the soul of the Cossacks vanished in an instant; their hearts were fluttering like birds.

The further they went, the lovelier the steppe became. In those days the vast expanse which makes up the southern part of Russia, right down to the Black Sea, was green virgin wilderness. Never had plow cut through the immense waves of its wild flowers; they were only trampled by the horses who were hidden in them as in a forest. Nothing in nature could be fairer; the whole surface of the earth was an ocean of green and gold, glittering with millions of different flowers. Through the high slender stalks of grass slipped the pale blue, indigo, and lilac cornflowers; the yellow broom thrust up its pyramidal crest; the white meadowsweet studded the surface with its umbrella-shaped plumes; an ear of wheat, brought God knows whence, was ripening among them. Among their slender stems partridges scurried about craning their necks. The air was filled with a thousand different bird calls. Hawks hovered motionless in the sky with wings outspread and eyes fixed immovably on the grass. The cries of a flock of wild geese moving off echoed from God knows what faraway lake. A gull rose with measured sweep of its wings from the grass and luxuriously bathed in the blue ocean of the air. Now she vanished in the heights, passing into a tiny black dot; now she turned over and gleamed in the sun. . . . How lovely are the steppes, damn them!

Our travelers only halted for a few minutes for dinner, when the escort of ten Cossacks who accompanied them dismounted and untied the wooden kegs of vodka and the pumpkin shells which were used instead of bowls. They ate nothing but bread and lard, or biscuits, drank only one cupful of vodka to keep up their strength, for Taras Bulba never permitted drinking on the road, and then went on till the evening. Toward nightfall the whole steppe was completely transformed; all its multicolored surface was flooded with the last bright glow of the sun and gradually darkened, so that the shadow could be seen creeping over it and turning it dark green; the odors that arose were richer; every flower, every blade of grass exhaled fragrance, and the whole steppe was bathed in sweet scent. Over the dark blue sky broad streaks of rosy gold were flung as though by a gigantic brush; light and transparent clouds made white drifts here and there; and the freshest breath of wind, alluring as a wave of the sea, faintly stirred the tops of the grass and gently caressed the cheek. All the music that had resounded in the day was hushed and replaced by another. The spotted marmots crept out of their holes, stood upon their hind paws, and made the steppe resound with their whistling. The churring of the grasshoppers grew louder. At times from some secluded lake came the cry of a swan, ringing like silver in the air.

The travelers halted in the middle of the open steppe, picked out a resting place, made a fire, and set on it a cauldron in which they cooked a stew; the steam rose and floated slanting through the air. After supper the Cossacks lay down to sleep, leaving their fettered horses grazing in the grass. They stretched themselves on their jackets. The midnight stars looked straight at them. They heard the innumerable world of insects that filled the grass, their whirr and buzz and churring; all resounded musically in the night, grew clearer in the fresh air, and lulled the drowsy ear. If one of them rose and stood up for a moment, he saw the steppe dotted with the gleaming sparks of fireflies. Here and there the night sky was lighted up by the faraway glow of dry reeds being burned here and there in the meadows and by the rivers, and a dark string of swans flying to the north would suddenly gleam with silvery pink light, and then it looked as though red handkerchiefs were flying through the dark sky.

The travelers rode on without incident. They nowhere came upon trees: everywhere the same boundless, free, lovely steppe. But at times they saw on one side the dark blue tops of the faraway forest that stretches along the bank of the Dnieper. Only once did Taras point out to his sons a little black dot far away in the grass, saying: "Look, boys, there's a Tartar galloping there!" A little head fixed its narrow eyes straight upon them in the distance, sniffed the air above its mustaches like a hunting dog, and like an antelope vanished on seeing that the Cossacks were thirteen in number.

"Well now, lads, you may try to overtake the Tartar! But better not try, you'll never catch him: his horse is swifter than my Devil." Bulba, however, took precautions, fearing an ambush concealed somewhere. They galloped up to the Tatarka, a little stream that falls into the Dnieper, plunged into the water with their horses, and for a long time swam along to conceal their tracks, then clambered out onto the bank and went on their way.

Three days after that they were not far from the place which was the goal of their journey. There was a sudden chill in the air; they felt that the Dnieper was near. Then it gleamed in the distance and stood out, a dark streak against the horizon. A chill breath arose from its cold waves, and it stretched nearer and nearer, and at last covered half the surface of the land. It was that part of the Dnieper where, after being narrowed into rapids, it at last takes its own way, and, roaring like the sea, flows in freedom, where the islands scattered in mid-river force it still further from the banks, and its waters spread themselves wide over the land, meeting no crags or heights. The Cossacks dismounted from their horses, embarked on a ferry, and after three hours' sailing reached the shores of the Island of Khortitsa, where at that time the camp, which so often changed its location, was situated.

A group of people were wrangling with the ferrymen on the bank. The Cossacks looked after their horses. Taras drew himself up with dignity, tightened his belt, and haughtily stroked his mustaches. His young sons, too, looked themselves up and down with a sort of apprehension and vague pleasure, and all of them rode together into the outer village, which is half a mile from the camp. As they rode in, they were deafened by fifty smiths' hammers clanging upon twenty-five anvils covered with turf and sunk in the earth. Powerful leatherworkers were sitting under their porches in the street; they were kneading bulls' skins with their powerful arms. Hucksters were sitting in shanties with heaps of flints, tinder, and powder; an Armenian had hung out costly kerchiefs; a Tartar was turning upon spits fillets of mutton dipped in dough; a Jew, craning his head forward, was drawing vodka out of a barrel. But the first man they came across was a Dnieper Cossack asleep in the middle of the road, his arms and legs stretched out. Taras Bulba could not help stopping and admiring him. "Ah, how grandly he is sprawling! I swear, he is an impressive figure!" he said, stopping his horse. It was indeed a rather bold picture; the

Cossack lay full length like a lion in the road; his forelock, tossed proudly back, covered half a yard of ground; his trousers of expensive crimson cloth were smeared with tar, showing his complete disregard for them. After admiring him, Bulba made his way further along the narrow street, which was encumbered by craftsmen carrying on their trades there, and men of all nations, who crowded this outer village of the camp, which was like a fair and which clothed and fed the Cossacks, who could do nothing but carouse and shoot.

At last they had passed the outer village and saw a few scattered barracks,[2] roofed with turf or, in the Tartar fashion, with felt. There were cannons standing about some of them. Nowhere were fences to be seen, nor little low-pitched huts with porches on low wooden posts such as were in the outer village. A small rampart and barricade, not guarded by anyone, showed their fearful recklessness. A few sturdy Cossacks, lying with their pipes in their teeth, right on the road, looked at them rather unconcernedly and did not move. Taras rode carefully between them with his sons, saying: "Good health to you, gentlemen!"

"Good health to you too!" answered the Cossacks. Everywhere picturesque groups were dotted about the plain. From their tanned faces it could be seen that they all had been hardened in battle and had passed through privations of all sorts. So this was it, the camp! This was the nest from which all those heroes came forth as proud and vigorous as lions. This was the source from which freedom and Cossack chivalry flowed over the whole of the Ukraine!

The travelers came out into a spacious square where the Council[3] usually assembled. On a big cask turned upside down a Cossack was sitting without his shirt; he had it in his hands and was slowly mending the holes in it. Their way was barred again by a crowd of musicians in whose midst a young Cossack was dancing and flinging up his arms, his cap jauntily thrust on one side. He only shouted: "Play faster, musicians! Foma, don't grudge vodka to good Christians!" And Foma, who had a black eye, was ladling out an enormous mugful to every comer at random. Four old Cossacks near the young one were working their legs rather mincingly, flinging themselves like a whirlwind almost on the musicians'

---

[2] *Kurens*, a group of buildings within the camp (*sech*); a fortified village. Also applied to a detachment of men, a military unit. (ed.)
[3] *Rada*, assembly of Cossack elders. (ed.)

heads, and suddenly dropping into a squatting position, they flew around, stamping with their silver heels vigorously and resoundingly on the hard beaten ground. The earth resounded with a hollow echo far around and the air was ringing with the dance tunes struck out by the clinking heels of their boots. One more eager than the rest kept uttering shrieks and flying after the others in the dance. His long forelock fluttered in the wind, his powerful chest was revealed; but he was wearing a warm winter sheepskin and the sweat was dripping from him as from a pail.

"At least take off your sheepskin!" said Taras at last. "You see how hot it is!"

"I can't!" cried the Cossack.

"Why not?"

"I cannot; if I fling a thing off I swap it for drink; that's my way." The young warrior had long been without cap or girdle, or embroidered kerchief; all had gone the same road.

The crowd grew larger; others joined the dancers, and no one could have watched without being held spellbound by that most free, most furious dance the world has ever seen, the *Kozatchok*, named after its originators.

"Oh, if it weren't for my horse," cried Taras, "I'd join in, I'd really join in the dance!"

And meanwhile they began coming upon gray-headed old veterans who had more than once been elders and were respected by all in the camp for their services. Taras soon met a number of old acquaintances. Ostap and Andrei heard nothing but greetings. "Ah, is that you, Pecheritsa! Good day, Kozolup!" "From where has God brought you, Taras?" "How did you come here, Doloto? Good health to you, Kirdiaga! Good health to you, Gusty! I never thought to see you, Remen!" And warriors, gathered from all the turbulent world of South Russia, kissed each other, and questions followed at once. "And what of Kasian? Where's Borodavka? What news of Kolopior? What's Pidsyshok doing?" And all Taras Bulba heard in reply was that Borodavka had been hanged at Tolopan, that Kolopior had been flayed near Kizikirmen, that Pidsyshok's head had been pickled in a barrel and sent to Constantinople. Old Bulba's head drooped as he said pensively: "They were good Cossacks!"

III

Taras Bulba had been living with his sons for about a week in the camp. Ostap and Andrei were not much occupied in studying the military art. The Cossacks did not care to trouble themselves with drill or to waste time in maneuvers: the young men were taught and trained only by experience in the heat of battle, which was therefore almost continuous. The Cossacks thought it tedious to employ the intervals in practicing any sort of discipline except perhaps firing at a target and occasionally horse racing and hunting wild beasts in the steppes and the meadows. All the rest of the time was given up to revelry—the outward manifestation of the breadth and vigor of their unfettered spirits. The camp presented an extraordinary spectacle; it was an uninterrupted festivity, a ball that began noisily and never ended. Some of its inmates practiced crafts, others kept shops and traded; but the majority caroused from morning till evening, if the jingle in their pockets made it possible, and the booty they had won had not yet passed into the hands of dealers and tavern keepers. There was a fascinating charm in this carousing. It was not a gathering of people drinking to drown sorrow, but simply the frenzied recklessness of gaiety. Everyone who came here forgot and forsook everything that had occupied him before. He spat, one may say, upon his past, and carelessly abandoned himself to freedom and the companionship of other reckless revelers like himself, who had no kindred, no home nor family, nothing but the open sky and the eternal festivity. This produced a wild gaiety that could spring from no other source. The talk and storytelling among the crowd lazily resting on the ground was often so amusing, so full of life and vigor, that all the cool composure of the Cossacks was needed to maintain an unmoved expression without the twitch of a mustache —a conspicuous characteristic by which the Russian of the South is still distinguished from his fellow countrymen. The gaiety was drunken and noisy, but for all that it was not the gaiety of the gloomy tavern where a man seeks forgetfulness in dreary and depraving hilarity; it was like an intimate club of school comrades. The only difference was that instead of sitting spelling out words and listening to the dull teaching of a schoolmaster, they rode out on five thousand horses to the attack; instead of a field to play ball in, they had unguarded, insecure frontiers, over which the swift

Tartar showed his head and the Turk in his green turban looked steadily and menacingly. The difference was that, instead of being compulsorily kept at school, they had of their own free will forsaken their fathers and mothers and run away from their homes; that here there were men who had had the noose around their necks and who, escaping pale death, had plunged into life, and life in all its festive fullness; that here there were men whose honorable tradition it was never to keep a kopek in their pockets; that here there were men who had till then considered a gold coin a fortune, whose pockets, thanks to the Jewish leaseholders, might have been turned inside out without risk of losing anything. Here there were all the students who could not endure the floggings of the seminary and who had not learned one letter of the alphabet in school; but with them there were also men here who knew something of Horace, Cicero, and the Roman Republic. Here were many of the officers who afterward distinguished themselves in the Polish army; here, too, were numbers of experienced guerillas who had the conviction that it did not matter where they fought so long as they fought, since it was improper for a gentleman not to be engaged in warfare. There were many here, too, who had come to the camp in order to say afterward that they had been there, and were seasoned warriors. Who was not to be found there? The strange republic was a necessity of the age. Lovers of the military life, lovers of gold goblets, rich brocades, gold coins, could find work here at any time. Only those devoted to women could find nothing here, for not one woman dared to show herself even in the outer village of the camp.

To Ostap and Andrei it seemed exceedingly strange that numbers of people arrived at the camp and no one asked where these men came from, who they were, and what were their names. They came here as though returning to their own home which they had left but an hour before. The newcomer merely showed himself to the leader,[4] who usually said: "Good health to you! Do you believe in Christ?"

"I do!" answered the newcomer.

"And do you believe in the Holy Trinity?"

"I do!"

"And do you go to church?"

---

[4] *Koshevoy*, head of a camp. (ed.)

"I do!"

"Well, then, cross yourself!" The newcomer crossed himself.

"Good!" answered the leader. "Go to the unit which you choose."

With that the whole ceremony ended. And all of the camp prayed in one church and was ready to defend it to the last drop of their blood, though they would not hear of fasting and abstinence. Only Jews, Armenians, and Tartars, moved by intense desire of gain, ventured to live and trade in the outer village, for the Cossacks never liked bargaining and paid just as much money as their hand happened to pull out of their pockets. The lot of these covetous traders was most pitiful, however; they were like the villagers who live at the foot of Vesuvius, for as soon as the Cossacks had spent all their money, they smashed the dealers' stalls and took their goods for nothing.

The camp consisted of over sixty military units, which were very much like separate independent republics and still more like a children's boarding school or a seminary. No one kept anything to himself: everything was in the hands of the chief of the unit, who because of that was commonly addressed as "Father." He kept the money, the clothes, all the provisions, the boiled grain, the porridge, and even the fuel; the Cossacks gave him their money to take care of. Frequently a quarrel sprang up between one unit and another, and this at once led to a fight. Their inmates crowded the square and belabored each other's ribs with their fists, until at last one party proved the stronger and gained the upper hand; then followed a wild drinking party. Such was the camp which had such a fascination for young men.

Ostap and Andrei plunged with all the ardor of youth into this sea of reckless gaiety and instantly forgot their father's house and their seminary, and all that had stirred their hearts before this; they surrendered entirely to their new life. Everything interested them, the festive customs of the camp and the not very complicated rules and regulations which sometimes, indeed, struck them as too severe in such an independent republic. If a Cossack were a thief and stole any trifle, it was regarded as a disgrace to the whole body of Cossacks: he was bound to the whipping post as a thief, and beside him was laid an oak club with which each Cossack was obliged to deal him a blow, until in this way he was beaten to death. If a man did not pay his debts, he was chained to a cannon, where he had to remain until one of his comrades was moved to buy him off by paying the debt for him. But Andrei was most impressed by the fearful punishment laid down for murder. He saw a pit dug on the spot and the murderer lowered into it alive, and above him the coffin containing the body of his victim was laid, and then both were covered with earth. Long afterward he was haunted by this horrible form of punishment and kept picturing the man buried alive with the horrible coffin.

Soon the two young Cossacks were quite at home in the camp. Often with other comrades of their unit and sometimes with the whole of their unit and the neighboring ones, they went out to shoot immense numbers of the various wild birds of the steppe, of stags and goats; or they visited the lakes, rivers, and streams which were assigned by lot to the different units, dropped in their tackle and their nets, and drew out vast shoals of fish to supply their comrades. Though there were no maneuvers in which a Cossack could show his mettle, they had already attracted notice among the other young men by their reckless boldness and success in everything. They shot quickly and accurately at the target, and swam across the Dnieper against the current—a feat which wins for the novice a triumphant reception into Cossack circles.

But old Taras was preparing a different kind of activity for them. Such an idle life was not to his taste—he longed for action. He was always pondering how he could rouse the camp to some bold enterprise in which a warrior might fittingly enjoy himself. At last one day he went to the leader and said to him plainly: "Well, it's high time for the Dnieper Cossacks to go on an adventure."

"There's nowhere for them to have it," answered the leader, taking a little pipe out of his mouth and spitting aside.

"Nowhere? We could move against the Turks or the Tartars."

"We cannot go into Turkey nor to the Tartars," answered the leader, coolly putting his pipe back into his mouth.

"Why can't we?"

"Well, we promised the Sultan peace."

"But you know he is a pagan, and God and the Holy Scriptures bid us beat the infidels."

"We have not the right. If we had not sworn by our faith, then perhaps we might have; but now we cannot, it's impossible."

"How impossible? How can you say we have not the right? Here I have two sons, both young men. Neither has ever been once in battle, and you say we have not the right; and you say the Cossacks must not go to war."

"Well, it's not right to do so."

"Then it is right for the strength of the Cossacks to be wasted, for a man to rot like a dog without deeds of valor, for neither fatherland nor Christianity to get any good from him, is it? Then what the hell are we living for? Explain that to me. You're a clever man, it was not for nothing they chose you leader: explain what we are living for?"

The leader made no answer to this question. He was an obstinate Cossack. He was silent for a little while and then said:

"There won't be war, anyway."

"So there won't be war?" Taras asked him.

"No."

"So it's no use thinking about it?"

"It's no use even thinking about it."

"You wait, you tight-fisted devil!" said Bulba to himself: "I'll let you know!" And he determined on the spot to revenge himself on the leader.

After talking to one and then to another, he set up a drinking feast for them all, and several drunken Cossacks went straight to the square where, tied to posts, there were kettledrums on which they used to beat to summon the assembly. Not finding the sticks, which were always kept at the drummer's, they each snatched up a block of wood and began beating the drums. The first to run up at the sound was the drummer, a tall man with only one eye, and that one looking terribly sleepy.

"Who dares beat the drums?" he shouted.

"Hold your tongue! Take your drumsticks and beat the drum when you are told!" they answered.

The drummer at once took out of his pocket the sticks which he had brought with him, knowing well how such incidents ended. At the rat-a-tat of the drums, dark groups of Cossacks began swarming into the square like bees. They all gathered in a circle, and after a third tattoo had been beaten on the drums, the elders showed themselves at last: the leader with his mace, the badge of office, in his hand, the judge with the official seal, the clerk with his inkpot, and the captain with his staff. The leader and the other officials took off their caps and bowed in all directions to the Cossacks, who stood proudly with their arms akimbo.

"What is the meaning of this assembly? What do you want, comrades?" said the leader. The shouts and abuse would not let him go on.

"Put down your mace! Put down your mace this minute, son of the devil! We'll have no more of you!" the Cossacks shouted from the crowd. Some of the sober units wanted, it seemed, to protest, but the drunken and the sober came to blows. The noise and uproar became general.

The leader tried to speak, but knowing that the determined crowd, once roused to fury, might beat him to death for it (which almost always happened on such occasions), he made a very low bow, put down his mace, and disappeared into the crowd.

"Do you bid us, too, to put down our badge of office, comrades?" said the judge, the clerk, and the captain, and they made ready at once to lay down the inkpot, the seal, and the staff.

"No, you remain!" the crowd shouted. "We only wanted to throw out the leader because he is a woman and we want a man for a leader."

"Whom do you elect leader now?" asked the judge and the captain.

"Choose Kukubenko!" shouted some.

"We won't have Kukubenko!" shouted others. "It's too soon for him, the milk is not dry on his lips."

"Let Shilo be leader!" shouted some.

"A Shilo[5] in your back!" the crowd shouted with oaths. "A fine Cossack when he thieves like a Tartar, the son of a bitch! Into the devil's sack with drunken Shilo!"

"Borodaty, let us make Borodaty leader!"

"We won't have Borodaty! The devil's mother take him!"

"Shout Kirdiaga!" whispered Taras Bulba to several.

"Kirdiaga! Kirdiaga!" shouted the crowd. "Borodaty! Borodaty! Kirdiaga! Kirdiaga! Shilo! The hell with Shilo! Kirdiaga!"

All the candidates, hearing their names called, at once stepped out of the crowd to avoid giving any grounds for supposing that they were taking any personal part in their election.

"Kirdiaga! Kirdiaga!" sounded louder than the rest.

"Borodaty!" The question was put to a show of hands and Kirdiaga was the victor.

---

[5] "Bradawl." (ed.)

"Go and fetch Kirdiaga!" they shouted.

A dozen Cossacks, some hardly able to stand, they had drunk so heavily, moved out of the crowd and went at once to tell Kirdiaga of his election. Kirdiaga, a clever though rather elderly Cossack, had been sitting for some time in his barracks, as though he knew nothing of what was taking place.

"What is it, comrades? What do you want?" he asked.

"Come along, you have been elected leader!"

"Mercy on us!" said Kirdiaga. "How can I be worthy of such an honor? How can I be leader? Why, I haven't sense enough to fill such an office. Could no one better be found in the whole camp?"

"Come along, we tell you!" shouted the Cossacks. Two of them took him by the arms and, although he resisted, he was at last dragged along to the square, accompanied by abuse, punches in the back, kicks, and exhortations. "Don't resist, you son of a bitch! Accept the honor, you dog, when it's given to you!" In this way Kirdiaga was led into the circle of Cossacks.

"Well, comrades!" those who led him boomed out to the crowd: "do you agree that this Cossack should be our leader?"

"We all agree!" roared the crowd, and the whole plain resounded to their shout.

One of the elders picked up the mace of office and took it to the newly elected leader. Kirdiaga, as the custom was, at once refused it. It was brought him a second time, and only at the third time he at last accepted it. A shout of approval rang out through the whole crowd, and again the whole plain echoed far and wide from the Cossacks' shout. Then four of the oldest Cossacks, with gray mustaches and gray forelocks (there were no very old men in the camp, for no Dnieper Cossack died a natural death) stepped forward out of the crowd, and each, taking a handful of earth which had been turned into mud by recent rain, laid it on Kirdiaga's head. The wet earth trickled from his head over his mustache and cheeks, and his whole face was smeared with mud. But Kirdiaga stood without moving and thanked the Cossacks for the honor shown him.

Thus ended the noisy meeting. Bulba was very pleased with the results, perhaps more than the others: it was his revenge on the former leader; moreover, Kirdiaga was an old comrade of his and had been with him on campaigns by land and sea, sharing the toils and hardships of war. The crowd dispersed at once to celebrate the election, and a riotous debauch followed, such as Ostap and Andrei had not before seen. The drinking booths were smashed; mead, vodka, and beer were simply seized, without payment; the booth keepers were glad to get off alive. The whole night was spent in shouting and singing songs celebrating their exploits, and the rising moon for hours witnessed crowds of musicians parading through the streets with bandores, drums, and round balalaikas, together with church choristers who were kept at the camp to sing in church and to glorify the deeds of the Cossacks. At last drink and exhaustion overcame their stubborn heads. And here and there a Cossack was seen falling to the ground; another, embracing a comrade and even weeping with sentimentality, would roll over with him. Here a whole group were lying in a heap; here a Cossack looking out for the best place to lie down ended by lying on a block of wood. The last whose head was most stubborn still uttered incoherent words; at last he too was felled by the power of drink, he too fell sprawling—and all of the camp sank into slumber.

IV

Next day Taras Bulba was conferring with the new leader as to how to rouse the Cossacks to some deed of valor. The leader was a clever and crafty Cossack, he knew the Cossacks through and through, and at first he said: "We cannot go beyond our oath, it can't be done," but after a pause he added: "No matter, it can be done; we will not break our oath, but we will think of something. Only let the people assemble, but not at my command, but simply at their own pleasure—you know how to manage that—and we and the elders will hasten to the square, as though we knew nothing about it."

Not an hour after their conversation the kettledrums were sounding again. Both drunken and reckless Cossacks suddenly popped up. Thousands of Cossacks were hurrying at once to the square. Questions were asked: "Who? What for? Why is a meeting called?" No one answered. At last, first in one corner and then in another, men were heard saying: "Here the strength of the Cossacks is being wasted; there is no war! Here our elders have grown sluggish, their eyes are buried in fat! It seems there is no justice in the world!" Other Cossacks listened at first, and then they too began saying: "Indeed, there is no justice in the world!" The elders seemed astounded at these sayings. At last the leader stepped forward and said: "Allow me, comrades, to speak!"

"Speak!"

"What we have to discuss now, honorable sirs, and you, maybe, know this better than I do, is that many Cossacks are so deeply in debt to the Jews at the taverns and to their comrades that not even the devil will give them credit. Then again there are many fellows who have never seen what war is with their eyes, while no young man—you know it very well, comrades—can exist without war. What sort of Cossack will he make if he has not once fought a pagan?"

"He speaks well," thought Bulba.

"Don't imagine though, comrades, that I say this to break the peace. God forbid! I merely state it. Moreover we have a church—it's a disgrace to say what it's like: here by the grace of God the camp has been established so many years, and up to now not only the outside of the church but even the icons are devoid of adornment; someone might at least have thought to make them a silver frame; they have only received what some Cossacks have bequeathed, and indeed their offerings were poor, because they had drunk up almost everything they had in their lifetime. I am saying this not to urge the beginning of war with the heathens: we have promised the Sultan peace, and it would be a great sin for us, because we have taken an oath in accordance with our law."

"Why is he making such a muddle?" said Bulba to himself.

"So, as you see, comrades, it is not possible to begin a war: knightly honor forbids. So this is what in my poor judgment I suggest: let the young ones go alone with the boats, let them make a little visit to the shores of Anatolia.[6] What do you think, comrades?"

"Take us all, take us all!" the crowd shouted from all sides: "we are ready to lay down our lives for our faith."

The leader was alarmed; he had not at all wanted to arouse all the Cossacks: to break the peace seemed to him in this case to be wrong. "Will you allow me, comrades, to speak again?"

"Enough!" exclaimed the Cossacks. "You'll say nothing better."

"If that's how it is, so be it. I am the servant of your will. We all know, we know it from Scripture, that the voice of the people is the voice of God. Nothing wiser can be thought of than what the people has thought. But there is this: you know, comrades, that

---

[6] The Asiatic part of Turkey. (ed.)

the Sultan will not let our young men's diversion go unpunished. And by that time we should be ready and our strength would be fresh and we should be afraid of nobody. And while we are absent the Tartars may attack: they won't face us, the Turkish dogs, and dare not come to the house when the master is at home, but will bite our heels from behind and bite hard too. And if it has come to telling the whole truth, we have not boats enough in store nor powder enough ground for all to go. So be it: I am the servant of your will."

The crafty leader ceased speaking. The Cossacks began talking in groups, the chiefs of each unit consulted together; fortunately few were drunk, and so they decided to listen to the counsels of prudence.

That very hour several men set off to the opposite bank of the Dnieper to the treasury, where in inaccessible secret places, under water and in the reeds, the treasury of the army and some of the weapons taken from the enemy lay hidden. All the others rushed to the boats to overhaul them and get them ready for the journey. The bank was instantly crowded with men. Some carpenters arrived with axes in their hands. Old weather-beaten, broad-shouldered, sturdy-legged Cossacks, some with grizzled mustaches, some with black ones, tucking up their trousers, stood knee-deep in the water and dragged the boats with a strong rope from the shore. Others hauled dry logs and trees of all sorts. Here men were mending the boats with boards; here they had turned one upside down and were calking and tarring it; here, as the custom was with the Cossacks, they were binding bundles of long reeds to the sides of boats so that they would not be sunk by the sea waves; further up, campfires had been built all along the bank and tar was being boiled in copper cauldrons for tarring the vessels. The old and experienced directed the young. The tapping of hammers and the shouts of the workmen sounded all over the place; the whole bank was heaving with life and movement.

At that moment a big ferryboat began floating toward the bank. A group of men standing on it waved their hands from afar. They were Cossacks in tattered jackets. Their disordered dress—many had nothing but their shirt and the short pipe in their teeth—showed that they had just escaped from some disaster, or that they had been drinking so deeply that they had squandered everything that they had had upon them. A short, broad-shouldered Cossack of about

fifty stepped out from among them and stood in front. He shouted
and waved his arms more vigorously than the rest; but his words
could not be heard above the hammering and shouts of the workmen.

"What has brought you?" asked the leader, when the ferryboat
reached the bank. All the workmen stopped their work and with ax
and chisel in the air stared in expectation.

"Trouble!" the short Cossack shouted from the ferry.

"What trouble?"

"Will you allow me to speak, Cossack?"

"Speak!"

"Or maybe you will call the assembly?"

"Speak, we are all here."

They all crowded around.

"Can you have heard nothing of what is being done in the Hetman's land?"

"Why, what?" one of the unit chiefs asked.

"Ah! What? It seems the Tartars have glued up your ears that
you have heard nothing?"

"Tell us what is happening there?"

"Such doings have never been seen since we were born and
christened."

"But do tell us what has happened, you son of a bitch!" shouted
someone from the crowd, evidently losing patience.

"Such times have come that now even the holy churches are not
ours."

"How do you mean, not ours?"

"Nowadays they are leased out to the Jews. If you don't pay the
Jew beforehand, you cannot serve mass."

"What are you talking about?"

"And if a Jewish dog does not put a stamp with his unbaptized
hand on the Holy Easter Cake, one cannot consecrate the cake."

"He is lying, comrades; it cannot be that an unbaptized Jew
puts a stamp on the Holy Easter Cake."

"Listen! I've more to tell you: and the Catholic priests are driving now all over the Ukraine in their two-wheeled carts. And the
trouble is not that they ride in their carriages, but that Orthodox
Christians and not horses pull them. Listen! There's more to tell:
they say the Jewesses are making themselves petticoats out of the

priests' vestments. These are the things that are going on in the Ukraine, comrades! And you sit here in the camp and enjoy yourselves, and it seems the Tartar has given you such a fright that you have neither ears nor eyes—and you don't hear what is going on in the world."

"Stop, stop!" broke in the leader, who had stood till then with his eyes on the ground like all the Dnieper Cossacks, who in important matters never give way to their first impulse, but remain mute and let the power of their indignation accumulate in silence.

"Stop! I too will say a word. And what were you—may the devil beat your father all over!—what were you doing yourselves? Hadn't you swords, or what? How was it you allowed such lawlessness?"

"Aye, how did we allow such lawlessness . . . ! You should have tried it when there were fifty thousand Poles and—indeed, no use to hide a sin—there were dogs too among our own men who had already accepted their Roman faith."

"And your Hetman and the chiefs, what were they about?"

"What the chiefs were about God grant no man may see again!"

"How so?"

"Why, so that now the Hetman lies in Warsaw roasted in a copper pot, and the arms and heads of the chiefs are being carried about at the fairs as a show. That's what has come of our chiefs' deeds!"

The whole crowd heaved. At first a silence fell over the whole riverside such as is common before a violent storm, then all at once voices arose and the whole riverside was talking:

"What! Jews renting out the Orthodox churches! Polish priests harnessing Orthodox Christians! What! Allow such tortures in Russia at the hands of the cursed infidels? Let them treat the chiefs and Hetman like that? But that shall not be, that shall never be!" Such sayings flew from one end of the crowd to another. The Dnieper Cossacks were in an uproar and felt their strength. This was not the excitement of frivolous people; it was the excitement of slow strong characters who do not soon get hot, but, when they are hot, long and obstinately retain that inner fire.

"Hang all the Jews!" was heard from the crowd. "Don't let them make the priests' vestments into petticoats for the Jewesses! Don't let them put stamps on the Holy Easter Cakes! Drown them all, the heathens, in the Dnieper!" These words uttered by someone in the crowd flashed like lightning through the heads of all, and the crowd rushed to the outer village, intending to cut the throats of all the Jews.

The poor sons of Israel, losing what little courage they had, hid in empty vodka barrels, in ovens, and even crept under the skirts of their wives; but the Cossacks found them everywhere.

"Illustrious masters!" cried one tall Jew as long as a stick, thrusting his pitiful face, distorted by terror, from among a group of his companions: "Illustrious masters! A word, only let us say one word! We'll tell you something you have never heard before—so important that there is no saying how important!"

"Well, let them speak," said Bulba, who always liked to hear the accused.

"Noble lords!" the Jew articulated. "Such lords have never before been known, upon my soul, never! Such kind, good, valiant gentlemen have never been in the world before!" His voice failed and shook with terror. "How could we think any harm to the Dnieper Cossacks! Those who are leaseholders in the Ukraine are not our people at all! By God, they are not! They are not Jews at all! The devil knows what they are: such that one can but spit upon them and turn them out! Here they will say the same. Isn't it true, Shloma, or you, Shmuel?"

"By God, it's true!" answered Shloma and Shmuel from among the crowd, in tattered caps, both white as clay.

"We have never had any dealings with the enemy," the tall Jew went on, "and we don't want to know anything of the Catholics: may they dream of the devil! We have been like brothers with you. . . ."

"What? The Dnieper Cossacks are your brothers?" one of the crowd shouted. "You'll never see that, you damned Jews! Into the Dnieper with them, comrades, drown all the heathens!"

These words were the signal. They seized the Jews by their arms and began flinging them into the water. Pitiful cries rang out on all sides, but the hardhearted Cossacks only laughed at the sight of the Jews' legs in slippers and stockings kicking in the air.

The poor orator who had called down trouble on his own head, slipped out of the long coat by which he was being held, and in nothing but a narrow spotted jacket clutched at Bulba's feet and in a piteous voice besought him: "Great lord, illustrious master! I knew your brother, the lamented Dorosh! He was a warrior who brought honor to all knighthood. I gave him eight hundred sequins, when he had to be ransomed from the Turks. . . ."

"You knew my brother?" asked Taras.

"By God, I did! A greathearted gentleman he was."

"And what is your name?"

"Yankel."

"Good," said Taras, and after a moment's thought he turned to the Cossacks and said: "There will always be time to hang the Jew when need be; but today give him to me."

Saying this, Taras led him to his wagons beside which his Cossacks were standing; "Come, crawl under the cart, lie there and don't move, and you, boys, don't let the Jew go."

Then he started to the square, for the whole crowd had for some time been assembled there. Everyone had instantly abandoned the riverbank and the equipment of the boats, for now an expedition by land and not by sea was before them, and not boats and Cossack "sea gulls" but carts and horses were needed. Now all wanted to join, old and young; everyone, with the assent of all the elders, the unit chiefs, and by the will of all the Dnieper Cossacks, resolved to go straight to Poland, to revenge all the wrong and shame done to their faith and to the Cossack fame, to plunder the towns, to burn the villages and crops, and to spread their glory far and wide over the steppe. All were at once belted and armed. The leader seemed to have grown several feet taller. He was no longer the timid servant of the frivolous desires of the free people; he was an absolute ruler, he was a despot who knew how to command. All the independent and reveling warriors stood in orderly ranks respectfully looking down, not daring to raise their eyes when the leader gave an instruction: he gave them quietly without haste or shouting, like an old Cossack, much experienced in action, who was not for the first time carrying out a well-planned enterprise.

"Inspect yourselves, all of you. Inspect yourselves!" he said. "See that the baggage wagons and kegs of tar are in order; try your weapons. Do not take much clothing with you: a shirt and two pairs of trousers for each Cossack, and a pot of porridge and of crushed millet—let no one take more! Everything that is needed will be in the store-wagons. Let every Cossack have a pair of horses! And take two hundred oxen, for oxen will be needed at the fords and slippery places. And keep discipline, comrades, above everything. I know there are some among you who, as soon as

God sends them any booty, go at once tearing up cotton stuff and expensive velvets for leg wrappers. Give up that wretched habit, don't touch petticoats of any sort, but only take a weapon if you can get hold of a good one, and gold or silver pieces, for they go a long way and are of use in every emergency. And here, comrades, I tell you beforehand: if anyone gets drunk on the campaign, there will be no trial for him; I will have him tied by the collar to a wagon, whoever he may be, even though it should be the most valiant Cossack of the whole army; like a dog, he will be shot at once and left without burial for the birds to peck, for a man drunk on a campaign does not deserve Christian burial. Young men, obey your elders in everything! If you are grazed by a bullet or get a scratch on the head from a saber or anything else, don't pay much attention to it; mix a charge of powder in a goblet of vodka, drink it off at one breath, and it will all pass off, there will be no fever even; and on the wound, if it is not too big, simply put earth, mixing it with spittle in the palm of your hand, and the wound will dry up. Well, now to work, to work, lads, and without haste; do the thing thoroughly!"

So spoke the leader and as soon as he had finished his speech, all the Cossacks set to work at once. The whole camp was sober, and not a single drunken man could be found anywhere; it was as though there had never been any among the Cossacks. Some were mending the hoops of the wheels and changing the axles in the carts; some were carrying sacks of provisions to the wagons or heaping weapons on them; some were driving in horses and oxen. From all sides was heard the tramp of horses' hoofs, the firing of guns to test them, the clank of swords, the bellowing of bulls, the creaking of wagons being turned upside down, talk and loud shouting and driving. And soon the Cossack camp stretched in a long, long string over the whole plain. And anyone wanting to run from the head to the tail of it would have had to run a great way. In the little wooden church the priests conducted a service and sprinkled all with holy water; everyone kissed the cross. When they started off and filed out of the camp all the Cossacks looked back. "Farewell, our Mother!" they said almost in the same words: "May God keep thee from all calamity!"

As he rode through the outer village Taras Bulba saw that his Jew, Yankel, had already rigged up a sort of booth and was selling flints, screwdrivers, powder, and various military equipment necessary for the journey, even loaves and rolls. "What a devil of a Jew!" Taras thought to himself, and riding up to him on his horse said: "Fool, why are you sitting here? Do you want to be shot like a sparrow?"

Yankel, in answer to this, went closer up to him and, making a gesture with both hands as though he wanted to tell him something mysterious, said: "Let only my lord keep silent and say nothing to anyone: among the Cossack wagons is one wagon of mine; I am taking stores of everything necessary for the Cossacks, and on the way I will furnish provisions of all sorts at a cheaper price than any Jew has sold them yet; by God, yes; by God, yes!"

Taras Bulba shrugged his shoulders, marveled at the spontaneous resourcefulness of the Jewish character, and rode off to join the others.

V

Soon all the southwest of Poland was a prey to terror. From all sides flew the rumor: "The Dnieper Cossacks! The Dnieper Cossacks have appeared!" Everyone who could escape, escaped. All rose up and ran in different directions, after the manner of that reckless unorganized age, when nobody built fortresses or castles, but a man put up his thatched dwelling anyhow for a time. He thought: "Useless to waste labor and money on a hut when it will be carried off by invading Tartars anyway!" All was in commotion: some bartered oxen and plow for horse and gun and set off to join the troops; some went into hiding, driving away their cattle and carrying away what could be carried away. Sometimes they were met upon the way by men who greeted their visitors with weapons, but more often by others who had made their escape sooner. Everyone knew that it was hard to deal with the turbulent and warlike crowd that went under the name of the Dnieper Cossack army, which, for all its external freedom and lack of organization, had a discipline adapted for times of warfare. The horsemen rode on, not overstraining or overheating their horses; those on foot marched soberly behind the wagons; and the whole body moved only by night, resting by day and choosing for that purpose uninhabited places and forests, of which there were plenty in those days. Spies and scouts were sent on ahead to find out and learn where, what, and how. And often they suddenly appeared in

places where they could least be expected, and then everyone
there took leave of life: villages were wrapped in flames, what cattle and horses were not driven off with the troops were slaughtered
on the spot. It seemed as though they were carousing rather than
carrying on a campaign. One's hair stands on end nowadays at the
terrible evidence of the ferocity of that half-savage age displayed
everywhere by the Dnieper Cossacks. Slaughtered babes, women
with breasts cut off, men set free with the skin flayed from their
feet to their knees—in fact, the Cossacks paid off their old scores
with interest. The prelate of one monastery, hearing of their approach, sent two monks to tell them that they were not behaving
as they should, that there was an agreement between the Dnieper
Cossacks and the Government, that they were guilty of a breach of
their duty to the Polish King and at the same time infringing all
the people's rights. "Tell the bishop from me and all the Dnieper
Cossacks," said the leader, "not to be afraid: so far the Cossacks
are only lighting their pipes." And soon the stately monastery
was wrapped in flames and its colossal Gothic windows looked
out sullenly through waves of fire. The fleeing crowds of monks,
Jews, and women flooded the towns, where there was at least some
hope from the garrison and armed defense of the town. The belated help sent from time to time by the Government, consisting of
a few regiments, either could not find the enemy or feared them,
turned their backs at the first encounter, and fled on their swift
steeds. Sometimes it happened that many of the Polish generals who
had been victorious in previous wars resolved on joining their forces
and setting up a united front against the Cossacks. And then it was
that the young Cossacks proved themselves, shunning plunder, gain,
and helpless enemies, and burning to show what they could do before their older comrades and to measure themselves in single combat with some alert and boastful Pole, flaunting on his proud
steed, with his wide sleeves and cloak flying in the wind. It was
diverting practice; they carried off plenty of horses, trappings, expensive swords, and guns. In one month the callow fledglings
had grown hardy and been completely transformed; they had become men, their features in which a youthful softness had till then
been perceptible were now fierce and vigorous. And old Taras
was glad to see that his two sons were among the foremost. It
seemed as though Ostap were destined from birth for the career of
arms and the hard discipline of warlike deeds. Never losing his head

nor being disconcerted by any emergency, with a coolness almost unnatural in a lad of twenty-two, he could in one instant gauge all the hazards and circumstances of the situation, could on the spot find the means of escaping it, and in such a way as to overcome it more surely afterwards. His movements began to be marked by the confidence of experience, and the qualities of a future leader were apparent in them. His whole body was charged with energy, and there was a breadth and lionlike power about his knightly qualities. "Ah, that one with time will make a good colonel!" said old Taras to himself. "Aie, aie, he will make a good colonel and one that will outshine his father!"

Andrei was entirely absorbed in the fascinating music of the bullets and the swords. He did not know what it meant to consider or calculate, or to measure his own strength and that of others beforehand. He found in battle a wild thrill and enchantment; he seemed imbued with a joyous feeling in those moments when a man's mind is aflame, when all flits in confusion before his eyes, when heads are flying and horses falling to the earth with a crash, while he dashes, as though drunk, amid the whizz of bullets and the glitter of swords, and deals blows on all sides and does not feel those dealt him. More than once the father marveled at Andrei too, seeing how, urged on only by passionate enthusiasm, he rushed upon what a cool and prudent man would not have risked, and merely by his furious impetus achieved marvels at which veteran warriors could not but wonder. Old Taras was surprised and said: "And he is a good one too—may the devil not take him—he's not Ostap, but he's a good warrior too!"

It was decided to march straight upon the town of Dubno, where, so it was rumored, there were many wealthy inhabitants and plenty of treasure. In a day and a half the march was accomplished and the Cossacks appeared before the town. The inhabitants resolved to defend themselves to the last, and preferred to die in their squares and streets and at their thresholds, rather than admit the enemy into their homes. A high rampart of earth surrounded the town; where the rampart was lower a stone wall jutted out or a house that served as a battery or an oak palisade. The garrison was strong and felt the gravity of the position. The Cossacks eagerly tried to clamber on the rampart but were met with volleys of grapeshot. The tradespeople and inhabitants apparently did not care to remain idle and they stood in crowds on the rampart. A spirit of desperate

resistance could be discerned in their eyes; the women, too, resolutely assisted, and stones, barrels, and pots flew down on the heads
of the Cossacks, followed by boiling liquid and finally by sacks of
sand which blinded them. The Cossacks did not like to deal with
fortified places; besieging was not in their line. The leader ordered
them to retreat, and said: "It is no matter, comrades, our retreating; may I be an unclean Tartar and not a Christian if we let a
single one of them out of the town. Let them all rot with hunger,
the dogs!" The troops, retreating, surrounded the whole town, and,
having nothing better to do, spent their time in devastating the surrounding neighborhood, burning the villages and shocks of uncar-
ried wheat, turning their droves of horses into the crops yet un-
touched by the sickle, where, as luck would have it, the waving
ears were heavy with grain, the fruit of an extraordinarily good
season, that should have brought a lavish reward to all the peasants.
The besieged saw with horror from the town the destruction of the
means of their subsistence. Meanwhile the Cossacks, after drawing a
double ring with their carts around the whole town, settled down
as though at the camp in units, smoked their pipes, exchanged the
weapons they had carried off as plunder, played leapfrog or odd
and even, and looked with exasperating unconcern at the town. At
night they lighted campfires; the cooks in each unit boiled porridge
in immense copper cauldrons; a guard stood watch by the fires
which burned all night. But soon the Cossacks began to be bored by
their inactivity and prolonged sobriety, now unaccompanied by action. The leader indeed ordered the ration of drink to be doubled,
a concession sometimes made when no difficult exploits or maneuvers were required of the troops. The young men, especially the
sons of Taras Bulba, disliked such a life. Andrei was unmistakably
bored. "Silly fellow," Taras said to him, "be patient as a Cossack
and you will be a leader! He is not a good warrior who keeps up
his spirits only in affairs of great moment; he is a good warrior who
is not weary in idleness, who endures everything and will still
stick to his point, do what you will to him." But a fiery youth
cannot be like an old man: their characters are different and they
look with different eyes on the same thing.

Meanwhile Taras' regiment arrived, led by Tovkach; with him
there were two other captains, a clerk, and other officers; all the
Cossacks made up over four thousand. Among them were not a
few volunteers who had joined of their own free will without a

summons, as soon as they heard what was doing. The captains brought Taras' sons a blessing from their old mother and a cypruswood icon to each of them from the Mezhigorsky Monastery at Kiev. Both the brothers put the holy images around their necks and could not help being sad as they thought of their old mother. What did that blessing predict and tell them? Was it a blessing for victory over the enemy and then a joyous return home with booty and everlasting glory in the songs of the bandore players, or . . . ? But the future is unknown, and it stands before man like the autumn fog that rises from the swamp; in it the birds fly senselessly up and down flapping their wings, not recognizing one another, the dove not seeing the hawk, the hawk not seeing the dove, and not one knowing how far he is flying from his doom.

Ostap was already busily employed and had long ago gone off to his unit; but Andrei felt a vague depression at heart, though he could not have said why. Already the Cossacks had finished their supper. The evening had long ago faded into dusk, the air was enfolded in the marvelous night of July; but still Andrei did not go to his unit, he did not lie down to sleep, but still unconsciously he gazed at the picture spread out before him. Stars innumerable twinkled with a delicate bright gleam in the sky. The plain was covered far and wide with the wagons scattered about it with hanging pails of pitch and with all sorts of goods and provisions taken from the enemy. Beside the carts, under the carts, and at a little distance from them everywhere, the Cossacks stretched on the grass. They were all sleeping in picturesque attitudes: one with a bag for a pillow under his head, another with a cap, another simply using the ribs of a comrade. A saber, a matchlock gun, a short pipe with copper disks, a metal rod and tinder lay invariably by each Cossack. The heavy oxen lay, their legs bent under them, like great whitish masses, and might in the distance have been taken for gray rocks scattered about the slopes of the steppe. On all sides the bass snore of the sleeping warriors rose up from the grass, and the horses, indignant at their hobbled legs, answered it with resounding neighs from the steppe. Meanwhile something grand and sinister was mingled with the beauty of the July night. This was the glow of the burning villages in the distance. In one place the flame spread calmly and majestically over the sky; in another, meeting something inflammable and at once flaring up, it hissed and flew whirling upward to the very stars, and shreds of flame flickered out in the faraway sky. Here a charred and blackened monastery stood fiercely like a grim Carthusian monk, displaying its gloomy magnificence at every flash; there the monastery garden was burning; it seemed as though one could hear the trees hissing amid the coils of smoke, and, when the flame leaped up, it threw a phosphorescent purplish light on ripe clusters of plums, or turned the yellow pears to red gold, and, hanging on the wall or the branch of a tree, the body of a poor Jew or monk who had perished with the building in the flames made a patch of black among them. Above the flames the birds hovered in the distance, looking like a heap of tiny dark crosses upon a field of fire. The besieged town, it seemed, was sleeping; its spires and roofs and the palisade and the walls were all glowing with the reflection of the faraway fires.

Andrei made the round of the Cossack lines. The campfires, by which guards were sitting, were every minute on the point of going out, and the guards themselves were asleep after a meal eaten with Cossack appetite. He wondered a little at such carelessness, thinking: "It's as well that no powerful enemy is near and there is nothing to be afraid of." At last, he too went up to one of the wagons, clambered on it, and lay down on his back with his hands folded under his head; but he could not go to sleep, and lay a long time gazing at the sky: it was all open before him; the air was pure and limpid; the multitude of stars that make up the Milky Way and lie like a slanting stripe across the sky were all bathed in light. At times Andrei seemed to sink into forgetfulness and a light mist of drowsiness screened the sky from him for a minute; then it grew clear and all was visible again.

At that moment he imagined that the strange image of a human face flitted before him. Thinking that it was simply an illusion of sleep, which would at once vanish, he opened his eyes wide and saw that a wan emaciated face was really bending down to him and looking straight into his eyes. Long coal-black hair hung in loose disorder from under the dark veil flung over the head; and the strange glitter in the eyes and the deathly pallor of the dark face with its sharp features made him think that it was a ghost. He unconsciously put his hand on his gun, and said almost with a shudder: "Who are you? If you are an evil spirit, begone; if a living man, you have chosen an ill time for a jest—I will kill you with one shot."

In answer to this, the apparition put its finger to its lips and seemed to be imploring silence. He dropped his hand and looked more closely at it. From the long hair and from the neck and dark half-naked bosom he saw it was a woman. But she was not a native of those parts: her face was swarthy, wasted, and wan; her broad cheekbones stood out sharply above the sunken cheeks; her narrow eyes slanted upward. The more he gazed at her features the more he fancied something familiar in them. At last he could not refrain from asking: "Tell me, who are you? It seems to me that I know you, or have seen you somewhere."

"Two years ago in Kiev."

"Two years ago in Kiev," repeated Andrei, trying to ransack all that remained in his memory of his old student life. He looked at her intently once more and all at once cried out aloud: "You are the Tartar woman! The servant of the Polish lady, the governor's daughter . . ."

"Hush!" the Tartar woman said, folding her hands with a supplicating air, trembling all over, and at the same time turning her head to see whether anyone had been awakened by the loud cry uttered by Andrei.

"Tell me, tell me, why are you here?" Andrei, almost breathless, asked in a whisper broken by emotion. "Where is your lady? Is she still living?"

"She is here, in the town."

"In the town?" he repeated, almost crying out again, and he felt all his blood rush to his heart. "How is it she is in the town?"

"Because the old master is in the town: he has been commander in Dubno for the last year and a half."

"Is she married? But tell me—how strange you are!—how is she now . . . ?"

"She has had nothing to eat for two days."

"What?"

"None of the inhabitants have had a bit of bread for a long time, for a long time they have eaten nothing but earth."

Andrei was stunned.

"My lady saw you with the Cossacks from the town rampart. She said to me: 'Go tell him, if he remembers me, to come to me; and, if he does not, to give you a piece of bread for my old mother, for I do not want to see my mother die before my eyes. Let me die first and her after me. Clasp his knees and his feet and entreat him; he, too, has an old mother—let him for her sake give us bread!' "

Many and varied feelings woke up and burned in the youthful heart of the Cossack.

"But how is it you are here? How did you come?"

"By an underground way."

"Is there an underground way?"

"There is."

"Where?"

"You will not betray us, sir?"

"I swear by the Holy Cross!"

"Going down the steep bank and crossing the stream there among the reeds."

"And it comes out in the town?"

"Straight to the town monastery."

"Let us go, let us go at once!"

"But, for the sake of Christ and Holy Mary, a bit of bread."

"Good, you shall have it. Stay here by the wagon, or, better still, lie down on it; nobody will see you, all are asleep. I will be back at once."

And he went off to the wagon where the provisions belonging to his unit were kept. His heart was throbbing. All the past, all that had been stifled by the Cossack bivouacking, by the harsh life of warfare—all floated to the surface again, in its turn drowning the present. Again there rose up before him, as though from the depths of a dark sea, the proud girl; her lovely hands, her eyes, her laughing lips, her thick dark nut-brown hair that fell in curls over her firm breasts, and all the supple harmonious lines of her girlish figure flashed in his memory again. No, they had never died away, they had never vanished from his heart, they had merely been laid aside for a time to make room for other powerful feelings; but often, very often, the deep sleep of the young Cossack had been troubled by them, and often waking up he had lain sleepless on his bed, though he had not fully understood the cause.

He walked on, while the throbbing of his heart grew more and more violent at the mere thought that he would see her again, and his strong young knees trembled. When he reached the wagons, he had entirely forgotten what he came for: he put his hand to his forehead and stood rubbing it, trying to remember what he had to do. At last he started, filled with horror: it suddenly came into his mind that she was dying of hunger. He rushed to a wagon and put under his arm several big black loaves; but at once wondered whether that food, well fitted for a strong and by no means dainty Cossack, would not be coarse and unsuitable for her tender constitution. Then he remembered that the leader had yesterday blamed the cooks for boiling all the buckwheat flour at once for porridge when there was fully enough for three meals. In the full conviction that he would find enough in the cauldrons, he pulled out his father's field cauldron and went with it to the cook of their unit who was asleep by two immense cauldrons, under which the embers were still warm. Glancing into them, he was amazed to see that both were empty. Superhuman powers were needed to eat all they had contained, especially as there were fewer men in their unit than in the others. He glanced into the cauldrons of the other units—nothing anywhere. He could not help recalling the saying, "The Dnieper Cossacks are like children: when there is little they eat it all, when there is much they leave nothing either." What was he to do? There was somewhere, he thought, in the stores of his father's regiment a sack of white bread which they had found when plundering the bakehouse of a monastery. He went at once to his father's wagon, but it was no longer on the wagon. Ostap had taken it for a pillow and, stretched on the ground near by, he was snoring for all the plain to hear. Andrei seized the sack with one hand and pulled it away so suddenly that Ostap's head fell on the ground and he sat up half-asleep, and, with his eyes still closed, shouted at the top of his voice:

"Hold him, hold the Polish bastard and catch his horse, catch his horse!"

"Be quiet, I'll kill you!" Andrei cried in terror, swinging the sack at him. But Ostap would not have gone on speaking anyway; he subsided with a snore which set the grass quivering where he lay. Andrei looked about him timidly to see whether Ostap's outbreak in his sleep had wakened any of the Cossacks. One head with a shock of hair was raised in the next unit, but after looking around it dropped back again on the ground at once.

After waiting a few minutes, he set off with his burden. The Tartar woman was lying, hardly daring to breathe. "Get up, let us go! All are asleep, do not fear! Can you lift just one of those loaves, if I can't carry all?" Saying this, he heaped up sacks on his back and, passing by a wagon, dragged out another sack of millet, even took in his hands the loaves which he had meant to give the Tartar woman to carry, and, somewhat bowed under the weight, walked boldly between the rows of sleeping Cossacks.

"Andrei!" said old Bulba, as his son passed him. The young man's heart sank; he stood still and, trembling all over, asked softly "What is it?"

"There's a woman with you! Aye, I'll skin you when I get up! Women will bring you to no good!" Saying this he propped his head on his elbow and stared intently at the Tartar woman, muffled in her veil. Andrei stood more dead than alive and had not the courage to glance at his father's face. When at last he raised his eyes and looked at him, he saw that old Bulba was asleep again, his head lying on his open hand.

He crossed himself. The panic flew from his heart as quickly as it had swooped down upon it. When he turned to look toward the Tartar woman, she was standing before him like a statue of dark granite, all muffled in her veil, and the glow of the faraway fire flaring up gleamed only in her eyes, which looked lifeless as those of a corpse. He pulled her by the sleeve and they set off together, continually looking back, and at last went down the slope to a low hollow—almost a ravine, such as is called in some places a creek—at the bottom of which a stream trickled amid tufts of grass and sedge. Going down into this hollow, they were completely concealed from the view of the whole plain on which the Cossack camp was pitched. Anyway, when Andrei looked around he saw that the slope behind him rose up like a steep wall above the height of a man; at the top of it some stalks of wild flowers were swaying, and above them the moon was rising in the sky like a slanting sickle of bright red gold. A slight breeze rising from the steppe announced that the dawn was not far off. But nowhere was a cock-crow heard in the distance: neither in the town nor in the ruined villages around it was there one cock left. They crossed the water on a small log; the opposite bank seemed higher than the one they left behind and rose up like a cliff. It seemed as though this place was in itself a strong and trustworthy point of the town fortification; the earthen rampart was lower here and no garrison was looking out behind it. But at a little distance there rose up the thick wall of the monastery. The steep bank was all overgrown with rough grass, and in the little glade between it and the water tall reeds stood almost as high as a man. At the top of the steep bank the remains of a fence which had once enclosed a vegetable garden could be seen; in front of it were broad burdock leaves, behind it rose goosefoot, wild prickly thistle, and a sunflower tossing its head higher than them all. Here the Tartar woman slipped off her shoes and walked barefoot, pulling up her skirt, for the place was marshy and full of water. Making their way through the reeds, they stopped before a heap of brushwood and fagots. Moving aside the brushwood they found an opening in the earth—an opening hardly bigger than the doorway of a bread oven. The Tartar woman, bending her head, went in first; Andrei followed her, bending down as low as he could do to creep in with his sacks, and soon they found themselves in complete darkness.

VI

Andrei moved slowly in the dark and narrow underground passage, following the woman and carrying the sacks of bread. "Soon we shall be able to see," said his guide. "We are near the spot where I left the candlestick." And in fact the dark earthen walls began to be lighted up with a faint glimmer. They reached a rather wider place which seemed to be a chapel of sorts; anyway there was a little narrow table like an altar fixed to the wall, and a faded, almost completely effaced image of a Catholic Madonna could be discerned above it. A little silver lamp hanging before it gave a faint glimmer. The Tartar woman bent down and picked up from the ground a tall thin copper candlestick, with snuffers, a skewer to push up the wick, and an extinguisher hanging on little chains about it. Picking it up, she lighted it from the little lamp. The light grew brighter and, walking on together, now throwing a brilliant light, now casting a coal-black shadow, they were like a Gherardo delle notti.[7] The fresh handsome face of the young Cossack, brimming over with health and youth, was a striking contrast to the wan pale face of his companion. The passage grew a little wider so that it was possible for Andrei to stand a little more upright. He looked with curiosity at the earthen walls, which reminded him of the Kiev catacombs. Here, just as in the Kiev catacombs, there were recesses in the walls and coffins stood here and there; in places there were even human bones softened by the damp and dropping into powder. It

---

[7] Italian name ("Gherardo of the nights") of a Dutch painter, Gerard van Honthorst (1590-1656), who was fond of painting interiors dimly lighted. (ed.)

seemed that here, too, there had been holy men, who had hidden themselves from the turmoils, sorrows, and temptations of the world. The passage was in places very damp: sometimes there was standing water under their feet. Andrei had often to stop to let his companion rest, for she was continually overcome by weariness. Her stomach, unaccustomed to food, could not digest the small piece of bread she had swallowed, and often she stood still, motionless for several minutes.

At last a little iron door appeared before them. "Well, thank God, we have arrived!" said the Tartar in a faint voice, and she lifted her hand to knock, but had not the strength to do it. Andrei instead struck a violent blow on the door; there was a hollow echo which showed that there was a big open space beyond it. The sound changed in tone, resounding against the lofty domes. Two minutes later there was the jingle of keys and someone seemed to come down a staircase. At last the door was unlocked; they were met by a monk standing on a narrow flight of stairs with keys and a candle in his hands. Andrei involuntarily stood still at the sight of the Catholic monk, a figure that aroused hatred and contempt in the Cossacks, who treated monks more inhumanly than Jews. The monk too stepped back a little on seeing a Cossack; but a word indistinctly uttered by the Tartar woman reassured him. He locked the door after them and led them up the stairs; they found themselves under the dark lofty arches of the monastery church. At one of the altars decked with tall candlesticks and candles a priest was kneeling and praying in a low voice. Two young choristers in purple robes with white lace capes over them knelt on each side of him with censers in their hands. He prayed that a miracle might take place so that the town might be saved, so that the failing spirit of the people might be fortified, so that patience might be strengthened and the tempter confounded when he incited the people to utter weak-spirited and cowardly lamentations over their earthly misfortunes. A few women, looking like ghosts, knelt leaning with their weary heads sunk on the backs of chairs and dark wooden benches in front of them; a few men too knelt mournfully propped against the columns and pillars which supported the vaulted roof. The stained-glass window above the altar was lighted up with the pink flush of morning, and circles of light of blue, yellow, and many other hues fell from it on the floor, casting a sudden brightness into the dark church. The whole altar in its faraway

recess seemed all at once bathed in brilliance; the smoke of the in-
cense hovered in the air in a cloud of rainbow light. Andrei, from
his dark corner, gazed not without wonder at the marvelous effect
of light. At that moment the majestic strains of the organ suddenly filled the whole church; they grew richer and richer, swelling out and spreading out, changing into resounding peals of
thunder; then, suddenly transformed into heavenly music, floated
aloft under the arched roof, the melodious notes recalling the
high-pitched voices of girls; then, changing again to a bass roar
and thunder, died away. And the thundering echoes still floated
quivering under the roofs, and Andrei, with his mouth open, marveled at the majestic music.

At that moment he felt someone pull him by the lower half of
his jacket. "Come!" said the Tartar woman. They crossed the
church unnoticed by anyone, and then came out into the market
place which lay before it. The dawn had long been red in the sky.
Everything proclaimed the rising of the sun. The market place,
which was square in shape, was completely empty; there were still
wooden tables standing in the middle of it showing that here,
only perhaps a week before, a provision market had been held.
The street—in those days there was no pavement—was simply
heaped with dry mud. The market place was surrounded by little
one-story stone and clay houses with wooden posts and pillars visible in their walls all the way up, with slanting crosspieces of wood,
as men usually built their houses in those days and as they may be
seen even today in some parts of Lithuania and Poland. They were
all topped with disproportionately high roofs, and had numbers of
dormer windows and apertures in the walls. On one side, almost
next to the church, rose a higher building, quite different from the
rest, probably the town hall or some government office. It was a
two-story building, and above it there was a belvedere built in two
arches, and inside it a sentry standing watch. There was a big
clock face under the roof. The market place looked dead, but
Andrei thought he heard a faint moan. Looking more closely, he
noticed on the other side a group of two or three men lying on the
ground completely motionless. He looked steadily to find out
whether they were asleep or dead, and at that moment stumbled
over something lying at his feet. It was the dead body of a woman,
apparently a Jewess. She seemed to be young, though there was no
trace of youth in her distorted and emaciated features. There was a

red silk handkerchief on her head; two rows of pearls or beads adorned the lappets over her ears; two or three long curls fell below them on her wasted neck on which the veins stood out. Beside her lay a baby convulsively clutching her thin breast and pinching it with his fingers in unconscious anger at finding no milk. He no longer screamed or cried, and only from the slow heaving of his body it could be seen he was not dead or was perhaps just now expiring. They turned into the streets and were suddenly stopped by a frenzied figure, who, seeing Andrei's precious burden, flew at it like a tiger and clutched at him, shouting "Bread!" but his strength was not equal to his fury; Andrei pushed him away; he fell to the ground. Moved by compassion, he thrust on him one loaf, on which the poor wretch fell like a mad dog, gnawing at it, eating it up, and on the spot in the street expired in terrible convulsions through having been so long without food. Almost at every step they met the dreadful victims of famine. It seemed as though, unable to support their agonies within doors, many had run out into the streets in hope of finding something to sustain them. At the gate of a house sat an old woman, and no one could have said whether she was asleep or dead, or simply lost in forgetfulness; anyway she heard nothing and saw nothing, but sat motionless with her head sunk on her breast. A wasted body was hanging in a noose from the roof of another house: the poor wretch, unable to endure the agonies of hunger, had preferred to hasten his end by suicide. At the sight of this horrible evidence of starvation, Andrei could not refrain from asking the Tartar woman: "Surely they could have found something to maintain life? If a man is brought to the last extremity, then there is nothing he can do, he ought to eat what he has before looked upon with disgust: he can feed on the animals forbidden by law; anything can be turned into food at such a time."

"All are eaten up," said the Tartar woman: "every creature; you will find not a horse nor a dog nor even a mouse in the town. We have never kept stores in reserve in the town; everything used to be brought us from the villages."

"But how can you, when you are dying such a cruel death, still think of defending the town?"

"Well, maybe the commander would surrender, but yesterday morning the colonel, who is not far away, sent a hawk into the town with a note tied to it, telling us not to surrender the town, and say-

ing that he was coming to save us with a regiment and only waiting
for another colonel that they may come together. And now they
are expected every minute . . . but here we are at the house."

Andrei had already from the distance seen the house, which was
unlike the others and designed, so it seemed, by an Italian architect;
it was built of fine red bricks and was of two stories. The windows
of the lower story were set in high, jutting granite cornices; the
upper story consisted of small arches forming a gallery; between
them was a trellis with heraldic crests on it; there were crests too
on the corners of the house. A wide outer staircase of painted
bricks led into the market place itself. At the bottom of the staircase were two sentries, one on each side, who picturesquely and
symmetrically leaned with one hand on the halberd standing beside
them, and with the other supported their bowed heads, and so
looked more like carved images than living creatures. They were
not asleep nor dozing, but seemed insensible to everything. They
did not even notice who went up the steps. At the top of the stairs
they found a sumptuously equipped and dressed soldier holding
a prayer book in his hand. He raised his weary eyes to look at
them, but the Tartar woman said one word to him, and he dropped
them again on the open pages of his prayer book. They went into
the first room, a rather large one, which served as a waiting room, or
simply as a vestibule; it was filled with people sitting in different
positions around the walls; soldiers, servants, secretaries, butlers,
and all the retinue required to display the grandeur of a great Polish nobleman, who was not only a soldier but also a landowner.
There was the smell of a smoldering candle; two others were still
burning in two immense candlesticks almost as tall as a man, standing in the middle of the room, although the morning light had for
some time been looking into the broad latticed window. Andrei
would have gone straight up to a broad oak door decorated with a
crest and a number of carved ornaments; but the Tartar woman
pulled him by the sleeve and pointed to a little door in the side wall.
By this door they came out into the corridor and then into a room
which he began to scrutinize attentively. The light coming through
a crack in the shutter fell on something—a crimson curtain, a gilt
cornice, and a picture on the wall. Here the Tartar woman bade
Andrei wait, and opened the door into another room from which
there came a gleam of light. He heard a whisper and a soft voice
which thrilled him through and through. He caught through the

open door a rapid glimpse of a graceful feminine figure with a
wealth of long hair which fell on her raised arm. The Tartar woman
came back and told him to go in. He had no memory of how he
went in and how the door closed behind him. In the room two candles were burning and a little lamp glimmered before the holy
image; under it, after the Catholic fashion, stood a tall table with
steps to kneel on during prayer. But this was not what his eyes were
seeking. He glanced around and saw a woman who looked as though
frozen or turned to stone in rapid movement. It seemed as though
her whole figure had been darting toward him and had suddenly
stopped. And he, too, stood still before her in bewilderment. It was
not like this that he had imagined seeing her; this was not she,
not the lady he had known before; nothing in her was the same,
but now she was twice as beautiful and marvelous as before; then
there had been something unfinished, incomplete in her, now she
was the perfect picture to which the artist has given the finishing
touch. That had been a charming, frivolous girl; this was a lovely
woman in all the perfection of her beauty. Every depth of feeling
was expressed in her lifted eyes, not traces, not hints of feeling, but
its fullest intensity. The tears not yet dry upon them veiled them
with a brilliant mist which pierced the heart; her bosom, neck, and
shoulders had the lovely lines of perfectly developed beauty;
her hair, which had floated before in light curls about her face,
was now a thick luxuriant mass, part of which was done up and part
of which hung loose over the full length of her arm, and in delicate,
long, beautifully curling tresses fell over her bosom. It seemed as
though every one of her features was transformed. In vain he
strove to find one of those which had haunted his memory—not
one was the same. Terrible as was her paleness, it had not dimmed
her incredible beauty; on the contrary, it seemed to give it an intense, invincibly triumphant quality. And Andrei felt awed and
stood motionless before her. She, too, seemed impressed at the
sight of the ruggedly handsome and manly Cossack; even though
his limbs were motionless his figure seemed to reveal the ease and
freedom of his movements; his eyes flashed with clear firmness,
the velvety eyebrows rose in a bold arch, the tanned cheeks glowed
with all the brightness of youth, and the thin black mustache shone
like silk.

"No, I have not the strength to thank you fittingly, generous
knight," she said, and the silvery notes of her voice quivered.

"Only God can reward you; it's not for me, a weak woman . . ." She dropped her eyes; like lovely semicircles of snow, the eyelids, edged with lashes long as arrows, hid them; her lovely face was bowed, and a faint flush suffused it. Andrei could say nothing to this; he longed to utter all that was in his heart, to utter it with all the ardor which was in his heart, and could not. He felt something sealing his lips; the sound died away from the word; he felt that it was not for him, bred in the seminary and the rough life of the camp, to answer such words, and he raged inwardly at his Cossack nature.

At that moment the Tartar woman came into the room. She had already cut the loaf brought by the young knight into slices; she brought it on a golden dish and set it before her mistress. The beauty glanced at her, at the bread, and raised her eyes to Andrei and much was said in those eyes. That softened gaze that betrayed the helplessness and inability to express the feelings that were overwhelming her was easier for Andrei to understand than any words. His heart grew light at once; he felt that the knot in it was unraveled. The feelings and emotions of his soul, which had been as though shackled, now felt released and longed to find vent in a ceaseless flow of words, when the beauty, turning to the Tartar, asked her uneasily: "And Mother? Have you taken her some?"

"She is asleep."

"And Father?"

"Yes; he said that he would come himself to thank the knight."

She took the bread and raised it to her lips. With unutterable pleasure Andrei watched her break it with her gleaming white fingers and eat. All at once he remembered the man frenzied with hunger who had expired before his eyes after swallowing a piece of bread. He turned pale, and clutching her by the arm cried:

"Enough! Do not eat more! You have eaten nothing for so long, bread will be poison to you now." And she dropped her hand at once, laid the bread on the dish and, like an obedient child, looked into his eyes. And if but some word could tell . . . but no sculptor's chisel nor painter's brush nor the lofty might of words has power to express what is sometimes seen in the eyes of a maiden, nor the tenderness which overwhelms one who looks into them.

"My queen!" cried Andrei, his heart and soul and whole being brimming over. "What do you need, what do you wish? Command me! Set me the most impossible task in the world—I will hasten to carry it out! Tell me to do what no man can do—I will do it; I will go to perdition for you! I will, I will! And to perish for you, I swear by the Holy Cross, is so sweet for me . . . but I do not know how to say this! I have three farms, half of my father's herds, everything that my mother brought my father, what she even conceals from him—all is mine. No one of the Cossacks has weapons now like mine: for the handle of my sword alone they would give me the best herd of horses and three thousand sheep. And all that I renounce, I cast aside, I throw away, I fling into the fire or the water at one word from your lips, or one sign from your delicate black eyebrow! But I know that I may be uttering foolish words and out of season, and that all this is not fitting here; that it is not for me, who have spent my life in the seminary and in the camp, to speak as men speak in the company of kings, princes, and all who are foremost in the world of knighthood. I see that you are a different creation from all of us, and all other wives and daughters of boyars are far beneath you. We are not fit to be your slaves; only the heavenly angels can serve you."

Mutely attentive, hanging on each word, the maiden heard with growing amazement the frank earnest words in which a youthful soul brimming over with strength was reflected as in a mirror. And every simple word of that speech, uttered in a voice that came straight from the heart, was full of strength. And, her lovely face thrust forward, she flung back her unruly hair, opened her mouth, and gazed at him with parted lips. Then she tried to say something, and suddenly stopped short and remembered that the knight was bound to other duties, that his father, his brother, and all his fellow countrymen stood behind him like cruel avengers; that the terrible besiegers of the town were the Cossacks, that all of them, with their town, were doomed to a cruel death . . . and her eyes suddenly filled with tears. She quickly seized her silk-embroidered handkerchief, put it to her face, and in a minute it was all wet; and a long time she sat, her lovely head thrown back, biting her lower lip with her snow-white teeth—as though suddenly stung by a poisonous snake—and keeping the handkerchief to her face that he might not see her heart-rending grief.

"Say one word to me!" said Andrei, taking her by her hand, which was soft as satin. The touch of it sent fire thrilling through his veins, and he pressed the hand that lay lifeless in his. But still she stayed motionless and neither spoke nor took the handkerchief from her face.

"Why is it you are so sorrowful? Tell me, why is it you are so sorrowful?"

She threw away her handkerchief, flung back the long hair that crept into her eyes, and poured out pitiful words, uttering them in a soft, soft voice, like the breeze that rises on a fair evening and suddenly passes over the thick reeds by the waterside; they stir, they rustle, and all at once mournful whispers rise, and the wayfarer stands still to catch them with inexplicable sadness, heeding not the fading eventide, nor the gay songs of the peasants on their homeward way from harvest and field labor, nor the faraway rumble of some passing cart.

"Do I not deserve everlasting compassion? Is not the mother unhappy who brought me into the world? Is it not a bitter fate that has fallen to my lot? A cruel torturer is my harsh destiny! It brought all men to my feet: the foremost noblemen of all Poland, the wealthiest lords, counts, foreign barons, and all the flower of our knighthood. All of them were free to love me, and every one of them would have deemed my love great happiness. I had but to lift my finger, and any one of them, the fairest, the noblest in face and in family, would have been my husband. But not for one of them has my cruel fate bewitched my heart; passing by the noblest knights of our land, my heart is lost to a stranger, to our foe. Wherefore, Holy Mother of God, for what sins, for what terrible crimes dost Thou so harshly and mercilessly chastise me? My days have been spent in abundance and luxury; the best and costliest dishes and sweet wines have been my fare. And what has it all been for? To what end? Is it to die at last a bitter death, such as the poorest beggar in the land does not die? And it is not enough that I am destined to this dreadful doom; not enough that before my own end I must see dying in insufferable agonies the father and mother to save whom I would gladly give my life twenty times over; all that is not enough: before my end I must see and hear words and love such as I have never known. He must rend my heart with his words that my bitter lot may be bitterer still, that I may grieve the more for my young life, that death may seem to me more terrible, and that I may reproach more bitterly my cruel fate and Thee —forgive my transgression—Holy Mother of God!" And when she ceased, a feeling of utter hopelessness was reflected in her face;

every feature told of gnawing grief, and everything, from the mournfully bowed brow and downcast eyes to the tears lingering and drying on her flushed cheeks, all seemed saying, "There is no happiness in this face!"

"It is unheard of, it cannot be," said Andrei, "that the fairest and best of women should suffer a fate so bitter, when she is born for everything that is best in the world to bow down before her as before a shrine. No, you shall not die! It is not for you to die; I swear by my birth and all that is dear to me in the world—you shall not die! If it comes to that, if nothing—no strength, no prayer, no valor, can turn aside the bitter fate, we will die together and I will die first; I will die before you at your lovely knees, and even in death they shall not part me from you."

"Do not deceive yourself and me," she said, softly, shaking her lovely head. "I know, and to my great sorrow know too well, that you must not love me; and I know what is your sacred duty: your father, your comrades, your country are calling you, while we are your foes."

"And what are father, comrades, and country to me?" said Andrei, tossing his head and drawing his whole figure erect like a poplar. "If that is it, then let me tell you I have no one! No one, no one!" he repeated with the voice and movement of his hand with which the buoyant, indomitable Cossack expresses determination in face of a deed incredible and impossible for another. "Who says that my country is the Ukraine? Who gave it to me for my country? Our country is what our soul seeks, what is most precious of all things to it. My country is you! Here is my country! And I shall bear it in my heart, I shall bear it in my heart to the day of my death, and we shall see, let any Cossack tear it from me! And I will give up everything in the world, renounce all, and perish for this country!"

For an instant, petrified like a lovely statue, she gazed into his eyes, then suddenly, with the exquisite feminine impulsiveness of which only a spontaneously generous-hearted woman created for noble emotion is capable, she threw herself on his neck, flinging her exquisite snow-white arms about him, and broke into sobs. At that instant there came from the street the sound of confused shouts, accompanied by the blowing of trumpets and beating of drums: but he heard them not; he felt nothing but the fragrant warmth with which her exquisite lips breathed upon him, the tears that streamed on his face, and the sweetly perfumed hair in which he was held as in a net of dark and shining silk.

Then the Tartar woman ran in with a joyful cry. "Saved, saved!" she cried, beside herself. "Our soldiers are entering the town, they have brought bread, millet, flour, and Cossack prisoners!" But neither of them heard what soldiers had come into the town, what they had brought with them, and what Cossacks were prisoners. Full of emotions transcending all things earthly, Andrei kissed the fragrant lips that pressed his cheek, and warmly those lips responded. And in that mutual kiss they felt what man feels but once in a lifetime.

And ruined is the Cossack! He is lost for all the chivalry of the Cossacks! He will see the camp no more; nor his father's farms, nor the church of God. The Ukraine will see no more of the bravest of the sons who undertook to defend her. Old Taras will tear the gray hair from his head and curse the day and hour when he begot such a son to shame him.

VII

There was noise and confusion in the camp of the Cossacks. At first no one could explain how the Polish troops had succeeded in entering the town. Then it appeared that all the men of the Pereiaslav unit, stationed in front of the side gate of the town, were dead drunk; so there was no cause for wonder that half of them had been killed and the other half taken prisoner before they all understood what was happening. While the next units, awakened by the noise, were seizing their weapons, the troops were already entering the town, and their rear guard drove off with their fire the sleepy and only half-sober Cossacks, who were pursuing them in disorder.

The leader gave the order for all to assemble, and, when all were standing in a circle and had taken off their caps, amid general silence he said: "See, comrades, what has come to pass during this night; see what drunkenness leads to! See what a disgrace the enemy has done us! If you are allowed a double portion, it's your way, it seems, to get so drunk that the enemy of Christ's army pull off your trousers and even sneeze in your face without your noticing it."

All the Cossacks stood hanging their heads, knowing that they

were to blame; only one, Kukubenko, the chief of the Nezamaikovsky unit, replied. "Wait a moment, little father!" he said,
"though it is not the rule to make reply when the leader
speaks before the face of the whole company; but the thing was
not so, and one must say it. You have upbraided the Christian soldiers not quite justly. The Cossacks would be to blame and de-
serving of death if they had been drunk on the march, in the
field, or at hard heavy labor; but we were sitting with nothing to
do, idly sauntering to and fro before the town. There was no fast
nor other Christian ordinance: what was there to prevent a man
drinking in idleness? There is no sin in that. We had much better
show them what it costs to attack innocent people. Before this we
fought well, but now let us fight so that there will be nothing left
of them."

The chief's speech pleased the Cossacks. They raised their hanging heads and many nodded approval, saying: "Well said, Kukubenko!" And Taras Bulba, standing not far from the leader, said:
"Well, it seems Kukubenko has spoken the truth? What do you say
to it?"

"What do I say? I say blessed the father who begot such a son:
there is no great wisdom in uttering words of blame, but great
wisdom in uttering a word which instead of upbraiding a man
after misfortune cheers him up and gives him courage, as the
spur gives courage to the horse, refreshed by a drink of water. I myself meant to say a word of comfort to you afterwards, but Kukubenko has forestalled me."

"The leader has spoken well, too!" resounded among the ranks
of the Cossacks. "Well said!" repeated others. And even the elders,
gray-headed like pigeons, nodded, and, twitching their gray mustaches, said quietly: "Well said!"

"Listen, comrades!" the leader went on. "To take fortresses, to
scale walls and mine under them, as the German craftsmen of foreign lands do—may the devil confound them!—is not a task befitting Cossacks. But seemingly the enemy has entered the town with
no great stores. They had but few carts with them. The people in
the town are hungry, so they will eat it all up in no time, and there's
hay which the horses need, too . . . of course I don't know,
maybe some saint of theirs will pitch it to them from heaven . . .
God knows about that; but their priests are good but for words.
For that cause or another they will come out of the town. Divide

into three detachments and stand on the three roads before the three gates. Before the chief gate five units, before each of the other gates three units. The Diadkivsy and Korsunsky units into ambush! The Tytarevsky and Tymoshevsky units to the reserve on the right side of the wagons! The Sherbinovsky and upper Steblikivsky units to the left side! And you fine fellows who are most violent in speech, step out of the ranks to provoke the enemy! The Poles are an empty-headed lot; they can't stand abuse, and maybe they will all come out of the gates this very day. Chiefs of the units, each inspect his men: if you are short of men, fill up your ranks with what are left of the Pereiaslavsky. Inspect everything anew! Give every man a cupful to sober him, and a loaf to every Cossack, though I dare say they all had enough yesterday, for, to tell the truth, they all overate themselves, till it's a wonder no one burst in the night. And here is one more warning: if any Jewish tavern owner sells a Cossack a single mug of vodka, I'll nail a pig's ear to the dog's forehead, and will hang him upside down! To work, brothers! Get to work!"

Such were the leader's orders, and all bowed low to him and went bareheaded to their wagons and their horses, and not till they were quite a long way off did they put on their caps again. All began arming themselves: they tested their sabers and their double-edged swords, poured powder from the sacks into their powder pouches, rolled the wagons to their proper places, and picked out their horses.

Going off to his regiment, Taras wondered in vain what had become of Andrei: "Was he captured with the rest and bound when he was asleep? But no, Andrei is not a man to let himself be taken prisoner alive." He was not to be seen among the slain Cossacks either. Taras was greatly perplexed, and he marched at the head of his regiment without noticing that someone had been for a good time calling him by name. "Who needs me?" he said at last, coming to himself. The Jew Yankel stood before him.

"Noble colonel, noble colonel!" the Jew said in a hurried and broken voice, as though he wanted to communicate a matter not quite unimportant: "I have been in the town, noble colonel." Taras looked at the Jew and wondered how he had managed to get into the town.

"What devil took you there?"

"I'll tell you at once," said Yankel. "As soon as I heard the up-

roar at dawn and the Cossacks began firing, I caught up my long
coat and ran there without putting it on! I only put my arms in the
sleeves on the way, because I wanted to find out as quickly as I
could the reason of the uproar, the reason that the Cossacks were
firing at daybreak. I ran up to the town gates at the moment when
the last company was entering the town. I look, and at the head of
a division, I see the standard bearer Galiandovich. He is a man I
know; for the last three years he has owed me a hundred gold
pieces. I followed him with the notion of getting him to pay
me, and went into the town together with them."

"How could you go into the town and expect them to pay you,
too?" said Bulba. "And didn't he order you to be hanged on the spot
like a dog?"

"Oh, dear, yes, he meant to hang me," answered the Jew. "His
servants caught me and put the rope around my neck; but I besought the gentleman; I said that I would wait for the money as long
as the gentleman wished, and promised to lend him more if only he
would help me to get from the other knights what they owe me;
for Galiandovich—I am telling you everything, noble sir—has not
a single gold piece in his pocket, though he has farms and estates
and four castles and steppe land right up to the Shklov; like a Cossack he has nothing, not a kopek, and now, if the Jews of Breslau
had not equipped him, he would have had nothing to go to the war
in. That is why he was at the Diet. . . ."

"What were you doing in the town? Did you see our men?"

"To be sure! There are lots of our men there: Yitzchak, Ra-
chum, Shmuel, the Jewish contractor . . ."

"Confound them, the bastards!" cried Taras, flying into a rage.
"Why do you foist your scurvy kindred on me? I am asking you
about our Cossacks."

"Our Cossacks I did not see; I saw only the lord Andrei."

"You saw Andrei?" cried Bulba. "What are you saying? Where
did you see him? In a dungeon? In a pit? Dishonored? Bound?"

"Who would dare bind the lord Andrei? Now he is such a
great knight . . . My word, yes! I did not know him! And his
shoulderpieces are of gold and his armguards of gold and his breast-
plate is of gold and his cap is of gold and there is gold on his belt and
everywhere gold and all gold. So that he is all shining in gold, like
the sun in the spring when every bird chirps and sings in the
garden and the wild flowers smell sweet. And the general has

given him the very best horse to ride; the horse alone cost two hundred gold pieces."

Bulba was dumbfounded.

"Why has he put on other dress?"

"Because it is better, that's why he has put it on. And he is riding about and the others are riding about; and he is teaching them and they are teaching him, like the richest Polish nobleman!"

"Who has forced him to do it?"

"I don't know that anyone has forced him. Does my lord not know that he has gone over to them of his own will?"

"Who has gone over?"

"Why, the lord Andrei!"

"Gone over? Where?"

"Gone over to their side; he is one of them now."

"You are lying, you swine!"

"How can I be lying? Am I a fool to tell you a lie? Would I tell a lie to my own ruin? Don't I know that a Jew will be hanged like a dog if he tells a lie to a gentleman?"

"So according to you, then, he has sold his fatherland and his faith?"

"I don't say he has sold anything; I only said that he has gone over to them!"

"You are lying, you devil of a Jew! Such a thing has never been in a Christian land! You are mistaken, you dog!"

"May the grass grow on the threshold of my house if I am. May everyone spit on the tomb of my father and my mother, of my father-in-law, and the father of my father and the father of my mother if I am mistaken. If my lord wishes I will even tell him why he has gone over to them."

"Why?"

"The general has a beautiful daughter. Holy God, what a beauty!" Here the Jew did his utmost to portray her beauty in his own face, flinging wide his arms, screwing up his eyes, and twisting his mouth as though tasting something.

"Well, what of that?"

"It is for her sake he has done it all and has gone over. If a man is in love he is like the sole of a shoe: when it has been soaked in water, take and bend it, it will bend."

Bulba pondered deeply. He remembered how great is the power of weak woman, how many strong men she has ruined, how sus-

ceptible Andrei's nature was on that side; and for some time he
stood without moving from the spot as though struck dumb.

"If my lord will listen, I will tell him more," the Jew went on.
"As soon as I heard the uproar and saw that they were going in at
the town gates, I snatched up a string of pearls in case of need, for
there are noble and beautiful ladies in the town; and if there are
noble and beautiful ladies, I said to myself, though they have nothing to eat, yet they will buy pearls. And when the gentleman's
servants let me go, I ran to the general's courtyard to sell the pearls.
I questioned the Tartar servingwoman. 'There will be a wedding
directly,' she said, 'as soon as they drive off the Cossacks. The
lord Andrei has promised to drive back the Cossacks!' "

"And you did not kill him on the spot, the son of a bitch?"
cried Bulba.

"What for? He has gone over of his own will. How is the man to
blame? He is happier there, so he has gone over there."

"And you saw him face to face?"

"Oh dear, yes! Such a glorious warrior! The most splendid of
them all. God give him good health, he knew me at once; and
when I went up to him, he said at once . . ."

"What did he say?"

"He said—first he beckoned with his finger, and then he said:
'Yankel!' 'Lord Andrei?' said I. 'Yankel! Tell my father, tell my
brother, tell all the Cossacks, tell everyone that my father is no
father to me now, my brother is no brother, my comrade no
comrade, and that I will fight against all of them, all of them I will
fight!' "

"You are lying, damned Judas!" Taras shouted, beside himself.
"You are lying, you son of a bitch! You crucified Christ, you
man accursed of God! I will kill you—you bastard! Be off—or you
will meet your death!" Taras snatched up his sword as he said it.
The terrified Jew took to his heels and fled as fast as his thin spare
legs would carry him. For a long time he ran without looking back,
through the Cossack camp and far away over the open plain,
though Taras did not pursue him, reflecting that it was senseless to
vent his fury on the first comer. Now he remembered that on the
previous night he had seen Andrei walking about the camp with
some woman, and he bowed his gray head and still refused to believe that so great a disgrace could have come to pass and that his
own son had sold his faith and soul.

At last he led his regiment into ambush and concealed himself with them behind a wood, the only one not yet burned by the Cossacks.

Meanwhile the Dnieper Cossacks, both on foot and on horse, came out on the three roads to the three gates of the city. One after the other the chiefs filed by: the Umansky, the Popovichevsky, the Kanevsky, the Steblikivsky, the Nezamaikovsky, the Gurguziv, the Tytarevsky, and the Tymoshevsky. Only the Pereiaslavsky unit was absent. The Cossacks of that unit had drunk deep and drunk away their lives. Some awoke, bound in the foes' hands; some, without waking, had passed asleep into the damp earth; and Khlib, their chief, himself, without his trousers and upper attire, was in the Polish camp.

The Cossacks' movements were heard in the city. All streamed out on the rampart, and a picture came alive before the Cossacks; the Polish knights, one handsomer than the other, stood on the wall. Copper helmets flashed like the sun, plumed with feathers white as the swan's. Others wore light caps of pink and blue, with the tops bent over on one side, full coats with hanging sleeves embroidered with gold and garnished with little cords; some had sabers and weapons in sumptuous settings, for which their masters had paid great sums—and there were many other sumptuous things of all sorts. Foremost of all stood the colonel of the new troops in a red cap decked with gold. The colonel was a heavy man, taller and stouter than any, and the ample folds of his costly full coat barely met around him. On the other side, almost at the side gate, stood another colonel, a small dried-up man: but his keen little eyes looked out sharply from under his overhanging brows, and he turned rapidly from side to side, pointing briskly with his thin sinewy hand, and giving orders; it could be seen that in spite of his frail body he was well versed in the arts of war. Near him stood a standard bearer, a tall lanky figure with thick mustaches, with no lack of color in his face: he was a man fond of strong mead and carousing. And behind them there were many Polish nobles of all sorts, some equipped at the cost of their own gold pieces, some at the Crown's expense, some by loans from Jews, after pledging all that was left in their ancestral castles. There were not a few also of the various parasites, whom the senators used to take with them to banquets to add to their own consequence, and who stole silver goblets from the table and the sideboards, and, after being gentlemen one day, would be sitting on the coachman's box the next. There were some of all sorts. There were some who at times had not a drop to drink, but all had been equipped for the war.

The Cossack ranks stood silent before the walls. There was no gold on any one of them; there was but a gleam of it here and there on the hilts of swords and stocks of guns. The Cossacks did not like to be richly attired for battle; they wore plain coats of mail and jackets, and far into the distance could be seen the black astrakhan and red tops of their caps.

Two Cossacks rode out in front of their ranks: one quite young, the other older, both bitter in speech and not bunglers in action: Okhrim Nash and Mykyta Golokopytenko. After them rode out Demid Popovich, too, a powerful Cossack who had been at the camp for years, had been at Adrianopolis and suffered many hardships in his day—he had been burned in the fire and escaped to the camp with his head singed and blackened and his mustaches burned off—but Popovich had regained his strength, grown a love-lock over his ear, and thick pitch-black mustaches. And a bitter and biting tongue had Popovich.

"Ah, red coats on all the troops, but I should like to know whether there is any red blood in the soldiers?"

"I'll show you!" the stout colonel shouted from above. "I'll bind you all! Hand over your guns and horses, you peasants. Have you seen how I've bound your fellows captive? Bring the Cossacks onto the rampart to show them!"

And they led the Cossacks out on the rampart tightly bound with ropes. Foremost of them was the chief of a unit, Khlib, without his trousers and shirt, just as they had captured him drunk. The chief hung his head, ashamed of being naked before his own Cossacks and of having been caught like a dog, asleep. And his head had turned gray in a single night.

"Don't grieve, Khlib! We will rescue you!" the Cossacks shouted to him from below.

"Don't grieve, old friend!" the unit chief Borodaty called out: "you're not to blame that you were taken naked; a misfortune may happen to any man; the shame is theirs for displaying your nakedness."

"Your soldiers are brave at fighting men asleep, it seems," said Golokopytenko, looking up at the rampart.

"You wait a bit, we'll shave off your forelocks!" they shouted from above.

"I should like to see them shave off our forelocks," said Popovich, turning to face them on his horse, and then looking at his own men, he said: "But maybe the Poles are right: if that fat man there leads them they will all have a good defense."

"Why do you think they'll have a good defense?" said the Cossacks, knowing that Popovich doubtless had some sally ready.

"Because they can all hide behind him and no lance could get at them behind his belly!"

All the Cossacks laughed; and long afterward many of them shook their heads, saying: "Well, he is something, Popovich! If anyone can twist a word, well . . ." But what the Cossacks meant by "well" they did not say.

"Move back, move back at once from the walls!" cried the leader; for the Poles seemed exasperated by the sarcasm and the colonel waved his hand.

Scarcely had the Cossacks moved aside when there came a volley of grapeshot from the rampart. There was a stir and bustle; the gray-headed commander in chief rode up himself on his horse. The gates were opened and the troops marched out. Foremost in straight ranks the embroidered hussars rode out on their horses; after them came men in coats of mail and then those in plated armor with lances, then others in copper helmets; then the Poles of the highest nobility rode apart, each dressed after his own taste. The proud nobles would not mingle in the ranks with the others, and those of them who were not in command rode apart with their servants. Then again came rows of soldiers, followed by Galiandovich; after him came ranks of soldiers again and then the stout colonel, and in the rear the little short colonel rode last of all.

"Don't let them! Don't let them form into ranks!" shouted the leader. "All units press upon them at once! Leave all the other gates! Tytarevsky unit, attack on the flank! Diadkiv unit, attack on the other flank! Bear on them in the rear, Kukubenko, Palyvoda! Harass them, harass them and keep them apart!"

And the Cossacks rushed from all sides, attacked the Poles and threw them into disorder, and were thrown into disorder themselves. They did not even let it come to firing; the fighting was with swords and lances. All were thrown together in confusion, and every man had a chance to show his mettle.

Demid Popovich stabbed three of the rank and file with his lance and threw two Polish noblemen from their horses, saying: "Those are good horses! I've wanted to get hold of such for a long time." And he drove the horses far away into the plain, shouting to the Cossacks standing there to catch them. Then he forced his way back into the turmoil and again set upon the Poles he had thrown from their horses; one he killed, on the neck of the other he flung a noose, tied him to his saddle, and dragged him across the field, taking from him a saber with a costly hilt, and untying from his belt a whole pouch of gold pieces.

Kobita, a brave, still young Cossack, engaged in combat with one of the most valiant of the Polish army, and long they struggled. They fought hand to hand. The Cossack had already nearly vanquished his assailant and, knocking him down, stabbed him with a sharp Turkish knife in the breast: but he did not escape himself; at the same instant a hot bullet struck him on the temple. He was felled by one of the most illustrious, most handsome of the Polish knights, of an ancient princely family. Swaying like a slender poplar, he darted hither and thither on his dun-colored steed. And many more feats of knightly valor he performed: two Cossacks he hacked in pieces; he threw Fiodor Korzh, a brave Cossack, to the ground, horse and all, fired at the horse, and struck the Cossack behind the horse with his lance; he smote off many a head and many a hand, and he it was that felled the Cossack Kobita with a bullet in his head.

"That's the man I would try my strength with!" shouted Kukubenko, the chief of the Nezamaikovsky unit. Giving his horse the rein, he pounced straight upon him from behind, uttering a loud scream so that all standing by shuddered at the unnatural sound. The Pole tried to turn his horse and face him; but the horse would not obey. Terrified by the dreadful scream, he started to one side, and Kukubenko caught him with a bullet from his gun. The molten lead passed in between his shoulder blades and he fell from his horse. But even then the Pole would not yield, he still strove to deal a blow at his foe; but the hand that held the sword sank powerless to the ground. And Kukubenko, taking his heavy lance in both hands, drove it right between his blanching lips; the pike knocked out two teeth, white as sugar, cleft the tongue in twain, smashed the neckbone, and drove far into the earth. So he pinned him there to the damp earth forever. The noble blood, crimson as the guelder-rose berry, spurted up in streams and stained his yellow gold-embroidered jacket all red. Kukubenko left him and made his way with his Nezamaikovsky Cossacks to another group.

"Oh, what precious trappings he has left unstripped!" said Borodaty, the chief of the Umansky unit, riding away from his followers to the spot where lay the Pole slain by Kukubenko. "Seven Poles have I killed with my own hand, but such trappings I have not seen yet on any." And Borodaty coveted them: he bent down to take the costly armor from the dead Pole; already he had pulled out a Turkish knife, set with gems all of one hue, and untied a pouch of gold pieces from the belt, and lifted from the breast a knapsack containing fine linen, sumptuous silver, and a maiden's curl, carefully treasured in remembrance. And Borodaty did not hear the red-nosed standard bearer, whom he had thrown down once from the saddle and at whom he had had a good slash, fly up behind him. The standard bearer swung his sword and smote him on the neck as he bowed down. Greed brought the Cossack to no good; the mighty head flew off and the dead man fell headless, wetting the earth with blood far and wide. Up into the heights flew the stern Cossack's soul, frowning and indignant, and at the same time marveling that it had so quickly parted from so strong a body. The standard bearer had not time to seize the chief's head by the forelock to tie it to his saddle before a fierce avenger was upon him.

As a hawk, soaring in the sky and circling around and around on its powerful wings, suddenly hovers suspended on one spot and then darts like an arrow on the quail calling to its mate, so Taras' son Ostap pounced on the standard bearer and cast a rope about his neck. The Pole's red face flushed a deeper crimson as the cruel noose tightened upon his throat. He gripped his pistol, but his convulsively twitching hand could not guide the shot and the bullet flew at random into the plain. In an instant Ostap untied from the man's own saddle the silken cord which the standard bearer took for binding prisoners, and with his own silken cord tied his hands and his feet, fastened the end of the cord to the saddle, and dragged him across the battlefield, calling loudly to the Cossacks of the Umansky unit to go and pay the last honors to their chief.

When the Umansky Cossacks heard that their chief, Borodaty, was among the dead, they left the battlefield and ran to take his body; and on the spot began discussing whom to choose to succeed him. At last they said: "But why discuss it? We could not find a better chief than Bulba's son Ostap: it is true he is younger than all of us, but he has the good sense of an old man."

Ostap, taking off his cap, thanked all his Cossack comrades for the honor done him; he did not urge his youth nor his inexperience, knowing that they were fighting and it was no time for that, but at once led them back to the fray and showed them that they had not been wrong to choose him as chief. The Poles felt that the battle was growing too fierce; they retreated, and were racing across the plain to rally at its other end. And the short colonel waved to four fresh divisions standing apart by the very gate, and from them came a volley of grapeshot into the Cossacks: but few were hit; the bullets struck the Cossacks' cattle who were staring wildly at the battle. The panic-stricken cattle bellowed, turned toward the Cossack encampment, broke the carts, and trampled many underfoot. But at that moment Taras, bursting out of ambush with his regiment, rushed with a loud shout to intercept them. All the frantic herd turned back, terrified by his shout, and stampeded the Polish regiments, scattering the cavalry and trampling and dispersing all.

"Oh, thanks to you, oxen!" shouted the Cossacks. "You did your work on the march and now you've done fighting service, too!" And they struck at the enemy with fresh energy. They overcame many of their foes at that time. Many Cossacks showed their mettle: Metelitsia, Shilo, the two Pysarenkos, Vovtuzenko, and many others. The Poles saw that things were going badly indeed; they lowered their standards and began shouting for the city gates to be opened. The ironshod gates opened with a creak and received the exhausted and dust-covered horsemen who crowded in like sheep into a fold. Many of the Cossacks would have pushed them, but Ostap checked his men, saying: "Keep back, keep back from the walls, comrades! You must not go close to them." And true were the words he spoke, for the enemy hurled and flung down from the walls anything they could lay their hands on, and many were struck. At that moment, the leader rode up and praised Ostap, saying: "Here is a new unit chief, but he leads his troops as though he were a veteran!" Old Bulba turned around to look what

new chief was there and saw Ostap on his horse at the head of all
the Umansky unit, with his cap crushed on one side and the commander's staff in his hand.

"What a son you are!" he said, looking at him; and the old man
was happy, and began thanking all of the troops of the unit for
the honor they had shown his son.

The Cossacks retreated once more, making ready to go to the
camps; and again the Poles appeared on the city rampart, this time
with tattered cloaks. There were stains of gore on many costly
coats, and the handsome copper helmets were thick with dust.

"Well, did you bind us?" the Cossacks shouted to them from
below.

"I've this for you!" the stout colonel kept shouting from above,
showing a rope; and the dusty, weary warriors still went on hurl-
ing threats, and the more defiant on both sides flung biting words at
one another.

At last they all dispersed. Some, worn out with the fight, went to
rest. Others sprinkled earth on their wounds and tore into bandages the kerchiefs and costly garments taken from the slain foe.
Others, who were a little less weary, began gathering up the dead
and paying them the last honors; with broadswords and lances
they dug graves; they brought earth in their caps and jackets; they
laid out their comrades' bodies with respect and scattered fresh
earth upon them that the crows and fierce eagles should not peck
their eyes. But the bodies of the Poles they bound by dozens to the
tails of wild horses and set them loose to race over the plain, and
for a long way pursued them, lashing them all the time. The frantic horses galloped over ridges and hillocks, across the hollows and
watercourses, and the dead bodies of the Poles were battered on
the earth and covered with blood and dust.

Then all the Cossacks sat down in circles to supper, and long
they talked of the deeds and feats that had fallen to the lot of
each to make an everlasting tale for strangers and posterity. It
was long before they lay down to sleep; and old Taras sat wakeful longer than all, pondering what it could mean that Andrei had
not been among the enemy. Had the Judas been ashamed to come
out to fight against his comrades, or had the Jew deceived him, and
was his son simply a prisoner? But then he remembered that Andrei's heart was excessively susceptible to women's words. He
was overcome with grief, and inwardly vowed vengeance against

the Polish woman who had ensnared his son. And he would have
carried out his vow: he would not have heeded her beauty; he
would have dragged her by her thick luxuriant hair and have
hauled her across the plain among all the Cossacks. And her
marvelous breasts and shoulders, dazzling as the unmelting snows
that cover the mountain heights, would have been crushed on the
earth, blood-stained and covered with dust. He would have torn
her glorious lovely body limb from limb. But Bulba knew not
what God prepares for man on the morrow, and he began sinking
into slumber and at last fell asleep. But the Cossacks still talked together, and all night long the guard, sober and wakeful, stood on
watch by the fires, gazing intently in all directions.

VIII

The sun had not yet reached the zenith when all the Cossacks
gathered in circles. News had come from the camp that in the
absence of the Cossacks the Tartars had plundered everything in
it, had dug out the goods which the Cossacks kept hidden underground, had overwhelmed and taken prisoner all who were left
behind, and with all the herds of cattle and droves of horses had
set off straight for Perekop. Only one Cossack, Maxim Golo-
dukha, had torn himself out of the Tartars' hands on the way,
stabbed the guard, unfastened his bag of sequins, and on a Tartar
horse, in Tartar dress, ridden away from his pursuers for a day and
a half and two nights, ridden the horse to death, mounted another
on the road, crippled that one too, and on a third reached the camp,
having learned on the way that the Cossacks were at Dubno. He
could only tell them that this misfortune had happened; but how it
had come to pass, whether the men left behind had been carousing
after the Cossack habit and been taken prisoner when they were
drunk, and how the Tartars had found the spot where the treasury was buried—that he did not tell them. The Cossack was terribly exhausted, he was swollen all over, his face was burned and
chapped by the wind; he sank down on the spot and fell into a
deep sleep.

In such cases it was the custom with Dnieper Cossacks to pursue the raiders instantly, trying to overtake them on the road; for
the prisoners might immediately be carried to the markets of Asia
Minor, to Smyrna or Crete, and there was no telling in what

places their Cossack heads with the long forelocks might not be seen. This was why they had assembled. They all, to the last man, stood with their caps on, for they had not come to listen to the commands of their superiors, but to consult together as equals. "Let the elders give counsel first!" they shouted in the crowd. "Let the leader give counsel!" said the others.

Then the leader, taking off his cap, not as their commanding officer but as their comrade, thanked all the Cossacks for the honor, and said: "Many among us are older and wiser in counsel, but, since you have done me the honor, my advice is not to lose time, comrades, but to pursue the Tartars; for you know yourselves what a Tartar is; they will not stand still with their plunder to await our arrival, but will dispose of it instantly, so that no trace may be found. So my advice is, go. We have had our fling here. The Poles know what the Cossacks are; we have avenged our faith so far as was in our power; there is little to be gained from the starved city. And so my advice is to go."

"Go!" rang out loudly in the Cossack ranks. But these words were not to Taras Bulba's taste, and he knitted his frowning black eyebrows, sprinkled with white, like bushes growing on the high crag of a mountainside with their tops always covered with the hoarfrost of the north.

"No, your counsel is not right," he said. "You are wrong; you seem to have forgotten that our comrades seized by the Poles are left in captivity. You would seemingly have us disregard the first sacred law of comradeship, would have us leave our mates to be flayed alive, or to be quartered and their Cossack limbs sent about from town to village, as the Poles did with the Hetman and the foremost Russian noblemen in the Ukraine. Have they not insulted our holy things enough? What are we made of? I ask you all. What is the Cossack worth who leaves a comrade in misfortune, leaves him like a dog to perish among aliens? If it has come to the point that Cossack honor is meaningless, that you will allow people to spit into your gray mustaches, to reproach you with words of infamy, then I will not risk such upbraiding. I will remain alone!"

All the standing Cossacks wavered.

"But have you forgotten, brave colonel," the leader said then, "that we have comrades in the Tartars' hands, also, that if we do not rescue them now they will be sold into lifelong slavery to heathens, which is worse than any cruel death? Have you forgotten that they have now all our treasure paid for with Christian blood?"

All the Cossacks hesitated and did not know what to say. No one of them was willing to face dishonor. Then Kasian Bovdiug, the oldest in years of all the army, stepped forward. He was held in honor by all the Cossacks; twice he had been elected leader, and in battle, too, had been a good Cossack, but for years now he had been too old to take part in any campaigns. He did not like to give advice either; what the old warrior liked best was lying on his side by the Cossack campfire, listening to tales of the adventures and campaigns of years gone by. He never took part in their talk, but only listened, pressing down with his finger the ash in his short pipe, which he never took out of his mouth. And for hours afterward he would sit screwing up his eyes, and the Cossacks did not know whether he was asleep, or still listening. He always remained behind them when there were campaigns, but this time something had roused the old man. Waving his hand in Cossack fashion, he had said: "Well! come what may! I'm coming too; perhaps I may be of some use to the Cossack cause!"

All the Cossacks sank into silence when he stepped out now before the assembly, for it was long since they had heard a word from him. Everyone wanted to know what Bovdiug would say.

"My turn has come to say a word, comrades!" was how he began. "Listen to an old man, children. The leader uttered words of wisdom; and, as the head of the Cossack army in duty bound to guard its safety and to take care of the army treasury, he could have said nothing better. I tell you that! Let that be my first speech! And now listen to what my second speech tells you. This is what my second speech tells you: Taras, the colonel, God grant him long years and may there be more colonels like him in the Ukraine, spoke a greater truth! The first duty and the chief honor of the Cossack is to be true to his comrades. Long as I have lived I have never, brothers, heard of a Cossack deserting or betraying his comrade. And both these and the others are our comrades—whether there are more or fewer of them does not matter—all are comrades, all are dear to us. So this is my counsel: let those who care more for the prisoners seized by the Tartars set off in pursuit of the Tartars, and those who care more for the friends who have been taken prisoners by the Poles, and who do not want to leave their true task, remain. The leader is in duty bound to go with the one half after the Tartars, while the other half will choose another leader. And that leader, if you care to listen to a white-headed comrade, could be no one but Taras Bulba. No one of us is his equal in valor."

So said Bovdiug and ceased; and all the Cossacks were pleased that the old man had brought them to sense like this. They all flung up their caps and shouted: "Thanks, old man! For years you have sat silent, but here at last you have spoken; well might you say when you set off on the march that you would be of use to the Cossack cause: so it has come to pass."

"Well, do you agree to it?" asked the leader.

"We all agree!" shouted the Cossacks.

"Then is the assembly over?"

"The assembly is over!" shouted the Cossacks.

"Then now listen to my orders," said the leader, and he stepped forward and put on his hat, while all the Cossacks took off their caps and stood with uncovered heads and downcast eyes, as was always done among the Cossacks when a superior officer was about to address them. "Now you must divide, comrades. Those who want to go, step to the right; those who want to remain, step to the left! Each unit chief will go where the greater number of his unit go; the lesser half of the unit will join other units."

And they all began to cross over, some to the right, some to the left. The leader passed over to the side to which the greater number of his unit had passed; the rest of the unit joined other units; and it turned out that the numbers to the right and to the left were almost equal. Among those who wanted to remain were almost the whole of the Nezamaikovsky unit, the larger part of the Popovichevsky unit, the whole Umansky unit, the whole Kanevsky unit, the greater part of the Steblikivsky unit, the greater part of the Tymoshevsky unit. All the others chose to go in pursuit of the Tartars. There were many brave and stalwart Cossacks on both sides. Among those who decided to go after the Tartars were: Cherevaty, a good old Cossack, Pokotypole, Lemish, Khoma Prokopovich; Demid Popovich, too, went to the right because he was a Cossack of a very restless character and would never stay long in one place; he had already tried his strength with the Poles and wanted to try it with the Tartars. The chiefs of the units were Nostiugan, Pokryshka, Nevylychsky; and many other famous and valiant Cossacks longed to try their sword and mighty arm in combat with the

Tartars. There were many extremely good Cossacks also who chose to remain: the unit chiefs Demytrovich, Kukubenko, Vertykhvist, Balaban, and Ostap Bulba. Then there were many other renowned and bold Cossacks: Vovtuzenko, Cherevychenko, Stepan Guska, Okhrim Guska, Mykola Gusty, Zadorozhny, Metelitsia, Ivan Zakrutyguba, Mosy Shilo, Diogtiarenko, Sydorenko, Pysarenko, and then the second Pysarenko and the third Pysarenko, and there were many other good Cossacks. All were men who had traveled far and wide; they had marched about the Anatolian coasts, about the salt marshes and steppes of the Crimea, along all the streams big and little which fall into the Dnieper, about all the pools and islands of that river; they had been in the Moldavian, Wallachian, and Turkish lands, and navigated all the Black Sea in the double-ruddered Cossack boats; in fifty such boats drawn up in a row they had attacked richly laden ships; they had sunk not a few of the Turkish galleys, and much powder they had fired in their day. Many a time they had torn up expensive silks and velvets for leg wrappers; many a time they had stuffed the purses in their trousers' girdles with sequins of pure gold. And there is no reckoning the wealth, enough to last another man a lifetime, which each one of them had squandered on drink and debauchery. They threw everything away in Cossack style, treating everybody and hiring musicians that everything in the world might be gay. Yet even now few of them had no hoard of wealth buried—mugs, silver ladles, and bracelets—under the reeds on the isles of the Dnieper that the Tartars might not succeed in finding it, if by ill-luck they made an unexpected attack on the camp; but it would be hard for the Tartars to find it, for the owner himself had by now almost forgotten where it was buried. Such were the Cossacks who prepared to remain and take vengeance on the Poles for their trusty comrades and the Christian faith.

The old Cossack Bovdiug, too, preferred to remain with them, saying: "I'm too old to pursue the Tartars, but this is the place in which to die a good Cossack death. Long have I prayed to God that when my time comes to end my life I may end it warring for a holy and Christian cause. And so it has come to pass. There could be in no other place a more glorious end for an old Cossack."

When all were divided and standing in two rows on opposite sides, the leader passed between them and said: "Well, comrades, is the one side content with the other?"

"All are content, old man!" answered the Cossacks.

"Well, then, kiss each other and say farewell, for God knows whether it will be your lot to meet again in this life. Obey your chief and do what you know yourselves: you know yourselves what Cossack honor dictates."

And all the Cossacks kissed one another. First the chiefs began, and, holding aside their gray mustaches, kissed each other three times, took each other's hands, and held them tight; each wanted to ask the other: "Well, comrade, shall we see each other again?" But they did not ask, they were silent, and both gray-headed warriors sank into thought. And all the Cossacks said farewell to one another knowing there was much work ahead for both; they could not, however, separate at once, but they had to wait for the darkness of night that the enemy might not see that their numbers were diminished. Then they all went off to dinner with their separate units.

After dinner all who had the journey before them lay down to rest and had a long sound sleep, as though feeling that it might be the last time they could sleep so freely. They slept till sunset: when the sun had gone down and it was beginning to get dark, they began greasing the cart wheels. After equipping themselves they sent the baggage on ahead and, taking off their caps once more to their comrades, set off quietly after the wagons; the cavalry quietly, with no shouting or whistling to the horses, tramped lightly after the foot soldiers, and quickly they vanished in the darkness. Only the hollow ring of the horses' hoofs and the creaking of the wheels, which had perhaps not been properly greased, resounded in the darkness of the night.

Their comrades, left behind, still waved their hands though nothing could be seen. And when they turned and went back to their places, when, as the stars came out, they saw that half the carts were gone, that many, many comrades were lost to them, everyone felt sad at heart, and none could help growing melancholy, and bowing their reckless heads.

Taras saw how troubled were the Cossack ranks and how a gloom, unseemly in the brave, was slowly overcoming them, but he said nothing; he wanted to give them time to get over the sadness of parting from their comrades. Meanwhile in silence he prepared himself to rouse them all at one moment by uttering the Cossack battle cry, so that courage might come back anew to the heart of each with greater force than before, a revitalization of which only the Slav race is capable, that richly endowed, vigorous race which, compared with all others, is as the ocean to shallow rivers; in time of tempest it is all uproar and commotion, tossing and flinging up billows as no impotent river can; in calm, still weather it stretches far and wide its limitless glassy surface, fairer than any river, an endless joy to the eye.

And Taras bade his servants unload one of the wagons that stood apart from the rest. It was larger and stronger than any of the others; its thick wheels were covered with strong double bands of iron; it was heavily laden, covered with horsecloths and strong ox-leathers and bound with stiffly tarred ropes. In the wagon were barrels and kegs of excellent old wine which had lain long in Bulba's cellars. He had held it in reserve for a solemn occasion, so that, if a great moment came and some deed worthy to be handed down to posterity should be awaiting them, every single Cossack should have a drink of precious wine, so that at a great moment a man might rise to the occasion. Hearing their colonel's command, the servants rushed to the wagon; with their broadswords they cut the strong cords, took off the stout ox-leathers and the horsecloths, and brought out the barrels and the kegs.

"All of you take as much as you want," said Bulba. "Each use what he has, ladle or bowl with which he waters his horse, or gauntlet, or cap, and if there's nothing better, then simply cup your hands."

One Cossack used a ladle, one a bowl for giving drink to the horses, another a gauntlet, another a cap, while some simply cupped their hands. Bulba's servants, going back and forth between the ranks, poured out from the barrels and the kegs for all. But Taras bade them await the signal for all to drink at once. They could see that he wanted to say something. Taras knew that strong as the good old wine was in itself and well fitted to fortify the spirit, yet if the right word went with it, the power of the wine and the spirit would be doubly strengthened.

"I am treating you, comrades!" said Bulba, "not in honor of your having made me your commander, great as such an honor is, nor in honor of our leave-taking from our comrades; no, at another time either would have been fitting, but a very different moment awaits us now. Deeds of great endeavor, of great Cossack valor, are awaiting us! And so, comrades, let us drink all together,

let us drink, first of all, to the holy Orthodox faith, that the time
may come at last when it will spread over the whole world and
everywhere there may be one holy religion and all the pagans
on earth will become Christian! And at the same time let us drink,
too, to the camp, that long it may stand to the destruction of all the
heathen world, that it may send out everywhere young heroes,
each better, each finer than the last. And let us drink, too, to our
own glory, that our grandsons and their sons after them may tell
how once there were men who were not false to their comrades and
did not betray them. So to our faith, comrades, to our faith!"

"To our faith!" all who stood in the front ranks boomed out with
their deep voices. "To our faith!" Those further away took it up—
and all, old and young, drank to their faith.

"To the camp!" said Taras, and raised his hand high above his
head.

"To the camp!" came the deep echo in the foremost ranks. "To
the camp!" the old men said quietly, twitching their gray mustaches; and with a flutter like young falcons the young Cossacks
repeated: "To the camp!" And the plain heard far away the Cossacks honoring their camp.

"Now the last drink, comrades, to glory and to all the Christians
in the world!"

And all the Cossacks to the last man tossed off the last drop to
glory and to all Christians in the world. Long afterward it was repeated through all the ranks among all the units: "To all the
Christians there are in the world!"

By now their drinking vessels were empty and still the Cossacks
stood with their hands raised; though the eyes of all, sparkling with
the wine, looked gay, yet they were full of brooding thought; it
was not of gain and the booty of war that they were thinking now,
nor were they wondering who would be lucky in winning gold
pieces, costly weapons, embroidered coats, and Circassian horses.
They were looking into the future, like eagles sitting on the topmost crags of rocky mountains, high precipitous mountains, from
which they can see the boundless expanse of the ocean, dotted
with galleys, ships, and all manner of vessels like tiny birds in the
sky, and bordered by faintly visible strips of coast with towns on
the shore like tiny insects, and sloping forests like fine grass. Like
eagles they scanned all the plain around them and looked into
their future that grew blacker in the distance. The whole plain with

its fields and roads will be covered with their bleaching bones,
be richly bathed in their Cossack blood and strewn with broken
wagons, shattered swords, and splintered lances; far and wide
will lie, scattered, their heads with hanging mustaches and long
forelocks tangled and stiff with blood; the eagles will fly down to
peck and tear out their Cossack eyes. But there will be great comfort in a deathbed so spacious and free! Not one noble deed will
perish, and the Cossack glory will not be lost like the little grain of
powder from the musket barrel. The bandore player will come with
the gray beard over his chest, a white-headed old man, though
maybe still full of ripe manhood, prophetic in spirit, and he will say
his rich powerful word about them. And the tale of them will race
over the whole world, and all who are born hereafter will talk of
them: for a mighty word resounds far and wide like the sonorous
copper of the bell into which the craftsman has blended much pure
precious silver, that its lovely chime may ring out afar through
cities, hovels, palaces, and plains, calling all alike to join in holy
prayer.

IX

No one in the city had learned that half of the Cossacks had set
off in pursuit of the Tartars. From the tower of the town hall the
sentinels only noticed that some of the wagons were moving out
beyond the forest, but they thought that the Cossacks were preparing to make an ambush; the French engineer thought the same.
Meanwhile the leader's words were coming true, and a shortage of
provisions was being felt in the city: as was common in past times
the soldiers had not considered how much they would need. They
tried to make a sortie, but half of the bold men who took part in it
were slain on the spot by the Cossacks, and the other driven back
into the city without having gained anything. The Jews, however,
took advantage of the sortie and sniffed out information: where
the Cossacks had gone and for what purpose, and under which
leaders, and how many of them had departed and how many of
them had been left behind, and what they were thinking of doing
—in fact, within a few minutes everything was known in the
town. The commanders recovered their spirits and prepared to
give battle: Taras saw it at once from the commotion and uproar
in the city, and he worked zealously, drew up his men, gave or-

ders, and stationed the units in three camps, surrounding them with the wagons by way of barricades—a form of battle in which the Dnieper Cossacks were invincible; he commanded two units to prepare an ambush; he covered part of the plain with short stakes, broken weapons, and splinters of lances, intending if possible to drive the enemy cavalry there. And when all was done that was needed, he made a speech to the Cossacks, not to encourage them and renew their vigor, but simply because he desired to utter all that was in his heart.

"I want to tell you, friends, what is meant by our comradeship. You have heard from your fathers and your grandfathers in what honor our land was once held among all men; she let the Greeks see what she could do, and took tribute from Constantinople, and her cities were rich, and her temples, and her princes were of Russian birth, her own princes and not Catholic heretics. All that was taken by the infidels, all was lost. We were left destitute, and, like a widow when her strong husband is dead, our country was destitute as we were! It was in those days that we, comrades, clasped our hands in brotherhood! It is on that that our comradeship stands! Nothing is holier than the love of comrades. The father loves his child, the mother loves her child, the child loves its father and mother; but that is not the same, brothers; the wild beast too loves its offspring, but only man can be akin in soul, though not in blood. There have been comrades in other lands, too, but such comrades as in Russia there have never been. More than one of you has had occasion to be for a little while in foreign lands; you see that there, too, are men! God's creatures, too, and you speak with them as with your own fellows; but when it comes to uttering a word from the heart—no! You see they are clever people, but not the same; they are men like us but not the same! No, comrades, to love as the Russian heart can love—to love not with the mind or anything else, but with all that God has given you, all that is in you —Ah! . . ." said Taras, and he waved his hand while his gray head trembled and his mustache twitched. "No!" he said. "No one can love like that! I know that mean ways have come into our land now; men think only of having sheaves of grain and stacks of wheat and of their droves of horses, and of their mead sealed up safe in their cellars. The devil knows what pagan habits they are adopting; they disdain their own language, they do not care to talk with their own people; they sell their own countrymen, as men sell a

soulless beast in the market. The favor of an alien king, and, indeed, not of a king, but the paltry favor of a Polish nobleman who
kicks them in the face with his yellow boot, is more precious to
them than any brotherhood. But even the lowest wretch, whatever
he may be, even though he may be groveling in grime and servility,
even he, comrades, has a grain of Russian feeling; it will awaken
one day—and he, poor wretch, will clasp his hands in horror, will
clutch at his head cursing aloud his abject life, ready by tortures to
expiate his shameful deeds. Let them all know what comradeship
means in Russia! If it comes to dying, not one of them will have
the luck to meet with such a death! Not one, not one! Mice like
them can't rise to that!"

So spoke the chief and, when he ended his speech, his head which
had grown silvery in Cossack service still trembled. All who stood
around were deeply moved by such a speech, which went straight
to their hearts; the eldest in the ranks stood motionless, their gray
heads bowed; a tear quietly gathered in their old eyes; they slowly
wiped it away with their sleeve. And then all, as though by common agreement, waved their hands at the same instant and tossed
their heads. Clearly old Taras had brought back to them much
that was familiar and best in those who had gained wisdom by sorrow, toils, daring, and all the hardships of life, and stirred those
whose youthful souls, pure as a pearl, understood much instinctively, to the everlasting joy of the old parents who gave them life.

Already the enemy's troops were marching out of the city to the
din of drums and the blowing of trumpets, and the Polish nobles,
with their arms akimbo, rode forth, surrounded by innumerable
servants. The stout colonel was giving orders. As they began in
close ranks to advance upon the Cossack camps, with flashing eyes
and glittering copper armor, they took aim with their rifles. As
soon as the Cossacks saw that they had come within reach of
their guns, they all fired in return, unceasingly. The clamor
floated over all the surrounding fields and meadows, blending into
one continuous roar: the smoke covered the whole plain. The
Cossacks still fired without taking breath; those in the rear did
nothing but load and hand the weapons to those in the front ranks,
so that the enemy were amazed and could not understand how the
Cossacks fired without loading their guns. By now nothing could
be seen for the dense smoke in which both armies were wrapped;
no one could see how first one and then another dropped in the

ranks. But the Poles felt that the bullets were flying thickly and that things were getting hot; and when they staggered back to move out of the smoke and look about them, many were missing from their ranks; while of the Cossacks only perhaps two or three were killed out of a hundred. And still the Cossacks went on firing without stopping. Even the French engineer marveled and had never seen the like, saying on the spot before all of them: "They are gallant fellows, the Dnieper Cossacks! That's how others should fight in other lands!" And he advised the Poles to turn their cannon at once upon the camp. Loud was the roar from the throats of the iron cannon; the earth trembled, resounding afar, and twice as much smoke rolled over the plain. Men smelled the gunpowder in the squares and streets of cities far and near. But the Poles aimed too high, the blazing hot balls made too wide a sweep; tearing through the air, they flew over the heads of those in the camp and sank deeply into the ground, ripping and flinging up the black earth. The French engineer tore at his hair at such blundering and began firing the cannon himself, disregarding the incessant hail of bullets from the Cossacks.

Taras saw from a distance the danger threatening the Nezamaikovsky and Steblikivsky units, and he shouted in a booming voice: "Quickly, away from the wagons! and let each man mount his horse!" But the Cossacks would not have had time to carry out either command if Ostap had not rushed into the very midst of the Polish gunners; he beat out the fuses of six gunners, but four he could not cope with; the Poles drove him back. Meanwhile the Frenchman himself took a fuse in his hand to fire off the biggest cannon, which no one of the Cossacks had seen before. Terrible it looked with its huge throat, and a thousand deaths looked down from it: and when it boomed out, and after it three others, making the earth shake four times with hollow echo, terrible was the destruction they dealt! Many an old mother will sob for her Cossack son, beating her bony hands on her aged bosom; many a widow will be left in Glukhov, Nemirov, Chernigov, and other cities. She will run out every day to the market place, scanning all who pass by, looking into the face of each one of them, seeking for one dearer than all; but many warriors will pass through the town and never will she find among them the one dearer than all.

It was as though half of the Nezamaikovsky unit had never been! As suddenly as a field, where every ear of wheat shines bright as a heavy gold piece, is beaten down by the hail, so they were beaten down and laid low.

How the Cossacks raged! How they all rushed to the rescue! How the chief Kukubenko boiled with fury seeing that more than half of his unit was no more! With those who were left he fought his way into the midst of the fray. In his wrath he chopped into mincemeat the first Pole he came upon; many he flung down from their horses, driving his lance through rider and horse; he made his way to the gunners and carried off one cannon. Then he saw the Umansky chief was busy, and Stepan Guska was already capturing the chief cannon. He left those Cossacks and returned with his men to another part where the enemy were thickest: where the Nezamaikovsky Cossacks passed they left an open way, where they turned there was an open space! It could be seen that the ranks were thinner and that the Poles had fallen in stacks. Vovtuzenko was by the wagons, while Cherevychenko was in front, and Diogtiavenko was at the furthest wagons, and beyond him was the chief Vertykhvist. Diogtiavenko had tossed two Poles on his lance, but fell at last on a third who was not easy to overcome. The Pole was resourceful and stalwart, he was adorned with sumptuous accouterments, and brought with him no less than fifty servants. He pressed Diogtiavenko hard, felled him to the ground, and as he swung his sword over him, shouted: "There is not one among you, dogs of Cossacks, who would dare to face me in combat!"

"Here is one!" said Mosy Shilo, and he stepped forward. He was a mighty Cossack; more than once he had been in command on the sea and had suffered many hardships. The Turks had captured him with his followers at Trebizond and had taken them all as galley slaves, had kept them with iron chains on their arms and legs, given them no grain for weeks at a time, and nothing to drink but putrid seawater. The poor prisoners had suffered and endured it all rather than give up their Orthodox faith. But their chief, Mosy Shilo, could not hold out; he trampled underfoot the holy law, bound the unholy turban around his sinful head, gained the confidence of the Pasha, became the steward on the ship, and was put in charge of all the prisoners. Greatly the poor captives grieved over it, for they knew that, if their own comrade would betray his faith and go over to the oppressors, their lot would be harder and more bitter in his power than under any other infidel; and so indeed it came to pass. Mosy Shilo put them all into fresh chains, three in a row, bound them with cords that cut them to their very bones; he beat them with blows upon their necks. And when the Turks, delighted at having gained such a servant, began feasting and, forgetting their own religious law, all got drunk, he took all the sixty-four keys and gave them to the prisoners that they might unlock their fetters, cast them with their chains into the sea, take up swords instead, and slaughter the Turks. The Cossacks took much booty then and returned with glory to their country, and long afterward the bandore players sang the praises of Mosy Shilo. He would have been elected leader, but he was a peculiar Cossack. Sometimes he performed exploits such as the best of them would not have dreamed of; at other times some crazy whim took possession of him. He squandered everything in drink and revelry, was in debt to everyone in the camp, and stole, moreover, like a gutter thief; he would by night carry off all the equipment of a Cossack from another unit and pawn it. For such a shameful deed he was tied to a post in the market place and an oak cudgel was put beside him, so that every man might deal him a blow according to his strength: but there was not one among all the Cossacks who would lift the cudgel against him, for they all remembered his services in the past. Such was the Cossack Mosy Shilo.

"There are men who can destroy you, dog!" he said, setting upon him. And how they hacked at each other then! And the shoulderpieces and breastplates of both were dented by the blows. The Polish foe cleft Shilo's coat of mail, driving the blade right into his body; the Cossack's shirt was stained red. But Shilo heeded it not; he swung his sinewy arm (he had a powerful muscular arm) and dealt the Pole a blow upon the head. The copper helmet flew in pieces, the Pole staggered and fell with a thud, and Shilo began hacking and quartering the stunned foe. Slay him not, Cossack, but rather turn around! The Cossack did not turn, and one of the slain man's servants stabbed him in the neck with a knife. Shilo turned and the bold fellow would have been badly handled, but he vanished in the smoke. From all sides came the sound of guns. Shilo staggered, and felt that his wound was mortal. He fell to the ground, put his hand on his wound, and said, turning to his comrades: "Farewell, comrades! May Holy Russia live forever, and may her glory be eternal!" And he closed his dimming eyes, and his Cossack soul soared out of his rough body. But by then Zadorozhny had ridden out with his men, Vertykhvist had broken the ranks, and Balaban had moved forward.

"Well, comrades," said Taras, calling to the leaders of the units, "is there powder left in your flasks? Has the Cossack might failed? Are the Cossacks giving way?"

"We have powder still in our flasks, old man; the Cossack might has not failed yet! The Cossacks are not giving way!"

And the Cossacks pressed hard; all the enemy's ranks were thrown into confusion. The short colonel sounded a rallying call, and ordered eight painted standards to be unfurled to gather his men, who were scattered far and wide over the plain. All the Poles hastened to the standards, but before they had time to form into ranks again the chief Kukubenko with his Nezamaikovsky Cossacks dashed into their midst and flew straight for the fat colonel. The colonel could not hold out, but, turning his horse, put it into a gallop; and Kukubenko pursued him far into the plain, not letting him join his regiment. Seeing this from a unit on the flank, Stepan Guska galloped to intercept him, a noose in his hand, riding with his head on his horse's neck, and seizing the moment, with one throw he cast the noose about the Pole's neck. The colonel turned crimson, clutching at the rope with both hands and struggling to tear it apart, but a mighty thrust drove the fatal lance straight into his stomach. There he was left pinned to the earth. But Guska fared no better! The Cossacks hardly had time to look around when they saw Stepan Guska lifted on four lances. The poor Cossack had only breath to say: "Down with all foes, and may Russia rejoice forever and ever!" And with that he gave up his soul.

The Cossacks looked around, and on one side the Cossack Metelitsia was entertaining the Poles, knocking down one and then another; while on the other side the chief Nevylychky and his Cossacks were pressing them hard; while at the wagons Zakrutyguba was turning the enemy and beating them; while Pysarenko the third had already driven back a whole crowd from the furthest wagons. In another place there was hand-to-hand fighting on the wagons.

"Well, comrades," their chief Taras shouted to them as he rode ahead of them all, "have you still powder left in the flasks? Is the Cossack force still strong? The Cossacks are not giving way yet?"

"We've still powder left in our flasks; the Cossack force is still strong; the Cossacks are not giving way yet!"

But Bovdiug had fallen from the wagon. The bullet had caught him just under the heart; yet the old man rallied all his strength and said: "I am not sorry to part with life. God grant every man such a death! May Russia be glorious to the end of time!" And Bovdiug's soul fled to the heavenly heights to tell the old men who had departed long before how men can fight in Russia and, better still, how they can die for their holy faith.

Balaban also fell to the ground soon after. Three mortal wounds were dealt him from a spear, from a bullet, and from a heavy broadsword. He was one of the most valiant Cossacks; many exploits he had performed when in command of expeditions by sea, but most famous of all was his raid on the coasts of Anatolia. That time the Cossacks carried off many sequins, precious Turkish possessions, robes and trappings of all sorts, but they met with trouble on their homeward way: they came, poor fellows, under Turkish fire. When the ship fired at them, half the boats whirled around and turned over, throwing more than one Cossack into the water; but the reeds bound to the sides saved the boats from sinking. Balaban rowed off as fast as he could, steered straight toward the sun, and so could not be seen by the Turkish ship. All the night after, with ladles and with their caps they baled out the water, stuffing up the broken places; from their Cossack trousers they cut out sails, and so sailed off and escaped from the swift Turkish ship. And not only did they reach the camp unharmed, but brought with them a gold embroidered chasuble for the Archimandrite of the Mezhigorsky Monastery at Kiev, and for the icon of the Church of the Intercession at camp they brought a setting of pure silver. And long afterward the bandore players celebrated the Cossacks' success.

Now he bowed his head, feeling the death agonies, and said quietly: "It seems to me, comrades, I am dying a fine death: seven have I slain with the sword, nine I have stabbed with the lance, I have trampled under my horse's hoofs plenty, and I know not how many I have shot. May Russia flourish forever . . ." And his soul fled from his body.

Cossacks! Cossacks! abandon not the flower of your army! By now Kukubenko was surrounded: only seven men were left of the Nezamaikovsky unit, and by now they were overpowered; already their chief's garments were stained with blood. Taras himself, seeing his plight, hastened to his assistance. But the Cossacks were too late: a lance had stabbed him to the heart before the enemy surrounding him were driven off. Slowly he sank into the arms of

the Cossacks who supported him, and the young blood spurted out
in a stream like precious wine brought in a glass vessel from the cellar by careless servants who slip at the entrance and shatter the
costly flagon, the wine spilling upon the ground; and the master,
running up, clutches his head in despair, since he has kept it for the
best moment of his life, so that, if God should grant in his old age
a meeting with the comrades of his youth, they might celebrate together those old other days when men made merry otherwise and
better. . . . Kukubenko looked around and said: "I thank God
that it is my lot to die before your eyes, comrades! May men better than we live after us, and may Russia, beloved of Christ, flourish
forever . . . !" And his young soul fled. The angels received it in
their arms and bore it to heaven. It will be good for him there. "Sit
at my right, Kukubenko!" Christ will say to him, "thou hast not
betrayed thy comrades; thou hast wrought no deed of dishonor;
thou hast forsaken no man in trouble; thou hast guarded and saved
My Church."

Kukubenko's death was a blow to everyone. The Cossack ranks
were by now very thin; many, very many valiant men were missing; but still the Cossacks stood firm and held their own.

"Well, comrades," Taras shouted to the units that were left, "is
there still powder in your flask? Are not your sabers blunted? Is
not the Cossack force weary? Have not the Cossacks given way?"

"We still have powder, old man; our sabers are still sharp; the
Cossack force is not weary; the Cossacks have not given way yet!"

And the Cossacks charged again as though they had suffered
no losses. By now only three leaders of the units were left alive;
streams of blood ran red on every side; the mounds of Cossack and
Polish dead rose high. Taras glanced at the sky and already a string
of vultures stretched across it. Well, there would be a harvest for
someone! And over there Metelitsia was tossed on a lance, and the
head of one of the Pysarenkos rolled to the ground, severed from
the body, and Okhrim Guska, overwhelmed and thrown to the
earth, was hacked in quarters. "Now!" said Taras, and waved his
handkerchief. Ostap understood the signal and, dashing out of ambush, charged the cavalry. The Poles could not stand against his
furious onslaught, and Ostap chased and drove them straight to
the place where stakes and broken lances were driven into the
ground. The horses stumbled and fell and the Poles flew over their
heads. At the same moment the Cossacks who stood last behind the

wagons, seeing that the Poles were within range, opened fire. All the Poles were overwhelmed and thrown into confusion, and the Cossacks' spirits rose. "Victory is ours," the voices of Cossacks rang out on all sides, trumpets were sounded, and a banner of victory was unfurled. The defeated Poles were running in all directions seeking cover.

"Oh, no, not quite victory yet!" said Taras, looking toward the city gates, and he was right.

The gates were flung open and a regiment of hussars, the flower of all the cavalry regiments, darted out. All were mounted on dun-colored stallions, all alike; at their head rode a young noble more alert and handsomer than any; his black hair strayed from under his copper helmet; a costly scarf embroidered by the hands of the greatest beauty in the city was twisted around his arm. Taras was thunderstruck when he saw that it was Andrei. And Andrei, meanwhile, caught up in the fire and ardor of battle, eager to be worthy of the gift tied to his arm, bounded forward like a young wolfhound, the handsomest, swiftest, and youngest of the pack. The practiced huntsman calls to him—and he races on, his legs forming one straight line in the air, his whole body slanting sideways as he flings up the snow and a dozen times runs beyond the hare in the heat of his course. Old Taras stood still and looked at the way in which he cleared a road before him, dispersing the Cossacks, hacking and dealing blows to right and to left. Taras could not stand it and shouted: "What? Your own men? You are striking your comrades, you devil's son?" But Andrei saw not who was before him, he knew not whether they were his comrades or others; he saw nothing. Tresses, long tresses were all that he saw, and a breast like a river swan and a snowy neck and shoulders, and all that is created for wild embraces.

"Hey, Cossacks! Lure him into the wood, lure him!" shouted Taras. And at once thirty of the swiftest Cossacks undertook to lure him there. And, setting straight their high caps, they galloped on their horses right across the path of the hussars. They struck the foremost on the flank and threw them into confusion, parted them from those behind, dealt a blow to two or three, while Golokopytenko dealt Andrei a blow flat on the back, and at once the Cossacks galloped away from them at their utmost speed. How Andrei flew at them! How the young blood boiled in all his veins! Driving his sharp spurs into his horse, he dashed full speed after the Cossacks, not looking back, not seeing that only twenty men were following him; while the Cossacks galloped like the wind and made straight for the wood. Andrei overtook them and had almost caught Golokopytenko, when suddenly a mighty hand clutched at his horse's bridle. Andrei looked around: Taras was facing him! The young man trembled all over and turned pale, as a schoolboy who has heedlessly been teasing a companion and has been struck by him on the forehead with a ruler flares up, leaps from the bench in a rage and chases his terrified schoolfellow, ready to tear him to pieces, when he suddenly stumbles against the teacher as he is entering the classroom: instantly his rage is over and his impotent fury subsides. So Andrei's anger passed away instantly, as though it had never been. And he was aware of no one but his terrifying father.

"Well, what are we going to do now?" said Taras, looking him straight in the face. But Andrei stood with downcast eyes and said nothing in reply.

"Well, son, have your Poles helped you?"

Andrei was speechless.

"So you would betray? Betray your faith? Betray your comrades? Stop! Dismount!"

Obediently, like a child, Andrei slipped off his horse and stood more dead than alive before Taras.

"Stand still, stir not! I begot you, and now I shall kill you!" said Taras, and stepping back he took the gun from his shoulder. Andrei was pale as a sheet; his lips could be seen to move and he uttered a name, but it was not the name of his country, nor of his mother or brother; it was the name of the Polish beauty. Taras fired.

Like a stalk of wheat cut by the sickle, like a young lamb with the deadly steel at its heart, Andrei hung his head and sank upon the grass, not uttering one word.

His murderer stood still, and long he gazed at the lifeless corpse. He was handsome even in death; his manly face, lately so full of strength and irresistible charm for women, was still magnificent; the black eyebrows like mourning velvet cast a shadow over his blanching features.

"What a Cossack he might have been!" said Taras. "Tall in stature and black-browed and a face like a nobleman, and his arm was strong in battle! He has perished! Dying shamefully like a vile dog!"

"Father, what have you done! Was it you who killed him?" said Ostap, riding up.

Taras bowed his head.

Steadily Ostap gazed into the dead man's eyes. He grieved for his brother and said at once: "Let us give him honorable burial, father, that the enemy may not cast ignominy upon him, nor birds of prey tear his body."

"They will bury him without our help!" said Taras. "There will be plenty to weep and mourn for him!"

And for two minutes he pondered whether to leave him to be torn by the wolves or to honor in him the knightly valor which a brave man ought to respect in anyone, when he saw Golokopytenko galloping up to him: "Bad news: the Poles are reinforced, fresh troops have come to their support!" Before Golokopytenko had finished speaking, Vovtuzenko galloped up: "Bad news: more reinforcements are coming . . . !" Before Vovtuzenko had finished Pysarenko ran up without his horse, crying: "Where are you? The Cossacks are looking for you, the chief Nevylychsky is slain, Zadorozhny is slain, Cherevychenko is slain; but the Cossacks stand firm. They do not want to die without looking at your face; they want you to glance at them before the hour of death."

"Mount, Ostap!" said Taras, and he made haste that he might find the Cossacks still there, that he might yet look upon them and that they might see their chief again before their death. But they had not ridden out of the wood before the forces of the enemy had surrounded the wood on all sides, and everywhere between the trees horsemen appeared with swords and lances.

"Ostap! Ostap! Do not surrender!" shouted Taras, and drawing his sword he began to tackle the first he came upon. But six had pounced on Ostap all at once. But it was an unlucky hour for them, it seemed: the head of the first flew off; the second was sent whirling back; the third had a thrust from a lance in his ribs; the fourth was more daring: he bent his head to escape a bullet and the lead went into his horse's chest—the frenzied beast reared, fell to the earth, and crushed his rider under him. "Well done, son! Well done, Ostap!" shouted Taras; "here I am behind you!" And he still beat off his assailants. Taras struggled and slashed away, dealt blows on many a head, while he gazed before him at Ostap and saw that he was attacked again by almost eight at once.

"Ostap! Ostap! Do not surrender!" But by now Ostap was overpowered; by now one had cast a noose about his neck; they were binding him, carrying him off.

"Oh, Ostap, Ostap!" shouted Taras, struggling to him and making mincemeat of all he met.

"Oh, Ostap, Ostap . . . !" But at that very minute something like a heavy stone struck him. Everything went around in a whirl before his eyes. For an instant he had a confused vision of heads, lances, smoke, gleams of fire, branches covered with leaves, flashing before his eyes. Then he sank to the earth like a felled oak. And a mist covered his eyes.

X

"I have had a long sleep!" said Taras, waking as from a heavy drunken slumber, and trying to recognize the objects around him. A terrible weakness overpowered his limbs. The walls and corners of an unfamiliar room seemed hovering before him. At last he saw that Tovkach was sitting before him and seemed to be listening to every breath he took.

"Yes," thought Tovkach to himself, "you might perhaps have slept forever!" But he said nothing, only held up his finger and gestured to him to be silent.

"But tell me, where am I now?" asked Taras, racking his brains and trying to remember what had happened.

"Be silent!" his comrade shouted sternly at him. "What more do you want to know? Don't you see you are covered with wounds? For the last two weeks we have been galloping with you, not stopping to take breath, and you have been raving in fever and delirium. This is the first time you have waked up quietly. Be quiet if you don't want to do yourself harm."

But Taras kept on striving and struggling to remember what had happened. "But didn't the Poles surround me altogether and seize me? There was no possibility of my fighting my way out of the crowd, was there?"

"Be quiet, I tell you, son of a devil!" shouted Tovkach angrily, as a nurse driven out of all patience shouts at a disobedient child. "What good is it to you to know how you escaped? It's enough that you have escaped. There were men who would not abandon you—well, and that's enough for you! We have many a night yet to gallop together. You think they rate you a simple Cossack? No, they have set a price of two thousand gold pieces on your head."

"And Ostap?" Taras cried suddenly. He had striven his utmost to remember, and suddenly he recalled that Ostap had been captured and bound before his eyes and now was in the hands of the Poles. And the old man's mind was overwhelmed with grief. He tore and pulled off all the bandages on his wounds; he flung them far away, tried to say something aloud, but fell to raving instead. Fever and delirium overpowered him again and senseless babble flowed incoherently from his lips. And meanwhile his faithful comrade stood before him, cursing and uttering harsh words of reproach. At last he seized him by the hands and feet, rolled him up like a baby, fixed all his bandages, wrapped him in a wolf skin, bound him in splints of bark and, fastening him with cords to his saddle, galloped along the road with him again.

"I will bring you home even dead! I will not let the Poles dishonor your Cossack name, tear your body to pieces, and fling it into the water. If an eagle is to peck out your eyes, let it be at least our eagle of the steppes and not the Polish one, not the one that flies from Poland. Even though dead, I will bring you to the Ukraine."

So spake his faithful comrade. He galloped on day and night without resting and brought Taras unconscious to the camp of the Dnieper Cossacks. There he began treating him persistently with herbs and ointments; he found a wise Jewess who for a month gave him potions to drink, and at last Taras was better. Whether it was the treatment or his iron strength that gained the day, within six weeks he was on his legs again; the wounds had healed, and only the scars left by the sword showed how deeply once the old Cossack had been wounded. But he had grown noticeably gloomy and melancholy. Three sorrowful lines furrowed his brow and never left it. He looked about him now: all was new at the camp, all his old comrades were dead. Not one was left of those who had fought for justice, for faith, and for brotherhood. And those who had gone with the leader in pursuit of the Tartars—those, too, had long passed away. All had laid down their lives, all had perished; some had been killed honorably in battle, others had perished from lack of food and water in the salt wastes of the Crimea; some had perished in captivity, unable to bear disgrace; the old leader himself was no more, not one of his old comrades was left, and the strong Cossacks that had once been brimming over with life had long been laid to rest under the grass. All he felt was that there had been a mighty feast, a noisy feast: all the drinking vessels had been smashed to bits; not one drop of wine was left; the guests and the servants had carried off all the costly goblets and drinking bowls —and the giver of the feast was left at home in confusion, thinking: "Better had there never been that feast." All efforts to entertain and to cheer Taras were in vain; in vain the gray-headed, bearded bandore players, who passed by in twos and in threes, sang the praises of his Cossack feats. He looked with gloom and indifference at everything, and his passive face bore traces of hopeless grief and suffering, as with bowed head he murmured: "My son! My Ostap!"

The Cossacks made ready for an expedition by sea. Two hundred boats were lowered into the Dnieper and Asia Minor saw them with shaven heads and long forelocks putting her flourishing coasts to fire and sword; she saw the turbans of her Moslem inhabitants scattered like her innumerable flowers on the blood-soaked fields and floating on her shores. She saw many Cossack trousers smeared with tar, many muscular arms holding black whips. The Cossacks devoured and laid waste all the vineyards; they left dung heaps in the mosques; they used costly Persian shawls for leg wrappers and encircled their mud-stained jackets with them. For years afterward their short pipes were picked up in those parts. Gaily they set sail back; a Turkish ship with ten cannon pursued them and dispersed their light canoes like birds with a volley from all ten at once. A third of their number were drowned in the depths of the sea; but the rest met together again at the mouth of the Dnieper with twelve barrels full of sequins. But Taras cared nothing for all this now. He went off into the water meadows and the steppes as if to go hunting, but his gun was not discharged. And laying it on the ground he would sit on the seashore, full of grief. For hours he would sit there with bowed head, murmuring: "My Ostap! My Ostap!" Before him the Black Sea stretched sparkling; the sea gull called in the faraway reeds; his white mustache glistened like silver as one tear after another dropped on it.

At last Taras could bear it no longer: "Come what may, I will go to find out what has happened to him, whether he is alive or in the tomb, or whether there is no trace of him, even in the grave. Come what may, I will find out!" he said.

And a week later he was in the town of Uman on his horse, fully

armed, with a lance and a sword, a bottle at his saddle, a pot of porridge, cartridges, horse's harness, and other equipment. He rode
straight up to a dirty, mud-stained little hut whose little windows
were so begrimed that they could scarcely be seen; the chimney
was stuffed up with a rag, and the roof was full of holes and covered with sparrows. A garbage heap lay before the very door. The
face of a Jewess wearing a headpiece adorned with faded pearls
peeped out of the window.

"Is your husband at home?" said Bulba, dismounting and tying
the reins to an iron hook in the doorpost.

"Yes," said the Jewess, and made haste to come out with grain in
a ladle for the horse and a bottle of beer for the horseman.

"Where is your Jew?"

"He is in the other room, saying his prayers," said the Jewess,
bowing and wishing Bulba good health as he lifted the bottle to his
lips.

"Stay here, feed and water my horse, while I will go and speak
with him alone. I have business with him."

This Jew was our friend Yankel. By now he rented a bit of land
and kept a little tavern; he had by degrees got all the gentry and
nobility of the neighborhood into his hands, had gradually extracted
almost all their money, and the presence of this Jew was having a
profound influence in the district. For three miles in every direction there was not a single hut left in decent condition; they were
all tumbling down and falling into ruins; everything was being
squandered in drink, and nothing was left but poverty and rags; the
whole countryside was laid bare as though by fire or pestilence.
And if Yankel had stayed there another ten years, he would certainly have laid bare the whole province.

Taras went into the inner room. The Jew was saying his prayers,
covered with his rather dirty blanket,[8] and in accordance with the
rites of his religion turned to spit for the last time, when his eyes
suddenly fell on Bulba standing behind him. First of all, the two
thousand gold pieces promised as a reward for Bulba's head seemed
to leap up before the Jew's eyes; but he was ashamed of his greed
and strove to conquer the everlasting thought of gold which twines
like a worm about the soul of a Jew.

"Listen, Yankel," said Taras to the Jew, who began by bowing

---

[8] I.e., prayer shawl. (ed.)

down before him, and then carefully locked the door that they might not be seen. "I saved your life—the Cossacks would have torn you to pieces like a dog. Now it is your turn: now do me a service!"

The Jew's face clouded over a little.

"What service? If it is something I can do, why not do it?"

"Say nothing. Take me to Warsaw."

"To Warsaw? How, to Warsaw?" said Yankel. His eyebrows and his shoulders jerked in amazement.

"Don't tell me anything. Take me to Warsaw. Come what may, I want to see him once more, to say one word to him."

"Say one word to whom?"

"To him, Ostap, my son."

"Has not his honor heard that . . ."

"I know, I know all about it; they offered two thousand gold pieces for my head. They give it a value, the fools! I'll give you five thousand. Here are two thousand on the spot"—Bulba shook two thousand gold pieces out of his leather purse—"and the rest when I come back."

The Jew instantly seized a towel and covered the gold pieces with it.

"Aie, the wonderful money! Aie, the gold coin!" he said, turning a gold piece over in his hands and trying it with his teeth. "I expect that the man from whom your honor seized such good gold pieces did not live another hour, he went at once to the river and drowned himself there, after losing such splendid gold pieces."

"I would not have asked you. I could, perhaps, have found the road to Warsaw by myself; but the damned Poles may recognize me somehow and seize me; for I am not good at strategy, while you Jews have been created for it. You can cheat the very devil; you know every dodge; so that's why I have come to you! And indeed I should gain nothing in Warsaw by myself. Bring out your cart at once and take me!"

"And does your honor expect me to harness the nag right away and say 'Hey, gee up!' Does your honor suppose that I can take your honor just as he is without hiding him?"

"Well then, hide me, hide me as best you can, in an empty barrel or something."

"Aie, aie! And does your honor think he could be hidden in a barrel? Surely your honor knows that everyone supposes that there is vodka in a barrel."

"Well, let them suppose that there is vodka in it."

"What? Let them suppose there is vodka!" said the Jew, and he seized his earlocks in both hands and then threw up both hands in dismay.

"Why, what are you so worked up about?"

"Why, surely your honor knows that God created vodka for everyone to taste it. They are all greedy and fond of dainties there; a Polish gentleman would run four miles after a barrel, pierce a hole in it on the spot and see at once that nothing runs out, and say: 'A Jew doesn't carry a barrel empty; there is sure to be something in it! Seize the Jew, bind the Jew, take all the Jew's money, throw the Jew into prison!' For everyone wicked pounces on the Jew; everyone takes a Jew for a dog, for they think he is not a man, if he's a Jew!"

"Well, then, put me in a load of fish!"

"I can't, your honor, I really can't. The folks are hungry as dogs now through all Poland, and they'll steal the fish and feel your honor under them."

"Well, take me to the devil, only take me."

"Listen, listen, your honor!" said the Jew, tucking up the cuffs of his sleeves and going up to him with outspread hands. "This is what we will do. Fortresses and castles are being built everywhere now; French engineers have come from Germany, and so lots of bricks and stones are being carted along the road. Let your honor lie at the bottom of the cart and I'll lay the bricks above; your honor looks strong and sturdy and so he won't mind if it's a little heavy; and I'll make a hole in the load below to pass food to your honor."

"Do as you like, only take me!"

And an hour later a brick cart was driven out of Uman with two horses in the shafts. On one of them sat lanky Yankel, and his long curly earlocks danced under his Jewish skullcap as he jolted up and down on the horse, looking as thin as a signpost.

XI

At the time when the events described took place there were as yet none of the customs officials and excise officers who are such a terrible menace to enterprising people now, and so everyone could take any goods he thought fit anywhere. If somebody made a raid upon them and inspected them, he did so mostly for his own satisfaction, especially if there were objects alluring to the eye among the goods, and if his own arm was of fair weight and strength. But bricks aroused no covetousness and were driven without hindrance through the principal gate of the town. Bulba, in his narrow cage, could hear only the noise of the traffic, the shouts of wagoners, and nothing more. Yankel, jogging up and down on his short-shanked dusty nag, turned, after taking several roundabout ways, into a dark narrow thoroughfare, known by the name of Mud Street and also Jew Street, because almost all the Jews of Warsaw were to be found there. This street was very much like a backyard turned inside out. It seemed as though the sun never entered it at all. The completely blackened wooden houses, with numbers of poles stretched from the windows, made the street even darker. At rare intervals a brick wall showed red between them, and even that had turned black in many places. Only here and there the stucco top of a wall, catching the sunlight, made a glaring patch of white that hurt the eyes. Here there was a striking selection of articles: pipes, rags, shells, broken pots. Everyone flung into the street whatever was of no use to him, so affording the passer-by the agreeable possibility of thrilling his esthetic sensibility. A man on horseback could almost reach with his hand the poles which were stretched across the street from one house to another with long Jewish stockings, short trousers, and a smoked goose hanging on them. Sometimes the rather attractive face of a Jewess, adorned with tarnished beads, peeped out of a decrepit window. A group of muddy, tattered Jew boys with curly heads shouted and lolled in the mud. A red-haired Jew with freckles all over his face, which made him look like a sparrow's egg, peeped out of a window; at once he addressed Yankel in his unintelligible jargon, and Yankel at once drove into a yard. Another Jew came down the street, stopped, and also entered into conversation; and when Bulba emerged at last from under the bricks, he saw three Jews talking with great animation.

Yankel turned to him and said that everything would be arranged, that his Ostap was in the city dungeon, and that though it would be a hard task to persuade the guards, yet he hoped to obtain an interview for him.

Bulba went with the three Jews into the house.

The Jews began talking among themselves again in their incomprehensible language. Taras looked at each one of them. It seemed as though he were deeply moved; an overmastering flame of hope —that hope which sometimes visits a man in the utmost depths of despair—gleamed in his harsh and apathetic face; his old heart began beating as violently as a young man's.

"Listen, Jews!" he said. And there was something of passion in his words. "You can do anything in the world, you can dig a thing up from the bottom of the sea, and there is an old saying that a Jew will steal himself if he can steal nothing else. Set free my Ostap for me! Give him a chance to escape from the devil's hands. Here, I've promised this man twelve thousand gold pieces; I will add another twelve. Everything I have, costly goblets and gold buried in the earth; my house and my last garment I will sell, and will make a contract with you for all my life that whatever I take in war I will share it in equal halves with you."

"Oh, it can't be done, your honor, it can't be done!" Yankel said with a sigh.

"No, it can't!" said another of the Jews.

All three of them looked at one another.

"We might try," said the third, looking sheepishly at the other two. "Maybe God will help us."

The three Jews began talking in German.[9] Though Bulba strained his ears he could make out nothing; he could only distinguish the word "Mordechai" uttered several times.

"Listen, your honor!" said Yankel. "We must take counsel with a man the like of whom has never been seen in this world. Oo, oo! He is as wise as Solomon, and if he can do nothing no one in the world can do it. Stay here; here is the key and don't let anyone in."

The Jews went out into the street. Taras locked the door and looked through the little window at the filthy scene. The three Jews had stopped in the middle of the street and had begun talking rather excitedly; they were soon joined by a fourth and finally by a fifth. He heard "Mordechai, Mordechai," repeated again. The Jews kept continually looking toward one side of the street; at last from a wretched-looking house at the end of it a foot appeared in a Jewish slipper, and he saw the flutter of the skirts of a long coat. "Ah! Mordechai! Mordechai!" the Jews all cried with one voice. A

---

[9] Yiddish. (ed.)

scrawny Jew, somewhat shorter than Yankel and far more wrin-
kled, with an immense upper lip, drew near the impatient group;
and all the Jews vied with one another in hurriedly telling him the
story, while Mordechai glanced several times toward the little
window. Mordechai gesticulated, listened, interrupted, often spat
to one side, and lifting up the skirts of his coat, thrust his hand into
his pocket and drew out some jingling coins, displaying his very
shabby trousers. At last all the Jews set up such an uproar that the
one who was standing on the lookout had to signal to them to be
silent, and Taras was beginning to be anxious about his own safety,
till, remembering that Jews can discuss nothing except in the
street, and that the devil himself could not understand their language, he felt reassured. Two minutes later the Jews came into the
room together. Mordechai went up to Taras, patted him on the
shoulder, and said: "When we and God mean to do a thing, it will
come out right."

Taras looked at this Solomon, the like of whom had never been
seen in the world, and some hope revived in him. His appearance
was certainly calculated to inspire some confidence. His upper lip
was something fearful to look at; its thickness was undoubtedly
not all due to nature. This Solomon only had fifteen hairs in his
beard—and those on the left side. His face bore so many traces of
blows he had received for his temerity, that he had doubtless lost
count of them long ago and grown used to regarding them as something natural.

Mordechai went away with the companions who were so filled
with wonder at his wisdom. Bulba was left alone. He was in a
strange and novel situation; for the first time in his life he was
conscious of anxiety. His soul was in a feverish state. He was not
the same man as of old, inflexible, unwavering, steadfast as an oak;
he was timid, he was weak now. He shuddered at every rustle, at
every fresh figure of a Jew appearing at the end of the street. In
this condition he spent the whole day; he neither ate nor drank,
and never took his eyes off the little window looking on the street.
At last, late in the evening, Mordechai and Yankel appeared. Taras'
heart stood still.

"Well? Successful?" he asked them with the restive eagerness of
a wild horse. But, before the Jews had recovered breath to answer,
Taras noticed that Mordechai was without one of his earlocks
which had hung down in ringlets somewhat untidily below his

skullcap. It could be seen that he wanted to say something, but he mumbled out such drivel that Taras could make nothing of it. And Yankel himself kept putting his hand to his mouth, as though he were suffering from a cold.

"Oh! Honored sir!" said Yankel. "Now it is utterly impossible! I swear it is! Such wicked people that one ought to spit on their heads. Here, Mordechai will tell you. Mordechai did what no one in the world has done yet; but it is not God's will it should be so. Three thousand soldiers are stationed there, and tomorrow all the prisoners will be executed."

Taras looked into the Jew's eyes; there was no impatience or anger in his face now.

"And if your honor wants to see him you must go early tomorrow before the sun has risen. The guards have agreed, and one officer has promised. But may they have no happiness in the world to come! *Oy weh mir!*[10] What greedy folks they are! There are none such even among us: fifty gold pieces I gave to each one of them and to the officer . . ."

"Very good, take me to him!" Taras pronounced resolutely, and all his firmness came back to him. He agreed to Yankel's proposal that he should be disguised as a foreign count who had arrived from Germany. The farsighted Jew had already provided clothes for the purpose. By now it was night. The master of the house, the red-haired, freckled Jew whom the reader knows already, pulled out a thin mattress covered with a sort of sacking and laid it on a bench for Bulba. Yankel lay down on the floor on a similar mattress. The red-haired Jew drank a small goblet of some beverage, threw off his full coat, and, looking in his slippers and stockings rather like a chicken, retreated with his Jewess into a sort of cupboard. Two little Jew boys lay down on the floor beside the cupboard like two little puppies. But Taras did not sleep; he sat motionless, faintly drumming with his fingers on the table; he kept his pipe in his mouth and blew out smoke, which started the Jew sneezing in his sleep and tucking his nose into the quilt. The sky was hardly touched by the first pale glimmer of dawn when he poked Yankel with his foot. "Get up, Jew," he said, "and give me the disguise."

In an instant he had dressed himself; he blackened his mustache and his eyebrows, put a little dark cap on his head, and not one of

---

[10] A common Yiddish expression: "Woe is me!" (ed.)

the Cossacks who knew him best could have recognized him. He did not look more than thirty-five. A ruddy flush of health played on his cheeks, and the scars on his face gave it a commanding air. The gold-embroidered coat was very becoming to him.

The streets were still asleep. Not a single figure with a tradesman's basket was yet to be seen in the town. Bulba and Yankel reached a building which looked like a nesting heron. It was lowpitched, broad, huge, blackened, and on one side of it a long narrow tower like the neck of a stork was thrust up with a bit of roof sticking up on the top of it. This building served a number of different purposes: in it were barracks, a prison, and even a court of justice. Our friends went in at the gate and found themselves in the middle of a spacious hall or covered court. About a thousand men were asleep in it. Directly opposite the entrance was a low door before which two sentinels were sitting, playing a sort of game which consisted in one of them striking the other on the palm of the hand with two fingers. They only turned their heads when Yankel said: "It's us; listen, gentlemen, it's us."

"Go in!" said one of them, opening the door with one hand while he held out the other to his comrade to receive his blows. They went into a dark, narrow corridor, which led them again into a similar hall with little windows high up.

"Who goes there?" shouted several voices, and Taras saw a considerable number of soldiers fully armed. "We are forbidden to admit anyone," they said.

"It's us!" shouted Yankel. "Us, noble gentlemen!" But no one would listen to him. Luckily at that moment there walked in a fat man who was apparently a commanding officer, for he swore louder than any.

"Noble sir, here we are; you know us, and his honor the count will show his gratitude too."

"Let them in, you damned bastards! And admit no one else. And let no one take off his sword nor make a mess on the floor . . ."

The rest of his eloquent orders our friends did not hear. "You know us, it's me; we are your own people!" said Yankel to everyone he met.

"Well, can we go in now?" he asked one of the guards when they had at last reached the end of the corridor.

"You can, only I don't know whether they'll admit you right

into the prison. Jan is not there now; there's another man on guard in his place," answered the sentry.

"Aie, aie," the Jew pronounced softly. "That's bad, your honor!"

"Lead the way!" Taras pronounced stubbornly. The Jew obeyed.

At the door of the dungeon, which ran up to a point at the top, stood a soldier with mustaches in three stories. The upper story of the mustaches turned backward, the second straight forward, the third downward, which made him look very much like a tomcat.

The Jew approached him, cringing, and almost sideways. "Your Serene Highness! Illustrious lord!"

"Are you speaking to me, Jew?"

"To you, your high nobility."

"Hm . . . and I am just a simple soldier!" said he with the mustaches, his eyes beginning to twinkle.

"Why, upon my word, I thought you were the general himself. Aie, aie, aie . . . !" With this the Jew wagged his head and twiddled his fingers. "Aie, how grand you look! Upon my word, a colonel, a regular colonel! Another touch and he'd be a colonel! Your honor only needs to be mounted on a horse as swift as a fly and to drill the regiments!"

The soldier stroked the lowest tier of his mustaches, while his eyes gleamed with pleasure.

"What fine fellows soldiers are!" the Jew went on. "*Oy weh mir,* what splendid fellows! The gold lacings and brass plates, they fairly glitter like the sun; and the girls—as soon as they see the soldiers . . . Aie, aie . . . !" The Jew wagged his head again.

The soldier twisted the upper stage of his mustaches and let out through his teeth a sound not unlike the neigh of a horse.

"I beg your honor to do me a service!" the Jew said. "This prince here has come from foreign lands, he wants to have a look at the Cossacks. He has never in his life seen what the Cossacks are like."

The arrival of foreign counts and barons was a fairly common event in Poland; they were often attracted solely by curiosity to see this half-Asiatic corner of Europe; they looked upon Muscovy and the Ukraine as almost a part of Asia. And so the soldier, making a rather low bow, thought proper to add a few words from himself.

"I don't know, Your Highness," he said, "why you care to look at them. They are dogs, not men, and their religion is one that everyone despises."

"You lie, you bastard!" said Bulba. "You are a dog yourself! How dare you say our faith is despised? It's your heretical belief that is despised!"

"Ah, ha!" said the soldier. "I know, friend, who you are; you are one of the same lot I have in prison. Wait while I call our men here."

Taras saw his indiscretion, but obstinacy and some annoyance prevented him from thinking how to correct it. Happily Yankel intervened instantly.

"Your High Nobility! How could the count be a Cossack? And if he were a Cossack, how could he come to be dressed and look like a count?"

"Tell that to others . . . !" And the soldier was opening his mouth to shout.

"Your Royal Majesty! Hush, for God's sake!" cried Yankel. "Don't speak! We will pay you for it beyond anything you have even seen. We'll give you two gold pieces."

"Ah, ha! Two gold pieces! Two gold pieces are nothing to me; I pay the barber that for shaving only half my chin. A hundred gold pieces, Jew!" Here the soldier twisted his mustache. "And if you don't give the hundred I'll call at once!"

"And why so much?" said the Jew, mournfully, untying his leather purse. He had turned quite pale, but he was glad there was no more in his purse, and that the soldier could not count beyond a hundred.

"Your honor, your honor! Let us make haste and go! You see what bad people they are!" said Yankel, observing that the soldier was fingering the money, as though regretting he had not asked more.

"Why, you Polish swine," said Bulba, "you have taken the money and you don't intend to show me the prisoners? No, you must show me. Since you've taken the money you have no right to refuse now."

"Go along, go to hell! Or I'll call out this minute and then you'll . . . Look sharp and be off, I tell you!"

"Your honor, let us go, do let us go! Curse them! May they spit with horror in their dreams!" cried poor Yankel.

Slowly, with bowed head, Bulba turned and walked back, followed by reproaches from Yankel, who was consumed by grief at the thought of the wasted gold pieces.

"And what did he get them for! Let him swear, the dog, they are folk that always must be swearing! *Oy!* What luck God sends some people! A hundred gold pieces simply for turning us out! While the likes of us have our hair torn off and our faces made unfit to look at and no one gives us a hundred gold pieces. Oh, my God! Merciful God!"

But their failure had far more effect on Bulba; it was shown in the violently burning flame in his eyes.

"Let us go!" he said suddenly as though shaking himself. "Let us go to the market place. I want to see how they will torture him."

"*Oy*, your honor! Why go? That will be no good to us now, you know."

"Come along!" said Bulba, stubbornly; and the Jew, sighing, trailed after him like a nurse.

It was not difficult to find the square in which the execution was to take place; people were flocking to it from all sides. In that brutal age such occasions were regarded as among the most interesting spectacles not only by the ignorant mob but even by the upper classes. Numbers of old women, most devout; numbers of young girls and young women, so timid that all night afterward they dreamed of blood-stained corpses and cried out in their sleep as loudly as a drunken hussar, never missed a chance of satisfying their curiosity. "Oh, what torture!" many of them cried with hysterical frenzy, shutting their eyes and turning away, yet they would go on standing, often for hours. One man stood with his mouth open and his arms stretched out before him, as though he meant to leap on the heads of the crowd to get a better view. A butcher thrust his fat face above the mass of narrow, small, and ordinary heads; he watched the whole process with the air of a connoisseur and talked in monosyllables with a gunsmith, whom he addressed as "old friend," because on some holiday he had been drinking with him in the same tavern. Some of the people kept up an eager discussion, others were even making bets; but the majority were the sort of people who look at the whole world and everything that happens in it and go on picking their noses. In the front, close to the whiskered warriors who made up the town guard, was standing a young gentleman, or youth who looked like a gentleman in military uniform, who had put on absolutely everything he had, so that nothing was left in his lodging but a tattered shirt and an old pair of boots. Two chains with some sort of coin on them hung

about his neck, one above the other. He was standing with his
sweetheart, and was continually looking around for fear someone
should soil her silk dress. He explained everything to her so thoroughly that not a word could have been added: "All these people
that you see, Juzysya darling," he told her, "have come to look at
the execution of criminals. And this man, darling, who is holding
an ax and other instruments in his hand, is the executioner, and he
will punish them. And when he begins to break them on the wheel
and inflict other tortures, the criminal will still be alive; but when
his head is cut off, he will die at once, darling. At first he will
scream and move, but as soon as his head is cut off then he will not
be able to scream nor eat nor drink, because he won't have any
head, darling." And the girl heard it all with awe and curiosity.

The roofs of the houses were dotted with people. Strange faces
decked with whiskers or wearing something like a cap were poked
out of attic windows. The aristocracy sat on the balconies under
awnings. The pretty little hand of a Polish lady, smiling and sparkling, lay white as sugar on the railing. Illustrious nobles, rather
stout, gazed at the scene with a dignified air. A footman in gorgeous livery with flowing sleeves was handing them various beverages and edibles. Often a black-eyed roguish girl would seize a cake
or fruit in her little white hand and throw it into the crowd. A
throng of hungry knights held out their caps to catch it, and a tall
one, whose head stood out above the crowd, in a faded red coat
with tarnished gold braid on it, was the first to catch one, thanks to
his long fingers; he kissed the prize, pressed it to his heart, and then
put it in his mouth. A falcon, hanging in a gilt cage under the balcony, was also a spectator; with his beak on one side and one claw
in the air, he too scrutinized the people attentively from his perch.
But all at once a stir passed through the crowd, and voices were
heard on all sides:

"They are bringing them! The Cossacks!"

They came, bareheaded, with long forelocks and beards that had
been left to grow. They moved with no sign of fear nor sullenness,
but with a sort of quiet pride; their garments of costly cloth were
worn threadbare and hung in ancient rags about them; they did not
greet the people nor look at them. Foremost of all walked Ostap.

What were old Taras' feelings when he saw his Ostap? What
passed in his heart? He gazed at him from the crowd, not one
movement escaped him. The Cossacks drew near the scaffold. Os-

tap stopped. He was to be the first to face the terrible ordeal. He looked at his comrades, raised his hand, and pronounced in a loud voice: 'O God! grant that none of the heretics standing here may hear, the unclean wretches, how a Christian is tortured! That not one of us may utter one word!" After this he went up to the scaffold.

"Good, son, good!" said Bulba softly, and he bowed his gray head.

The executioner stripped Ostap of his old rags; his arms and legs were bound in a frame made for the purpose and . . . We will not horrify our readers with a picture of the fiendish tortures, which would make their hair stand on end. These atrocities were the product of that coarse, savage age, when man led a bloody life spent entirely in violence, and his heart was hardened by this till he lost all sense of humanity. In vain some few, who stand out as exceptions in their age, opposed these horrors. In vain the King and many nobles of enlightened heart and intelligence urged that such cruel punishments could only inflame the vengeance of the Cossacks. But the influence of the King and of wise counsels was of no avail beside the turbulence and unbridled violence of the nobles, whose imprudent, incredible lack of foresight, childish vanity, and trivial pride turned the Diet into a parody of government.

Ostap bore the tortures and agonies like a hero. No cry or moan was heard, even when the bones of his arms and legs were being broken, when the awful cracking sound made by them was heard by the farthest spectators in the deathly silence of the crowd, while the Polish ladies turned away their eyes—there was no flinching in his face, nothing like a moan broke from his lips. Taras stood in the crowd with bowed head, though he proudly raised his eyes, and only said approvingly: "Good, son, good!"

But when Ostap was brought to the last mortal agonies, it seemed as though his strength was beginning to give way. And he turned his eyes in all directions about him: good God! all unknown, all alien faces! If only someone akin to him could have been present at his death! He did not wish to hear the sobs and desolation of a weak mother, or the frantic wails of a wife tearing her hair and beating her white breasts; he longed now to see a strong man who with a word of wisdom might have strengthened and comforted him at his end. And his heart failed him and he cried out:

"Father, where are you, do you hear all this . . . ?"

"I hear!" rang forth out of the absolute stillness, and a million people shudder. A division of cavalry dashed to make a careful inspection of the crowd. Yankel turned pale as death; and when the cavalry moved on a little way from him, he turned around in horror to glance at Taras. But Taras was no longer beside him; all trace of him had vanished.

XII

Taras had reappeared. A hundred and twenty thousand Cossacks appeared on the frontiers of the Ukraine. This was no small division, no company that had come out in search of booty or in pursuit of the Tartars. No, the whole nation had risen up, for the patience of the people was exhausted; they had risen up to avenge the flouting of their rights, the disgraceful mockery of their customs, the outraging of the faith of their forefathers and their sacred traditions, the desecrating of their churches, the licentiousness of the foreign nobles, the religious persecutions, the shameful domination of Jews in a Christian land: everything that had accumulated from old days and swollen the sum of sullen hatred in the Cossacks. The young but stouthearted headman Ostranitsa[11] was in command of the vast numbers of Cossacks. His old experienced comrade and adviser, Gunia, was conspicuous at his side. Eight colonels commanded regiments of twelve thousand each. Two captains and another staff-bearing officer rode after the headman. The chief standard bearer was in command of the principal flag; many other flags and banners fluttered in the distance; the assistant staff-bearing officers bore the badges of office. There were many of other grades in the regiments: quartermaster and transport officers, regimental clerks, and with them detachments of cavalry and infantry; there were almost as many volunteers as there were regular enrolled Cossacks. The Cossacks had risen up from all sides: from Chigirin, from Pereiaslav, from Baturin, from Glukhov, from the Lower Dnieper, and from all the districts and islands about its upper reaches. Horses beyond number and immense cavalcades of carts trailed over the fields. And among those Cossacks, and among those eight regiments, was one regiment finer than all the rest; and

---

[11] Several of the secondary characters are based on historical figures. Ostranitsa, for example, was a leader of the Cossacks who was beheaded by the Poles in 1638. (ed.)

that regiment was commanded by Taras Bulba. Everything gave him the foremost place—his age, his experience, his skill in moving his troops, and his hatred of the foe, more intense than anyone's. His ruthless ferocity and cruelty seemed excessive even to the Cossacks. The gray-headed warrior would set no punishment but the fire and the gallows, and his voice in the military councils was always for slaughter.

No need to describe the battles in which the Cossacks displayed their bravery, nor the course of the campaign in detail; all that is recorded in the pages of the chronicles. We all know what war waged for religion is like in Russia; no force is stronger than faith. It is as fierce and invincible as the unhewn rock in the midst of the stormy, ever treacherous sea. From the very midst of the ocean depths it raises to the heavens its indestructible walls, all fashioned of one single stone. It can be seen from all sides, and it looks straight in the face of the racing billows. And woe to the ship which falls foul of it! Its weak masts and rigging fly into chips, everything in it is smashed to atoms, and the shuddering air resounds with the pitiful screams of the drowning.

The chronicles give a detailed picture of the flight of the Polish garrisons from the towns set free by the Cossacks; of the hanging of the shameless Jewish contractors; of the weakness of the Polish commander, Nikolai Pototsky, with his immense army, against the invincible force of the Cossacks; of the way in which, defeated and pursued, he lost the greater part of his army in a little river, and the fierce Cossacks besieged him in the little town of Polonnoe; and how the Polish commander in the last extremity solemnly vowed in the name of the King and the nobles that the Cossacks should be satisfied in full and all their rights and privileges should be restored. But the Cossacks were not such fools as to be taken in by that; they knew what Polish vows were worth. And Pototsky would not have flaunted again on his six-thousand-ruble racehorse, the mark for all the great ladies and the envy of the nobles; he would not have made a noise at the Diets and given gorgeous banquets to the senators, had he not been saved by the Russian clergy of the district. When all the priests in their shining gold chasubles, bearing crosses and icons, and the bishop at the head of them in his pastoral miter, cross in hand, came out to meet the Cossacks, they all bowed and took off their caps. They would have disregarded anyone at that time, even the King himself; but they dared not oppose their Orthodox Church and they revered their clergy. The Cossack leader and his colonel agreed together to release Pototsky, taking from him a solemn oath to leave all Orthodox churches in freedom, to renounce his old enmity, and to do nothing to harm the Cossack power. Only one colonel would not agree to such a peace. That one was Taras. He tore a handful of hair from his head and cried:

"Aie, leaders, colonels! Do no such womanish deed! Trust not the Poles; they will betray you, the dogs!"

When the regimental clerk presented the terms of the peace, and the leader signed it, Taras took off his trusty blade, a costly Turkish saber of the finest steel, broke it in two like a stick, and flung the parts far away in different directions, saying: "Farewell! As the two parts of that sword cannot be united and make up one blade again, so shall we comrades never meet again in this world! Remember my farewell words . . ." (At this word his voice rose higher, gathering uncanny strength, and all were confounded at his prophetic words.) "You will remember me at your dying hour! Do you think you have bought peace and tranquillity; do you think you are going to live at ease? A strange sort of ease you will enjoy: they will flay the skin from your head, leader, they will stuff it with chaff, and for years it will be seen at the fairs! Nor will you Cossacks keep your heads! You will perish in damp dungeons, buried within stone walls, if you are not all boiled alive in cauldrons like sheep!

"And you, lads!" he went on, turning to his followers: "who among you wants to die a genuine death, not on the stove or on a woman's bed, or drunk under a tavern fence like any carcass, but an honest Cossack death, all in one bed like bride and bridegroom? Or maybe you will go back home and turn infidels and carry the Catholic priests upon your backs?"

"We're with you, we're with you, colonel! We'll follow you!" cried all who were in Taras' regiment, and many others hastened to join them.

"Since you will follow me, then follow me!" said Taras, pulling his cap down on his head; he looked fiercely at all those who stayed behind, straightened himself on his horse, and shouted to his men: "No one shall insult us with words of reproach! And now, lads, off to pay a visit to the Catholics!" And then he lashed his horse, and a string of a hundred wagons trailed behind him, and with him were many Cossacks on horse and foot; and he turned around to look menacingly at those who stayed behind, and his eyes were full of wrath. No one dared to stop them. The regiment marched off in sight of the whole army, and for a long way Taras still turned and gazed menacingly back.

The leader and the colonels stood confounded, all sank into thought, and were silent as though oppressed by some gloomy foreboding. Taras' prophecy was not an idle one: everything came true as he had predicted. A little later, after the treachery at Kanev, the leader's head was stuck upon a pole, and many of the foremost commanders shared his fate.

And what of Taras? Taras marched all over Poland with his regiment, burned eighteen villages and nearly forty churches, and arrived as far as Cracow. He slaughtered numbers of Poles of all sorts, and sacked the finest and wealthiest castles; the Cossacks unsealed and poured away barrels of mead and wine hundreds of years old that had been carefully preserved in Polish noblemen's cellars; they slashed to bits and burned the sumptuous cloth of garments and the vessels that were in the storerooms. "Spare nothing!" was all Taras said. The Cossacks did not spare the black-browed damsels, the white-bosomed, fair-faced maidens; even at the altar they could find no safety; Taras burned them together with the altars. More than once snow-white arms were raised from the flames to the heavens accompanied with pitiful cries which would have moved the very earth and set the grass of the steppes shuddering with pity. But the cruel Cossacks heeded nothing; picking up the babes from the streets on their lances, they flung them too into the flames. "That's for you, accursed Poles, in memory of Ostap!" Taras would say. And such sacrifices he made to Ostap's memory in every village, until the Polish government saw that Taras' exploits were something more than common brigandage, and the same Pototsky was sent with five regiments to capture Taras.

For six days the Cossacks retreated by byroads from their pursuers; their horses saved them, but they were almost worn out by this headlong flight. But this time Pototsky was equal to the charge laid upon him; he pursued them without flagging and overtook them on the bank of the Dniester, where Bulba had halted to rest in a deserted ruined fortress.

It stood conspicuous above the precipitous bank at the edge of the Dniester, with its broken rampart and dilapidated walls. The topmost crag, that looked on the point of breaking off and flying down, was strewn with rubble and broken bricks. The Polish commander Pototsky assailed him here on the two sides that looked out to the open plain. For four days the Cossacks fought and struggled, beating back the Poles with bricks and stones. But their stores and their strength were exhausted, and Taras decided to fight his way through the ranks of the foe. And the Cossacks were making their way through, and their swift horses would perhaps have served them faithfully once more, when suddenly Taras stopped in full flight and shouted: "Stop! I've dropped my pipe; I won't have even my pipe fall into the hands of the accursed Poles!" And the old chief bent down and began looking in the grass for the pipe which had been his inseparable companion, by land and by sea, on the march, and at home. And at that moment a gang suddenly dashed up and seized him under his mighty shoulders. He struggled with every limb, but the soldiers who had captured him were not thrown to the ground, as had happened in the past.

"Ah, old age, old age!" he said, and the stout old Cossack burst into tears. But old age was not to blame; his strength was overcome by greater strength. There were nearly thirty men hanging on to his arms and legs. "The crow is caught!" cried the Poles. "Now we've only to think how best to do him honor, the dog." And with Pototsky's sanction they decided to burn him alive in the sight of all. A leafless tree which had been struck by lightning stood at hand. They dragged him by iron chains to the tree trunk, nailed his hands to it, and raising him on high so that he could be seen from all parts, began to build a fire under the tree. But Taras looked not at the pile, he thought not of the fire by which they were going to burn him; he looked where the Cossacks were making a stand; from his height he could see everything plainly.

"Make for the mountain, Cossacks, make swiftly for the mountain beyond the forest," he shouted, "they will not reach you there!" But the wind did not carry his words. "They will be lost for nothing!" he said in despair, and glanced below where the Dniester sparkled. Joy gleamed in his eyes. He saw four boats peeping out from behind the bushes, and, straining his voice to the utmost, he shouted: "To the river! To the river, Cossacks, go down by the path on the left. There are boats by the bank; take all, that they may not pursue!"

This time the wind blew from the other quarter and all he said was heard by the Cossacks. But for such counsel he was given a blow on the head which made everything hazy.

The Cossacks raced full gallop by the path downhill with the Poles in full pursuit just behind them. They saw that the path turned and twisted, going around and around. "Ah, comrades! here goes!" they all said; they halted for an instant, raised their whips, whistled, and their Tartar steeds, rising from the earth and stretching themselves in the air like snakes, flew over the precipice and splashed into the Dniester. Only two fell short of the river, and they were dashed on the rocks, and perished there with their horses, without time to cry out. The rest were swimming with their horses in the river and unmooring the boats. The Poles stopped short at the precipice, marveling at the incredible feat of the Cossacks, and hesitating whether to leap down or not. One young colonel, an eager, hot-blooded fellow, the brother of the lovely lady who had bewitched poor Andrei, did not hesitate but rushed headlong on his horse after the Cossacks: he turned over three times in the air and fell straight upon the jagged rocks. He was torn to pieces falling over the precipice, and his brains, mixed with blood, bespattered the bushes that covered the rugged walls of the cliff.

When Taras Bulba recovered from the blow and looked at the Dniester, the Cossacks were in their boats and rowing hard; bullets were flying after them from above, but did not reach them. And the old chief's eyes glittered joyfully.

"Farewell, comrades!" he shouted to them. "Remember me and come here again next spring and have a fine time of it! What have you gained, you Polish bastards? Think you there is anything in the world that a Cossack would fear? Wait a while, the time is coming, the time is at hand when you will learn what the Orthodox Russian faith can do! Already the nations far and near have an inkling that their ruler will rise up from Russia, and there will be no power on earth that will not submit to him . . . !"

By now the fire was rising about his legs, and wrapping the tree in flames. . . . But there are no fires, no tortures in the world, no force indeed that can break the Russian spirit!

The Dniester is no small river, and many are the backwaters, the thick sedges, the sandbanks, and the deep pools in it; the river glimmers like a mirror, resounding with the ringing cry of the swans, and the proud golden-eye duck soars swiftly above it, and many marsh birds, and red-breasted sandpipers and other wildfowl abound among its reeds and on its banks. The Cossacks plied their oars in unison, moved rapidly in their narrow boats, and cautiously avoided the sandbanks, rousing the fluttering birds and talking of their chief.

VIY [1]

As soon as the rather lilting seminary bell which hung at the gate of the Bratsky Monastery rang out every morning in Kiev, school-boys and students hurried there in crowds from all parts of the town. Students of grammar, rhetoric, philosophy, and theology trudged to their classrooms with exercise books under their arms. The grammarians* were very small boys: they shoved each other as they went along and quarreled in a shrill alto; they almost all wore muddy or tattered clothes, and their pockets were full of all manner of garbage, such as knucklebones, whistles made of feathers, or a half-eaten pie, sometimes even little sparrows, one of whom, suddenly tweeting at an exceptionally quiet moment in the classroom, would cost its owner some sound whacks on both hands and sometimes a thrashing. The rhetoricians walked with more dignity; their clothes were often quite free from holes; on the other hand, their faces almost all bore some decoration: either one eye

---

[1] Viy is a colossal creation of the popular imagination. It is the name among the Little Russians for the chief of the gnomes, whose eyelids droop down to the earth. This whole story is folklore. I was unwilling to change it, and I tell it almost in the simple words in which I heard it. (N. Gogol) [Gogol probably never heard it at all. No discovery has been made of the folklore source of Viy. (ed.)]

* I.e., freshmen; rhetoricians = sophomores; philosophers = juniors; theologians = seniors. (ed.)

had sunk right under the forehead, or there was a monstrous swelling in place of a lip, or some other disfigurement. They talked and swore among themselves in tenor voices. The philosophers conversed an octave lower in the scale; they had nothing in their pockets but strong, cheap tobacco. They prepared no provisions of any sort but ate on the spot anything they came across; they smelled of pipes and vodka to such a distance that a passing workman would sometimes stop a long way off and sniff the air like a hound.

As a rule the market was just beginning to stir at that hour, and the women with pretzels, rolls, melon seeds, and poppy cakes would tug at the skirts of those whose coats were of fine cloth or some cotton material.

"This way, young gentlemen, this way!" they kept saying from all sides: "here are pretzels, poppy cakes, twists, good white rolls. They are really good! Made with honey! I baked them myself."

Another woman, lifting up a sort of long twist made of dough, would cry: "Here's a pretzel! Buy my pretzel, young gentlemen!"

"Don't buy anything from her: see what a disgusting woman she is, her nose is horrible and her hands are dirty. . . ."

But the women were afraid to bother the philosophers and the theologians, for the latter were fond of taking samples, and always a good handful.

On reaching the seminary, the crowd dispersed to their various classes, which were held in low-pitched but fairly large rooms with little windows, wide doorways, and dirty benches. The classroom was at once filled with all sorts of buzzing sounds: the "auditors" heard their pupils repeat their lessons; the shrill alto of a grammarian rang out, and the windowpane responded with almost the same note; in a corner a rhetorician, whose mouth and thick lips should have belonged at least to a student of philosophy, was droning something in a bass voice, and all that could be heard at a distance was "Boo, boo, boo . . ." The "auditors," as they heard the lesson, kept glancing with one eye under the bench, where a roll or a cheesecake or some pumpkin seeds were peeping out of a scholar's pocket.

When this learned crowd managed to arrive a little too early, or when they knew that the professors would be later than usual, then by general consent they got up a fight, and everyone had to take part in it, even the monitors whose duty it was to maintain discipline and look after the morals of all the students. Two theologians usually settled the arrangements for the battle: whether each class was to defend itself individually, or whether all were to be divided into two parties, the bursars and the seminarists.[2] In any case, the grammarians first began the attack, and, as soon as the rhetoricians entered the fray, they ran away and stood at points of vantage to watch the contest. Then the devotees of philosophy, with long black mustaches, joined in, and finally those of theology, very thick in the neck and attired in shocking trousers, took part. It commonly ended in theology beating all the rest, and the philosophers, rubbing their ribs, would be forced into the classroom and sat down on the benches to rest. The professor, who had himself at one time taken part in such battles, could, on entering the class, see in a minute from the flushed faces of his audience that the battle had been a good one, and, while he was caning a rhetorician on the fingers, in another classroom another professor would be smacking philosophy's hands with a ruler. The theologians were dealt with in quite a different way: they received, to use the expression of a professor of theology, "a peck of peas apiece"—in other words, a liberal drubbing with short leather thongs.

On holidays and ceremonial occasions the bursars and the seminarists went from house to house as mummers. Sometimes they acted a play, and then the most distinguished figure was always some theologian, almost as tall as the belfry of Kiev, who took the part of Herodias or Potiphar's wife.[3] They received in payment a piece of linen, a sack of millet, or half a boiled goose, or something of the sort. All in this crowd of students—the seminarists as well as the bursars, with whom they maintained a hereditary feud—were exceedingly badly off for means of subsistence, and at the same time had extraordinary appetites, so that to reckon how many dumplings each of them tucked away at supper would be utterly impossible, and therefore the voluntary offerings of prosperous citizens could not be sufficient for them. Then the "senate" of the philosophers and theologians dispatched the grammarians and rhet-

---

[2] Both bursars and seminarists studied for the priesthood. Bursars were partly sponsored by the government and partly by private donations; they lived on the premises of the seminary. Seminarists were fully sponsored by the state and did not necessarily reside on the premises. (ed.)

[3] Herodias was the wife of Herod, ruler of Palestine at the time of Christ's death. Potiphar's wife falsely accused Joseph of attempting to seduce her (Genesis 39). (ed.)

oricians, under the supervision of a philosopher (who sometimes took part in the raid himself), with sacks on their shoulders to plunder the vegetable gardens—and pumpkin porridge was made in the bursars' quarters. The members of the "senate" ate such masses of melons that the next day their "auditors" heard two lessons from them instead of one, one coming from their lips, another muttering in their stomachs. Both the bursars and the seminarists wore long garments resembling frock coats, "prolonged to the utmost limit," a technical expression signifying below their heels.

The most important event for the seminarists was the coming of the vacation: it began in June, when they usually dispersed to their homes. Then the main road was dotted with philosophers, grammarians, and theologians. Those who had nowhere to go went to stay with some comrade. The philosophers and theologians took a situation, that is, undertook the tutoring of the children in some prosperous family, and received in payment a pair of new boots or sometimes even a coat. The whole crowd trailed along together like a gypsy encampment, boiled their porridge, and slept in the fields. Everyone hauled along a sack in which he had a shirt and a pair of leg wrappers. The theologians were particularly careful and precise: to avoid wearing out their boots, they took them off, hung them on sticks, and carried them on their shoulders, particularly if it was muddy; then, tucking their trousers up above their knees, they splashed fearlessly through the puddles. When they saw a village, they turned off the main road and, going up to any house that seemed a little better looking than the rest, stood in a row before the windows and began singing a chant at the top of their voices. The master of the house, some old Cossack villager, would listen to them for a long time, his head propped on his hands; then he would sob bitterly and say, turning to his wife: "Wife! What the scholars are singing must be very profound. Bring them bacon and anything else that we have." And a whole bowl of dumplings was emptied into the sack; a big piece of bacon, several flat loaves, sometimes a trussed hen, would go into it, too. Fortified with such supplies, the grammarians, rhetoricians, philosophers, and theologians went on their way again. Their numbers lessened, however, the further they went. Almost all wandered off toward their homes, and only those were left whose parental homes were further away.

Once, at the time of such a migration, three students turned off the main road in order to replenish their store of provisions at the first homestead they could find, for their sacks had long been empty. They were the theologian Khaliava, the philosopher Khoma Brut, and the rhetorician Tibery Gorobets.

The theologian was a tall, broad-shouldered fellow; he had an extremely odd habit—anything that lay within his reach he invariably stole. In other circumstances, he was of an excessively gloomy temper, and when he was drunk he used to hide in the rank grass, and the seminarists had a lot of trouble finding him there.

The philosopher, Khoma Brut, was of a cheerful temper, he was very fond of lying on his back, smoking a pipe; when he was drinking he always engaged musicians and danced the *trepak*. He often had a taste of the "peck of peas" but took it with perfect philosophical indifference, saying that there is no escaping what has to be. The rhetorician, Tibery Gorobets, had not yet the right to wear a mustache, to drink vodka, and to smoke a pipe. He only wore a curl around his ear, and so his character was as yet hardly formed; but, judging from the big bumps on the forehead, with which he often appeared in class, it might be presumed that he would make a good fighter. The theologian, Khaliava, and the philosopher, Khoma, often pulled him by the forelock as a sign of their favor, and employed him as their messenger.

It was evening when they turned off the main road; the sun had only just set and the warmth of the day still lingered in the air. The theologian and the philosopher walked along in silence smoking their pipes; the rhetorician, Tibery Gorobets, kept knocking off the heads of the wayside thistles with his stick. The road ran between scattered groups of oak and nut trees standing here and there in the meadows. Sloping uplands, little hills, green and round as cupolas, were interspersed here and there about the plain. The fields of ripening wheat, which came into view in two places, showed that some village must soon be seen. However, it was more than an hour since they had passed the wheatfields and still they had come upon no dwelling. The sky was now completely wrapped in darkness, and only in the west was there a pale streak left of the glow of sunset.

"What the hell does it mean?" said the philosopher, Khoma Brut. "It looked as though a village would appear in a minute."

The theologian did not speak; he gazed at the surrounding country, then put his pipe back in his mouth, and they continued on their way.

"I swear!" the philosopher said, stopping again, "not even the fist of a devil is to be seen."

"Maybe some village will turn up further on," said the theologian, not removing his pipe.

But meantime night had come on, and a rather dark night it was. Small storm clouds increased the gloom, and by every sign they could expect neither stars nor moon. The students noticed that they had lost their way and for a long time had been walking off the road.

The philosopher, after feeling about with his feet in all directions, said at last, abruptly: "Where's the road?"

The theologian did not speak for a while, then after pondering, he said: "Yes, it is a dark night."

The rhetorician walked off to one side and tried on his hands and knees to feel for the road, but his hands came upon nothing but foxes' holes. On all sides of them there was the steppe, which, it seemed, no one had ever crossed.

The travelers made another effort to press on a little, but there was the same wilderness in all directions. The philosopher tried shouting, but his voice seemed completely lost on the steppe, and met with no reply. All they heard was, a little afterward, a faint moaning like the howl of a wolf.

"What are we to do?" said the philosopher.

"Why, stop and sleep in the open!" said the theologian, and he felt in his pocket for flint and tinder to light his pipe again. But the philosopher could not agree to this: it was always his habit at night to put away a quarter-loaf of bread and four pounds of bacon, and he was conscious on this occasion of an insufferable sense of loneliness in his stomach. Besides, in spite of his cheerful temper, the philosopher was rather afraid of wolves.

"No, Khaliava, we can't," he said. "What, stretch out and lie down like a dog, without having eaten anything? Let's make another try for it; maybe we'll stumble on some dwelling place and get at least a drink of vodka for supper."

At the word "vodka" the theologian spat to one side and said: "Well, of course, it's no use staying in the open."

The students walked on, and to their intense delight, they caught the sound of barking in the distance. Listening which way it came from, they walked on more boldly and a little later saw a light.

"A village! It really is a village!" said the philosopher.

He was not mistaken in his supposition; in a little while they actually saw a small homestead consisting of only two huts looking into the same farmyard. There was a light in the windows; a dozen plum trees stood by the fence. Looking through the cracks in the gates made of paling the students saw a yard filled with carts of merchants. Stars peeped out here and there in the sky at the moment.

"Look, fellows, let's not be put off! We must get a night's lodging somehow!"

The three learned gentlemen banged on the gates together and shouted, "Open!"

The door of one of the huts creaked, and a minute later they saw before them an old woman in sheepskin.

"Who is there?" she cried, with a hollow cough.

"Give us a night's lodging, granny; we have lost our way; a night in the open is as bad as a hungry belly."

"What manner of folks may you be?"

"Oh, harmless folks: Khaliava, a theologian; Brut, a philosopher; and Gorobets, a rhetorician."

"I can't," grumbled the old woman. "The yard is crowded with folk and every corner in the hut is full. Where am I to put you? And such great hulking fellows, too! Why, it would knock my hut to pieces if I put such fellows in it. I know these philosophers and theologians; if one began taking in these drunken fellows, there'd soon be no home left. Be off, be off! There's no place for you here!"

"Have pity on us, granny! How can you let Christian souls perish for no rhyme or reason? Put us where you please; and if we do anything wrong or anything else, may our arms be withered, and God only knows what befall us—so there!"

The old woman seemed somewhat softened.

"Very well," she said, as though reconsidering. "I'll let you in, but I'll put you all in different places; for my heart won't be in peace if you are all lying together."

"That's as you please; we'll make no objection," answered the students.

The gate creaked and they went into the yard.

"Well, granny," said the philosopher, following the old woman, "how would it be, as they say . . . I swear I feel as though somebody were driving a cart in my stomach: not a morsel has passed my lips all day."

"What next will he want!" said the old woman. "No, I've nothing to give you, and the oven's not been heated today."

"But we'd pay for it all," the philosopher went on, "tomorrow morning, in hard cash. Yes!" he added in an undertone, "the devil you'll get!"

"Go in, go in! and you must be satisfied with what you're given. Fine young gentlemen the devil has brought us!"

Khoma the philosopher was thrown into utter dejection by these words, but his nose was suddenly aware of the odor of dried fish; he glanced toward the trousers of the theologian, who was walking at his side, and saw a huge fishtail sticking out of his pocket. The theologian had already succeeded in requisitioning a whole carp from a wagon. And as he had done this from no selfish motive but simply from habit, and, quite forgetting his carp, was already looking about for anything else he could carry off, having no mind to miss even a broken wheel, the philosopher slipped his hand into his friend's pocket, as though it were his own, and pulled out the carp.

The old woman put the students in their several places: the rhetorician she kept in the hut, the theologian she locked in an empty closet, the philosopher she assigned a sheep's pen, also empty.

The latter, on finding himself alone, instantly devoured the carp, examined the walls of the pen, kicked an inquisitive pig that woke up and thrust its snout in from the next pen, and turned over on his right side to fall into a sound sleep. All at once the low door opened, and the old woman, bending down, stepped into the pen.

"What is it, granny, what do you want?" said the philosopher.

But the old woman came toward him with outstretched arms.

"Aha, ha!" thought the philosopher. "No, my dear, you are too old!"

He turned away a little, but the old woman unceremoniously approached him again.

"Listen, granny!" said the philosopher. "It's a fast time now; and I am a man who wouldn't sin in a fast for a thousand gold pieces."

But the old woman opened her arms and tried to catch him without saying a word.

The philosopher was frightened, especially when he noticed a strange glitter in her eyes. "Granny, what is it? Go—go away—God bless you!" he cried.

The old woman said not a word, but tried to clutch him in her arms.

He leaped to his feet, intending to escape; but the old woman stood in the doorway, fixed her glittering eyes on him, and again began approaching him.

The philosopher tried to push her back with his hands but, to his surprise, found that his arms would not rise, his legs would not move, and he perceived with horror that even his voice would not obey him: words hovered on his lips without a sound. He heard nothing but the beating of his heart. He saw the old woman approach him. She folded his arms, bent his head down, leaped with the swiftness of a cat upon his back, and struck him with a broom on the side; and he, prancing like a horse, carried her on his shoulders. All this happened so quickly that the philosopher scarcely knew what he was doing. He clutched his knees in both hands, trying to stop his legs from moving, but, to his extreme amazement, they were lifted against his will and executed capers more swiftly than a Circassian racer. Only when they had left the farm, and the wide plain lay stretched before them with a forest black as coal on one side, he said to himself: "Aha! she's a witch!"

The waning crescent of the moon was shining in the sky. The timid radiance of midnight lay mistily over the earth, light as a transparent veil. The forests, the meadows, the sky, the dales, all seemed as though slumbering with open eyes; not a breeze fluttered anywhere; there was a damp warmth in the freshness of the night; the shadows of the trees and bushes fell on the sloping plain in pointed wedge shapes like comets. Such was the night when Khoma Brut, the philosopher, set off galloping with a mysterious rider on his back. He was aware of an exhausting, unpleasant, and at the same time, voluptuous sensation assailing his heart. He bent his head and saw that the grass which had been almost under his feet seemed growing far below him, and that above it there lay water, transparent as a mountain stream, and the grass seemed to be at the bottom of a clear sea, limpid to its very depths; anyway, he saw clearly in it his own reflection with the old woman sitting on his back. He saw shining there a sun instead of the moon; he heard the bluebells ringing as they bent their little heads; he saw a water sprite float out from behind the reeds, there was the gleam of her leg and back, rounded and firm, all brightness and shimmering. She turned toward him and now her face came nearer, with eyes clear, sparkling, keen, with singing that pierced the heart; now it was on the surface, and shaking with sparkling laughter it moved away; and now she turned on her back, and her cloudlike breasts, dead white like unglazed china, gleamed in the sun at the edges of their white, soft, and supple roundness. Little bubbles of water like beads bedewed them. She was all quivering and laughing in the water. . . .

Did he see this or did he not? Was he awake or dreaming? But what was that? The wind or music? It was ringing, ringing and reverberating and ever closer, piercing his heart with an unendurable trill. . . .

"What does it mean?" the philosopher wondered, looking down as he flew along, full speed. The sweat was streaming from him. He was aware of a fiendishly voluptuous feeling; he felt a stabbing, exhaustingly terrible delight. It often seemed to him as though his heart had melted away, and with terror he clutched at it. Worn out, desperate, he began trying to recall all the prayers he knew. He went through all the exorcisms against evil spirits, and all at once felt somewhat refreshed; he felt that his step was growing slower, the witch's hold upon his back seemed feebler, thick grass touched him, and now he saw nothing extraordinary in it. The clear, crescent moon was shining in the sky.

"Good!" the philosopher Khoma thought to himself, and he began repeating the exorcisms almost aloud. At last, quick as lightning, he sprang from under the old woman and in his turn leaped on her back. The old woman, with a tiny tripping step, ran so fast that her rider could scarcely breathe. The earth flashed by under him; everything was clear in the moonlight, though the moon was not full; the ground was smooth, but everything flashed by so rapidly that it was confused and indistinct. He snatched up a piece of wood that lay on the road and began whacking the old woman with all his might. She uttered wild howls; at first they were angry and menacing, then they grew fainter, sweeter, clearer, then rang out

gently like delicate silver bells that went straight to his heart; and
the thought flashed through his mind: was it really an old woman?

"Oh, I can do no more!" she murmured, and sank exhausted on
the ground.

He stood up and looked into her face (there was the glow of
sunrise, and the golden domes of the Kiev churches were gleaming
in the distance): before him lay a beautiful girl with luxuriant
tresses all in disorder and eyelashes as long as arrows. Senseless, she
tossed her bare white arms and moaned, looking upward with eyes
full of tears.

Khoma trembled like a leaf on a tree; he was overcome by pity
and a strange emotion and timidity, feelings he could not himself
explain. He began running, full speed. His heart throbbed uneasily
as he went, and he could not account for the strange new feeling
that had taken possession of it. He did not want to go back to the
farm; he hastened to Kiev, thinking all the way of this incomprehensible adventure.

There was scarcely a student left in the town. All had dispersed
about the countryside, either to jobs as tutors, or simply without
them; because in the villages of Little Russia they could get dumplings, cheese, sour cream, and puddings as big as a hat without
paying a kopek for them. The big rambling house in which the students were lodged was absolutely empty, and although the philosopher rummaged in every corner, and even felt in all the holes and
cracks in the roof, he could not find a bit of bacon or even a stale
roll such as were commonly hidden there by the students.

The philosopher, however, soon found means to improve his lot:
he walked whistling three times through the market, finally winked
at a young widow in a yellow bonnet who was selling ribbons,
shot, and wheels—and was that very day regaled with wheat dumplings, a chicken . . . in short, there is no telling what was on the
table laid for him in a little mud hut in the middle of a cherry
orchard.

The same evening the philosopher was seen in a tavern; he was
lying on the bench, smoking a pipe as his habit was, and in the
sight of all he flung the Jew who kept the tavern a gold coin. A
mug stood before him. He looked at all that came in and went out
with cool, contented eyes, and thought no more of his extraordinary adventure.

Meanwhile rumors were circulating everywhere that the daughter of one of the richest Cossack captains,[4] who lived nearly forty miles from Kiev, had returned one day from a walk, terribly injured, hardly able to crawl home to her father's house, was lying at the point of death, and had expressed a wish that one of the Kiev seminarists, Khoma Brut, should read the prayers over her and the psalms for three days after her death. The philosopher heard of this from the rector himself, who summoned him to his room and informed him that he was to set off on the journey without any delay, that the Cossack captain had sent servants and a carriage to fetch him.

The philosopher shuddered from an unaccountable feeling which he could not have explained to himself. A dark presentiment told him that something evil was awaiting him. Without knowing why, he bluntly declared that he would not go.

"Listen, Domine Khoma!" said the rector. (On some occasions he expressed himself very courteously with those under his authority.) "Who the hell is asking you whether you want to go or not? All I have to tell you is that if you go on flaunting your wit and making trouble, I'll order you such a whacking with a young birch tree, on your back and the rest of you, that there will be no need for you to go to the bath[5] after."

The philosopher, scratching behind his ear, went out without uttering a word, proposing at the first suitable opportunity to put his trust in his heels. Plunged in thought he went down the steep staircase that led into a yard shut in by poplars, and stood still for a minute, hearing quite distinctly the voice of the rector giving orders to his butler and someone else—probably one of the servants sent to fetch him by the officer.

"Thank his honor for the grain and the eggs," the rector was saying: "and tell him that as soon as the books about which he writes are ready I will send them at once, I have already given them to a scribe to be copied, and don't forget, my good man, to mention to his honor that I know there are excellent fish at his place, especially sturgeon, and he might on occasion send some; here in

[4] *Sotniks*, Cossack officers who commanded one hundred troops originally, a greater number in later times. (ed.)
[5] *Bania*, a bathhouse where birch twigs are used to massage and cleanse the skin. (ed.)

the market the fish are bad and expensive. And you, Yavtukh, give the young fellows a cup of vodka each, and tie up the philosopher or he'll run off directly."

"There, the devil's son!" the philosopher thought to himself. "He got wind of it, the long-legged charlatan!" He went down and saw a covered chaise, which he almost took at first for a baker's oven on wheels. It was, indeed, as deep as the oven in which bricks are baked. It was only the ordinary Cracow carriage in which Jews travel fifty together with their wares to all the towns where they smell out a fair. Six healthy and powerful Cossacks, no longer young, were waiting for him. Their coats of fine cloth, with tassels, showed that they belonged to a rather important and wealthy master; some small scars proved that they had at some time been in battle, not ingloriously.

"What's to be done? What is to be must be!" the philosopher thought to himself and, turning to the Cossacks, he said aloud: "Good day to you, comrades!"

"Good health to you, master philosopher," some of the Cossacks replied.

"So I am to get in with you? It's a large chaise!" he went on, as he clambered in, "we need only hire some musicians and we might dance here."

"Yes, it's a carriage of ample proportions," said one of the Cossacks, seating himself on the box beside the coachman, who had tied a rag over his head to replace the cap which he had managed to leave behind at a tavern. The other five and the philosopher crawled into the recesses of the chaise and settled themselves on sacks filled with various purchases they had made in the town. "It would be interesting to know," said the philosopher, "if this chaise were loaded up with goods of some sort, salt for instance, or iron wedges, how many horses would be needed then?"

"Yes," the Cossack sitting on the box said after a pause, "it would need a sufficient number of horses."

After this satisfactory reply the Cossack thought himself entitled to hold his tongue for the remainder of the journey.

The philosopher was extremely desirous of learning more in detail, who this captain was, what he was like, what had been heard about his daughter who in such a strange way returned home and was found on the point of death, and whose story was now connected with his own, what was being done in the house, and how things were there. He addressed the Cossacks with inquiries, but no doubt they too were philosophers, for by way of a reply they remained silent, smoking their pipes and lying on their backs. Only one of them turned to the driver on the box with a brief order: "Take care, Overko, you old buzzard, when you are near the tavern on the Chukhrailovski road, don't forget to stop and wake me and the other fellows if any should happen to drop asleep."

After this he fell asleep rather noisily. These instructions were, however, quite unnecessary, for as soon as the gigantic chaise drew near the tavern all the Cossacks shouted together: "Stop!" Moreover, Overko's horses were already trained to stop themselves at every tavern.

In spite of the hot July day, they all got out of the chaise and went into the low-pitched dirty room, where the Jew who kept the tavern hastened to receive his old friends with every sign of delight. The Jew brought from under the skirt of his coat some ham sausages, and putting them on the table, turned his back at once on this food forbidden by the Talmud. All the Cossacks sat down around the table; earthenware mugs were set for each of the guests. Khoma had to take part in the general festivity, and, as Little Russians infallibly begin kissing each other or weeping when they are drunk, soon the whole room resounded with smacks. "Come, Spirid, a kiss." "Come here, Dorosh, I want to embrace you!"

One Cossack with gray mustaches, a little older than the rest, propped his cheek on his hand and began sobbing bitterly at the thought that he had no father nor mother and was all alone in the world. Another one, much given to moralizing, persisted in consoling him, saying: "Don't cry; please don't cry! What is there in it . . . ? The Lord knows best, you know."

The one whose name was Dorosh became extremely inquisitive, and, turning to the philosopher Khoma, kept asking him: "I should like to know what they teach you in the seminary. Is it the same as what the deacon reads in church, or something different?"

"Don't ask!" the sermonizing Cossack said emphatically: "let it be as it is. God knows what is wanted, God knows everything."

"No, I want to know," said Dorosh, "what is written there in those books? Maybe it is quite different from what the deacon reads."

"Oh, my goodness, my goodness!" said the sermonizing worthy, "and why say such a thing; it's as the Lord wills. There is no changing what the Lord has willed!"

"I want to know all that's written. I'll go to the seminary, I will. Do you suppose I can't learn? I'll learn it all, all!"

"Oh my goodness . . . !" said the sermonizing Cossack, and he dropped his head on the table, because he was utterly incapable of supporting it any longer on his shoulders. The other Cossacks were discussing their masters and the question of why the moon shone in the sky. The philosopher, seeing the state of their minds, resolved to seize his opportunity and make his escape. To begin with he turned to the gray-headed Cossack who was grieving for his father and mother.

"Why are you blubbering, uncle?" he said. "I am an orphan myself! Let me go in freedom, fellows! What do you want with me?"

"Let him go!" several responded. "Why, he is an orphan, let him go where he likes."

"Oh, my goodness, my goodness!" the moralizing Cossack articulated, lifting his head. "Let him go!"

"Let him go where he likes!"

And the Cossacks meant to lead him out into the open air themselves, but the one who had displayed his curiosity stopped them, saying: "Don't touch him. I want to talk to him about the seminary: I am going to the seminary myself. . . ."

It is doubtful, however, whether the escape could have taken place, for when the philosopher tried to get up from the table his legs seemed to have become wooden, and he began to perceive such a number of doors in the room that he could hardly discover the real one.

It was evening before the Cossacks realized that they had further to go. Clambering into the chaise, they trailed along the road, urging on the horses and singing a song of which nobody could have made out the words or the sense. After trundling on for the greater part of the night, continually straying off the road, though they knew every inch of the way, they drove at last down a steep hill into a valley, and the philosopher noticed a fence that ran alongside, low trees and roofs peeping out behind it. This was a big village belonging to the captain. By now it was long past midnight; the sky was dark, but there were little stars twinkling here and there. No light was to be seen in a single hut. To the accompaniment of the barking of dogs, they drove into the courtyard. Thatched barns and little houses came into sight on both sides; one of the latter, which stood exactly in the middle opposite the gates, was larger than the others, and was apparently the officer's residence. The chaise drew up before a little shed that served as a barn, and our travelers went off to bed. The philosopher, however, wanted to inspect the outside of the officer's house; but, though he stared his hardest, nothing could be seen distinctly; the house looked to him like a bear; the chimney turned into the rector. The philosopher gave up the idea and went to sleep.

When he woke up, the whole house was in commotion: the captain's daughter had died during the night. Servants were hurriedly running back and forth; some old women were crying; an inquisitive crowd was looking through the fence at the house, as though something might be seen there. The philosopher began leisurely examining the objects he could not discern in the night. The captain's house was a little, low-pitched building, such as was usual in Little Russia in old days; its roof was of thatch; a small, high, pointed gable with a little window that looked like an eye turned upward, was painted in blue and yellow flowers and red crescents; it was supported on oak posts, rounded above and hexagonal below, with carving at the top. Under the gable was a little porch with seats on each side. There were verandas around the house resting on similar posts, some of them carved in spirals. A tall pyramidal pear tree, with trembling leaves, made a patch of green in front of the house. Two rows of barns for storing grain stood in the middle of the yard, forming a sort of wide street leading to the house. Beyond the barns, close to the gate, stood facing each other two three-cornered storehouses, also thatched. Each triangular wall was painted in various designs and had a little door in it. On one of them was depicted a Cossack sitting on a barrel, holding a mug above his head with the inscription: "I'll drink it all!" On the other, there was a bottle, flagons, and at the sides, by way of ornament, a horse upside down, a pipe, a tambourine, and the inscription: "Wine is the Cossack's comfort!" A drum and brass trumpets could be seen through the huge window in the loft of one of the barns. At the gates stood two cannons. Everything showed that the master of the house was fond of merrymaking, and that the yard often resounded with the shouts of revelers. There were two windmills outside the gate. Behind the house stretched gardens, and through the treetops the dark caps of chimneys were all that could be seen of huts smothered in green bushes. The whole village lay on the broad sloping side of a hill. The steep side, at the very foot of which lay the courtyard, made a screen from the north. Looked at from below, it seemed even steeper, and here and there on its tall top uneven stalks of rough grass stood out black against the clear sky; its bare aspect was somehow depressing; its clay soil was hollowed out by the fall and trickle of rain. Two huts stood at some distance from each other on its steep slope; one of them was overshadowed by the branches of a spreading apple tree, banked up with soil and supported by short stakes near the root. The apples, knocked down by the wind, were falling right into the master's courtyard. The road, coiling about the hill from the very top, ran down beside the courtyard to the village. When the philosopher scanned its terrific steepness and recalled their journey down it the previous night, he came to the conclusion that either the captain had very clever horses or that the Cossacks had very strong heads to have managed, even when drunk, to escape flying head over heels with the immense chaise and baggage. The philosopher was standing on the highest point in the yard. When he turned and looked in the opposite direction he saw quite a different view. The village sloped away into a plain. Meadows stretched as far as the eye could see; their brilliant verdure was deeper in the distance, and whole rows of villages looked like dark patches in it, though they must have been more than fifteen miles away. To the right of the meadowlands was a line of hills, and a hardly perceptible streak of flashing light and darkness showed where the Dnieper ran.

"Ah, a wonderful spot!" said the philosopher, "this would be the place to live, fishing in the Dnieper and the ponds, birdcatching with nets, or shooting kingsnipe and little bustards. Though I do believe there would be a few great bustards too in those meadows! One could dry lots of fruit, too, and sell it in the town, or, better still, make vodka of it, for there's no drink to compare with fruit vodka. But it would be just as well to consider how to slip away from here."

He noticed outside the fence a little path completely overgrown with weeds; he was mechanically setting his foot on it with the idea of simply going first out for a walk, and then stealthily passing between the huts and dashing out into the open country, when he suddenly felt a rather strong hand on his shoulder.

Behind him stood the old Cossack who had on the previous evening so bitterly bewailed the death of his father and mother and his own solitary state.

"It's no good your thinking of running away, Mr. Philosopher!" he said: "this isn't the sort of establishment you can run away from; and the roads are bad, too, for anyone on foot; you had better come to the master: he's been expecting you for a long time in the parlor."

"Let's go! To be sure . . . I'm delighted," said the philosopher, and he followed the Cossack.

The officer, an elderly man with gray mustaches and an expression of gloomy sadness, was sitting at a table in the parlor, his head propped on his hands. He was about fifty; but the deep despondency on his face and its wan pallor showed that his soul had been crushed and shattered at one blow, and all his old gaiety and noisy merrymaking had disappeared forever. When Khoma went in with the old Cossack, he removed one hand from his face and gave a slight nod in response to their low bows.

Khoma and the Cossack stood respectfully at the door.

"Who are you, where do you come from, and what is your calling, good man?" said the captain, in a voice neither friendly nor ill-humored.

"A bursar, student in philosophy, Khoma Brut . . ."

"Who was your father?"

"I don't know, honored sir."

"Your mother?"

"I don't know my mother either. It is reasonable to suppose, of course, that I had a mother; but who she was and where she came from, and when she lived—I swear, good sir, I don't know."

The old man paused and seemed to sink into a reverie for a minute.

"How did you come to know my daughter?"

"I didn't know her, honored sir, I swear, I didn't. I have never had anything to do with young ladies, never in my life. Bless them, begging your pardon!"

"Why did she select you and no other to read the psalms over her?"

The philosopher shrugged his shoulders. "God knows how to explain that. It's a well-known thing, the gentry are forever taking fancies that the most learned men couldn't explain, and the proverb says: 'The devil himself must dance at the master's bidding.' "

"Are you telling the truth, philosopher?"

"May I be struck down by thunder on the spot if I'm not."

"If she had only lived one brief moment longer," the captain said to himself mournfully, "I should have learned all about it. 'Let no one else read over me, but send, Father, at once to the Kiev Seminary and fetch the bursar, Khoma Brut; let him pray three nights for my sinful soul. He knows . . . !' But what he knows, I did not hear: she, poor darling, could say no more before she died. You, good man, are no doubt well known for your holy life and pious works, and she, maybe, heard tell of you."

"Who? I?" said the philosopher, stepping back in amazement. "I —holy life!" he articulated, looking straight in the officer's face. "God be with you, sir! What are you talking about! Why—though it's not a decent thing to speak of—I paid the baker's wife a visit on Holy Thursday."

"Well . . . I suppose there must be some reason for selecting you. You must begin your duties this very day."

"As to that, I would tell your honor . . . Of course, any man versed in Holy Scripture may, as far as in him lies . . . but a deacon or a sacristan would be better fitted for it. They are men of understanding, and know how it is all done, while I . . . Besides I haven't the right voice for it, and I myself am good for nothing. I'm not the figure for it."

"Well, say what you like, I shall carry out all my darling's wishes; I will spare nothing. And if for three nights from today you duly recite the prayers over her, I will reward you; if not . . . I don't advise the devil himself to anger me!"

The last words were uttered by the captain so vigorously that the philosopher fully grasped their significance.

"Follow me!" said the captain.

They went out into the hall. The captain opened the door into another room, opposite the first. The philosopher paused a minute in the hall to blow his nose and crossed the threshold with unaccountable apprehension.

The whole floor was covered with red cotton material. On a high table in the corner under the holy images lay the body of the dead girl on a coverlet of dark blue velvet adorned with gold fringe and tassels. Tall wax candles, entwined with sprigs of guelder rose, stood at her feet and head, shedding a dim light that was lost in the brightness of daylight. The dead girl's face was hidden from him by the inconsolable father, who sat down facing her with his back to the door. The philosopher was impressed by the words he heard:

"I am grieving, my dearly beloved daughter, not that in the flower of your age you have left the earth, to my sorrow and mourning, without living your allotted span; I grieve, my darling, that I know not him, my bitter foe, who was the cause of your death. And if I knew the man who could but dream of hurting you, or even saying anything unkind of you, I swear to God he should not see his children again, if he be old as I, nor his father and mother, if he be of that time of life, and his body should be cast out to be devoured by the birds and beasts of the steppe! But my grief it is, my wild marigold, my bird, light of my eyes, that I must live out my days without comfort, wiping with the skirt of my coat the trickling tears that flow from my old eyes, while my enemy will be making merry and secretly mocking the feeble old man. . . ."

He came to a standstill, due to an outburst of sorrow, which found vent in a flood of tears.

The philosopher was touched by such inconsolable sadness; he coughed, uttering a hollow sound in the effort to clear his throat. The captain turned around and pointed him to a place at the dead girl's head, before a small lectern with books on it.

"I shall get through three nights somehow," thought the philosopher: "and the old man will stuff both my pockets with gold pieces for it."

He drew near, and clearing his throat once more, began reading, paying no attention to anything else and not venturing to glance at the face of the dead girl. A profound stillness reigned in the room. He noticed that the captain had withdrawn. Slowly he turned his head to look at the dead, and . . .

A shudder ran through his veins: before him lay a beauty whose like had surely never been on earth before. Never, it seemed, could features have been formed in such striking yet harmonious beauty. She lay as though living: the lovely forehead, fair as snow, as silver, looked deep in thought; the even brows—dark as night in the midst of sunshine—rose proudly above the closed eyes; the eyelashes, that fell like arrows on the cheeks, glowed with the warmth of secret desires; the lips were rubies, ready to break into the laugh of bliss, the flood of joy . . . But in them, in those very

features, he saw something terrible and poignant. He felt a sicken-
ing ache stirring in his heart, as though, in the midst of a whirl of
gaiety and dancing crowds, someone had begun singing a funeral
dirge. The rubies of her lips looked like blood surging up from her
heart. All at once he was aware of something dreadfully familiar in
her face. "The witch!" he cried in a voice not his own, as, turning
pale, he looked away and fell to repeating his prayers. It was the
witch that he had killed!

When the sun was setting, they carried the corpse to the church.
The philosopher supported the coffin swathed in black on his shoulder, and felt something cold as ice on it. The captain walked in
front, with his hand on the right side of the dead girl's narrow
coffin. The wooden church, blackened by age and overgrown with
green lichen, stood disconsolately, with its three cone-shaped domes,
at the very end of the village. It was evident that no service had
been performed in it for a long time. Candles had been lighted before almost every image. The coffin was set down in the center
opposite the altar. The old captain kissed the dead girl once more,
bowed down to the ground, and went out with the coffin bearers,
giving orders that the philosopher should have a good supper
and then be taken to the church. On reaching the kitchen all the
men who had carried the coffin began putting their hands on
the stove, as the custom is with Little Russians, after seeing a dead
body.

The hunger of which the philosopher began at that moment to
be conscious made him for some minutes entirely oblivious of the
dead girl. Soon all the servants began gradually assembling in the
kitchen, which in the captain's house was something like a club,
where all the inhabitants of the yard gathered together, including
even the dogs, who, wagging their tails, came to the door for bones
and scraps. Wherever anybody might be sent, and with whatever
duty he might be charged, he always went first to the kitchen to
rest for at least a minute on the bench and smoke a pipe. All the
unmarried men in their smart Cossack coats lay there almost all day
long, on the bench, under the bench, or on the stove—anywhere,
in fact, where a comfortable place could be found. Then everybody invariably left behind in the kitchen either his cap or a whip
to keep stray dogs off or some such thing. But the biggest crowd
always gathered at suppertime, when the coachman who had taken

the horses to the paddock, and the herdsman who had brought the cows in to be milked, and all the others who were not to be seen during the day, came in. At supper, even the most taciturn tongues were moved to loquacity. It was then that all the news was discussed: who had got himself new trousers, and what was hidden in the bowels of the earth, and who had seen a wolf. There were witty talkers among them; indeed, there is no lack of them anywhere among the Little Russians.

The philosopher sat down with the others in a big circle in the open air before the kitchen door. Soon a peasant woman in a red bonnet popped out, holding in both hands a steaming bowl of dumplings, which she set down in their midst. Each pulled out a wooden spoon from his pocket, or, for lack of a spoon, a wooden stick. As soon as their jaws began moving more slowly, and the wolfish hunger of the whole party was somewhat assuaged, many of them began talking. The conversation naturally turned on the dead maiden.

"Is it true," said a young shepherd who had put so many buttons and copper disks on the leather strap on which his pipe hung that he looked like a small haberdasher's shop, "is it true that the young lady, pardon the expression, was on friendly terms with the Evil One?"

"Who? The young mistress?" said Dorosh, a man our philosopher already knew, "why, she was a witch! I'll take my oath she was a witch!"

"Hush, hush, Dorosh," said another man, who had shown a great disposition to soothe the others on the journey, "that's no business of ours, forget it. It's no good talking about it."

But Dorosh was not at all inclined to hold his tongue; he had just been to the cellar on some job with the butler, and, having applied his lips to two or three barrels, he had come out extremely merry and talked away without ceasing.

"What do you mean? Me to be quiet?" he said. "Why, I've been ridden by her myself! I swear I have!"

"Tell us, uncle," said the young shepherd with the buttons, "are there signs by which you can tell a witch?"

"No, you can't," answered Dorosh, "there's no way of telling; you might read through all the psalm books and you couldn't tell."

"Yes, you can, Dorosh, you can; don't say that," the former com-

forter objected; "it's with good purpose God has given every creature its peculiar habit; folks that have studied say that a witch has a
little tail."

"When a woman's old, she's a witch," the gray-headed Cossack
said coolly.

"Oh! you're a nice bunch!" retorted the peasant woman, who
was at that instant pouring a fresh lot of dumplings into the empty
pot; "regular fat hogs!"

The old Cossack, whose name was Yavtukh and nickname Kov-
tun, gave a smile of satisfaction, seeing that his words had cut the
old woman to the quick; while the herdsman gave vent to a guffaw,
like the bellowing of two bulls as they stand facing each other.

The beginning of the conversation had aroused the philosopher's
curiosity and made him intensely anxious to learn more details about
the captain's daughter, and so, wishing to bring the conversation
back to that subject, he turned to his neighbor with the words: "I
should like to ask why all the folk sitting at supper here look upon
the young mistress as a witch? Did she do mischief to anybody or
bring anybody to harm?"

"There were all sorts of doings," answered one of the company,
a man with a flat face strikingly resembling a spade. "Everybody
remembers the huntsman Mikita and the . . ."

"What about the huntsman Mikita?" said the philosopher.

"Stop! I'll tell about the huntsman Mikita," said Dorosh.

"I'll tell about him," said the coachman, "for he was a great
crony of mine."

"I'll tell about Mikita," said Spirid.

"Let him, let Spirid tell it!" shouted the company.

Spirid began: "You didn't know Mikita, Mr. Philosopher Khoma.
Ah, he was a man! He knew every dog as well as he knew his own
father. The huntsman we've got now, Mikola, who's sitting next
but one from me, isn't worth the sole of his shoe. Though he
knows his job, too, but beside the other he's trash, garbage."

"You tell the story well, very well!" said Dorosh, nodding his
head approvingly.

Spirid went on: "He'd see a hare quicker than you'd wipe the
snuff from your nose. He'd whistle: 'Here, Breaker! Here, Swift-
foot!' and he in full gallop on his horse; and there was no saying
which would outrace the other, he the dog, or the dog him. He'd
toss off a mug of vodka without winking. He was a fine huntsman!"

Only a little time back he began to be always staring at the young
mistress. Whether he had fallen in love with her, or whether she
had simply bewitched him, anyway the man was done for, he became stupid; the devil only knows what he turned into . . . pfoo!
No decent word for it. . . ."

"That's good," said Dorosh.

"As soon as the young mistress looks at him, he drops the bridle
out of his hand, calls Breaker 'Bushybrow,' is all of a fluster and
doesn't know what he's doing. One day the young mistress comes
into the stable where he is rubbing down a horse.

" 'Mikita,' says she, 'let me put my little foot on you.' And he,
foolish fellow, is pleased at that. 'Not your foot only,' says he,
'you may sit on me altogether.' The young mistress lifted her foot,
and, as soon as he saw her bare, plump white leg, he went fairly
crazy, so he said. He bent his back, silly fellow, and clasping her
bare legs in his hands, ran galloping like a horse all over the countryside. And he couldn't say where he was driven, but he came
back more dead than alive, and from that time he withered up like
a chip of wood; and one day when they went into the stable, instead of him they found a heap of ashes lying there and an empty
pail; he had burned up entirely, burned up by himself. And he was
a huntsman such as you couldn't find another all the world over."

When Spirid had finished his story, reflections upon the rare qualities of the deceased huntsman followed from all sides.

"And haven't you heard tell of Sheptun's wife?" said Dorosh,
addressing Khoma.

"No."

"Well, well! You are not taught with too much sense, it seems, in
the seminary. Listen, then. There's a Cossack called Sheptun in our
village—a good Cossack! He is given to stealing at times, and telling
lies when there's no occasion, but . . . he's a good Cossack. His
place is not so far from here. Just about the very hour that we sat
down this evening at the table, Sheptun and his wife finished their
supper and lay down to sleep, and, as it was fine weather, his wife
lay down in the yard, and Sheptun in the hut on the bench; or no
. . . it was the wife lay indoors on the bench and Sheptun in the
yard . . ."

"Not on the bench; she was lying on the floor," said a peasant
woman, who stood in the doorway with her cheek propped in her
hand.

Dorosh looked at her, then looked down, then looked at her again, and after a brief pause, said: "When I strip off your petticoat before everybody, you won't be pleased."

This warning had its effect; the old woman held her tongue and did not interrupt the story again.

Dorosh went on: "And in the cradle hanging in the middle of the hut lay a baby a year old—whether of the male or female sex I can't say. Sheptun's wife was lying there when she heard a dog scratching at the door and howling fit to make you run out of the hut. She was scared, for women are such foolish creatures that, if toward evening you put your tongue out at one from behind a door, her heart's in her mouth. However, she thought: 'Well, I'll go and give that damned dog a whack on its nose, and maybe it will stop howling,' and taking the poker she went to open the door. She had hardly opened it when a dog dashed in between her legs and straight to the baby's cradle. She saw that it was no longer a dog, but the young mistress, and, if it had been the young lady in her own shape as she knew her, it would not have been so bad. But the peculiar thing is that she was all blue and her eyes glowing like coals. She snatched up the child, bit its throat, and began sucking its blood. Sheptun's wife could only scream: 'Oh, horror!' and rushed toward the door. But she sees the door's locked in the passage; she flies up to the loft and there she sits trembling, the foolish woman; and then she sees the young mistress coming up to her in the loft; she pounced on her, and began biting the foolish woman. When Sheptun pulled his wife down from the loft in the morning she was bitten all over and had turned black and blue; and next day the foolish woman died. So you see what uncanny and wicked doings happen in the world! Though it is of the gentry's breed, a witch is a witch."

After telling the story, Dorosh looked about him complacently and thrust his finger into his pipe, preparing to fill it with tobacco. The subject of the witch seemed inexhaustible. Each in turn hastened to tell some tale of her. One had seen the witch in the form of a haystack come right up to the door of his cottage; another had had his cap or his pipe stolen by her; many of the girls in the village had had their hair cut off by her; others had lost several quarts of blood which she had sucked from them.

At last they pulled themselves together and saw that they had been chattering too long, for it was quite dark in the yard. They all began wandering off to their sleeping places, which were either in the kitchen, or the barns, or the middle of the courtyard.

"Well, Mr. Khoma! now it's time for us to go to the deceased lady," said the gray-headed Cossack, addressing the philosopher; and with Spirid and Dorosh they set off to the church, lashing with their whips at the dogs, of which there were a great number in the road, and which gnawed their sticks angrily.

Though the philosopher had managed to fortify himself with a good mugful of vodka, he felt a fearfulness creeping stealthily over him as they approached the lighted church. The stories and strange tales he had heard helped to work upon his imagination. The darkness under the fence and the trees grew less thick as they came into the more open place. At last they went into the church enclosure and found a little yard, beyond which there was not a tree to be seen, nothing but open country and meadows swallowed up in the darkness of night. The three Cossacks and Khoma mounted the steep steps to the porch and went into the church. Here they left the philosopher with the best wishes that he might carry out his duties satisfactorily, and locked the door after them, as their master had bidden them.

The philosopher was left alone. First he yawned, then he stretched, then he blew into both hands, and at last he looked about him. In the middle of the church stood the black coffin; candles were gleaming under the dark images; the light from them only lit up the icon stand and shed a faint glimmer in the middle of the church; the distant corners were wrapped in darkness. The tall, old-fashioned icon stand showed traces of great antiquity; its carved fretwork, once gilt, only glistened here and there with splashes of gold; the gilt had peeled off in one place, and was completely tarnished in another; the faces of the saints, blackened by age, had a gloomy look. The philosopher looked around him again. "Well," he said, "what is there to be afraid of here? No living man can come in here, and to guard me from the dead and ghosts from the other world I have prayers that I have but to read aloud to keep them from laying a finger on me. It's all right!" he repeated with a wave of his hand, "let's read." Going up to the lectern he saw some bundles of candles. "That's good," thought the philosopher; "I must light up the whole church so that it may be as bright as daylight. Oh, it is a pity that one must not smoke a pipe in the temple of God!"

And he proceeded to stick up wax candles at all the cornices, lecterns, and images, not stinting them at all, and soon the whole church was flooded with light. Only overhead the darkness seemed somehow more profound, and the gloomy icons looked even more sullenly out of their antique carved frames, which glistened here and there with specks of gilt. He went up to the coffin, looked timidly at the face of the dead—and could not help closing his eyelids with a faint shudder: such terrible, brilliant beauty!

He turned and tried to move away; but with the strange curiosity, the self-contradictory feeling, which dogs a man especially in times of terror, he could not, as he withdrew, resist taking another look. And then, after the same shudder, he looked again. The striking beauty of the dead maiden certainly seemed terrible. Possibly, indeed, she would not have overwhelmed him with such fear if she had been a little less lovely. But there was in her features nothing faded, tarnished, dead; her face was living, and it seemed to the philosopher that she was looking at him with closed eyes. He even fancied that a tear was oozing from under her right eyelid, and, when it rested on her cheek, he saw distinctly that it was a drop of blood.

He walked quickly away to the lectern, opened the book, and to give himself more confidence began reading in a very loud voice. His voice beat upon the wooden church walls, which had so long been deaf and silent; it rang out, forlorn, unechoed, in a deep bass in the absolutely dead stillness, and seemed somehow uncanny even to the reader himself. "What is there to be afraid of?" he was saying meanwhile to himself. "She won't rise up out of her coffin, for she will fear the word of God. Let her lie there! And a fine Cossack I am, if I should be scared. Well, I've drunk a drop too much—that's why it seems dreadful. I'll have a pinch of snuff!" However, as he turned over the pages, he kept taking sidelong glances at the coffin, and an involuntary feeling seemed whispering to him: "Look, look, she is going to get up! See, she'll sit up, she'll look out from the coffin!"

But the silence was deathlike; the coffin stood motionless; the candles shed a perfect flood of light. A church lighted up at night with a dead body in it and no living soul near is full of terror!

Raising his voice, he began singing in various keys, trying to drown the fears that still lurked in him, but every minute he turned his eyes to the coffin, as though asking, in spite of himself: "What if she does sit up, if she gets up?"

But the coffin did not stir. If there had but been some sound! some living creature! There was not so much as a cricket churring in the corner! There was nothing but the faint sputter of a distant candle, the soft sound of a drop of wax falling on the floor.

"What if she were to get up . . . ?"

She was raising her head . . .

He looked at her wildly and rubbed his eyes. She was, indeed, not lying down now, but sitting up in the coffin. He looked away, and again turned his eyes with horror on the coffin. She stood up . . . she was walking about the church with her eyes shut, moving her arms back and forth as though trying to catch someone.

She was coming straight toward him. In terror he drew a circle around him; with an effort he began reading the prayers and pronouncing the exorcisms which had been taught him by a monk who had all his life seen witches and evil spirits.

She stood almost on the very line; but it was clear that she had not the power to cross it, and she turned livid all over like one who has been dead for several days. Khoma had not the courage to look at her; she was terrifying. She ground her teeth and opened her dead eyes; but, seeing nothing, turned with fury— that was apparent in her quivering face—in another direction, and flinging her arms, clutched in them each column and corner, trying to catch Khoma. At last, she stood still, holding up a menacing finger, and lay down again in her coffin.

The philosopher could not recover his self-possession, but kept gazing at the narrow coffin of the witch. At last the coffin suddenly sprang up from its place and with a hissing sound began flying all over the church, zigzagging through the air in all directions.

The philosopher saw it almost over his head, but at the same time he saw that it could not cross the circle he had drawn, and he redoubled his exorcisms. The coffin dropped down in the middle of the church and stayed there without moving. The corpse got up out of it, livid and greenish. But at that instant the crow of the cock was heard in the distance; the corpse sank back in the coffin and closed the lid.

The philosopher's heart was throbbing and the sweat was

streaming down him; but, emboldened by the cock's crowing, he read on more rapidly the pages he ought to have read through before. At the first streak of dawn the sexton came to relieve him, together with old Yavtukh, who was at that time performing the duties of a beadle.

On reaching his distant sleeping place, the philosopher could not for a long time get to sleep; but weariness gained the upper hand at last and he slept on till it was time for dinner. When he woke up, all the events of the night seemed to him to have happened in a dream. To keep up his strength he was given a mug of vodka.

Over dinner he soon grew lively, made a remark or two, and devoured a rather large sucking pig almost unaided; but some feeling he could not have explained made him unable to bring himself to speak of his adventures in the church, and to the inquiries of the inquisitive he replied, "Yes, all sorts of strange things happened." The philosopher was one of those people who, if they are well fed, are moved to extraordinary benevolence. Lying down with his pipe in his teeth, he watched them all with a sweet look in his eyes and kept spitting to one side.

After dinner the philosopher was in excellent spirits. He went around the whole village and made friends with almost everybody; he was kicked out of two huts; indeed, one good-looking young woman caught him a good smack on the back with a spade when he took it into his head to feel her chemise and skirt, and inquire what stuff they were made of. But as evening approached the philosopher grew more pensive. An hour before supper almost all the servants gathered together to play *kragli*—a sort of skittles in which long sticks are used instead of balls, and the winner has the right to ride on the loser's back. This game became very entertaining for the spectators; often the coachman, a man as broad as a pancake, was mounted on the swineherd, a feeble little man, who was nothing but wrinkles. Another time it was the coachman who had to bow his back, and Dorosh, leaping on it, always said: "What a fine bull!" The more dignified of the company sat in the kitchen doorway. They looked on very gravely, smoking their pipes, even when the young people roared with laughter at some witty remark from the coachman or Spirid. Khoma tried in vain to give himself up to this game; some gloomy thought stuck in his head like a nail. At supper, in spite of his efforts to be merry, terror grew within him as the darkness spread over the sky.

"Come, it's time to start, Mr. Seminarist!" said his friend, the gray-headed Cossack, getting up from the table with Dorosh; "let us go to our task."

Khoma was taken to the church again in the same way; again he was left there alone and the door was locked upon him. As soon as he was alone, fear began to take possession of him again. Again he saw the dark icons, the gleaming frames, and the familiar black coffin standing in menacing stillness and immobility in the middle of the church.

"Well," he said to himself, "now there's nothing amazing to me in this marvel. It was only alarming the first time. Yes, it was only rather alarming the first time, and even then it wasn't so alarming; now it's not alarming at all."

He made haste to take his stand at the lectern, drew a circle around him, pronounced some exorcisms, and began reading aloud, resolving not to raise his eyes from the book and not to pay attention to anything. He had been reading for about an hour and was beginning to cough and feel rather tired; he took his horn out of his pocket and, before putting the snuff to his nose, stole a timid look at the coffin. His heart turned cold; the corpse was already standing before him on the very edge of the circle, and her dead, greenish eyes were fixed upon him. The philosopher shuddered, and a cold chill ran through his veins. Dropping his eyes to the book, he began reading the prayers and exorcisms more loudly, and heard the corpse again grinding her teeth and waving her arms trying to catch him. But, with a sidelong glance out of one eye, he saw that the corpse was feeling for him where he was not standing, and that she evidently could not see him. He heard a hollow mutter, and she began pronouncing terrible words with her dead lips; they gurgled hoarsely like the bubbling of boiling pitch. He could not have said what they meant; but there was something fearful in them. The philosopher understood with horror that she was making an incantation.

A wind blew through the church at her words, and there was a sound as of multitudes of flying wings. He heard the beating of wings on the panes of the church windows and on the iron window frames, the dull scratching of claws upon the iron, and numberless evil creatures thundering on the doors and trying to break in. His heart was throbbing violently all this time; closing his eyes, he kept reading prayers and exorcisms. At last there was a sudden shrill sound in the distance; it was a distant cock crowing. The philosopher, utterly spent, stopped and took breath.

When they came in to fetch him, they found him more dead than alive; he was leaning with his back against the wall while, with his eyes almost popping out of his head, he stared at the Cossacks as they came in. They could scarcely get him along and had to support him all the way back. On reaching the courtyard, he pulled himself together and bade them give him a mug of vodka. When he had drunk it, he stroked down the hair on his head and said: "There are lots of foul things of all sorts in the world! And the fright they give one, there . . ." With that the philosopher waved his hand in despair.

The company sitting around him bowed their heads, hearing such sayings. Even a small boy, whom everybody in the servants' quarters felt himself entitled to depute in his place when it was a question of cleaning the stables or fetching water, even this poor youngster stared openmouthed at the philosopher.

At that moment the old cook's assistant, a peasant woman, not yet past middle age, a terrible coquette, who always found something to pin to her cap—a bit of ribbon, a carnation, or a little paper, if she had nothing better—passed by, in a tightly tied apron, which displayed her round, sturdy figure.

"Good day, Khoma!" she said, seeing the philosopher. "Aie, aie, aie! what's the matter with you?" she shrieked, clasping her hands.

"Why, what is it, silly woman?"

"Oh, my goodness! Why, you've become quite gray!"

"Aha! why, she's right!" Spirid pronounced, looking attentively at the philosopher. "Why, you have really become as gray as our old Yavtukh."

The philosopher, hearing this, ran headlong to the kitchen, where he had noticed on the wall a fly-spattered triangular bit of mirror before which were stuck forget-me-nots, periwinkles, and even wreaths of marigolds, testifying to its importance for the toilet of the finery-loving coquette. With horror he saw the truth of their words: half of his hair had in fact turned white.

Khoma Brut hung his head and abandoned himself to reflection.

"I will go to the master," he said at last. "I'll tell him all about it and explain that I cannot go on reading. Let him send me back to Kiev straight away."

With these thoughts in his mind he bent his steps toward the porch of the house.

The captain was sitting almost motionless in his parlor. The same hopeless grief which the philosopher had seen in his face before was still apparent. Only his cheeks were more sunken. It was evident that he had taken very little food, or perhaps had not eaten at all. The extraordinary pallor of his face gave it a look of stony immobility.

"Good day!" he pronounced on seeing Khoma, who stood, cap in hand, at the door. "Well, how goes it with you? All satisfactory?"

"It's satisfactory, all right; such devilish doings that one can but pick up one's cap and take to one's heels."

"How's that?"

"Why, your daughter, your honor . . . Looking at it reasonably, she is, to be sure, of noble birth, nobody is going to deny it; only, if I may, God rest her soul . . ."

"What of my daughter?"

"She had dealings with Satan. She gives one such horrors that there's no reading Scripture at all."

"Read away! read away! She did well to send for you; she took much care, poor darling, about her soul and tried to drive away all evil thoughts with prayers."

"That's your right to say, your honor; but I swear I cannot go on with it!"

"Read away!" the captain persisted in the same persuasive voice, "you have only one night left; you will do a Christian deed and I will reward you."

"But whatever rewards . . . Do as you please, your honor, but I will not read!" Khoma declared resolutely.

"Listen, philosopher!" said the captain, and his voice grew firm and menacing. "I don't like these pranks. You can behave like that in your seminary, but with me it is different. When I flog, it's not the same as your rector's flogging. Do you know what good leather whips are like?"

"I should think I do!" said the philosopher, dropping his voice; "everybody knows what leather whips are like: in a large dose, they're quite unendurable."

"Yes, but you don't know yet how my fellows can lay them on!" said the captain menacingly, rising to his feet, and his face assumed an imperious and ferocious expression that betrayed the unbridled violence of his character, only subdued for the time by sorrow.

"Here they first give a sound flogging, then sprinkle with vodka, and begin over again. Go along, go along, finish your task! If you don't—you'll never get up again. If you do—a thousand gold pieces!"

"Oho, ho! he's a rough one!" thought the philosopher as he went out: "he's not to be trifled with. Wait a moment friend; I'll cut and run, so that you and your hounds will never catch me."

And Khoma made up his mind to run away. He only waited for the hour after dinner when all the servants were accustomed to lie about in the hay in the barns and to give vent to such snores and wheezing that the back yard sounded like a factory.

The time came at last. Even Yavtukh closed his eyes as he lay stretched out in the sun. With fear and trembling, the philosopher stealthily made his way into the garden, from which he thought he could more easily escape into the open country without being observed. As is usual with such gardens, it was dreadfully neglected and overgrown, and so made an extremely suitable setting for any secret enterprise. Except for one little path, trodden by the servants on their tasks, it was entirely hidden in a dense thicket of cherry trees, elders, and burdock, which thrust up their tall stems covered with clinging pinkish burs. A network of wild hop was flung over this medley of trees and bushes of varied hues, forming a roof over them, clinging to the fence and falling, mingled with wild bellflowers, from it in coiling snakes. Beyond the fence, which formed the boundary of the garden, there came a perfect forest of tall grass and weeds, which looked as though no one cared to peep enviously into it, and as though any scythe would be broken to bits trying to mow down the stout stubbly stalks.

When the philosopher tried to get over the fence, his teeth chattered and his heart beat so violently that he was frightened at it. The skirts of his long coat seemed to stick to the ground as though someone had nailed them down. As he climbed over, he fancied he heard a voice shout in his ears with a deafening hiss: "Where are you off to?" The philosopher dived into the long grass and started running, frequently stumbling over old roots and trampling upon moles. He saw that when he came out of the tall weeds he would have to cross a field, and that beyond it lay a dark thicket of blackthorn, in which he thought he would be safe. He expected after making his way through it to find the road leading straight to Kiev. He ran across the field at once and found himself in the thicket.

He crawled through the prickly bushes, paying a toll of rags from his coat on every thorn, and came out into a little hollow. A willow with spreading branches bent down almost to the earth. A little brook sparkled pure as silver. The first thing the philosopher did was to lie down and drink, for he was insufferably thirsty. "Good water!" he said, wiping his lips; "I might rest here!"

"No, we had better go straight ahead; they'll be coming to look for you!"

These words rang out above his ears. He looked around—before him was standing Yavtukh. "Curse Yavtukh!" the philosopher thought in his wrath; "I could take you and fling you . . . And I could batter in your ugly face and all of you with an oak post."

"You needn't have gone such a long way around," Yavtukh went on, "you'd have done better to keep to the road I have come by, straight by the stable. And it's a pity about your coat. It's a good cloth. What did you pay a yard for it? But we've walked far enough; it's time to go home."

The philosopher trudged after Yavtukh, scratching himself. "Now the cursed witch will give it to me!" he thought. "Though, after all, what am I thinking about? What am I afraid of? Am I not a Cossack? Why, I've been through two nights, God will help me the third also. The cursed witch committed a fine lot of sins, it seems, since the Evil One makes such a fight for her."

Such were the reflections that absorbed him as he walked into the courtyard. Keeping up his spirits with these thoughts, he asked Dorosh, who through the patronage of the butler sometimes had access to the cellars, to pull out a keg of vodka; and the two friends, sitting in the barn, put away not much less than half a pailful, so that the philosopher, getting on his feet, shouted: "Musicians! I must have musicians!" and without waiting for the latter fell to dancing a jig in a clear space in the middle of the

yard. He danced till it was time for the afternoon snack, and
the servants who stood around him in a circle, as is the custom on
such occasions, at last spat on the ground and walked away,
saying: "Good gracious, how long the fellow keeps it up!" At
last the philosopher lay down to sleep on the spot, and a good
dousing with cold water was needed to wake him up for supper.
At supper he talked of what it meant to be a Cossack, and how
he should not be afraid of anything in the world.

"Time is up," said Yavtukh, "let us go."

"A splinter through your tongue, you damned hog!" thought
the philosopher, and getting to his feet he said: "Come along."

On the way the philosopher kept glancing from side to side
and made faint attempts at conversation with his companions.
But Yavtukh said nothing; and even Dorosh was disinclined to
talk. It was a hellish night. A whole pack of wolves was howling
in the distance, and even the barking of the dogs had a dreadful
sound.

"I imagine something else is howling; that's not a wolf," said
Dorosh. Yavtukh was silent. The philosopher could find nothing
to say.

They drew near the church and stepped under the decaying
wooden domes that showed how little the owner of the place
thought about God and his own soul. Yavtukh and Dorosh withdrew as before, and the philosopher was left alone.

Everything was the same, everything wore the same sinister
familiar aspect. He stood still for a minute. The horrible witch's
coffin was still standing motionless in the middle of the church.

"I won't be afraid; by God, I will not!" he said, and, drawing
a circle around himself as before, he began recalling all his spells
and exorcisms. There was an awful stillness; the candles spluttered
and flooded the whole church with light. The philosopher turned
one page, then turned another, and noticed that he was not reading
what was written in the book. With horror he crossed himself and
began chanting. This gave him a little more courage; the reading
made progress, and the pages turned rapidly one after the other.

All of a sudden . . . in the midst of the stillness . . . the iron
lid of the coffin burst with a crash and the corpse rose up. It was
more terrible than the first time. Its teeth clacked horribly against
each other, its lips twitched convulsively, and incantations came
from them in wild shrieks. A whirlwind swept through the church,

the icons fell to the ground, broken glass came flying down from the windows. The doors were burst from their hinges and a countless multitude of monstrous beings flew into the church of God. A terrible noise of wings and scratching claws filled the church. All flew and raced about looking for the philosopher.

All trace of drink had disappeared, and Khoma's head was quite clear now. He kept crossing himself and repeating prayers at random. And all the while he heard evil creatures whirring around him, almost touching him with their loathsome tails and the tips of their wings. He had not the courage to look at them; he only saw a huge monster, the whole width of the wall, standing in the shade of its matted locks as of a forest; through the tangle of hair two eyes glared horribly with eyebrows slightly lifted. Above it something was hanging in the air like an immense bubble with a thousand claws and scorpion stings stretching from the center; black earth hung in clods on them. They were all looking at him, seeking him, but could not see him, surrounded by his charmed circle. "Bring Viy! Fetch Viy!" he heard the corpse cry.

And suddenly a stillness fell upon the church; the wolves' howling was heard in the distance, and soon there was the thud of heavy footsteps resounding through the church. With a sidelong glance he saw they were bringing a squat, thickset, bandy-legged figure. He was covered all over with black earth. His arms and legs grew out like strong sinewy roots. He trod heavily, stumbling at every step. His long eyelids hung down to the very ground. Khoma saw with horror that his face was of iron. He was supported under the arms and led straight to the spot where Khoma was standing.

"Lift up my eyelids. I do not see!" said Viy in a voice that seemed to come from deep in the earth, and all the creatures flew to raise his eyelids.

"Do not look!" an inner voice whispered to the philosopher. He could not restrain himself, and he looked.

"There he is!" shouted Viy, and thrust an iron finger at him. And all pounced upon the philosopher together. He fell expiring to the ground, and his soul fled from his body in terror.

There was the sound of a cock crowing. It was the second cockcrow; the first had been missed by the gnomes. In panic they rushed to the doors and windows to fly out; but they could not; and so they remained there, stuck in the doors and windows.

When the priest went in, he stopped short at the sight of this defamation of God's holy place, and dared not serve the requiem on such a spot. And so the church was left forever, with monsters stuck in the doors and windows, overgrown with forest trees, roots, rough grass, and wild thorns, and no one can now find the way to it.

When the rumors of this reached Kiev, and the theologian, Khaliava, heard at last of the fate of the philosopher Khoma, he spent a whole hour plunged in thought. Great changes had befallen him during that time. Fortune had smiled on him; on the conclusion of his course of study, he was made bellringer of the very highest belfry, and he was almost always to be seen with a damaged nose, as the wooden staircase to the belfry had been extremely carelessly made.

"Have you heard what has happened to Khoma?" Tibery Gorobets, who by now was a philosopher and had a newly grown mustache, asked, coming up to him.

"Such was the lot God sent him," said Khaliava the bellringer. "Let us go to the tavern and drink to his memory!"

The young philosopher, who was beginning to enjoy his privileges with the ardor of an enthusiast, so that his full trousers and his coat and even his cap reeked of spirits and coarse tobacco, instantly signified his readiness.

"He was a fine fellow, Khoma!" said the bellringer, as the lame tavern keeper placed the third mug before him. "He was a fine man! And he came to grief for nothing."

"I know why he came to grief: it was because he was afraid; if he had not been afraid, the witch could not have done anything to him. You have only to cross yourself and spit right on her tail, and nothing will happen. I know all about it. Why, the old women who sit in our market in Kiev are all witches."

To this the bellringer bowed his head in token of agreement. But, observing that his tongue was incapable of uttering a single word, he cautiously got up from the table, and, lurching to right and to left, went to hide in a remote spot in the rough grass; from the force of habit, however, he did not forget to carry off the sole of an old boot that was lying on the bench.

THE TALE OF HOW IVAN IVANOVICH QUARRELED WITH IVAN NIKIFOROVICH

CHAPTER I

IVAN IVANOVICH AND IVAN NIKIFOROVICH

Ivan Ivanovich has a splendid coat.[1] Superb! And what astrakhan! Phew, damn it all, what astrakhan! Purplish-gray with a frost on it! I'll bet anything you please that nobody can be found with one like it! Now just look at it—particularly when he is standing talking to somebody—look from the side: isn't it delicious? There is no finding words for it. Velvet! Silver! Fire! Merciful Lord! St. Nikolai the Wonder-Worker, Holy Saint! Why don't I have a coat like that! He had it made before Agafya Fedoseevna went to Kiev. You know Agafya Fedoseevna, who bit off the tax assessor's ear?

An excellent man is Ivan Ivanovich! What a house he has in Mirgorod! There's a porch all round it on oak posts, and there

---

[1] *Bekesha,* a short hunting coat made of fur or astrakhan. (ed.)

are seats under the porch everywhere. When the weather is too hot, Ivan Ivanovich casts off his coat and his underwear, remaining in nothing but his shirt, and rests under his porch watching what is passing in the yard and in the street. What apple trees and pear trees he has under his very windows! You need only open the window—and the branches thrust themselves into the room. That is just in the front of the house; but you should see what he has in the garden at the back! What hasn't he got there? Plums, white and black cherries, vegetables of all sorts, sunflowers, cucumbers, melons, peas, even a threshing barn and a forge.

An excellent man is Ivan Ivanovich! He is very fond of a melon: it is his favorite dish. As soon as he has dined and come out into the porch, wearing nothing but his shirt, he at once bids Gapka bring him two melons, and with his own hands cuts them into slices, collects the seeds in a special piece of paper, and begins eating them. And then he tells Gapka to bring the inkstand, and with his own hand writes an inscription on the paper containing the seeds: "This melon was eaten on such and such a date." If some visitor happens to be there, he adds: "So and so was present."

The late Mirgorod judge always looked at Ivan Ivanovich's house with admiration. Yes, the little house is very nice. What I like is that barns and sheds have been built on every side of it so that, if you look at it from a distance, there is nothing to be seen but roofs, lying one over another, very much like a plateful of pancakes or even like those funguses that grow upon a tree. All the roofs are thatched with reeds, however; a willow, an oak tree, and two apple trees lean their spreading branches on them. Little windows with carved and whitewashed shutters peep through the trees and even wink into the street.

An excellent man is Ivan Ivanovich! The Poltava Commissar, Dorosh Tarasovich Pukhivochka, knows him too; when he comes from Khorol, he always goes to see him. And whenever the chief priest, Father Piotr, who lives at Koliberda, has half a dozen visitors, he always says that he knows no one who fulfills the duty of a Christian and knows how to live as Ivan Ivanovich does.

Goodness, how time flies! He had been a widower ten years even then. He had no children. Gapka has children and they often run about the yard. Ivan Ivanovich always gives each of them a slice of melon, or a pear. His Gapka carries the keys of the cupboards and cellars; but the key to the big chest standing in his bedroom, and of the middle cupboard, Ivan Ivanovich keeps himself, and he does not like anyone to go to them. Gapka is a sturdy wench, she goes about in a skirt, has fine healthy calves and fresh cheeks.

And what a devout man Ivan Ivanovich is! Every Sunday he puts on his coat and goes to church. When he goes in Ivan Ivanovich bows in all directions and then usually installs himself in the choir and sings a very good bass. When the service is over, Ivan Ivanovich cannot bear to go away without making the round of the beggars. He would, perhaps, not care to go through this tedious task, if he were not impelled to it by his innate kindliness. "Hello, poor woman!" he commonly says, seeking out the most crippled beggar woman in a tattered gown made up of patches. "Where do you come from, poor thing?"

"I've come from the hamlet, kind sir; I've not had a drop to drink or a morsel to eat for three days; my own children turned me out."

"Poor creature! what made you come here?"

"Well, kind sir, I came to ask alms, in case anyone would give me a copper for bread."

"Hm! Then I suppose you want bread?" Ivan Ivanovich usually inquires.

"Yes I do! I am as hungry as a dog."

"Hm!" Ivan Ivanovich usually replies, "so perhaps you would like meat too?"

"Yes and I'll be glad of anything your honor may be giving me."

"Hm! Is meat better than bread?"

"Is it for a hungry beggar to be choosy? Whatever you kindly give will be greatly appreciated." With this the old woman usually holds out her hand.

"Well, go along and God be with you," says Ivan Ivanovich. "What are you staying for? I am not beating you, am I?"

And after addressing similar inquiries to a second and a third, he at last returns home or goes to drink a glass of vodka with his neighbor, Ivan Nikiforovich, or to see the judge or the police captain.

Ivan Nikiforovich is a very good man, too. His garden is next door to Ivan Ivanovich's. They are such friends as the world has never seen. Anton Prokofievich Golopuz,[2] who goes about to this day in his cinnamon-colored coat with light blue sleeves, and dines on Sundays at the judge's, used frequently to say that the devil himself had tied Ivan Nikiforovich and Ivan Ivanovich together with a string; where the one went the other would turn up also.

Ivan Nikiforovich has never been married. Though people used to say he was going to be married, it was an absolute falsehood. I know Ivan Nikiforovich very well and can say that he has never had the faintest idea of getting married. What does all this gossip spring from? For instance, it used to be rumored that Ivan Nikiforovich was born with a tail. But this invention is so absurd, and at the same time disgusting and improper, that I do not even think it necessary to disprove it to enlightened readers, who must doubtless be aware that none but witches, and only very few of them, in fact, have a tail. Besides, witches belong rather to the female than to the male sex.

In spite of their great affection, these rare friends were not at all alike. Their characters can be best understood by comparison. Ivan Ivanovich has a marvelous gift for speaking extremely pleasantly. Goodness! How he speaks! Listening to him can only be compared with the sensation you have when someone is searching in your hair for lice, or gently passing a finger over your heel. One listens and listens and grows drowsy. It is pleasant! Extremely pleasant! Like a nap after bathing. Ivan Nikiforovich, on the other hand, is rather silent. But if he does rap out a word, one must look out, that's all! He is more cutting than any razor. Ivan Ivanovich is thin and tall; Ivan Nikiforovich is a little shorter, but makes up for it in breadth. Ivan Ivanovich's head is like a radish, tail downwards; Ivan Nikiforovich's head is like a radish, tail upwards. Ivan Ivanovich only lies in the porch in his shirt after dinner; in the evening he puts on his coat and goes off somewhere, either to the town shop which he supplies with flour, or into the country to catch quail. Ivan Nikiforovich lies all day long on his steps, usually with his back to the sun—if it is not too hot a day—and he does not care to go anywhere. If the whim takes him in the morning, he will walk about the yard, see how things are going in the garden and the house, and then go back to rest again. In the old days he used to go around to Ivan Ivanovich sometimes. Ivan Ivanovich is an ex-

[2] "Naked Belly." (ed.)

ceedingly refined man, he never utters an improper word in gentlemanly conversation, and takes offense at once if he hears one. Ivan Nikiforovich is sometimes not so prudent. On those occasions Ivan Ivanovich usually gets up from his seat and says: "That's enough, that's enough, Ivan Nikiforovich; we had better make haste out into the sun instead of uttering such ungodly words." Ivan Ivanovich is very angry if a fly gets into his borsht: he is quite beside himself then—he will throw the plate and his host is sure to catch hell! Ivan Nikiforovich is exceedingly fond of bathing and, when he is sitting up to his neck in water, he orders the table and the samovar to be set in the water too, and is very fond of drinking tea in such refreshing coolness. Ivan Ivanovich shaves his beard twice a week; Ivan Nikiforovich only once. Ivan Ivanovich is exceedingly inquisitive. God forbid that you should begin to tell him about something and not finish the story! If he is displeased with anything, he lets you know it. It is extremely difficult to tell from Ivan Nikiforovich's face whether he is pleased or angry; even if he is delighted at something he will not show it. Ivan Ivanovich is rather of a meek character. Ivan Nikiforovich, on the other hand, wears trousers with such ample folds that if they were blown out you could put the whole courtyard with the barns and the outhouses into them. Ivan Ivanovich has big expressive snuff-colored eyes and a mouth like the letter V; Ivan Nikiforovich has little yellowish eyes completely lost between his thick eyebrows and chubby cheeks, and a nose that looks like a ripe plum. If Ivan Ivanovich offers you snuff, he always first licks the lid of the snuffbox, then taps on it with his finger, and offering it to you, says, if you are someone he knows: "May I make so bold as to ask you to help yourself, sir?" Or if you are someone he does not know: "May I make so bold as to ask you to help yourself, sir, though I have not the honor of knowing your name and your father's and your rank in the service?"

Ivan Nikiforovich puts his horn of snuff straight into your hands and merely adds: "Help yourself." Both Ivan Ivanovich and Ivan Nikiforovich greatly dislike fleas, and so neither Ivan Ivanovich nor Ivan Nikiforovich ever let a Jew with his merchandise pass without buying from him various little bottles of an elixir protecting them from those insects, though they abuse him soundly for professing the Jewish faith. In spite of some dissimilarities, however, both Ivan Ivanovich and Ivan Nikiforovich are excellent people.

CHAPTER II

FROM WHICH MAY BE LEARNED
THE OBJECT OF IVAN IVANOVICH'S DESIRE,
THE SUBJECT OF A CONVERSATION BETWEEN
IVAN IVANOVICH AND IVAN NIKIFOROVICH,
AND IN WHAT WAY IT ENDED

One morning—it was in July—Ivan Ivanovich was lying under his porch. The day was hot, the air was arid and vibrating. Ivan Ivanovich had already been out into the country to see the hay cutters and the farm, and had already asked the peasants and the women he met from where they had come, where they were going, how, and when, and why; he was terribly tired and lay down to rest. As he lay down, he looked around at the storehouses, the yard, the barns, the hens running about the yard, and thought to himself: "Good Lord, what a manager I am! What is there that I have not got? Fowls, buildings, barns, everything I want, herb and berry vodka; pears and plum trees in my orchard; poppies, cabbage, peas in my vegetable garden . . . What is there that I have not got? . . . I should like to know what there is I have not got?"

After putting so profound a question to himself, Ivan Ivanovich sank into thought; meanwhile his eyes were in search of a new object, and, passing over the fence into Ivan Nikiforovich's yard, were involuntarily caught by a curious spectacle. A lean peasant woman was carrying out clothes that had been stored away, and was hanging them out on a line to air. Soon an old uniform with frayed facings stretched its sleeves out in the air and embraced a brocade blouse; after it, a gentleman's dress coat with a crest on the buttons and a moth-eaten collar displayed itself behind it; white cashmere trousers, covered with stains, which had once been drawn over the legs of Ivan Nikiforovich, though now they could scarcely have been drawn on his fingers. After them other garments in the shape of an inverted V were suspended, then a dark blue Cossack coat which Ivan Nikiforovich had had made twenty years before when he had been preparing to enter the military and was already letting his mustaches grow. At last, to put the finishing touch, a sword was displayed that looked like a spire sticking up in the air. Then the tails of something resembling a coat fluttered, grass-green in color and with copper buttons as big as a five-kopek piece. From behind peeped a vest trimmed with gold braid and cut low in front. The vest was soon concealed by the old petticoat of a deceased grandmother with pockets in which one could have stowed a watermelon. All this taken together made up a very interesting spectacle for Ivan Ivanovich, while the sunbeams, catching here and there a blue or a green sleeve, a red cuff or a bit of gold brocade, or playing on the sword that looked like a spire, turned it into something extraordinary, like the show played in the villages by strolling vagrants, when a crowd of people closely packed looks at King Herod in his golden crown or at Anton leading the goat.[3] Behind the scenes[4] the fiddle squeaks; a gypsy claps his hands on his lips by way of a drum, while the sun is setting and the fresh coolness of the southern night imperceptibly creeps closer to the fresh shoulders and full bosoms of the plump village women.

Soon the old woman emerged from the storeroom, sighing and groaning as she hauled along an old-fashioned saddle with broken stirrups, with shabby leather cases for pistols, and a saddlecloth that had once been crimson, embroidered in gold and with copper disks. "That's a stupid woman!" thought Ivan Ivanovich, "next she'll pull out Ivan Nikiforovich and air him!"

And indeed Ivan Ivanovich was not entirely mistaken in this surmise. Five minutes later Ivan Nikiforovich's nankeen trousers were swung up, and filled almost half of the courtyard. After that she brought out his cap and his gun.

"What is the meaning of it?" thought Ivan Ivanovich. "I have never seen a gun at Ivan Nikiforovich's. What does he want with that? He never shoots, but keeps a gun! What use is it to him? But it is a nice thing! I have been wanting to get one like that for a long time past. I should very much like to have that gun; I like to amuse myself with a little gun. Hey, woman!" Ivan Ivanovich shouted, nodding with his finger.

The old woman went up to the fence.

"What's that you have got there, granny?"

"You see yourself—a gun."

---

[3] King Herod and Anton were common figures on the puppet stage. (ed.)

[4] Of the puppet stage. Puppet shows were extremely popular, and the puppet theater was carried from town to town in a large wooden box. The puppet tradition influenced Gogol considerably, most especially in the earliest volume. (ed.)

"What sort of gun?"

"Who can say what sort! If it were mine, I might know, maybe, what it is made of; but it is the master's."

Ivan Ivanovich got up and began examining the gun from every point of view, and even forgot to scold the old woman for hanging it and the sword out to air.

"It's made of iron, one would think," the old woman went on.

"Hm! made of iron. Why is it made of iron?" Ivan Ivanovich said to himself. "Has your master had it long?"

"Maybe he has."

"It's a fine thing!" Ivan Ivanovich went on. "I'll ask him for it. What can he do with it? Or I'll trade him something for it. Granny, is your master at home?"

"Yes."

"What is he doing, lying down?"

"Yes."

"Well, that's all right, I'll come and see him."

Ivan Ivanovich dressed, took his gnarled stick to keep off the dogs, for there are many more dogs in the streets of Mirgorod than there are men, and went out.

Though Ivan Nikiforovich's courtyard was next to Ivan Ivanovich's and one could climb over the fence from one into the other, Ivan Ivanovich went by way of the street. From the street he had to pass into an alley which was so narrow that, if two one-horse carts happened to meet in it, they could not pass, but had to remain in that position until they were each dragged by their back wheels in the opposite direction into the street; as for anyone on foot, he was as apt to be adorned with burdocks, as with flowers. Ivan Ivanovich's cart shed looked into this lane on the one side, and Ivan Nikiforovich's barn, gates, and dovehouse on the other. Ivan Ivanovich went up to the gate and rattled the latch. Dogs began barking from within, but soon a crowd of dogs of various colors ran up, wagging their tails on seeing that it was a person they knew. Ivan Ivanovich crossed the courtyard in which Indian pigeons, fed by Ivan Nikiforovich with his own hand, melon rinds, with here and there green stuff or a broken wheel or a hoop off a barrel, or a boy sprawling in a soiled shirt—made up a picture such as painters love! The shadow cast by the garments on the clothesline covered almost the whole courtyard and gave it some degree of coolness. The woman met him with a bow and stood still, gaping.

Before the house a little porch was adorned with a roof on two oak posts—an unreliable shelter from the sun which at that season in Little Russia shines in deadly earnest and bathes a pedestrian from head to foot in scalding sweat. From this can be seen how strong was Ivan Ivanovich's desire to obtain the indispensable article, since he had even brought himself to break his invariable rule of walking only in the evening by going out at this hour in such weather!

The room into which Ivan Ivanovich stepped was quite dark, because the shutters were closed and the sunbeam that penetrated through a hole in the shutter was broken into rainbow hues and painted upon the opposite wall a multicolored landscape of thatched roofs, trees, and clothes hanging in the yard, but all upside down. This made an uncanny twilight in the whole room.

"God's blessing!" said Ivan Ivanovich.

"Ah, good day, Ivan Ivanovich!" answered a voice from the corner of the room. Only then did Ivan Ivanovich observe Ivan Nikiforovich lying on a rug spread out upon the floor.

"You must excuse my being in a state of nature." Ivan Nikoforovich was lying without anything on, not even his shirt.

"Never mind. Have you slept well today, Ivan Nikiforovich?"

"I have. And have you slept, Ivan Ivanovich?"

"I have."

"So now you have just got up?"

"Just got up? Good gracious, Ivan Nikiforovich! How could I sleep till now! I have just come from the farm. The wheatfields along the roadside are splendid! Magnificent! And the hay is so high and soft and golden!"

"Gorpina!" shouted Ivan Nikiforovich, "bring Ivan Ivanovich some vodka and some pies with sour cream."

"It's a very fine day."

"Don't praise the weather, Ivan Ivanovich. The devil take it! There's no doing anything for the heat!"

"So you must bring the devil in. Aie, Ivan Nikiforovich! you will remember my words, but then it will be too late; you will suffer in the next world for your ungodly language."

"What have I done to offend you, Ivan Ivanovich? I've not referred to your father or your mother. I don't know in what way I have offended you!"

"That's enough, that's enough, Ivan Nikiforovich!"

"I swear I have done nothing to offend you, Ivan Ivanovich!"

"It's strange that the quails still don't come at the birdcall."

"You may think what you like, but I have done nothing to offend you."

"I don't know why it is they don't come," said Ivan Ivanovich as though he did not hear Ivan Nikiforovich; "whether it is not quite time yet . . . though the weather one would think is just right."

"You say the wheatfields are good . . ."

"Magnificent! Magnificent!"

Then followed a silence.

"How is it you are hanging the clothes out, Ivan Nikiforovich?" Ivan Ivanovich said at last.

"Yes, that damned woman has let splendid clothes, almost new, get mildewy; now I am airing them; it's excellent fine cloth, they only need turning and I can wear them again."

"I liked one thing there, Ivan Nikiforovich."

"What's that?"

"Tell me, please, what do you want that gun for that's been hung out to air with the clothes?" At this point Ivan Ivanovich held out a snuffbox. "May I beg you to help yourself?"

"Not at all, you help yourself. I'll take a pinch of my own." With this Ivan Nikiforovich felt about him and got hold of his horn. "There's a stupid woman! So she has hung the gun out, too, has she? Wonderful snuff the Jew makes in Sorochintsy. I don't know what he puts in it, but it's so fragrant! It's a little like balsam. Here, take some, chew a little in your mouth. Isn't it like balsam? Do take some, help yourself!"

"Please tell me, Ivan Nikiforovich, I am still talking of the gun; what are you going to do with it? It's no use to you, you know."

"No use to me, but what if I go shooting?"

"Lord bless you, Ivan Nikiforovich, whenever will you go shooting? At the Second Coming, perhaps? You have never yet killed a single duck as far as I know and as others tell me, and you have not been created by the Lord for shooting. You have a dignified figure and deportment. How could you go trailing about the bogs when that article of your apparel which it is not quite proper to mention is in holes on every occasion as it is? What would it be like then? No, what you want is rest and peace." (Ivan Ivanovich, as we have mentioned already, was extremely picturesque in his speech when he wanted to persuade anyone. How he talked! Goodness, how he talked!) "Yes, you must behave accordingly. Listen, give it to me!"

"What an idea! It's an expensive gun. You can't get guns like that nowadays. I bought it from a Turk when I was going into the military; and to think of giving it away now all of a sudden! Impossible! It's an indispensable thing!"

"What is it indispensable for?"

"What for? Why, if burglars should break into the house . . . Not indispensable, indeed! Now, thank God, my mind is at rest and I am afraid of nobody. And why? Because I know I have a gun in my cupboard."

"A fine gun! Why, Ivan Nikiforovich, the lock is ruined."

"What if it is ruined? It can be repaired; it only needs a little hemp oil to get the rust off."

"I see no kind feeling for me in your words, Ivan Nikiforovich. You won't do anything to show your goodwill."

"What do you mean, Ivan Ivanovich, saying I show you no goodwill? Aren't you ashamed? Your oxen graze on my meadow and I have never once interfered with them. When you go to Poltava you always ask me for my cart, and have I ever refused it? Your little boys climb over the fence into my yard and play with my dogs—I say nothing. Let them play, so long as they don't touch anything! Let them play!"

"Since you don't care to give it to me, perhaps you might exchange it for something?"

"What will you give me for it?" With this Ivan Nikiforovich sat up, leaning on his elbow, and looked at Ivan Ivanovich.

"I'll give you the gray sow, the one that I fed up in the sty. A splendid sow! You'll see if she won't give you a litter of suckling pigs next year."

"I don't know how you can suggest that, Ivan Ivanovich. What use is your sow to me? Am I going to give a banquet at the devil's wake?"

"Again! You must keep bringing the devil in! It's a sin, it really is a sin, Ivan Nikiforovich!"

"How could you really, Ivan Ivanovich, give me for the gun the devil knows what—a sow?"

"Why is she the devil knows what, Ivan Nikiforovich?"

"Why is she? I should think you might know that for yourself.

This is a gun, a thing everyone knows; while that—the devil only knows what to call it—is a sow! If it had not been you speaking, I might have taken it as an insult."

"What fault have you found in the sow?"

"What do you take me for? That I should take a pig . . . ?"

"Sit still, sit still! I will say no more. . . . You may keep your gun, let it rust and rot standing in the corner of the cupboard—I don't want to speak of it again."

A silence followed upon that.

"They say," began Ivan Ivanovich, "that three kings have declared war on our Czar."

"Yes, Piotr Fiodorovich told me so. What does it mean? And what's the war about?"

"There is no saying for certain, Ivan Nikiforovich, what it's about. I imagine that the kings want us all to accept the Turkish faith."

"My word, the fools, what a thing to want!" Ivan Nikiforovich commented, raising his head.

"So you see, and our Czar has declared war on them for that. 'No,' he says, 'you accept the Orthodox faith!' "

"Well, our men will beat them, Ivan Ivanovich, won't they?"

"They certainly will. So you won't trade the gun, Ivan Nikiforovich?"

"I'm surprised at you, Ivan Ivanovich: I believe you are a man noted for your culture and education, but you talk like a boy. Why should I be such a fool . . . ?"

"Sit still, sit still. Forget it! Plague take it; I won't speak of it again."

At that moment some lunch was brought in. Ivan Ivanovich drank a glass of vodka and ate a pie with sour cream.

"I say, Ivan Nikiforovich, I'll give you two sacks of oats besides the sow; you have not sown any oats, you know. You would have to buy oats this year, anyway."

"I swear, Ivan Ivanovich, one should talk to you only after eating beans." (That was nothing; Ivan Nikiforovich would let off phrases worse than that.) "Who has ever heard of swapping a gun for two sacks of oats? I'll bet you won't offer your coat."

"But you forget, Ivan Nikiforovich, I am giving you the sow, too."

"What, two sacks of oats and a sow for a gun!"

"Why, isn't it enough?"

"For the gun?"

"Of course for the gun!"

"Two sacks for a gun?"

"Two sacks, not empty, but full of oats; and have you forgotten the sow?"

"You can go and kiss your sow or the devil, if you prefer him!"

"Oh! You'll see, your tongue will be pierced with red-hot needles for such ungodly sayings. One has to wash one's face and hands and fumigate oneself after talking to you."

"Excuse me, Ivan Ivanovich: a gun is a gentlemanly thing, a very interesting entertainment, besides being a very agreeable ornament to a room . . ."

"You go on about your gun, Ivan Nikiforovich, like a crazy child with a new toy," said Ivan Ivanovich with annoyance, for he was really beginning to feel angry.

"And you, Ivan Ivanovich, are a regular gander."

If Ivan Nikiforovich had not uttered that word, they would have quarreled and have parted friends as they always did; but now something quite different happened. Ivan Ivanovich turned crimson.

"What was that you said, Ivan Nikiforovich?" he asked, raising his voice.

"I said you were like a gander, Ivan Ivanovich!"

"How dare you, sir, forget propriety and respect for a man's rank and family and insult him with such an infamous name?"

"What is there infamous about it? And why are you waving your hands about like that, Ivan Ivanovich?"

"I repeat, how dare you, regardless of every rule of propriety, call me a gander?"

"I sneeze on your head, Ivan Ivanovich. What are you cackling about?"

Ivan Ivanovich could no longer control himself; his lips were quivering; his mouth lost its usual resemblance to the letter V and was transformed into an O; his eyes blinked until it was positively alarming. This was extremely rare with Ivan Ivanovich; he had to be greatly exasperated to be brought to this pass. "Then I beg to inform you," Ivan Ivanovich articulated, "that I do not want to know you."

"No great loss! Upon my word, I won't weep for that!" answered Ivan Nikiforovich.

He was lying, I swear he was! He was very much upset by it.

"I will never set foot in your house again."

"Aha, ah!" said Ivan Nikiforovich, so vexed that he did not know what he was doing, and, contrary to his habit, he rose to his feet. "Hey, woman, boy!" At this the same lean old woman and a small boy muffled in a long and full coat appeared in the doorway.

"Take Ivan Ivanovich by the arms and lead him out of the door!"

"What! A gentleman!" Ivan Ivanovich cried out indignantly, full of a sense of injured dignity. "You only dare! You approach! I will annihilate you together with your stupid master! Even the crows will not find your pieces!" (Ivan Ivanovich used to speak with extraordinary force when his soul was agitated.)

The whole group presented a striking picture: Ivan Nikiforovich, standing in the middle of the room in full beauty completely unadorned! The servingwoman, with her mouth wide open and an utterly senseless terror-stricken expression on her face! Ivan Ivanovich, as the Roman tribunes are depicted, with one arm raised! It was an extraordinary moment, a magnificent spectacle! And meanwhile there was but one spectator: that was the boy in an enormous coat, who stood very tranquilly picking his nose.

At last Ivan Ivanovich took his cap.

"Very nice behavior on your part, Ivan Nikiforovich! Excellent! I will not let you forget it!"

"Go along, Ivan Ivanovich, go along! And mind you don't cross my path. If you do, I will smash your ugly mug, Ivan Ivanovich!"

"So much for that, Ivan Nikiforovich," answered Ivan Ivanovich, making a fig and slamming the door, which squeaked loudly and sprang open again.

Ivan Nikiforovich appeared in the doorway and tried to add something, but Ivan Ivanovich flew out of the yard without looking back.

CHAPTER III

WHAT HAPPENED AFTER THE QUARREL OF IVAN IVANOVICH AND IVAN NIKIFOROVICH

And so two worthy men, the honor and ornament of Mirgorod, had quarreled! And over what? Over a trifle, over a gander. They refused to see each other, and broke off all relations, though they had before this been known as the most inseparable friends! Before this Ivan Ivanovich and Ivan Nikiforovich had sent every day to inquire after each other's health, and used often to converse together from their respective balconies and would say such agreeable things to each other than it warmed the heart to hear them.

On Sundays, Ivan Ivanovich in his cloth coat and Ivan Nikiforovich in his yellowish-brown nankeen Cossack coat used to set off to church almost arm in arm. And if Ivan Ivanovich, who had extremely sharp eyes, first noticed a puddle or filth of any sort in the middle of the street—a thing which sometimes does happen in Mirgorod—he would always say to Ivan Nikiforovich: "Be careful, don't put your foot down here, for it is unpleasant." Ivan Nikiforovich for his part, too, showed the most touching signs of affection, and, however far off he might be standing, always stretched out his hand with his horn of snuff and said: "Help yourself!" And how wonderfully they both managed their lands . . . ! And now these two friends . . . I was thunderstruck when I heard of it! For a long time I refused to believe it. Merciful Heavens! Ivan Ivanovich has quarreled with Ivan Nikiforovich! Such important men! Is there anything in this world one can depend on after that?

When Ivan Ivanovich reached home he was for a long time in a state of violent agitation. It was his habit to go first of all to the stable to see whether the mare was eating her oats (Ivan Ivanovich had a roan mare with a bald patch on her forehead, a very good little beast); then to feed the turkeys and suckling pigs with his own hand; and only then to go indoors, where he either would make wooden bowls (he was very skillful, as good as a turner, at carving things out of wood), or would read a book published by Liuby, Gary, and Popov[5] (Ivan Ivanovich did not remember the title of it, because the servant had long ago torn off the upper part of the title page to amuse a child with it), or would rest in the porch. Now he paid no heed to any of his usual occupations. Instead of doing so, on meeting Gapka he began scolding her for dawdling about doing nothing, though she was dragging grain into the kitchen; he shook his stick at the cock which came to the front steps for its usual tribute; and when a grubby little boy in a tattered shirt ran up to him, shouting, "Daddy, daddy! give me a

---

[5] Early nineteenth-century publishers of popular literature, i.e., cheap illustrated books for the half-literate. (ed.)

cake!" he threatened him and stamped his foot so alarmingly that the terrified boy fled.

At last, however, he recovered himself and began to follow his usual pursuits. He sat down to dinner late, and it was almost evening when he lay down to rest under the porch. The good borsht with pigeons in it which Gapka had cooked completely erased the incident of the morning. Ivan Ivanovich began to look after his garden and household with pleasure again. At last his eyes rested on the neighboring courtyard and he said to himself: "I haven't been to see Ivan Nikiforovich today: I'll go around to him." Saying this, Ivan Ivanovich took his stick and his cap and was going out into the street; but he had scarcely walked out of the gate when he remembered the quarrel, spat on the ground, and turned back. Almost the same action took place in Ivan Nikiforovich's yard. Ivan Ivanovich saw the servingwoman put her foot on the fence with the intention of climbing over into his yard, when suddenly the voice of Ivan Nikiforovich was audible, shouting: "Come back, come back! No need!"

· Ivan Ivanovich felt very dreary, however. It might very well have happened that these worthy men would have been reconciled the very next day, had not a particular event in the house of Ivan Nikiforovich destroyed every hope of reconciliation and poured oil on the fire of resentment when it was on the point of going out.

On the evening of the very same day Agafya Fedoseevna arrived on a visit to Ivan Nikiforovich. Agafya Fedoseevna was neither a relative nor a sister-in-law, nor, indeed, any connection of Ivan Nikiforovich's. One would have thought that she had absolutely no reason to visit him, and he was, indeed, not particularly pleased to see her. She did visit him, however, and used to stay with him for whole weeks at a time and occasionally longer. Then she carried off the keys and took the whole housekeeping into her own hands. This was very disagreeable to Ivan Nikiforovich, but, strange to say, he obeyed her like a child and, though he attempted sometimes to quarrel with her, Agafya Fedoseevna always got the best of it.

I must admit I do not understand why it has been ordained that women should take us by the nose as easily as they take hold of the handle of a teapot: either their hands are so created or our noses are fit for nothing better. And, although Ivan Nikiforovich's nose was rather like a plum, she took him by that nose and made him follow her about like a little dog. Indeed, he reluctantly changed his whole manner of life when she was there: he did not lie so long in the sun, and, when he did lie there, it was not in a state of nature; he always put on his shirt and his trousers, though Agafya Fedoseevna was far from insisting upon it. She was not one to stand on ceremony and, when Ivan Nikiforovich had a feverish attack, she used to rub him herself with her own hands from head to foot with vinegar and turpentine. Agafya Fedoseevna wore a cap on her head, three warts on her nose, and a coffee-colored jacket with yellow flowers on it. Her whole figure resembled a tub, and it was as hard to find her waist as it is to see one's nose without a mirror. Her legs were very short and shaped on the pattern of two cushions. She used to talk scandal and eat pickled beetroot in the mornings, and was a wonderful hand at scolding; and through all these varied pursuits, her face never for one moment changed its expression, a strange peculiarity only found as a rule in women.

As soon as she arrived, everything was turned upside down. "Don't you be reconciled with him, Ivan Nikiforovich, and don't you beg his pardon; he wants to be your ruin; he is that sort of man! You don't know him!" The damned woman went on whispering and whispering, till she brought Ivan Nikiforovich to such a state that he would not hear Ivan Ivanovich's name.

Everything assumed a different aspect. If the neighbor's dog ran into the yard, it was whacked with whatever was handy; if the children climbed over the fence, they came back howling with their little grubby shirts held up and marks of a switch on their backs. Even the servingwoman, when Ivan Ivanovich would have asked her some question, was so rude that Ivan Ivanovich, a man of extreme refinement, could only spit and say: "What a nasty woman! Worse than her master!"

At last, to put the finishing touches to all his offenses, the detested neighbor put up directly opposite, at the spot where the fence was usually climbed, a goose pen, as though specially planned to emphasize the insult. This revolting pen was put up with diabolical rapidity in a single day.

This excited fury and a desire for revenge in Ivan Ivanovich. He did not, however, show any sign of annoyance, although part of the pen was actually on his land; but his heart throbbed so violently that it was extremely hard for him to maintain this outward composure.

So he spent the day. Night came on. . . . Oh, if I were a painter, how wonderfully I could portray the charm of the night! I would picture all Mirgorod sleeping; the countless stars looking down on it immovably; the quiet streets resounding with the barking of the dogs far and near; the lovesick sexton hastening by them and climbing over a fence with chivalrous fearlessness; the white walls of the houses still whiter in the moonlight, while the trees that canopy them are darker, the shadows cast by the trees blacker, the flowers and silent grass more fragrant; while from every corner the crickets, the tireless minstrels of the night, set up their churring song in unison. I would describe how in one of those low-pitched clay houses a black-browed maiden, tossing on her lonely bed, dreams with heaving young breasts of a hussar's spurs and mustache, while the moonlight smiles on her cheeks. I would describe how the black shadow of a bat that settled on the white chimneys flits across the white road. . . . But even so I could hardly have depicted Ivan Ivanovich as he went out that night with a saw in his hand, so many were the different emotions written on his face! Quietly, stealthily, he slunk up and crept under the goose pen. Ivan Nikiforovich's dogs knew nothing as yet of the quarrel between them, and so allowed him as a friend to approach the pen, which stood firmly on four oak posts. Creeping up to the nearest post, he put the saw to it and began sawing. The noise of the saw made him look around every minute, but the thought of the insult revived his courage. The first post was sawn through; Ivan Ivanovich set to work on the second. His eyes were burning and could see nothing because of terror. All at once he uttered a cry and almost fainted; he thought he saw a corpse, but soon he recovered on perceiving that it was the goose, craning its neck at him. Ivan Ivanovich spat with indignation and went on with his work again. The second post, too, was sawn through; the goose house tottered. Ivan Ivanovich's heart began beating so violently as he attacked the third post, that several times he had to stop. More than half of the post was sawn through when all at once the tottering pen lurched violently. . . . Ivan Ivanovich barely had time to leap aside when it came down with a crash. Snatching up the saw in a terrible panic, he ran home and flung himself on his bed, without even courage to look out of the window at the results of his terrible act. He imagined that all Ivan Nikiforovich's household were assembled: the old servingwoman, Ivan Nikiforovich, the boy in the immense overcoat, were all led by Agafya Fedoseevna, coming with clubs to break down and smash his house.

Ivan Ivanovich passed all the following day in a kind of fever. He kept thinking that in revenge his detested neighbor would at least set fire to his house; and so he gave Gapka orders to keep a continual lookout to see whether dry straw had been put down anywhere. At last, to anticipate Ivan Nikiforovich, he made up his mind to be ahead of him and to lodge a complaint against him in the Mirgorod district court. What this meant the reader may learn from the following chapter.

CHAPTER IV

OF WHAT TOOK PLACE IN THE
MIRGOROD DISTRICT COURT

A delightful town is Mirgorod! There are all sorts of buildings in it. Some thatched with straw and some with reeds, some even with a wooden roof. A street to the right, a street to the left, everywhere an excellent fence; over it twines the hop, upon it hang pots and pans, behind it the sunflower displays its sunlike head and one catches glimpses of red poppies and fat pumpkins. . . . Splendid! The fence is always adorned with objects which make it still more picturesque—a checked petticoat stretched out on it or a smock or trousers. There is no thieving nor robbery in Mirgorod, and so everyone hangs on his fence what he thinks fit. If you come from the square, you will certainly stop for a moment to admire the view. There is a pool in it—a wonderful pool! You have never seen one like it! It fills up almost the whole square. A lovely pool! The houses, which might in the distance be taken for haystacks, stand around admiring its beauty.

But to my thinking there is no better house than the district court. Whether it is built of oak or birch wood does not matter to me, but, honored friends, there are eight windows in it! Eight windows in a row, looking straight on the square and onto that stretch of water of which I have spoken already and which the police captain calls the lake! It is the only one painted the color of granite; all the other houses in Mirgorod are simply whitewashed. Its roof is all made of wood, and would, indeed, have been painted red, if the oil intended for that purpose had not been eaten by the office clerks with onions, for, as luck would have it, it was Lent, and so the roof was left unpainted. There are steps leading out to the square, and the hens often run up them, because there are almost always grains or other things eatable scattered on the steps; this is not done on purpose, however, but simply from the carelessness of the petitioners coming to the court. The building is divided into two parts: in one there is the court, in the other there is the jail. In the first part, there are two clean, whitewashed rooms; one the outer room for petitioners to wait in, while in the other there is a table adorned with five inkstands; on the table stands the image of the two-headed eagle, the symbol of office; there are four oak chairs with high backs, and along the walls stand ironbound chests in which the records of the lawsuits of the district are piled up. On one of these chests a polished boot was standing at the moment.

The court had been sitting since early morning. The judge, a rather stout man, though considerably thinner than Ivan Nikiforovich, with a good-natured face and a greasy vest, was talking over a pipe and a cup of tea with the court assessor. The judge's lips were close under his nose, and so his nose could sniff his upper lip to his heart's content. This upper lip served him instead of a snuff-box, for the snuff aimed at his nose almost always settled upon it. And so the judge was talking to the court assessor. At one side a barefooted wench was holding a trayful of cups. At the end of the table the secretary was reading the summing up of a case, but in such a monotonous and depressing tone that the very man whose case it was would have fallen asleep listening to him. The judge would no doubt have been the first to do so if he had not been engaged in an interesting conversation.

"I purposely tried to find out," said the judge, taking a sip of tea, though the cup was by now cold, "how they manage to make them sing so well. I had a wonderful blackbird two years ago. And do you know, it suddenly went off completely and began singing God knows what; and the longer it went on, the worse it got; it took to lisping, wheezing—good for nothing! And you know it was the merest trifle! I'll tell you how it's done. A little pimple no bigger than a pea grows under the throat; this must be pricked with a needle. I was told that by Zakhar Prokofievich, and if you like I'll tell you just how it happened: I was going to see him . . ."

"Am I to read the second, Demyan Demyanovich?" the secretary, who had finished reading some minutes before, broke in.

"Oh, have you finished it already? Imagine, how quick you have been! I haven't heard a word of it! But where is it? Give it here! I'll sign it! What else have you got there?"

"The case of the Cossack Bokitko's stolen cow."

"Very good, read away! Well, so I arrived at his house . . . I can even tell you exactly what he gave me. With the vodka some sturgeon was served, unique! Yes, not like the sturgeon . . ." (At this the judge put out his tongue and smiled, while his nose sniffed his invariable snuffbox) ". . . to which our Mirgorod shop treats us. I didn't taste the herring because, as you are aware, it gives me heartburn; but I tried the caviar—splendid caviar! there can be no two words about it, superb! Then I drank peach vodka distilled with centaury. There was saffron vodka, too; but, as you are aware, I never touch it. It's very nice, you know; it whets the appetite before a meal, they say, and puts a finishing touch afterwards . . . Ah! what do my ears hear, what do my eyes behold . . . !" the judge cried out all at once on seeing Ivan Ivanovich walk in.

"God be with you! I wish you good health!" Ivan Ivanovich pronounced, bowing in all directions with the urbanity which was his peculiar characteristic. My goodness, how he could fascinate us all with his manners! I have never seen such refinement anywhere. He was very well aware of his own consequence, and so looked upon the universal respect in which he was held as his due. The judge himself handed Ivan Ivanovich a chair; his nose drew in all the snuff from his upper lip, which was always a sign with him of great satisfaction.

"What may I offer you, Ivan Ivanovich?" he inquired. "Will you take a cup of tea?"

"No, thank you very much!" answered Ivan Ivanovich; and he bowed and sat down.

"Oh, please do, just a cup!" repeated the judge.

"No, thank you. Very grateful for your hospitality!" answered Ivan Ivanovich. He bowed and sat down.

"Just one cup!" repeated the judge.

"Oh, do not trouble, Demyan Demyanovich!" At this Ivan Ivanovich bowed and sat down.

"One little cup?"

"Well, perhaps just one cup!" pronounced Ivan Ivanovich, and he put out his hand to the tray.

Merciful heavens! The height of refinement in that man! There is no describing the pleasing impression made by such manners!

"May I offer you another cup?"

"No, thank you very much!" answered Ivan Ivanovich, putting the cup turned upside down upon the tray and bowing.

"To please me, Ivan Ivanovich!"

"I cannot; I thank you!" With this Ivan Ivanovich bowed and sat down.

"Ivan Ivanovich! Come now, as a friend, just one cup!"

"No, very much obliged for your kindness!" Saying this, Ivan Ivanovich bowed and sat down.

"Just one cup! One cup!"

Ivan Ivanovich put out his hand to the tray and took a cup.

Bless me! How that man could keep up his dignity!

"I have," said Ivan Ivanovich, after drinking the last drop, "urgent business with you, Demyan Demyanovich: I wish to lodge a complaint." With this Ivan Ivanovich put down his cup and took from his pocket a sheet of stamped paper covered with writing. "A complaint against my enemy, my sworn foe."

"Against whom is that?"

"Against Ivan Nikiforovich Dovgochkhun!"

At these words the judge almost fell off his chair. "What are you saying!" he articulated, flinging up his hands; "Ivan Ivanovich! is this you?"

"You see for yourself it is I!"

"The Lord be with you and all the Holy Saints! What! You, Ivan Ivanovich, have become the enemy of Ivan Nikiforovich! Was it your lips that uttered those words? Say it again! Was not someone hiding behind you and speaking with your voice . . . ?"

"What is there so incredible in it? I cannot bear the sight of him: he has done me a deadly injury, he has insulted my honor!"

"Holy Trinity! How shall I ever tell my mother? She, poor old dear, says every day when my sister and I quarrel: 'You live like cats and dogs, children. If only you would take example from Ivan Ivanovich and Ivan Nikiforovich: once friends, always friends! To be sure they are friends! To be sure they are excellent people!' Fine friends after all! Tell me, what's it all about? How is it?"

"It's a delicate matter, Demyan Demyanovich! It cannot be told by word of mouth: better bid your secretary read my petition. Take it in that way; it would be more proper here."

"Read it aloud, Taras Tikhonovich!" said the judge, turning to the secretary. Taras Tikhonovich took the petition and, blowing his nose as all secretaries in district courts do blow their noses, that is, with the help of two fingers, began reading:

"From Ivan, son of Ivan Pererepenko, gentleman and landowner of the Mirgorod district, a petition; whereof the following points ensue:

"(1) Whereas the gentleman Ivan, son of Nikifor Dovgochkhun, notorious to all the world for his godless lawfully-criminal actions which overstep all bounds and provoke aversion, did, on the seventh day of July of the present year 1810, perpetrate a deadly insult upon me, both personally affecting my honor and likewise for the humiliation and confusion of my rank and family. The said gentleman is, moreover, of loathsome appearance, has a quarrelsome temper, and abounds with blasphemous and abusive words of every description . . ."

Here the reader made a slight pause to blow his nose again, while the judge folded his arms with a feeling of reverence and said to himself: "What a clever pen! Lord have mercy on us! How the man does write!"

Ivan Ivanovich begged the secretary to read on, and Taras Tikhonovich continued:

"The said gentleman, Ivan, son of Nikifor Dovgochkhun, when I went to him with friendly propositions, called me publicly by an insulting name derogatory to my honor, to wit, 'gander,' though it is well known to all the district of Mirgorod that I have never had the name of that disgusting animal and do not intend to be so named in the future. The proof of my gentle origin is the fact that in the register in the church of the Three Holy Bishops, there is recorded both the day of my birth and likewise the name given me in baptism. A 'gander,' as all who have any knowledge whatever of science are aware, cannot be inscribed in the register, seeing that a 'gander' is not a man but a bird, a fact thoroughly well known to everyone, even though he may not have been to a seminary. But the aforesaid pernicious gentleman, though fully aware of all this, abused me with the aforesaid foul name for no other purpose than to inflict a deadly insult to my rank and station.

"(2) This same unmannerly and ungentlemanly gentleman has inflicted damage, moreover, upon my private property, inherited by me from my father of the clerical calling, Ivan of blessed memory, son of Onisy Pererepenko, inasmuch as in contravention of every law he has moved a goose pen precisely opposite my front entrance, which was done with no other design but to emphasize the insult paid me, forasmuch as the said goose pen had till then been standing in a suitable place and was fairly solid. But the abominable plan of the aforesaid gentleman was solely to compel me to witness unseemly incidents: forasmuch as it is well known that no man goes into a pen, above all a goose pen, for any proper purpose. In carrying out this illegal action the two foremost posts have trespassed upon my private property, which passed into my possession in the lifetime of my father, Ivan of blessed memory, son of Onisy Pererepenko, which runs in a straight line from the barn to the place where the women wash their pots.

"(3) The gentleman described above, whose very name inspires aversion, cherishes in his heart the wicked design of setting fire to me in my own house. Whereof unmistakable signs are manifest from what follows: in the first place, the said pernicious gentleman has taken to emerging frequently from his apartments, which he never did in the past by reason of his slothfulness and the repulsive corpulence of his person; in the second place, in the servants' quarters adjoining the very fence which is the boundary of my land inherited by me from my late father, Ivan of blessed memory, son of Onisy Pererepenko, there is a light burning every day and for an exceptional length of time, which same is manifest proof thereof; inasmuch as hitherto through his niggardly stinginess not only the tallow candle but even the little oil lamp was always put out.

"And therefore I petition that the said gentleman, Ivan, son of Nikifor Dovgochkhun, as being guilty of arson, of insulting my rank, name, and family, and of covetously appropriating my property, and above all for the vulgar and reprehensible coupling with my name the title of 'gander,' be condemned to the payment of a fine together with all costs and expenses, and himself be thrown into fetters as a lawbreaker, and put in the prison of the town, and that this my petition may meet with prompt and immediate attention. Written and composed by Ivan, son of Ivan Pererepenko, gentleman and landowner of Mirgorod."

When the petition had been read, the judge drew nearer to Ivan Ivanovich, took him by a button, and began addressing him in somewhat this fashion: "What are you doing, Ivan Ivanovich? Have some fear of God! Drop the petition, the devil take it! (Let Satan enjoy it!) Much better shake hands with Ivan Nikiforovich and kiss him, and buy some santurin or nikopol wine or simply make some punch and invite me! We'll have a good drink together and forget it all!"

"No, Demyan Demyanovich, this is not a matter," said Ivan Ivanovich with the dignity which always suited him so well, "this is not a matter which admits of an amicable settlement. Goodbye! Goodbye to you, too, gentlemen!" he continued with the same dignity, turning to the rest of the company: "I trust that the necessary steps will in due course be taken in accordance with my petition." And he went out, leaving everyone present in amazement.

The judge sat without saying a word; the secretary took a pinch of snuff; the clerks upset the broken bottle which served them for an inkstand, and the judge himself was so absent-minded that he enlarged the pool of ink on the table with his finger.

"What do you say to this, Dorofei Trofimovich?" said the judge after a brief silence, turning to the assessor.

"I say nothing," said the assessor.

"What things people do!" the judge went on. He had hardly uttered the words when the door creaked and the front half of Ivan Nikiforovich landed in the office—the remainder of him was still in the hall. That Ivan Nikiforovich should appear, and in the court, too, seemed so extraordinary that the judge cried out, the secretary interrupted his reading, one clerk, in a frieze semblance of a dress coat, put his pen in his lips, while another swallowed a fly. Even the veteran with a stripe on his shoulder who discharged the duties of messenger and house porter, and who had before this been standing at the door scratching himself under his dirty shirt—even he gaped and stepped on somebody's foot.

"What fate has brought you? How and why? How are you, Ivan Nikiforovich?"

But Ivan Nikiforovich was more dead than alive, for he had become stuck in the doorway and could not take a step backwards or forwards. In vain the judge shouted to anyone who might be in the waiting room to shove Ivan Nikiforovich from behind into the court. There was nobody in the waiting room but an old woman who had come with a petition, and in spite of all her efforts she could do nothing with her skinny hands. Then one of the clerks, a broad-shouldered fellow with thick lips and a thick nose, with a drunken look in his squinting eyes, and ragged elbows, approached the foremost half of Ivan Nikiforovich, folded the latter's arms across his chest as though he were a baby, and winked to the veteran, who shoved with his knee in Ivan Nikiforovich's belly, and in spite of the latter's piteous moans he was squeezed out into the waiting room. Then they drew back the bolts and opened the second half of the door, during which operation the united efforts and heavy breathing of the clerk and his assistant, the veteran, diffused such a powerful odor about the room that the court seemed transformed for a time into a tavern.

"I hope you are not hurt, Ivan Nikiforovich? I'll tell my mother and she'll send you a lotion; you only rub it on your back and it will all pass off."

But Ivan Nikiforovich flopped into a chair, and except for prolonged sighs and groans could say nothing. At last in a faint voice hardly audible from exhaustion he said: "Would you like some?" and taking his snuff horn from his pocket added: "take some, help yourself!"

"Delighted to see you," answered the judge, "but still I cannot imagine what has led you to take so much trouble and to oblige us with such an agreeable surprise."

"A petition . . ." was all Ivan Nikiforovich could articulate.

"A petition? What sort of petition?"

"A complaint . . ." (Here breathlessness led to a prolonged pause.) "Oh! . . . a complaint against that scoundrel . . . Ivan Ivanovich Pererepenko!"

"Good Lord! You at it too! Such rare friends! A complaint against such an exemplary man . . . !"

"He is the devil himself!" Ivan Nikiforovich pronounced abruptly.

The judge crossed himself.

"Take my petition, read it!"

"There is nothing we can do, read it aloud, Taras Tikhonovich," said the judge, addressing the secretary with an expression of displeasure, though his nose unconsciously sniffed his upper lip, which it commonly did only from great satisfaction. Such perversity on the part of his nose caused the judge even more vexation: he took out his handkerchief and swept from his upper lip all the snuff, to punish its insolence.

The secretary, after going through his usual performance, which he invariably did before beginning to read, that is, blowing his nose without the assistance of a handkerchief, began in his ordinary voice, as follows:

"The petition of Ivan, son of Nikifor Dovgochkhun, gentleman of the Mirgorod district, whereof the following points ensue:

"(1) Whereas by his spiteful hatred and undisguised ill-will, the self-styled gentleman, Ivan, son of Ivan Pererepenko, is committing all sorts of mean, injurious, malicious, and shocking actions against me, and yesterday, like a robber and a thief, broke—with axes, saws, screwdrivers, and all sorts of carpenter's tools—at night into my yard and into my private pen situate therein, and with his own hand, and infamously hacked it to pieces, whereas on my side I had given no cause whatever for so lawless and burglarious a proceeding.

"(2) The said gentleman Pererepenko has designs upon my life, and, concealing the said design until the seventh of last month, came to me and began in cunning and friendly fashion begging from me a gun, which stands in my room, and with his characteristic meanness offered me for it many worthless things such as a gray sow and two measures of oats. But, guessing his criminal design at the time, I tried in every way to dissuade him therefrom; but the aforesaid blackguard and scoundrel, Ivan, son of Ivan Pererepenko, swore at me like a peasant and from that day has cherished an implacable hostility toward me. Moreover, the often aforementioned ferocious gentleman and brigand, Ivan, son of Ivan Pererepenko, is of a very ignoble origin: his sister was known to all the world as a strumpet, and left the place with the regiment of light cavalry stationed five years ago at Mirgorod and registered her husband as a peasant; his father and mother, too, were exceedingly lawless people, and both were incredible drunkards. But the aforementioned gentleman and robber, Pererepenko, has surpassed all his family in his beastly and reprehensible behaviour, and under a show of piety is guilty of the most profligate conduct: he does not keep the fasts, seeing that on St. Philip's Eve the godless man bought a sheep and next day bade his illegitimate wench Gapka slaughter it, alleging that he had need at once for tallow for lamps and candles.

"Wherefore I petition that the said gentleman may, as guilty of robbery, sacrilege, and cheating, and caught in the act of theft and burglary, be thrown into fetters and cast into the jail of the town or prison of the province, and there as may seem best, after being deprived of his grades and nobility, be soundly flogged and be sent to hard labor in Siberia if need be, and be ordered to pay all costs and expenses, and that this my petition may receive immediate attention. To this petition, Ivan, son of Nikifor Dovgochkhun, gentleman of the Mirgorod district, herewith puts his hand."

As soon as the secretary had finished reading, Ivan Nikiforovich picked up his cap and bowed with the intention of going away.

"Where are you off to, Ivan Nikiforovich?" the judge called after him. "Stay a little! Have some tea! Oryshko! Why are you standing there, foolish girl, winking at the clerks? Go and bring some tea!"

But Ivan Nikiforovich, terrified at having come so far from home and having endured so dangerous a quarantine, was already through the doorway saying: "Don't put yourself out, with pleasure I'll . . ." and he shut the door after him, leaving all the court in amazement.

There was no helping the situation. Both petitions had been received and the case seemed likely to awaken considerable interest, when an unforeseen circumstance gave it an even more remarkable character. When the judge had gone out of the court, accompanied by the assessor and the secretary, and the clerks were stowing away into a sack the various fowls, eggs, pies, rolls, and other trifles brought by the petitioners, the gray sow ran into the room and, to the surprise of all present, seized—not a pie or a crust of bread, but Ivan Nikiforovich's petition, which was lying at the end of the table with its pages hanging over the edge. Snatching up the petition, the gray grunter ran out so quickly that not one of the clerks could overtake her, in spite of the rulers and inkpots that were thrown after her.

This extraordinary incident caused a terrible commotion, because they had not taken a copy of the petition. The judge, his secretary, and the assessor spent a long time arguing over this unprecedented event; at last it was decided to write a report on it to the police captain, since proceedings in this matter were more the concern of the city police. The report, No. 389, was sent to him the same day and led to rather an interesting explanation, of which the reader may learn from the next chapter.

CHAPTER V

IN WHICH IS DESCRIBED A CONSULTATION
BETWEEN TWO PERSONAGES HIGHLY RESPECTED
IN MIRGOROD

Ivan Ivanovich had only just seen after his household duties and gone out, as his habit was, to lie down in the porch, when to his unutterable surprise he saw something red at the garden gate. It was the police captain's red cuff which, like his collar, had acquired a glaze, and at the edges was being transformed into polished leather. Ivan Ivanovich thought to himself: "It's just as well that Piotr Fiodorovich has come for a little talk"; but he was much surprised to see the police captain walking extremely fast and waving his hands, which he did not do as a rule. There were eight buttons on the police captain's uniform; the ninth had been torn off during the procession at the consecration of the church two years before, and the police constables had not yet been able to find it; though when the superintendents presented the police captain with their daily reports he invariably inquired whether the button had been found. These eight buttons had been sewn on as peasant women sow beans, one to the right and the next to the left. His left leg had been struck by a bullet in his last campaign, and so, as he limped along, he flung it so far to one side that it almost canceled all the work done by the right leg. The more rapidly the police captain forced the march the less he advanced, and so, while he was approaching the porch, Ivan Ivanovich had time enough to lose himself in conjecture why the police captain was waving his arms so vigorously. This interested him all the more as he thought the latter's business must be of exceptional importance, since he was actually wearing his new sword.

"Good day, Piotr Fiodorovich!" cried Ivan Ivanovich, who, as we have said already, was very inquisitive and could not restrain his impatience at the sight of the police captain attacking the step, still not raising his eyes, but struggling with his unruly legs which were utterly unable to take the step at one assault.

"A very good day to my dear friend and benefactor, Ivan Ivanovich!" answered the police captain.

"Pray be seated. You are tired I see, for your wounded leg hinders . . ."

"My leg!" cried the police captain, casting upon Ivan Ivanovich a glance such as a giant casts on a pigmy or a learned pedant on a dancing master. With this he stretched out his foot and stamped on the floor with it. This display of valor, however, cost him dear, for his whole person lurched forward and his nose pecked the railing; but the sage guardian of order, to preserve appearances, at once righted himself and felt in his pocket as though to get out his snuffbox.

"I can assure you, my dearest friend and benefactor, Ivan Ivanovich, that I have made worse marches in my time. Yes, seriously I have. For instance during the campaign of 1807 . . . Ah, I'll tell you how I climbed over a fence to visit a pretty German." With this the police captain screwed up one eye and gave a fiendishly sly smile.

"Where have you been today?" asked Ivan Ivanovich, desirous of cutting the police captain short and bringing him as quickly as possible to the occasion of his visit. He would very much have liked to ask what it was the police captain intended to tell him; but a refined *savoir faire* made him feel the impropriety of such a question, and Ivan Ivanovich was obliged to control himself and to wait for the solution of the mystery, though his heart was throbbing with unusual violence.

"By all means, I will tell you where I have been," answered the police captain; "in the first place I must tell you that it is beautiful weather today . . ."

The last words were almost too much for Ivan Ivanovich.

"But excuse me," the police captain went on, "I've come to you today about an important matter." Here the police captain's face and deportment resumed the anxious expression with which he had attacked the steps. Ivan Ivanovich revived, and trembled as though he were in a fever, though as his habit was, he promptly asked:

"What is it? Important? Is it really important?"

"Well, you will see: first of all, I must hasten to inform you, dear friend and benefactor, Ivan Ivanovich, that you . . . for my part kindly observe I say nothing, but the laws of government, the laws of government demand it: you have committed a breach of public order!"

"What are you saying, Piotr Fiodorovich? I don't understand a word of it."

"I swear, Ivan Ivanovich! How can you say you don't understand a word of it? Your own beast has carried off a very important legal document, and after that you say you don't understand a word of it!"

"What beast?"

"If I may say so, your own gray sow."

"And how am I to blame? Why did the court porter open the door?"

"But, Ivan Ivanovich, the beast is your property; so you are to blame."

"I am very much obliged to you for putting me on a level with a sow."

"Come, I did not say that, Ivan Ivanovich! Dear me, I did not say that! Kindly consider the question yourself with an open mind. You are undoubtedly aware that, in accordance with the laws of government, unclean animals are prohibited from walking about in the town, especially in the principal streets. You must admit that that's prohibited."

"God knows what you are talking about. As though it mattered a sow going out into the street!"

"Allow me to put to you, allow me, allow me, Ivan Ivanovich; it's utterly impossible. What can we do? It's the will of the government, we must obey. I do not dispute the fact that fowls and geese sometimes run into the street and even into the square—fowls and geese, mind; but even last year I issued a proclamation that pigs and goats were not to be allowed in public squares, and I ordered that proclamation to be read aloud before the assembled people."

"Well, Piotr Fiodorovich, I see nothing in all this but that you are trying to insult me in every way possible."

"Oh, you can't say that, my dear friend and benefactor, you can't say that I am trying to insult you! Think yourself: I didn't say a word to you last year when you put up a roof fully a yard higher than the legal height. On the contrary, I pretended I hadn't noticed it at all. Believe me, dearest friend, on this occasion, too, I would absolutely, so to speak . . . but my duty, my office, in fact, requires me to look after public cleanliness. Only consider when all at once there rushes into the main street . . ."

"Your main street, indeed! Why, every peasant woman goes there to fling away what she does not want."

"Allow me to say, Ivan Ivanovich, that it's you who are insulting me! It is true it does happen at times, but mostly under a fence, or behind barns or sheds; but that a sow in farrow should run into the main street, the square, is a thing that . . ."

"Good gracious, Piotr Fiodorovich! Why, a sow is God's creation!"

"Agreed. All the world knows that you are a learned man, that you are versed in the sciences and all manner of subjects. Of course, I have never studied any sciences at all. I began to learn to write only when I was thirty. You see, I rose from the ranks, as you are aware."

"Hm!" said Ivan Ivanovich.

"Yes," the police captain went on, "in 1801 I was in the forty-second regiment of light cavalry, an ensign in the fourth company. Our company commander was—if you will allow me to say so—Captain Eremeev." At this the police captain put his finger into the snuffbox which Ivan Ivanovich held open and fiddled with the snuff.

Ivan Ivanovich answered: "Hm."

"But my duty," the police captain went on, "is to obey the commands of government. Are you aware, Ivan Ivanovich, that anyone who steals a legal document in a court of law is liable like any other criminal to be tried in a criminal court?"

"I am so well aware of it that if you like I will teach you. That applies to human beings; for instance, if you were to steal a document; but a sow is an animal, God's creation."

"Quite so, but the law says one guilty of stealing . . . I beg you to note attentively, one guilty! Nothing is here defined as to species, sex, or calling; therefore an animal, too, may be guilty. Say what you like, but until sentence is passed on it, the animal ought to be handed over to the police, as guilty of a breach of order."

"No, Piotr Fiodorovich," retorted Ivan Ivanovich coolly, "that will not be so!"

"As you like, but I am bound to follow the regulations of government."

"Why are you threatening me? I suppose you mean to send the

one-armed soldier for her? I'll bid my servant girl show him out with the poker; his remaining arm will be broken."

"I will not venture to argue with you. In that case, if you will not hand her over to the police, make what use you like of her; cut her up, if you like, for Christmas, and make her into ham or eat her as fresh pork. Only I should like to ask you, if you will be making sausages, to send me just a couple of those your Gapka makes so nicely of the blood and fat. My Agrafena Trofimovna is very fond of them."

"Certainly I'll send you a couple of sausages."

"I shall be very grateful to you, dear friend and benefactor. Now allow me to say just one more word. I am charged by the judge and, indeed, by all our acquaintances, so to speak, to reconcile you with your friend, Ivan Nikiforovich."

"What! That boor! Reconcile me with that ruffian! Never! That will never be! Never!" Ivan Ivanovich was in an extremely resolute mood.

"Have it your own way," answered the police captain, regaling both nostrils with snuff. "I will not venture to advise you; however, allow me to put it to you: here you are now on bad terms, while if you are reconciled . . ."

But Ivan Ivanovich began talking about catching quails, which was his usual resource when he wanted to change the subject.

And so the police captain was obliged to go about his business without having achieved any success whatever.

CHAPTER VI

FROM WHICH THE READER MAY EASILY LEARN ALL THAT IS CONTAINED THEREIN

In spite of all the efforts of the court to conceal the affair, the very next day all Mirgorod knew that Ivan Ivanovich's sow had carried off Ivan Nikiforovich's petition. The police captain himself, in a moment of forgetfulness, first let slip a word. When Ivan Nikiforovich was told of it, he made no comment; he only asked: "Wasn't it the gray one?"

But Agafya Fedoseevna, who was present at the time, began needling Ivan Nikiforovich again: "What are you thinking about, Ivan Nikiforovich? You'll be laughed at as a fool if you let it pass!

A fine gentleman you'll be after this! You'll be lower than the peasant woman who sells the doughnuts you are so fond of."

And the pertinacious woman talked him around! She picked up a swarthy middle-aged man with pimples all over his face, in a dark blue coat with patches on the elbows, a typical scribbling pettifogger! He smeared his high boots with tar, wore three pens in his ear and a glass bottle by way of an inkpot tied on a string to a button. He would eat nine pies at a sitting and put the tenth in his pocket, and would write so much of all manner of legal chicanery on a single sheet of stamped paper that nobody could read it aloud straight off without intervals of coughing and sneezing. This little image of a man rummaged about, racked his brains and wrote, and at last concocted the following document:

"To the Mirgorod district court from the nobleman Ivan, son of Nikifor Dovgochkhun.

"Concerning the aforesaid my petition the which was from me, the gentleman Ivan, son of Nikifor Dovgochkhun, relating to the gentleman Ivan, son of Ivan Pererepenko, wherein which the district court of Mirgorod has manifested its partiality. And the same brash arbitrariness of the gray sow which was kept a secret and has reached our ears from persons in no way concerned therewith. Whereto the partiality and connivance, as of evil intention, falls within the jurisdiction of the law; inasmuch as the aforesaid sow is a foolish creature and thereby the more apt for the stealing of papers. Wherefrom it is evidently apparent that the sow frequently aforementioned, could not otherwise than have been incited to the same by the opposing party, the self-styled gentleman, Ivan, son of Ivan Pererepenko, the same having been already detected in housebreaking, attempted murder, and sacrilege. But the aforesaid Mirgorod court with its characteristic partiality manifested its tacit connivance; without the which connivance the aforesaid sow could by no manner of means have been admitted to the stealing of the paper, inasmuch as the Mirgorod district court is well provided with service; to which intent it is sufficient to name one soldier present on all occasions in the reception room, who, though he has a cross-eye and a somewhat useless arm, is yet fully capable of driving out a sow and striking her with a stick. Wherefrom the connivance of the aforesaid Mirgorod court thereto is proven and the partition of the ill-gotten profits therefrom on mutual terms is abundantly evident. The aforesaid robber and gentleman, Ivan, son of Ivan Pererepenko, is manifestly the scoundrelly accomplice therein. Wherefore, I, the gentleman Ivan, son of Nikifor Dovgochkhun, do herewith inform the said district court that if the petition above-mentioned shall not be recovered from the aforesaid gray sow, or from the gentleman Pererepenko, her accomplice, and if proceedings shall not be taken upon it in accordance with justice and in my favor, then I, the gentleman, Ivan, son of Nikifor, will lodge a complaint with the higher court concerning such illegal connivance of the aforesaid district court, transferring the case thereto with all due formalities.

"Ivan, son of Nikifor Dovgochkhun, gentleman of the Mirgorod district."

This petition produced its effect. The judge, like good-natured people as a rule, was a man of cowardly disposition. He appealed to the secretary. But the secretary emitted a bass "Hm" through his lips, while his face wore the expression of unconcern and diabolical ambiguity which appears only on the face of Satan when he sees the victim who has appealed to him lying at his feet. One resource only was left: to reconcile the two friends. But how approach that when all attempts had up to now been unsuccessful? However, they decided to try again; but Ivan Ivanovich declared point-blank that he would not hear of it, and was, indeed, very much incensed. Ivan Nikiforovich turned his back instead of answering, and did not utter a word. Then the case went forward with the extraordinary rapidity for which our courts of justice are so famous. A document was registered, inscribed, docketed, filed, copied, all in one and the same day; and then the case was laid on a shelf, where it lay and lay and lay for one year and a second and a third. Numbers of young girls had time to get married; a new street was laid down in Mirgorod, the judge lost one molar and two side teeth; more small children were running about Ivan Ivanovich's yard than before (goodness only knows where they sprang from); to spite Ivan Ivanovich, Ivan Nikiforovich built a new goose pen, though a little further away than the first, and so completely screened himself from Ivan Ivanovich that these worthy gentlemen scarcely ever saw each others' faces—and still the case lay in perfect order, in the cupboard which had been turned to marble by inkstains.

Meanwhile there occurred an event of the greatest importance in Mirgorod. The police captain was giving a party! Where can I find brushes and colors to paint the variety of the assembly and the magnificence of the entertainment? Take a clock, open it, and look what is going on there! Terribly confusing, isn't it? Now imagine as many if not more wheels standing in the police captain's courtyard. What chaises and traveling carriages were not there! One had a wide back and a narrow front; another a narrow back but a wide front. One was a chaise and a covered trap both at once; another was neither chaise nor trap; one was like a huge haystack or a fat merchant's wife; another was like a disheveled Jew or a skeleton that had not quite got rid of its skin. One was in profile exactly like a pipe with a long mouthpiece; another a strange creation, utterly shapeless and fantastic, was unlike anything in the world. From the midst of this chaos of wheels and box seats rose the semblance of a carriage with a window like that of a room, with a thick bar right across it. The coachmen in gray Cossack coats, tunics, and gray jerkins, in sheepskin hats and caps of all patterns, with pipes in their hands, led the unharnessed horses about the courtyards. What a party it was that the police captain gave! Allow me, I will enumerate all who were there: Taras Tarasovich, Evpl Akinfovich, Evtikhy Evtikhievich, Ivan Ivanovich—not *the* Ivan Ivanovich, but the other—Savva Gavrilovich, our Ivan Ivanovich, Elevfery Elevferievich, Makar Nazaryevich, Foma Grigorievich . . . I cannot go on! It is too much for me! My hand is tired from writing! And how many ladies there were! Dark and fair, and long and short, stout as Ivan Nikiforovich, and so thin that it seemed as though one could hide each one of them in the scabbard of the police captain's sword. What hats! What dresses! Red, yellow, coffee-colored, green, blue, new, turned and remade —fichus, ribbons, reticules! Goodbye to my poor eyes! They will be no more use after that spectacle. And what a long table was drawn out! And how everybody talked; what an uproar there was! A mill with all its clappers, grindstones, and wheels going is nothing to it! I cannot tell you for certain what they talked about, but it must be supposed that they discussed many interesting and important topics, such as the weather, dogs, ladies' hats, wheat, horses. At last Ivan Ivanovich—not *the* Ivan Ivanovich but the other one who squinted—said: "I am very much surprised that my right eye" (the squinting Ivan Ivanovich always spoke ironically of himself) "does not see Ivan Nikiforovich."

"He would not come!" said the police captain.

"How is that?"

"Well, it's two years, thank God, since they had a quarrel, that is, Ivan Ivanovich and Ivan Nikiforovich, and wherever one goes the other won't come on any account!"

"What are you telling me!" At this the squinting Ivan Ivanovich turned his eyes upward and clasped his hands together.

"Well, now, if men with good eyes don't live in peace, how am I to see eye to eye with anyone!"

At these words everyone laughed heartily. We were all very fond of the squinting Ivan Ivanovich, because he used to make jokes that were precisely in the taste of the day. Even a tall lean man in a wadded overcoat with a plaster on his nose who had before this been sitting in the corner without the slightest change in the expression of his face, even when a fly flew up his nose—even this gentleman rose from his seat and moved nearer to the crowd surrounding the squinting Ivan Ivanovich.

"Do you know what," the latter said when he saw a goodly company standing around him, "instead of gazing at my cross-eye, as you are now, let us reconcile our two friends! At this moment Ivan Ivanovich is conversing with the ladies—let us send on the sly for Ivan Nikiforovich and bring them together."

All agreed with Ivan Ivanovich's suggestion and decided to send at once to Ivan Nikiforovich's house to beg him most particularly to come to dine with the police captain. But the important question to whom to entrust this weighty commission puzzled everyone. They discussed at length who was most capable and most skillful in the diplomatic line; at last, it was unanimously resolved to confide the task to Anton Prokofievich Golopuz.

But we must first make the reader a little acquainted with this remarkable person. Anton Prokofievich was a perfectly virtuous man in the full meaning of that word; if any of the worthy citizens of Mirgorod gave him a scarf or a pair of trousers, he thanked them; if any gave him a slight flip on the nose, he thanked them even then. If he were asked: "Why is it your frock coat is brown, Anton Prokofievich, but the sleeves are blue?" he almost always answered: "And you haven't one at all! Wait a little while, it will

soon be shabby and then it will be all alike!" And in fact the blue
cloth began, from the effect of the sun, to turn brown, and now it
goes perfectly well with the color of the coat. But what is strange
is that Anton Prokofievich has the habit of wearing cloth clothes
in the summer and cotton in the winter. He has no house of his
own. He used to have one at the end of the town, but he sold it
and with the money he got for it he bought three bay horses and
a small chaise, in which he used to ride about visiting the neighboring landowners. But as the horses gave him a great deal of trouble, and besides he needed money to buy them oats, Anton Prokofievich swapped them for a fiddle and a serf girl, receiving a
twenty-five ruble note in the bargain. Then Anton Prokofievich
sold the fiddle and swapped the girl for a morocco purse set with
gold, and now he has a purse the like of which no one else pos-
sesses. He pays for this gratification by not being able to drive
about the countryside, and is forced to remain in town and to spend
his nights at different houses, especially those of the gentlemen
who derive pleasure from flipping him on the nose. Anton Prokofievich is fond of good food and plays pretty well at "Fools"
and "Millers." [6] Obedience has always been his natural element,
and so, taking his cap and his stick, he set off immediately.

But as he went, he began thinking how he was to make Ivan
Nikiforovich come to the reception. The somewhat harsh character of that otherwise estimable individual made his task almost an
impossible one. And, indeed, how could he be induced to come
when even to get out of bed was a very great effort for him?
And even supposing that he did get up, was he likely to go where
—as he undoubtedly knew—his irreconcilable enemy was to be
found? The more Anton Prokofievich considered the subject, the
more difficulties he found. The day was sultry; the sun was scorch-
ing; the perspiration poured down him in streams. Anton Prokofievich, though he was flipped on the nose, was rather a wily man in
many ways. It was only in swapping that he was rather unlucky.
He knew very well when he had to pretend to be a fool, and
sometimes knew how to hold his own in circumstances and cases in
which a clever man cannot often steer his course.

While his resourceful mind was thinking out means for per-
suading Ivan Nikiforovich, and he was going valiantly to face

---

[6] *Durak* and *melnik*, popular card games. (ed.)

the worst, an unexpected circumstance somewhat disconcerted him. It will not be amiss at this juncture to inform the reader that Anton Prokofievich had, among other things, a pair of trousers with the strange peculiarity of attracting all the dogs to bite his calves whenever he put them on. As ill-luck would have it, he had put on those trousers that day, and so he had hardly abandoned himself to meditation when a terrible barking in all directions beat on his ears. Anton Prokofievich set up such a shout (no one could shout louder than he) that not only our friend the serving-woman and the inmate of the immense overcoat ran out to meet him, but even the urchins from Ivan Ivanovich's courtyard raced to him, and, though the dogs only succeeded in biting one leg, this greatly cooled his enthusiasm, and he went up the steps with a certain timidity.

CHAPTER VII

AND LAST

"Ah, good day! What have you been teasing my dogs for?" said Ivan Nikiforovich, on seeing Anton Prokofievich; for no one ever addressed the latter except humorously.

"Plague take them all! Who's teasing them?" answered Anton Prokofievich.

"That's a lie."

"I swear it isn't. Piotr Fiodorovich asks you to dinner."

"Hm!"

"I swear! I can't tell you how earnestly he begs you to come. 'What's the meaning of it?' he said. 'Ivan Nikiforovich avoids me as though I were an enemy; he will never come for a little chat or to sit a bit.' "

Ivan Nikiforovich stroked his chin.

" 'If Ivan Nikiforovich will not come now,' he said, 'I don't know what to think: he must have something in his mind against me! Do me the favor, Anton Prokofievich, persuade Ivan Nikiforovich!' Come, Ivan Nikiforovich, let us go! There is a delightful group there now!"

Ivan Nikiforovich began scrutinizing a cock, who was standing on the steps crowing his loudest.

"If only you knew, Ivan Nikiforovich," the zealous delegate

continued, "what oysters, what fresh caviar has been sent to Piotr Fiodorovich!"

At this Ivan Nikiforovich turned his head and began listening attentively.

This encouraged the delegate.

"Let us make haste and go; Foma Grigorievich is there, too! What are you doing?" he added, seeing that Ivan Nikiforovich was still lying in the same position. "Well, are we going or not?"

"I don't want to."

That "I don't want to" was a shock to Anton Prokofievich; he had already imagined that his urgent representations had completely prevailed on this really worthy man; but he heard instead a resolute "I don't want to."

"Why don't you want to?" he asked almost with annoyance, a feeling he very rarely displayed, even when he had burning paper put on his head, which was a trick the judge and the police captain were particularly fond of.

Ivan Nikiforovich took a pinch of snuff.

"It's your business, Ivan Nikiforovich, but I don't know what prevents you."

"Why should I go?" Ivan Nikiforovich said at last. "The ruffian will be there!" That was what he usually called Ivan Ivanovich now . . . Merciful heavens! And not long ago . . .

"I swear, he won't! By all that's holy he won't! May I be struck dead on the spot with a thunderbolt!" answered Anton Prokofievich, who was ready to take this oath a dozen times in an hour. "Let us go, Ivan Nikiforovich!"

"But you are lying, Anton Prokofievich, he is there, isn't he?"

"He's not! May I never leave the spot if he is! And think yourself what reason have I to tell a lie! May my arms and legs be withered! . . . What, don't you believe me even now? May I drop here dead at your feet! May neither father nor mother nor myself ever see the kingdom of heaven! Do you still disbelieve me?"

Ivan Nikiforovich was completely appeased by these assurances, and bade his valet in the enormous overcoat to bring him his trousers and his nankeen Cossack coat.

I imagine that it is quite superfluous to describe how Ivan Nikiforovich put on his trousers, how his cravat was tied, and how, finally, he put on his Cossack coat which had split under the left sleeve. It is enough to say that during that time he maintained a decorous composure and did not answer one word to Anton Prokofievich's proposition that he should swap something with him for his Turkish purse.

Meanwhile the assembled company were, with impatience, awaiting the decisive moment when Ivan Nikiforovich would make his appearance, and the universal desire that these worthy men should be reconciled might at last be gratified. Many were almost positive that Ivan Nikiforovich would not come. The police captain even offered to take a wager with squinting Ivan Ivanovich that he would not come, and only gave it up because the latter insisted that the police captain should stake his wounded leg and he his cross-eye—at which the police captain was extremely offended and the company laughed on the sly. No one had yet sat down at the table, though it was long past one o'clock—an hour at which people have got some way with their dinner at Mirgorod, even on grand occasions.

Anton Prokofievich had hardly appeared at the door when he was instantly surrounded by all. In answer to all questions he shouted one decisive phrase: "Won't come!" He had scarcely uttered this, and a shower of reproaches and abuse and possibly flips, too, was about to descend on his head for the failure of his mission, when the door opened suddenly and—Ivan Nikiforovich walked in.

If Satan himself or a corpse had suddenly appeared he would not have produced such amazement as that into which Ivan Nikiforovich's entrance plunged the whole company; while Anton Prokofievich went off into guffaws of laughter, holding his sides with glee that he had so taken them in.

Anyway, it was almost incredible to everyone that Ivan Nikiforovich could, in so short a time, have dressed as befits a gentleman. Ivan Ivanovich was not present at this moment; he had left the room. Recovering from their stupefaction, all the company showed their interest in Ivan Nikiforovich's health and expressed their pleasure that he had grown stouter. Ivan Nikiforovich kissed everyone and said: "Much obliged."

Meanwhile the smell of borsht floated through the room and agreeably tickled the nostrils of the starving guests. All streamed into the dining room. A string of ladies, talkative and silent, lean and stout, filed in ahead, and the long table was dotted with every hue. I am not going to describe all the dishes on the table! I shall say nothing of the cheese cakes and sour cream, nor of the sweet-bread served in the borsht, nor of the turkey stuffed with plums and raisins, nor of the dish that looked very much like a boot soaked in kvass, nor of the sauce which is the swansong of the old cook, the sauce which is served in flaming spirit to the great diversion, and, at the same time, terror of the ladies. I am not going to talk about these dishes because I greatly prefer eating them to expatiating on them in conversation.

Ivan Ivanovich was very much pleased with the fish prepared with horse-radish sauce. He was entirely engrossed in the useful and nutritious exercise of eating it. Picking out the smallest fish-bones, he laid them on the plate, and somehow chanced to glance across the table. Heavenly Creator! How strange it was! Opposite him was sitting Ivan Nikiforovich!

At the very same instant Ivan Nikiforovich looked up, too . . . ! No . . . ! I cannot! Give me another pen! My pen is feeble, dead; it has too thin a point for this picture! Their faces were as though turned to stone with amazement reflected on them. Each saw the long-familiar face, at the sight of which, one might suppose, each would advance as to an unexpected friend, offering his snuffbox with the words: "Help yourself," or, "I venture to ask you to help yourself"; and yet that very face was terrible as some evil portent! Drops of sweat rolled down the faces of Ivan Ivanovich and Ivan Nikiforovich.

All who were sitting at the table were mute with attention and could not take their eyes off the friends of days gone by. The ladies, who had till then been absorbed in a rather interesting conversation on the method of preparing capons, suddenly ceased talking. All was hushed! It was a picture worthy of the brush of a great artist.

At last Ivan Ivanovich took out his handkerchief and began to blow his nose, while Ivan Nikiforovich looked around and rested his eyes on the open door.

The police captain at once noticed this movement and bade the servant shut the door securely. Then each of the friends began eating, and they did not once glance at each other again.

As soon as dinner was over, the two old friends rose from their seats and began looking for their caps to slip away. Then the police captain gave a wink, and Ivan Ivanovich—not *the* Ivan Ivanovich but the other, the one who squinted—stood behind Ivan Nikiforovich's back while the police captain went up behind Ivan Ivanovich's back, and both began shoving them from behind so as to push them toward each other and not to let them go till they had shaken hands. Ivan Ivanovich, the one who squinted, though he shoved Ivan Nikiforovich a little askew, yet pushed him fairly successfully to the place where Ivan Ivanovich was standing; but the police captain took a line too much to one side, because again he could not cope with his unruly leg which, on this occasion, would heed no command, and, as though to spite him, lurched a long way off in quite the opposite direction (this may possibly have been due to the number of liqueurs on the table), so that Ivan Ivanovich fell against a lady in a red dress who had been compelled by curiosity to thrust herself into their midst. Such an incident boded nothing good. However, to mend matters, the judge took the police captain's place and, sniffing up all the snuff from his upper lip, shoved Ivan Ivanovich in the other direction. This is the usual means of bringing about a reconciliation in Mirgorod; it is not unlike a game of ball. As soon as the judge gave Ivan Ivanovich a shove, the Ivan Ivanovich who squinted pushed with all his strength and shoved Ivan Nikiforovich, from whom the sweat was dropping like rain water from a roof. Although both friends resisted stoutly, they were thrust together, because both sides received considerable support from the other guests.

Then they were closely surrounded on all sides and not allowed to go until they consented to shake hands.

"God bless you, Ivan Nikiforovich and Ivan Ivanovich! Tell us truthfully now: what did you quarrel about? Wasn't it something trifling? Aren't you ashamed before men and before God!"

"I don't know," said Ivan Nikiforovich, panting with exhaustion (it was noticeable that he was by no means averse to reconciliation). "I don't know what I have done to Ivan Ivanovich; why did he cut down my goose pen and plot my ruin?"

"I am not guilty of any such evil designs," said Ivan Ivanovich, not looking at Ivan Nikiforovich. "I swear before God and before you, honorable gentlemen, I have done nothing to my enemy. Why does he defame me and cast ignominy on my rank and name?"

"How have I cast ignominy on you, Ivan Ivanovich?" said Ivan Nikiforovich. Another moment of explanation—another moment of reconciliation—and the long-standing feud was on the point of dying out. Already Ivan Nikiforovich was feeling in his pocket to get out his snuff horn and say: "Help yourself."

"Was it not damage," answered Ivan Ivanovich without raising his eyes, "when you, sir, insulted my rank and name with a word which it would be unseemly to repeat here?"

"Let me tell you as a friend, Ivan Ivanovich!" (At this Ivan Nikiforovich put his finger on Ivan Ivanovich's button, which was a sign of his complete goodwill.) "You took offense over the devil knows what, over my calling you a 'gander' . . ."

Ivan Nikiforovich was instantly aware that he had committed an indiscretion in uttering that word; but it was too late: the word had been uttered. All was ruined! Since Ivan Ivanovich had been beside himself and had flown into a rage, such as God grant one may never see, at the utterance of that word in private—think, dear readers, what it was now when this murderous word had been uttered in a company among whom there were a number of ladies, in whose society Ivan Ivanovich liked to be particularly punctilious. Had Ivan Nikiforovich acted otherwise, had he said "bird" and not "gander," the position might still have been saved. But—all was over!

He cast on Ivan Nikiforovich a glance—and what a glance! If that glance had been endowed with the power of action it would have reduced Ivan Nikiforovich to ashes. The guests understood that glance, and of their own accord made haste to separate them. And that man, a paragon of gentleness, who never let one beggar woman pass without questioning her, rushed out in a terrible fury. How violent are the tempests aroused by the passions!

For a whole month nothing was heard of Ivan Ivanovich. He shut himself up in his house. The sacred chest was opened, from the chest were taken—what? Silver rubles! Old ancestral silver rubles! And these silver rubles passed into the inky hands of scribblers. The case was transferred to the higher court. And when Ivan Ivanovich received the joyous tidings that it would be decided on the morrow, only then he looked out at the world and made up his mind to go out. Alas! for the next ten years the higher court informed him daily that the case would be settled on the morrow!

Five years ago I was passing through the town of Mirgorod. It was a bad time for traveling. Autumn had set in with its gloomy, damp weather, mud, and fog. A sort of unnatural greenness—the work of the tedious, incessant rains—lay in a thin network over the meadows and wheatfields, on which it seemed no more becoming than mischievous tricks in an old man, or roses on an old woman. In those days weather had a great effect upon me: I was depressed when it was dreary. But in spite of that I felt my heart beating eagerly as I drove into Mirgorod. Goodness, how many memories! It was twelve years since I had seen Mirgorod. Here, in those days, lived in touching friendship two unique men, two unique friends. And how many distinguished persons had died! The judge, Demyan Demyanovich, was dead by then; Ivan Ivanovich, the one who squinted, had taken leave of life, too. I drove into the principal street: posts were standing everywhere with wisps of straw tied to their tops: they were altering the streets! Several huts had been removed. Remnants of hurdles and fences remained standing disconsolately.

It was a holiday. I ordered my sack-covered chaise to stop before the church, and went in so quietly that no one turned around. It is true there was no one to do so: the church was deserted; there were scarcely any people about; evidently even the most devout were afraid of the mud. In the dull, or rather, sickly weather the candles were somehow strangely unpleasant; the dark side chapels were gloomy; the long windows with their round panes were streaming with tears of rain. I walked out into the side chapel and addressed an old man with grizzled hair. "Allow me to ask, is Ivan Nikiforovich living?" At that moment the lamp before the icon flared up and the light fell directly on the old man's face. How surprised I was when looking closely at it I saw familiar features! It was Ivan Nikiforovich himself! But how he had changed!

"Are you quite well, Ivan Nikiforovich? You look much older!"

"Yes, I am older. I have come today from Poltava," answered Ivan Nikiforovich.

"Good gracious! You have been to Poltava in such dreadful weather?"

"I was forced to! My lawsuit . . ."

At this I could not help dropping a sigh.

Ivan Nikiforovich noticed that sigh and said: "Don't be anxious: I have positive information that the case will be settled next week and in my favor."

I shrugged my shoulders and went to find out something about Ivan Ivanovich.

"Ivan Ivanovich is here!" someone told me. "He is in the choir."

Then I caught sight of a thin, wasted figure. Was that Ivan Ivanovich? The face was covered with wrinkles, the hair was completely white. But the coat was still the same. After the first greetings, Ivan Ivanovich, addressing me with the good-humored smile which so well suited his funnel-shaped face, said: "Shall I tell you my pleasant news?"

"What news?" I asked.

"Tomorrow my case will positively be settled; the court has told me so for certain."

I sighed still more heavily, and made haste to say goodbye—because I was traveling on very important business—and got into my chaise.

The lean horses, known in Mirgorod by the name of the post-express horses, set off, making an unpleasant sound as their hoofs sank into the gray mass of mud. The rain poured in streams onto the Jew who sat on the box covered with a sack. The damp pierced me through and through. The gloomy gate with the sentry box, in which a veteran was cleaning his gray equipment, slowly passed by. Again the same fields, in places black and furrowed and in places covered with green, the drenched cows and crows, the monotonous rain, the tearful sky without one gleam of light in it. —It is a dreary world, gentlemen.

Other Tales

THE NOSE

I

An extraordinarily strange incident took place in Petersburg on the twenty-fifth of March. The barber, Ivan Yakovlevich, who lives on Voznesensky Avenue (his surname is lost, and nothing more appears even on his signboard, where a gentleman is depicted with his cheeks covered with soapsuds, together with an inscription "also lets blood")—the barber Ivan Yakovlevich woke up rather early and was aware of a smell of hot bread. Raising himself in bed he saw his wife, a rather portly lady who was very fond of drinking coffee, engaged in taking out of the oven some freshly baked loaves.

"I won't have coffee today, Praskovia Osipovna," said Ivan Yakovlevich. "Instead I should like some hot bread with onions." (The fact is that Ivan Yakovlevich would have liked both, but he knew that it was utterly impossible to ask for two things at once, for Praskovia Osipovna greatly disliked such caprices.)

"Let the fool have bread: so much the better for me," thought his wife to herself. "There will be an extra cup of coffee left," and she flung one loaf on the table.

For the sake of propriety Ivan Yakovlevich put a jacket over his shirt, and, sitting down at the table, sprinkled some salt, peeled two onions, took a knife in his hand and, assuming an air of importance, began to cut the bread. After dividing the loaf into two halves he looked into the middle of it—and to his amazement saw something there that looked white. Ivan Yakovlevich probed at it carefully with his knife and felt it with his finger: "It's solid," he said to himself. "What in the world is it?"

He thrust in his fingers and pulled it out—it was a nose! . . . Ivan Yakovlevich's hand dropped with astonishment, he rubbed his eyes and felt it: it actually was a nose, and, what's more, it looked to him somehow familiar. A look of horror came into Ivan Ya-kovlevich's face. But that horror was nothing compared to the indignation with which his wife was overcome.

"Where have you cut that nose off, you monster?" she cried wrathfully. "You scoundrel, you drunkard, I'll go to the police myself to report you! You villain! I have heard from three men that when you are shaving them you pull at their noses till you almost tug them off."

But Ivan Yakovlevich was more dead than alive: he recognized that the nose belonged to none other than Kovaliov, the collegiate assessor whom he shaved every Wednesday and every Sunday.

"Wait, Praskovia Osipovna! I'll wrap it up in a rag and put it in a corner. Let it stay there for a while; I'll return it later on."

"I won't hear of it! As though I would allow a stray nose to lie about in my room. You dried-up biscuit! He can do nothing but sharpen his razors on the strop, but soon he won't be fit to do his duties at all, the strumpet, the good-for-nothing! As though I were going to answer to the police for you. . . . Oh, you dirt, you stupid blockhead. Away with it, away with it! Take it where you like! Don't let me set eyes on it again!"

Ivan Yakovlevich stood as though utterly crushed. He thought and thought, and did not know what to think. "The devil only knows how it happened," he said at last, scratching behind his ear. "Did I come home drunk last night or not? I can't say for certain now. But from all signs it seems that something extraordinary must have happened, for bread is a thing that is baked, while a nose is something quite different. I can't make head or tail of it." Ivan Yakovlevich sank into silence. The thought that the police might make a search there for the nose and throw the blame of it on him reduced him to complete prostration. Already the red collar, beautifully embroidered with silver, the saber, hovered before his eyes, and he trembled all over. At last he got his trousers and his boots, pulled on these wretched objects, and, accompanied by the stern reproaches of Praskovia Osipovna, wrapped the nose in a rag and went out into the street.

He wanted to thrust it out of sight somewhere, under a gate, or somehow accidentally to drop it and then turn off into a side street, but as ill-luck would have it he kept coming across people he knew, who would at once begin asking: "Where are you going?" or "Whom are you going to shave so early?" so that Ivan Yakovlevich could never find a moment to get rid of it. Another time he really did drop it, but a policeman pointed to it with his halberd from a long way off, saying as he did so: "Pick it up, you have dropped something!" and Ivan Yakovlevich was obliged to pick up the nose and put it in his pocket. He was overcome by despair, especially as the number of people in the street was continually increasing as the shops and stalls began to open.

He made up his mind to go to Isakievsky Bridge in the hope of being able to fling it into the Neva. . . . But I am afraid I am a little to blame for not having so far said more about Ivan Yakovlevich, a worthy man in many respects.

Ivan Yakovlevich, like every self-respecting Russian workman, was a terrible drunkard, and though every day he shaved other people's chins, his own went forever unshaven. Ivan Yakovlevich's jacket (he never wore any other shape) was motley, that is, it was black dappled all over with brown and yellow and gray; the collar was shiny, and instead of three buttons there was only one hanging on a thread. Ivan Yakovlevich was a great cynic, and when Kovaliov the collegiate assessor said to him while he was being shaved: "Your hands always stink, Ivan Yakovlevich," the latter would reply with the question: "What should make them stink?" "I can't tell, my good man, but they do stink," the collegiate assessor would say, and, taking a pinch of snuff, Ivan Yakovlevich lathered him for that on his cheeks and under his nose and behind his ears and under his beard—in fact, wherever he chose.

The worthy citizen found himself by now on Isakievsky Bridge. First of all he looked about him, then bent over the parapet as though to look under the bridge to see whether there were a great number of fish racing by, and stealthily flung in the rag with the nose. He felt as though a heavy weight had rolled off his back. Ivan Yakovlevich actually grinned. Instead of going to shave the chins of government clerks, he went to an establishment bearing the inscription "Tea and refreshments" and asked for a glass of punch, when he suddenly observed at the end of the bridge a police inspector of respectable appearance with full whiskers, a three-cornered hat, and a sword. He turned cold, and meanwhile the inspector beckoned to him and said: "Come this way, my good man."

Ivan Yakovlevich, knowing etiquette, took off his hat some way off and, as he approached, said: "I wish your honor good health."

"No, no, old fellow, I am not 'your honor': tell me what you were doing on the bridge?"

"I swear, sir, I was on my way to shave my customers, and I was only looking to see whether the current was running fast."

"That's a lie, that's a lie! You won't get off with that. Kindly answer!"

"I am ready to shave you, gracious sir, two or even three times a week with no conditions whatever," answered Ivan Yakovlevich.

"No, my friend, that is nonsense; I have three barbers to shave me and they think it a great honor, too. But be so kind as to tell me what you were doing there?"

Ivan Yakovlevich turned pale . . . but the incident is completely veiled in obscurity, and absolutely nothing is known of what happened next.

II

Kovaliov the collegiate assessor woke up early next morning and made the sound "brrrr . . ." with his lips as he always did when he woke up, though he could not himself have explained the reason for his doing so. Kovaliov stretched and asked for a little mirror that was standing on the table. He wanted to look at a pimple which had appeared on his nose the previous evening, but to his great astonishment there was a completely flat space where his nose should have been. Frightened, Kovaliov asked for some water and a towel to rub his eyes; there really was no nose. He began feeling with his hand, and pinched himself to see whether he was still asleep: it appeared that he was not. The collegiate assessor jumped out of bed, he shook himself—there was still no nose. . . . He ordered his clothes to be given him at once and flew off straight to the police commissioner.

But meanwhile we must say a word about Kovaliov in order that the reader may have some idea of what kind of collegiate assessor he was. Collegiate assessors who receive that title with the aid of academic diplomas cannot be compared with those who are created collegiate assessors in the Caucasus. They are two quite different species. The erudite collegiate assessors . . . But Russia is such a wonderful country that, if you say a word about one collegiate assessor, all the collegiate assessors from Riga to Kamchatka would certainly think you are referring to them; and it is the same, of course, with all grades and titles. Kovaliov was a collegiate assessor from the Caucasus. He had only been of that rank for the last two years, and so could not forget it for a moment; and to give himself greater weight and dignity he did not call himself simply collegiate assessor but always spoke of himself as a major. "Listen, my dear," he would usually say when he met a woman in the street selling shirt fronts, "you go to my house; I live in Sadovaya Street; just ask, does Major Kovaliov live here? Anyone will show you." If he met some pretty little baggage he would also give her a secret instruction, adding: "You ask for Major Kovaliov's flat, my love." For this reason we will for the future speak of him as the major.

Major Kovaliov was in the habit of walking every day up and down Nevsky Prospekt. The collar of his shirt front was always extremely clean and well starched. His whiskers were such as one may see nowadays on provincial and district surveyors, on architects and army doctors, also on those employed on special commissions, and in general on all such men as have full ruddy cheeks and are very good hands at a game of boston: these whiskers start from the middle of the cheek and go straight up to the nose. Major Kovaliov used to wear a number of cornelian seals, some with crests on them and others on which were carved Wednesday, Thursday, Monday, and so on. Major Kovaliov had come to Petersburg on business, that is, to look for a post befitting his rank: if he were successful, the post of a vice-governor, and failing that, the situation of an executive clerk in some prominent department. Major Kovaliov was not averse to matrimony, but only on condition he could find a bride with a fortune of two hundred thousand. And so the reader may judge for himself what was the major's position when he saw, instead of a nice-looking, well-proportioned nose, an extremely absurd flat space.

As misfortune would have it, not a cab was to be seen in the street, and he was obliged to walk, wrapping himself in his cloak and hiding his face in his handkerchief, as though his nose were bleeding. "But perhaps it was my imagination: it's impossible: I couldn't have been idiotic enough to lose my nose," he thought, and went into a café to look at himself in the mirror. Fortunately there was no one in the shop; some boys were sweeping the floor and arranging all the chairs; others with sleepy faces were bringing in hot pastries on trays; yesterday's papers covered with coffee stains were lying about on the tables and chairs. "Well, thank God, there is nobody here," he thought; "now I can look." He went timidly up to the mirror and looked. "What the hell's the meaning of it? Damn it!" he said, spitting. "If only there had been something instead of a nose, but there is nothing! . . ."

Biting his lips with vexation, he went out of the café and resolved, contrary to his usual practice, not to look or smile at anyone. All at once he stood as though rooted to the spot before the door of a house. Something inexplicable took place before his eyes: a carriage was stopping at the entrance; the carriage door flew open; a gentleman in uniform, bending down, sprang out and ran up the steps. What was the horror and at the same time amazement of Kovaliov when he recognized that this was his own nose! At this extraordinary phenomenon it seemed to him that everything was swimming before his eyes; he felt that he could scarcely stand; but he made up his mind, come what may, to await the gentleman's return to the carriage, and he stood trembling all over as though in a fever. Two minutes later the nose actually did come out. He was in a gold-braided uniform with a high collar; he had on buckskin trousers and at his side was a sword. From his plumed hat it might be inferred that he was of the rank of a civil councilor. Everything showed that he was going somewhere to pay a visit. He looked to both sides, called to the coachman to open the carriage door, got in, and drove off.

Poor Kovaliov almost went out of his mind; he did not know what to think of such a strange occurrence. How was it possible for a nose—which had only yesterday been on his face and could neither drive nor walk—to be in uniform! He ran after the carriage, which luckily did not go far, but stopped before the entrance of Kazansky Cathedral.[1]

He hurried in that direction, made his way through a row of old beggar women with their faces tied up and two slits in place of their eyes at whom he used to laugh so merrily, and went into the church. There were not many people inside the church. Kovaliov felt so upset that he could not pray, and he looked for the gentleman. At last he saw him standing apart from the other worshippers. The nose was hiding his face completely in a high stand-up collar and was saying his prayers in an attitude of complete piety.

"How am I to approach him?" thought Kovaliov. "One can see by everything—from his uniform, from his hat—that he is a civil councilor. Damned if I know how to do it!"

He began by coughing at his side; but the nose never changed his pious attitude for a minute and continued genuflecting.

"Sir," said Kovaliov, inwardly forcing himself to speak confidently. "Sir . . ."

"What do you want?" answered the nose, turning around.

"It seems . . . strange to me, sir. . . . You ought to know your proper place, and all at once I find you in church, of all places! You will admit . . ."

"Excuse me, I cannot understand what you are talking about. . . . Explain."

"How am I to explain to him?" thought Kovaliov, and plucking up his courage he began: "Of course I . . . I am a major, by the way. For me to go about without a nose, you must admit, is improper. An old woman selling peeled oranges on Voskresensky Bridge may sit there without a nose; but having prospects of obtaining . . . and being besides acquainted with a great many ladies in the families of Chekhtariova the civil councilor and others . . . You can judge for yourself . . . I don't know, sir" (at this point Major Kovaliov shrugged his shoulders) ". . . excuse me

[1] One of Gogol's squabbles with the omnipresent and omnipotent Russian censor came about as a result of the "sacrilegious" presence of the nose in Kazansky Cathedral. Gogol, always extremely sensitive to criticism (even, at times, before it was delivered), wrote a note to a friend in which he anticipated the adverse reaction of the censor, and, he wrote, if the censor objected to the nose being in an Orthodox church, he might place it in a Catholic church instead. But Gogol yielded to the censor, and the nose found itself before a bazaar. Mrs. Garnett translated from the revised (censor-approved) version. The original text (which now appears in the Academy edition of Gogol's work) appears above. (ed.)

. . . if you look at the matter in accordance with the principles of duty and honor . . . you can understand of yourself . . ."

"I don't understand a word," said the nose. "Explain it more satisfactorily."

"Sir," said Kovaliov, with a sense of his own dignity, "I don't know how to understand your words. The matter appears to me perfectly obvious . . . either you wish . . . Why, you are my own nose!"

The nose looked at the major and his eyebrows slightly quivered.

"You are mistaken, sir. I am an independent individual. Moreover, there can be no sort of close relations between us. I see, sir, from the buttons of your uniform, you must be serving in a different department." Saying this, the nose turned away.

Kovaliov was utterly confused, not knowing what to do or even what to think. Meanwhile they heard the agreeable rustle of a lady's dress: an elderly lady was approaching, all decked out in lace, and with her a slim lady in a white dress which looked very charming on her slender figure, in a straw-colored hat as light as a pastry puff. Behind them stood, opening his snuffbox, a tall footman with big whiskers and a dozen collars.

Kovaliov came nearer, pulled out the cambric collar of his shirt front, arranged the seals on his gold watch chain, and smiling from side to side, turned his attention to the ethereal lady who, like a spring flower, faintly swayed forward and put her white hand with its half-transparent fingers to her brow. The smile on Kovaliov's face broadened when he saw under the hat her round, dazzlingly white chin and part of her cheek flushed with the hues of the first spring rose; but all at once he skipped away as though he had been scalded. He remembered that he had absolutely nothing on his face in place of a nose, and tears oozed from his eyes. He turned away to tell the gentleman in uniform straight out that he was only pretending to be a civil councilor, that he was a rogue and a scoundrel, and that he was nothing else than his own nose. . . . But the nose was no longer there; he had managed to gallop off, probably again to call on someone.

This reduced Kovaliov to despair. He went back and stood for a minute or two under the colonnade, carefully looking in all directions to see whether the nose was anywhere about. He remembered very well that there was plumage in his hat and gold braid on his uniform; but he had not noticed his overcoat nor the

color of his carriage, nor his horses, nor even whether he had a
footman behind him and if so in what livery. Moreover, such
numbers of carriages were driving backwards and forwards and
at such a speed that it was difficult even to distinguish them; and if
he had distinguished one of them he would have had no means of
stopping it. It was a lovely, sunny day. There were masses of
people on Nevsky Prospekt; ladies were scattered like a perfect
cataract of flowers all over the pavement from Politseysky to the
Anichkin Bridge. Here he saw coming toward him a court councilor
of his acquaintance whom he used to call "lieutenant colonel,"
particularly if he were speaking to other people. There he saw
Yarygin, a head clerk in the senate, a great friend of his, who always lost points when he went eight at boston. And here was
another major who had received the rank of assessor in the Caucasus, beckoning to him. . . .

"Hell!" said Kovaliov. "Hi, cab! drive straight to the police
commissioner's."

Kovaliov got into a cab and shouted to the driver:

"Drive like a house on fire."

"Is the commissioner at home?" he cried, going into the hall.

"No," answered the porter, "he has just gone out."

"Well, that's my luck."

"Yes," added the porter, "and he has not been gone so long:
if you had come but a tiny minute earlier you might have found
him."

Kovaliov, still keeping the handkerchief over his face, got into
the cab and shouted in a voice of despair: "Drive on."

"Where?" asked the cabman.

"Drive straight on!"

"How straight on? The street divides here; is it to the right
or to the left?"

This question forced Kovaliov to pause, to think, again. In
his position he ought first of all to address himself to the department of law and order, not because it had any direct connection
with the police but because the intervention of the latter might
be far more rapid than any help he could get in other departments.
To seek satisfaction from the higher officials of the department in which the nose had announced himself as serving would
have been unwise, since from the nose's own answers he had been
able to perceive that nothing was sacred to that man and that

he might tell lies in this case too, just as he had lied in declaring that he had never seen him before. And so Kovaliov was on the point of telling the cabman to drive to the police station, when again the idea occurred to him that this rogue and scoundrel who had at their first meeting behaved in such a shameless way might seize the opportunity and slip out of town—and then all his searches would be in vain, or might be prolonged, God forbid, for a whole month. At last it seemed that Heaven itself directed him. He decided to go straight to a newspaper office and without loss of time to publish a circumstantial description of the nose, so that anyone meeting it might at once present it to him or at least let him know where it was. And so, deciding upon this course, he told the cabman to drive to the newspaper office, and all the way never stopped hitting him with his fist on the back, saying as he did so, "Faster, you rascal; hurry, you scoundrel!"

"Ugh, sir!" said the cabman, shaking his head and flicking with the reins at the horse, whose coat was as long as a lapdog's. At last the cab stopped and Kovaliov ran panting into a little reception room where a gray-headed clerk in spectacles, wearing an old jacket, was sitting at a table and with a pen between his teeth was counting over some coppers he had before him.

"Who receives inquiries here?" cried Kovaliov. "Ah, good day!"

"I wish you good day," said the gray-headed clerk, raising his eyes for a moment and then dropping them again on the money lying in heaps on the table.

"I want to insert an advertisement . . ."

"Allow me to ask you to wait a minute," the clerk pronounced, with one hand noting a figure on the paper and with the finger of his left hand moving two beads on the abacus. A footman in a braided coat and of rather smart appearance, which betrayed that he had at some time served in an aristocratic family, was standing at the table with a written paper in his hand and thought fit to display his social abilities: "Would you believe it, sir, that the little bitch is not worth eighty kopeks; in fact I wouldn't give eight for it, but the countess is fond of it—my goodness, she is fond of it, and here she will give a hundred rubles to anyone who finds it! To speak politely, as you and I are speaking now, people's tastes are quite incompatible: when a man's a sportsman, then he'll keep a setter or a poodle; he won't mind giving five hundred or a thousand so long as it is a good dog."

The worthy clerk listened to this with a significant air, and at the same time was reckoning the number of letters in the advertisement brought him. Along the sides of the room stood a number of old women, shop assistants, and house porters who had brought advertisements. In one it was announced that a coachman of sober habits was looking for a situation; in the next a secondhand carriage brought from Paris in 1814 was offered for sale; next a maid, aged nineteen, experienced in laundry work and also competent to do other work, was looking for a situation; a strong carriage with only one spring broken was for sale; a spirited, young, dappled gray horse, only seventeen years old, for sale; a new consignment of turnip and radish seed from London; a summer villa with all conveniences, stabling for two horses, and a piece of land that might well be planted with fine birches and pine trees; there was also an appeal to those wishing to purchase old boot soles, inviting such to come for the same every day between eight o'clock in the morning and three o'clock in the morning. The room in which all this company was assembled was a small one and the air in it was extremely thick, but the collegiate assessor Kovaliov was incapable of noticing the stench both because he kept his handkerchief over his face and because his nose was goodness knows where.

"Dear sir, allow me to ask you . . . my case is very urgent," he said at last impatiently.

"In a minute, in a minute! . . . Two rubles, forty-three kopeks! . . . This minute! One ruble and sixty-four kopeks!" said the gray-headed gentleman, flinging the old women and house porters the various documents they had bought. "What can I do for you?" he said at last, turning to Kovaliov.

"I want to ask . . ." said Kovaliov. "Some robbery or swindle has occurred; I cannot understand it at all. I only want you to advertise that anyone who brings me the scoundrel will receive a handsome reward."

"Allow me to ask what is your surname?"

"No, why put my surname? I cannot give it to you! I have a large circle of acquaintances: Chekhtariova, wife of a civil councilor, Podtochina, widow of an officer . . . they will find out. God forbid! You can simply put: 'a collegiate assessor,' or better still, 'a person of major's rank.' "

"Is the runaway your house serf, then?"

"A house serf indeed! that would not be so bad! It's my nose
. . . has run away from me . . . my own nose."

"H'm, what a strange surname! And is it a very large sum
this Mr. Nosov has robbed you of?"

"Nosov! . . . you are on the wrong track. It is my nose, my
own nose that has disappeared. I don't know where. The devil
wanted to have a joke at my expense."

"But in what way did it disappear? There is something I can't
quite understand."

"And indeed, I can't tell you how it happened; the point is
that now it is driving about the town, calling itself a civil councilor. And so I beg you to announce that anyone who catches
him must bring him at once to me as quickly as possible. Only
think, really, how can I manage without such a conspicuous part
of my person? It's not like a little toe, the loss of which I could
hide in my boot and no one could say whether it was there or
not. I go on Thursdays to Chekhtariova's: Podtochina, an officer's
widow, and her very pretty daughter are great friends of mine;
and you can judge for yourself what a fix I am in now . . . I
can't possibly show myself now. . . ."

The clerk pondered, a fact which was obvious from the way
he compressed his lips.

"No, I can't put an advertisement like that in the paper," he
said at last, after a long silence.

"What? Why not?"

"Well. The newspaper might lose its reputation. If everyone
is going to write that his nose has run away, why . . . As it is,
they say we print lots of absurd things and false reports."

"But what is there absurd about this? I don't see anything
absurd in it."

"You think there is nothing absurd in it? But last week, now,
this was what happened. A government clerk came to me just
as you have; he brought an advertisement, it came to two
rubles seventy-three kopeks, and all the advertisement amounted
to was that a poodle with a black coat had strayed. You wouldn't
think that there was anything in that, would you? But it turned
out to be libelous: the poodle was the cashier of some department,
I don't remember which."

"But I am not asking you to advertise about poodles but about
my own nose; that is almost the same as about myself."

"No, such an advertisement I cannot insert."

"But since my nose really is lost!"

"If it is lost that is a matter for the doctor. They say there are people who can fit you with a nose of any shape you like. But I observe you must be a gentleman of merry disposition and are fond of having your little joke."

"I swear as God is holy! If you like, since it has come to that, I will show you."

"I don't want to trouble you," said the clerk, taking a pinch of snuff. "However, if it is no trouble," he added, moved by curiosity, "it might be desirable to have a look."

The collegiate assessor took the handkerchief from his face. "It really is extremely strange," said the clerk, "the place is perfectly flat, like a freshly fried pancake. Yes, it's incredibly smooth."

"Will you dispute it now? You see for yourself I must advertise. I shall be particularly grateful to you and very glad this incident has given me the pleasure of your acquaintance."

The major, as may be seen, made up his mind on this occasion to resort to a little flattery.

"To print such an advertisement is, of course, not such a very great matter," said the clerk. "But I do not foresee any advantage to you from it. If you do want to, put it in the hands of someone with a skillful pen, describe it as a rare freak of nature, and publish the little article in *The Northern Bee*" (at this point he once more took a pinch of snuff) "for the benefit of youth" (at this moment he wiped his nose), "or anyway as a matter of general interest."

The collegiate assessor felt quite hopeless. He dropped his eyes and looked at the bottom of the paper where there was an announcement of a theatrical event; his face was ready to break into a smile as he saw the name of a pretty actress, and his hand went to his pocket to feel whether he had a five-ruble note there, for an officer of his rank ought, in Kovaliov's opinion, to have a seat in the orchestra; but the thought of his nose spoiled it all.

Even the clerk seemed touched by Kovaliov's difficult position. Desirous of relieving his distress in some way, he thought it befitting to express his sympathy in a few words: "I am really very much grieved that such an incident should have occurred to you. Wouldn't you like a pinch of snuff? it relieves headache and dissipates depression; even in intestinal trouble it is of use." Saying this the clerk offered Kovaliov his snuffbox, rather deftly opening the lid with a portrait of a lady in a hat on it.

This thoughtless act exhausted Kovaliov's patience.

"I can't understand how you can think it proper to make a joke of it," he said angrily; "don't you see that I am without just what I need for sniffing? To hell with your snuff! I can't bear the sight of it now, not merely your miserable Berezinsky stuff but even if you were to offer me rappee itself!" Saying this he walked out of the newspaper office, deeply mortified, and went in the direction of the local police inspector.

Kovaliov walked in at the very moment when he was stretching and clearing his throat and saying: "Ah, I should enjoy a couple of hours' nap!" And so it might be foreseen that the collegiate assessor's visit was not very opportune. The police inspector was a great patron of all arts and manufactures; but he preferred money to everything. "That is a thing," he used to say; "there is nothing better than that thing; it does not ask for food, it takes up little space, there is always room for it in the pocket, and if you drop it, it does not break."

The police inspector received Kovaliov rather coldly and said that after dinner was not the time to make an inquiry, that nature itself had ordained that man should rest a little after eating (the collegiate assessor could see from this that the sayings of the ancient sages were not unfamiliar to the local inspector), and that a respectable man does not have his nose pulled off.

This was adding insult to injury. It must be said that Kovaliov was very easily offended. He could forgive anything said about himself, but could never forgive insult to his rank or his calling. He was even of the opinion that any reference to officers of the higher ranks might be allowed to pass in stage plays, but that no attack ought to be made on those of a lower grade. The reception given him by the local inspector so disconcerted him that he tossed his head and said with an air of dignity and a slight gesture of surprise: "I must observe that after observations so insulting on your part I can add nothing more . . ." and went out.

He went home hardly conscious of the ground under his feet. By now it was dusk. His lodgings seemed to him melancholy or rather utterly disgusting after all these unsuccessful efforts. Going into his hall he saw his valet, Ivan, lying on his dirty leather sofa; he was spitting on the ceiling and rather successfully aiming at the same spot. The nonchalance of his servant enraged him; he hit him

on the forehead with his hat, saying: "You pig, you are always doing something stupid."

Ivan jumped up and rushed headlong to help him off with his
cloak.

Going into his room, weary and dejected, the major threw himself into an easy chair, and at last, after several sighs, said:

"My God, my God! Why has this misfortune befallen me? If I
had lost an arm or a leg it would have been better; but without a
nose a man is goodness knows what: neither fish nor fowl nor human being, good for nothing but to be flung out of the window!
And if only it had been cut off in battle or in a duel, or if I had been
the cause of it myself, but as it is, it is lost for no cause or reason, it
is lost for nothing, absolutely nothing! But no, it cannot be," he
added after a moment's thought; "it's incredible that a nose should
be lost. It must be a dream or an illusion. Perhaps by some mistake
I drank instead of water the vodka I use to rub my chin with after
shaving. Ivan, the idiot, did not remove it and very likely I took it."
To convince himself that he was not drunk, the major pinched
himself so painfully that he shrieked. The pain completely convinced him that he was living and acting in real life. He slowly approached the mirror and at first screwed up his eyes with the idea
that maybe his nose would appear in its proper place; but at the
same minute sprang back, saying: "What a terrible sight!"

It really was incomprehensible; if a button had been lost or a
silver spoon or a watch or anything similar—but to have lost this,
and in one's own apartment too! Thinking over all the circumstances, Major Kovaliov reached the supposition that what might
be nearest the truth was that the person responsible for this could
be no other than Madame Podtochina, who wanted him to marry
her daughter. He himself liked flirting with her, but avoided a definite engagement. When the mother had informed him plainly that
she wished for the marriage, he had slyly put her off with his compliments, saying that he was still young, that he must serve for five
years so as to be exactly forty-two. And that Madame Podtochina
had therefore made up her mind, probably out of revenge, to ruin
him, and had hired for the purpose some peasant witches, because
it was impossible to suppose that the nose had been cut off in any
way; no one had come into his room; the barber Ivan Yakovlevich
had shaved him on Wednesday, and all Wednesday and even all
Thursday his nose had been all right—that he remembered and

was quite certain about; besides, he would have felt pain, and there could have been no doubt that the wound could not have healed so soon and been as flat as a pancake. He formed various plans in his mind: either to summon Madame Podtochina formally before the court or to go to her himself and confront her with it. These reflections were interrupted by a light which gleamed through all the cracks of the door and informed him that a candle had been lighted in the hall by Ivan. Soon Ivan himself appeared, holding it before him and lighting up the whole room. Kovaliov's first movement was to snatch up his handkerchief and cover the place where yesterday his nose had been, so that his really stupid servant might not gape at the sight of anything so peculiar in his master.

Ivan had hardly time to retreat to his lair when there was the sound of an unfamiliar voice in the hall, pronouncing the words: "Does the collegiate assessor Kovaliov live here?"

"Come in, Major Kovaliov is here," said Kovaliov, jumping up hurriedly and opening the door.

A police officer walked in. He was of handsome appearance, with whiskers neither too fair nor too dark, and rather fat cheeks, the same officer who at the beginning of our story was standing at the end of Isakievsky Bridge.

"Did you lose your nose, sir?"

"That is so."

"It is now found."

"What are you saying?" cried Major Kovaliov. He could not speak for joy. He stared at the police officer standing before him, on whose full lips and cheeks the flickering light of the candle was brightly reflected. "How?"

"By extraordinary luck: he was caught almost on the road. He had already taken his seat in the stagecoach and was intending to go to Riga, and had already taken a passport in the name of a government clerk. And the strange thing is that I myself took him for a gentleman at first, but fortunately I had my spectacles with me and I soon saw that it was a nose. You know I am shortsighted. And if you stand before me I only see that you have a face, but I don't notice your nose or your beard or anything. My mother-in-law, that is my wife's mother, doesn't see anything either."

Kovaliov was beside himself with joy. "Where? Where? I'll go at once."

"Don't disturb yourself. Knowing that you were in need of it I brought it along with me. And the strange thing is that the man who has had the most to do with the affair is a rascal of a barber on Voznesensky Avenue, who is now in our custody. I have long suspected him of drunkenness and thieving, and only the day before yesterday he carried off a strip of buttons from one shop. Your nose is exactly as it was." With this the police officer put his hand in his pocket and drew out the nose just as it was.

"That's it!" Kovaliov cried. "That's certainly it. You must have a cup of tea with me this evening."

"I should look upon it as a great pleasure, but I can't possibly manage it: I have to go from here to the penitentiary. . . . How the price of food is going up! . . . At home I have my mother-in-law, that is my wife's mother, and my children, the eldest particularly gives signs of great promise, he is a very intelligent child; but we have absolutely no means for his education . . ."

For some time after the policeman's departure the collegiate assessor remained in a state of bewilderment, and it was only a few minutes later that he was capable of feeling and understanding again: so reduced was he to stupefaction by this unexpected good fortune. He took the recovered nose carefully in his two hands, holding them together like a cup, and once more examined it attentively.

"Yes, that's it, it's certainly it," said Major Kovaliov. "There's the pimple that came out on the left side yesterday." The major almost laughed aloud with joy.

But nothing in this world is of long duration, and so his joy was not so great the next moment; and the moment after, it was still less, and in the end he passed imperceptibly into his ordinary frame of mind, just as a circle on the water caused by a falling stone gradually passes away into the unbroken smoothness of the surface. Kovaliov began to think, and reflected that the business was not finished yet; the nose was found, but it had to be put on, fixed in its proper place.

"And what if it won't stick?" Asking himself this question, the major turned pale.

With a feeling of irrepressible terror he rushed to the table and moved the mirror forward so that he might not put the nose on crooked. His hands trembled. Cautiously and gently he replaced it in its former position. Oh horror, the nose would not stick on! . . .

He put it to his lips, slightly warmed it with his breath, and again applied it to the flat space between his two cheeks; but nothing would make the nose stick.

"Come, come, stick on, you fool!" he said to it; but the nose seemed made of wood and fell on the table with a strange sound as though it were a cork. The major's face twisted convulsively.

"Is it possible that it won't grow on again?" But, however often he applied it to the proper place, the attempt was as unsuccessful as before.

He called Ivan and sent him for a doctor who lived in the best apartment on the first floor of the same house. The doctor was a handsome man; he had magnificent pitch-black whiskers, a fresh and healthy wife, ate fresh apples in the morning, and kept his mouth extraordinarily clean, rinsing it out for nearly three-quarters of an hour every morning and cleaning his teeth with five different sorts of brushes. The doctor appeared immediately. Asking how long ago the trouble had occurred, he took Major Kovaliov by the chin and with his thumb gave him a flip on the spot where the nose had been, making the major jerk back his head so abruptly that he knocked the back of it against the wall. The doctor said that that did not matter, and, advising him to move a little away from the wall, he told him to bend his head around first to the right, and feeling the place where the nose had been, said, "H'm!" Then he told him to turn his head around to the left side and again said "H'm!" And in conclusion he gave him another flip with his thumb, so that Major Kovaliov threw up his head like a horse when his teeth are being looked at. After making this experiment the doctor shook his head and said:

"No, it's impossible. You had better stay as you are, for it may be made much worse. Of course, it might be stuck on; I could stick it on for you at once, if you like; but I assure you it would be worse for you."

"That's a nice thing to say! How can I stay without a nose?" said Kovaliov. "Things can't possibly be worse than now. It's simply beyond everything. Where can I show myself with such a terrible face? I have a good circle of acquaintances. Today, for instance, I ought to be at two evening parties. I know a great many people; Chekhtariova, the wife of a civil councilor, Podtochina, an officer's widow . . . though after the way she has behaved, I'll have nothing more to do with her except through the police. Do me a favor,"

Kovaliov went on in a supplicating voice; "is there no way to stick it on? Even if it were not neatly done, as long as it would stay on; I could even hold it on with my hand at critical moments. I wouldn't dance in any case for fear of a sudden movement upsetting it. As for remuneration for your services, you may be assured that as far as my means allow . . ."

"Believe me," said the doctor, in a voice neither loud nor low but persuasive and magnetic, "that I never work from mercenary motives; that is opposed to my principles and my science. It is true that I accept a fee for my visits, but that is simply to avoid wounding my patients by refusing it. Of course I could replace your nose; but I assure you on my honor, since you do not believe my word, that it will be much worse for you. You had better wait for the action of nature itself. Wash it frequently with cold water, and I assure you that even without a nose you will be just as healthy as with one. And I advise you to put the nose in a bottle, in spirits or, better still, put two tablespoonfuls of sour vodka on it and heated vinegar—and then you might get quite a sum of money for it. I'd even take it myself, if you don't ask too much for it."

"No, no, I wouldn't sell it for anything," Major Kovaliov cried in despair; "I'd rather it were lost than that!"

"Excuse me!" said the doctor, bowing himself out, "I was trying to be of use to you. . . . Well, there is nothing I can do! Anyway, you see that I have done my best." Saying this the doctor walked out of the room with a majestic air. Kovaliov did not notice his face, and, almost unconscious, saw nothing but the cuffs of his immaculate white shirt peeping out from the sleeves of his black tail coat.

Next day he decided, before lodging a complaint with the police, to write to Madame Podtochina to see whether she would consent to return him what she had taken without a struggle. The letter was as follows:

Dear Madam,
    Aleksandra Grigorievna
I cannot understand this strange conduct on your part. You may rest assured that you will gain nothing by what you have done, and you will not get a step nearer forcing me to marry your daughter. Believe me, that business in regard to my nose is no secret, no more than it is that you and no other are the person chiefly responsible. The sudden parting of the same from its natural position,

its flight and masquerading, at one time in the form of a government clerk and finally in its own shape, is nothing else than the consequence of the sorceries engaged in by you or by those who are versed in the same honorable arts as you are. For my part I consider it my duty to warn you, if the above-mentioned nose is not in its proper place today, I shall be obliged to resort to the assistance and protection of the law.

I have, however, with complete respect to you, the honor to be

> Your respectful servant,
> PLATON KOVALIOV

DEAR SIR,
PLATON KUZMICH!

Your letter greatly astonished me. I must frankly confess that I did not expect it, especially in regard to your unjust reproaches. I assure you I have never received the government clerk of whom you speak in my house, neither in masquerade nor in his own attire. It is true that Filipp Ivanovich Potanchikov has been to see me, and although, indeed, he is asking me for my daughter's hand and is a well-conducted, sober man of great learning, I have never encouraged his hopes. You make some reference to your nose also. If you wish me to understand by that that you imagine that I meant to make a long nose at you, that is, to give you a formal refusal, I am surprised that you should speak of such a thing when, as you know perfectly well, I was quite of the opposite way of thinking, and if you are courting my daughter with a view to lawful matrimony I am ready to satisfy you immediately, seeing that has always been the object of my keenest desires, in the hopes of which I remain always ready to be of service to you.

> ALEKSANDRA PODTOCHINA

"No," said Kovaliov to himself after reading the letter, "she really is not to blame. It's impossible. The letter is written as it could not be written by anyone guilty of a crime." The collegiate assessor was an expert on this subject, as he had been sent several times to the Caucasus to conduct investigations. "In what way, by what fate, has this happened? Only the devil could understand it!" he said at last, letting his hands fall to his sides.

Meanwhile the rumors of this strange occurrence were spreading all over the town, and of course, not without special additions. Just at that time the minds of all were particularly interested in the marvelous: experiments in the influence of magnetism had been attracting public attention only recently. Moreover, the story of the dancing chair in Koniuchennaya Street was still fresh, and so

there is nothing surprising in the fact that people were soon beginning to say that the nose of a collegiate assessor called Kovaliov was
walking along Nevsky Prospekt at exactly three in the afternoon.
Numbers of inquisitive people flocked there every day. Somebody
said that the nose was in Yunker's shop—and near Yunker's there
was such a crowd and such a crush that the police were actually
obliged to intervene. One speculator, a man of dignified appearance with whiskers, who used to sell all sorts of cakes and tarts
at the doors of the theaters, purposely constructed some very
strong wooden benches, which he offered to the curious to stand
on, for eighty kopeks each. One very worthy colonel left home
earlier on account of it, and with a great deal of trouble made his
way through the crowd; but to his great indignation, instead of
the nose, he saw in the shop windows the usual woolen undershirt
and a lithograph depicting a girl pulling up her stocking while a
foppish young man, with a cutaway waistcoat and a small beard,
peeps at her from behind a tree; a picture which had been hanging
in the same place for more than ten years. As he walked away he
said with vexation: "How can people be led astray by such stupid
and incredible stories!" Then the rumor spread that it was not on
Nevsky Prospekt but in Tavrichersky Park that Major Kovaliov's
nose took its walks; that it had been there for a long time; that,
even when Khozrev-Mirza[2] used to live there, he was greatly surprised at this strange freak of nature. Several students from the
Academy of Surgery made their way to the park. One worthy lady
of high rank wrote a letter to the superintendent of the park asking
him to show her children this rare phenomenon with, if possible, an
explanation that should be edifying and instructive for the young.
   All the gentlemen who invariably attend social gatherings and
like to amuse the ladies were extremely thankful for all these
events, for their stock of anecdotes was completely exhausted. A
small group of worthy and well-intentioned persons were greatly
displeased. One gentleman said with indignation that he could not
understand how in the present enlightened age people could spread
abroad these absurd stories, and that he was surprised that the government took no notice of it. This gentleman, as may be seen, belonged to the number of those who would like the government to
meddle in everything, even in their daily quarrels with their wives.

---

[2] Persian prince who arrived in Russia in 1829 to offer an official apology for
the murder of A. S. Griboedov, Russian ambassador to Teheran. (ed.)

After this . . . but here again the whole adventure is lost in fog, and what happened afterward is absolutely unknown.

III

What is utterly absurd happens in the world. Sometimes there is not the slightest semblance of truth to it: all at once that very nose which had been driving about the place in the shape of a civil councilor, and had made such a stir in the town, turned up again as though nothing had happened, in its proper place, that is, precisely between the two cheeks of Major Kovaliov. This took place on the seventh of April. Waking up and casually glancing into the mirror, he sees—his nose! puts up his hands—actually his nose! "Aha!" said Kovaliov, and in his joy he almost danced a jig barefoot about his room; but the entrance of Ivan stopped him. He ordered Ivan to bring him water at once, and as he washed he glanced once more into the mirror—the nose! As he wiped himself with the towel he glanced into the mirror—the nose!

"Look, Ivan, I think I have a pimple on my nose," he said, while he thought: "How horrible it will be if Ivan says, 'No, indeed, sir, there's no pimple and, indeed, there is no nose either!' "

But Ivan said: "There is nothing, there is no pimple: your nose is quite clear!"

"Damn it, that's wonderful!" the major said to himself, and he snapped his fingers.

At that moment Ivan Yakovlevich the barber peeped in at the door, but as timidly as a cat who had just been beaten for stealing the bacon.

"Tell me first: are your hands clean?" Kovaliov shouted to him while he was still some way off.

"Yes."

"You are lying!"

"Upon my word, they are clean, sir."

"Well, be careful."

Kovaliov sat down. Ivan Yakovlevich covered him up with a towel, and in one instant with the aid of his brushes had smothered the whole of his beard and part of his cheek in cream, like that which is served at merchants' name-day parties.

"Look here!" Ivan Yakovlevich said to himself, glancing at the nose and then turning his customer's head on the other side and looking at it sideways. "There it is, sure enough. What can it mean?" He went on pondering, and for a long while he gazed at the nose. At last, lightly, with a cautiousness which may well be imagined, he raised two fingers to take it by the tip. Such was Ivan Yakovlevich's system.

"Now, now, now, careful!" cried Kovaliov. Ivan Yakovlevich let his hands drop, and was flustered and confused as he had never been confused before. At last he began gently tickling him with the razor under his beard, and, although it was difficult and not at all easy for him to shave without holding on to the olfactory portion of the face, yet he did at last somehow, pressing his rough thumb into his cheek and lower jaw, overcome all difficulties, and finish shaving him.

When it was all over, Kovaliov at once made haste to dress, took a cab, and drove to the café. Before he was inside the door he shouted: "Waiter, a cup of chocolate!" and at the same instant peeped at himself in the mirror. The nose was there. He turned around gaily and, with a satirical air, slightly screwing up his eyes, looked at two military men, one of whom had a nose hardly bigger than a vest button. After that he started off for the office of the department, in which he was urging his claims to a post as vice-governor or, failing that, the post of an executive clerk. After crossing the reception room he glanced at the mirror; the nose was there. Then he drove to see another collegiate assessor or major, who was very fond of making fun of people, and to whom he often said in reply to various biting observations: "Ah, you! I know you, you are as sharp as a pin!" On the way he thought: "If the major does not split with laughter when he sees me, then it is a sure sign that everything is in its place." But the sarcastic collegiate assessor said nothing. "Good, good, damn it all!" Kovaliov thought to himself. On the way he met Podtochina, the officer's wife, and her daughter; he was profuse in his bows to them and was greeted with exclamations of delight—so there could be nothing wrong with him, he thought. He conversed with them for a long time and, taking out his snuffbox, purposely put a pinch to each nostril while he said to himself: "So much for you, you foolish petticoats, you hens! but I am not going to marry your daughter anyway. This is only *par amour!*"

And from that time forth Major Kovaliov promenaded about, as though nothing had happened, on Nevsky Prospekt, and at the theaters and everywhere. And the nose, too, as though nothing had happened, sat on his face without even a sign of coming off at the sides. And after this Major Kovaliov was always seen in a good humor, smiling, resolutely pursuing all the pretty ladies, and even on one occasion stopping before a shop in the Gostiny Court[3] and buying the ribbon of some order, I cannot say for what purpose, since he was not himself a cavalier of any order.

So this is the strange event that occurred in the northern capital of our spacious empire! Only now, on thinking it all over, we perceive that there is a great deal that is improbable in it. Apart from the fact that it certainly is strange for a nose supernaturally to leave its place and to appear in various places in the guise of a civil councilor—how was it that Kovaliov did not grasp that he could not advertise about his nose in a newspaper office? I do not mean to say that I should think it too expensive to advertise: that is nonsense, and I am by no means a mercenary person: but it is improper, awkward, not nice! And again: how did the nose get into the loaf, and how about Ivan Yakovlevich himself? . . . no, that I cannot understand, I am absolutely unable to understand it! But what is stranger, what is more incomprehensible than anything is that authors can choose such subjects. I confess that is quite beyond my grasp, it really is . . . No, no! I cannot understand it at all. In the first place, it is absolutely without profit to our country; in the second place . . . but in the second place, too, there is no profit. I really do not know what to say of it. . . .

And yet, in spite of it all, though of course one may admit the first point, the second and the third . . . may even . . . but there, are there not absurd things everywhere?—and yet, when you think it over, there really is something in it. Despite what anyone may say, such things do happen—not often, but they do happen.

---

[3] Large shopping center in St. Petersburg. (ed.)

THE COACH

The little town of B—— has grown much more lively since a cavalry regiment began to be stationed in it. Before then it was incredibly dull. When one drove through it and glanced at the low-pitched, painted houses which looked into the street with a terribly sour expression . . . well, it is impossible to put into words what things were like there: it is as dejecting as though one had lost money at cards, or just said something stupid and inappropriate—in short, it is depressing. The plaster on the houses has peeled off with the rain, and the walls instead of being white are piebald; the roofs are for the most part thatched with reeds, as is usual in our southern towns. The gardens have long ago, by order of the mayor, been cut down to improve the look of the place. There is never a soul to be met in the streets; at most a cock crosses the road, soft as a pillow from the dust that lies on it eight inches thick and at the slightest drop of rain is transformed into mud, and then the streets of the town of B—— are filled with fat animals which the local mayor calls Frenchmen; thrusting out their huge snouts from their baths, they begin grunting so loudly that the traveler can do nothing but urge on his horses. It is not easy, however, to meet a traveler in the town of B——. On rare, very rare occasions, some country gentleman, owning eleven serfs and dressed in a full nankeen coat, jolts over the road in something which is a sort of compromise between a carriage and a cart, and peeps out from behind piled-up sacks of flour, as he lashes his mare beside which runs a colt. Even the market place has rather a melancholy air: the tailor's shop is idiotically located, not facing the street but meeting it sideways; facing it, a brick building with two windows has been under construction for fifteen years; a little further, standing all by itself, there is one of those paling fences once so fashionable, painted gray to match the mud, and erected as a model for other buildings by the mayor in the days of his youth, before he had formed the habit of sleeping immediately after dinner and drinking at night a beverage flavored with dry gooseberries. In other parts the fences are all of wattle. In the middle of the square, there are very tiny shops; in them one may always see a bunch of pretzels, a peasant woman in a red kerchief, forty pounds of soap, a few pounds of bitter almonds, buckshot, some cotton material, and two shopmen who spend all their time playing a sort of quoits near the door.

But as soon as the cavalry regiment was stationed at the little town of B—— everything was changed: the streets were full of life and color, in fact, they assumed quite a different aspect; the low-pitched little houses often saw a graceful, well-built officer with a plume on his head passing by on his way to discuss promotion or the best kind of tobacco with a comrade, or sometimes to play cards for the carriage, which might have been described as regimental because, without ever leaving the regiment, it had already gone the round of all the officers; one day the major rolled up in it, the next day it was to be seen in the lieutenant's stable, and a week later, lo and behold, the major's orderly was greasing its wheels again. The wooden fence between the houses was always studded with soldiers' caps hanging in the sun; a gray military overcoat was always conspicuous on some gate; in the side streets soldiers were to be seen with mustaches as stiff as boot brushes. These mustaches were on view everywhere; if workwomen gathered in the market with their tin mugs, one could always get a glimpse of a mustache behind their shoulders. The officers brought life into the local society which had until then consisted of a judge, who lived in the same house with a deacon's wife, and a mayor, who was a very sagacious person, but slept absolutely the whole day from lunch to supper and from supper to lunch. Society gained even more in numbers and interest when the headquarters of the general of the brigade were transferred to the town. Neighboring landowners, whose existence no one would previously have suspected, began visiting the district town more frequently to see the officers and sometimes to play "bank," a card game of which there was an extremely hazy notion in their brains, busy with thoughts of crops and hares and their wives' commissions.

I am very sorry that I cannot recall what circumstance it was that led the general of the brigade to give a big dinner; preparations for it were made on a vast scale; the clatter of the cooks' knives in the general's kitchen could be heard almost as far as the town gate. The whole market was completely drained for the dinner, so that the judge and his deaconess had nothing to eat but buckwheat cakes. The little courtyard of the general's quarters was packed with chaises and carriages. The company consisted of gentlemen —officers and a few neighboring landowners. Of the latter, the most noteworthy was Pythagoras Pythagorasovich Chertokutsky, one of the leading aristocrats of the district of B———, who made more noise than anyone at the elections and drove to them in a very smart carriage. He had once served in a cavalry regiment and had been one of its most important and conspicuous officers, anyway he had been seen at numerous balls and assemblies, wherever his regiment had been stationed; the young ladies of the Tambov and Simbirsk provinces, however, could tell us most about that. It is very possible that he would have gained a desirable reputation in other provinces, too, if he had not resigned his commission owing to one of those incidents which are usually described as "an unpleasantness"; either he had given someone a box on the ear in the old days, or was given it; which I don't remember for certain; anyway, the point is that he was asked to resign his commission. He lost nothing of his importance through this, however. He wore a high-waisted dress coat of military cut, spurs on his boots, and a mustache under his nose, since, but for that, the nobility of his province might have supposed that he had served in the infantry, which he always spoke of contemptuously. He visited all the much-frequented fairs, to which those who make up the heart of Russia, that is, the nurses and children, stout landowners and their daughters, flock to enjoy themselves, driving in chaises with hoods, gigs, wagonettes, and carriages such as have never been seen in the wildest dreams. He had a special talent for smelling out where a cavalry regiment was stationed, and always went to interview the officers, very nimbly leaping out of his light carriage in view of them and very quickly making their acquaintance. At the last election he had given the nobility of the provinces an excellent dinner, at which he had declared that, if only he were elected leader, he "would put the gentlemen on the best possible footing." Altogether he lived like a gentleman, as the expression goes in the provinces; he married a rather pretty wife, getting with her a dowry of two hundred serfs and some thousands in cash. The money was at once spent on a team of six really first-rate horses, gilt locks on the doors, a tame monkey, and a French butler for the household. The two hundred serfs, together with two hundred of his own, were mortgaged to the bank for the sake of some commercial operations.

In short, he was a proper sort of landowner, a very decent sort of landowner . . .

Apart from this gentleman, there were a few other landowners at the general's dinner, but there is no need to describe them. The other guests were the officers of the same regiment, besides two staff officers, a colonel, and a fat major. The general himself was a big, fat man, though an excellent commanding officer, so the others said of him. He spoke in a rather thick, important bass. The dinner was remarkable; sturgeon of various sorts, as well as sterlet, bustards, asparagus, quails, partridges, and mushrooms, testified to the fact that the cook had not had a drop of anything strong between his lips since the previous day, and that four soldiers had been at work with knives in their hands all night, helping him with the fricassee and the jelly. A multitude of bottles, tall ones with Lafitte and short ones with Madeira; a lovely summer day, windows wide open, plates of ice on the table, the crumpled shirt fronts of the owners of extremely roomy dress coats, a cross fire of conversation drowned by the general's voice and washed down by champagne—all was in harmony. After dinner they all got up from the table with a pleasant heaviness in their stomachs, and, after lighting pipes, some with long and some with short mouthpieces, went out onto the steps with cups of coffee in their hands.

"You can look at her now," said the general; "if you please, my dear boy," he went on, addressing his adjutant, a rather sprightly young man of agreeable appearance, "tell them to bring the bay mare around! here you shall see for yourself." At this point the general took a pull at his pipe and blew out the smoke: "She is not quite well-groomed; this wretched, damned little town! She is a very"—puff-puff—"decent mare!"

"And have you"—puff-puff—"had her long, your Excellency?" said Chertokutsky.

"Well" . . . puff-puff-puff . . . "not so long; it's only two years since I had her from the stud farm."

"And did you get her broken in, or have you been breaking her in here, your Excellency?"

Puff-puff-pu—ff-puff. "Here." Saying this the general completely disappeared in smoke.

Meanwhile a soldier skipped out of the stables, the thud of hoofs was audible, and at last another soldier with huge black mustaches, wearing a white smock, appeared, leading by the bridle a trembling and frightened mare, who, suddenly flinging up her head, almost lifted the soldier and his mustaches into the air.

"There, there, Agrafena Ivanovna!" he said, leading her up to the steps.

The mare's name was Agrafena Ivanovna. Strong and wild as a beauty of the south, she stamped her hoof upon the wooden steps, then suddenly stopped.

The general, laying down his pipe, began with a satisfied air to look at Agrafena Ivanovna. The colonel himself went down the steps and took Agrafena Ivanovna by the nose, the major patted Agrafena Ivanovna on the leg, the others made a clicking sound with their tongues.

Chertokutsky went down and approached her from behind; the soldier, drawn up to attention and holding the bridle, looked straight into the visitor's eyes as though he wanted to jump into them.

"Very, very fine," said Chertokutsky, "a horse with excellent points! And allow me to ask your Excellency, how does she trot?"

"Her action is very good, only . . . that fool of a doctor's assistant, damn the man, gave her pills of some sort and for the last two days she has done nothing but sneeze."

"Very fine horse, very; and have you a suitable carriage, your Excellency?"

"A carriage? . . . But she is a saddle horse, you know."

"I know that, but I asked your Excellency to find out whether you have a suitable carriage for your other horses."

"Well, I am not very well off for carriages, I must admit; I have long been wanting to get a modern one. I have written to my brother who is in Petersburg just now, but I don't know whether he'll send me one or not."

"I think, your Excellency, there are no better carriages than the Viennese."

"You are quite right there." Puff-puff-puff——

"I have an excellent carriage, your Excellency, of real Vienna make."

"What is it like? Is it the one you came here in?"

"Oh no, that's just for rough work, for my excursions, but the other . . . It is a wonder! light as a feather, and when you are in it, it is simply, if I may say so, as though your nurse were rocking you in the cradle!"

"So it is comfortable?"

"Very comfortable indeed; cushions, springs, like a picture."

"That's nice."

"And so roomy! As a matter of fact, your Excellency, I have never seen one like it. When I was in the service I used to put a dozen bottles of rum and twenty pounds of tobacco in the luggage compartment, and besides that I used to have about six uniforms and underwear and two pipes, the very long ones, your Excellency, while you could put a whole ox in the glove compartment."

"That's nice."

"It cost four thousand, your Excellency."

"At that price it ought to be good; and did you buy it yourself?"

"No, your Excellency, it came to me by chance; it was bought by my friend, the companion of my childhood, a rare man with whom you would have got on perfectly, your Excellency; we were on such terms that what was his was mine, it was all the same. I won it from him at cards. Would you care, your Excellency, to do me the honor to dine with me tomorrow, and you could have a look at the carriage at the same time?"

"I really don't know what to say . . . for me to come alone like that . . . would you allow me to bring the other officers?"

"I beg the other officers to come too. Gentlemen! I shall think it a great pleasure to see you in my house."

The colonel, the major, and the other officers thanked him with a polite bow.

"What I think, your Excellency, is that if one buys a thing it must be good; if it is not good there is no use having it. When you do me the honor of visiting me tomorrow, I will show you a few other practical things I have bought."

The general looked at him and blew smoke out of his mouth. Chertokutsky was highly delighted at having invited the officers: he was inwardly ordering pastries and sauces while he looked very good-humoredly at the gentlemen in question, who for their part, too, seemed to feel twice as amiably disposed to him, as could be discerned from their eyes and the small movements they made, such as half bows. Chertokutsky spoke with more familiarity, and there was a softness in his voice as though it were weighed down with pleasure.

"There, your Excellency, you will make the acquaintance of my wife."

"I shall be delighted," said the general, stroking his mustache.

After that Chertokutsky wanted to set off for home at once so that he might prepare everything for the reception of his guests and the dinner to be offered them; he took his hat, but, strangely enough, it happened that he stayed on for some time. Meanwhile card tables were set up in the room. Soon the whole company was divided into parties of four for whist and sat down in the different corners of the general's room. Candles were brought; for a long time Chertokutsky was uncertain whether to sit down to whist or not, but as the officers began to press him to do so, he felt that it would be a breach of the rules of etiquette to refuse, and he sat down for a little while. By his side there appeared from somewhere a glass of punch which, without noticing it, he drank off instantly. After winning two rubbers Chertokutsky again found a glass of punch at hand and again without observing it emptied the glass, though he did say first: "It's time for me to be getting home, gentlemen, it really is time," but again he sat down to the second game.

Meanwhile conversation assumed an entirely personal character in the different corners of the room. The whist players were rather silent, but those who were not playing sat on sofas at one side and kept up a conversation of their own. In one corner a captain, with a cushion thrust under his back and a pipe between his teeth, was recounting in a free and flowing style his amatory adventures, which completely absorbed the attention of a circle gathered around him. One extremely fat landowner with short hands rather like overgrown potatoes was listening with an extraordinary mawkish air, and only from time to time exerted himself to get his short arm behind his broad back and pull out his snuffbox. In another corner a rather heated discussion sprang up concerning squadron drill, and Chertokutsky, who about that time twice threw down a jack instead of a queen, suddenly intervened in this conversation, which was not addressed to him, and shouted from his corner: "In what year?" or "Which regiment?" without observing that the question had nothing to do with the matter under discussion. Finally, a few minutes before supper, they stopped playing, though the games went on verbally and it seemed as though the heads of all were full of whist. Chertokutsky remembered perfectly that he had won a great deal, but he picked up nothing, and getting up from the tables stood for a long time in the attitude of a man who has found he has no handkerchief. Meanwhile supper was served. It need hardly be said that there was no lack of wines and that Chertokutsky was almost obliged to fill up his own glass at times because there were bottles standing on the right and on the left of him.

A very long conversation dragged on at table, but it was rather oddly conducted. One colonel who had served in the campaign of 1812 described a battle such as had certainly never taken place, and then, I am quite unable to say for what reason, took the stopper out of the decanter and stuck it in the pudding. In short, by the time the party began to break up it was three o'clock, and the coachmen were obliged to carry some of the gentlemen in their arms as though they had been parcels of groceries, and in spite of all his aristocratic breeding Chertokutsky bowed so low and with such a violent lurch of his head, as he got into his carriage, that he brought two burrs home with him on his mustaches.

At home everyone was sound asleep. The coachman had some difficulty in finding a footman, who conducted his master across the drawing room and handed him over to a chambermaid, in whose charge Chertokutsky made his way to his bedroom and got into bed beside his young and pretty wife, who was lying in the most enchanting way in a snow-white nightgown. The jolt made by her husband falling upon the bed awakened her. Stretching, lifting her eyelashes, and three times rapidly blinking her eyes, she opened them with a half-angry smile, but seeing that he absolutely declined on this occasion to show any interest in her, she turned over on the other side in vexation, and laying her fresh little cheek on her arm, soon afterward fell asleep.

It was at an hour which would not in the country be described
as early that the young mistress of the house woke up beside her
snoring spouse. Remembering that it had been nearly four o'clock
in the morning when he came home, she did not like to wake him,
and so, putting on her bedroom slippers which her husband had
ordered for her from Petersburg, and with a white dressing gown
draped about her like a flowing stream, she washed in water as
fresh as herself and proceeded to dress for the day. Glancing at
herself a couple of times in the mirror, she saw that she was looking
very nice that morning. This apparently insignificant circumstance
led her to spend two hours extra before the mirror. At last she was
very charmingly dressed and went out to take an airing in the
garden. As luck would have it, the weather was as lovely as it can
only be on a summer day in the South. The sun, directly overhead, was blazing hot; but it was cool walking on the thick, dark
paths, and the flowers were three times as fragrant in the warmth
of the sun. The pretty young wife quite forgot that it was now
twelve o'clock and her husband was still asleep. Already she could
hear the after-dinner snores of two coachmen and one groom
sleeping in the stable beyond the garden, but she still sat in a
shady spot from which there was an open view of the road, and
was absent-mindedly watching it, stretching empty and deserted
into the distance, when all at once a cloud of dust appearing in that
distance attracted her attention. Gazing intently, she soon discovered several carriages. The foremost was a light open carriage with
two seats. In it was sitting a general with thick epaulets that
gleamed in the sun, and beside him a colonel. It was followed by
another carriage with seats for four in which were the major, the
general's adjutant, and two officers facing. Then came the regimental chaise, familiar to everyone, at the moment in the possession of the fat major. The chaise was followed by another vehicle
known as a *bon-voyage*, in which there were four officers seated
and a fifth on their knees; then came three officers on excellent,
dark bay dappled horses.

"Then they may be coming to us," thought the lady. "Oh, my
goodness, they really are! They have turned at the bridge!" She
uttered a shriek, clasped her hands, and ran right over the flower
beds straight to her husband's bedroom; he was sleeping like the
dead.

"Get up! Get up! Make haste and get up!" she shouted, tugging at his arm.

"What?" murmured Chertokutsky, not opening his eyes.

"Get up, angel! Do you hear, visitors!"

"Visitors? What visitors?" . . . Saying this he uttered a slight grunt such as a calf gives when it is looking for its mother's udder. "Mm . . ." he muttered: "stoop your neck, precious! I'll give you a kiss."

"Darling, get up, for goodness' sake, make haste! The general and the officers! Oh dear, you've got a burr on your mustache!"

"The general! So he is coming already, then? But why the devil did nobody wake me? And the dinner, what about the dinner? Is everything ready that's wanted?"

"What dinner?"

"Why, didn't I order it?"

"You came back at four o'clock in the morning and you did not say one word to me, however much I questioned you. I didn't wake you, precious, because I felt sorry for you, you had had no sleep! . . ."

The last words she uttered in an extremely supplicating and languishing voice.

Chertokutsky lay for a minute in bed with his eyes popping out of his head, as though struck by a thunderbolt. At last he jumped out of bed with nothing but his shirt on, forgetting that this was quite indecent.

"Oh, I am an ass!" he said, slapping himself on the forehead. "I invited them to dinner! What's to be done? Are they far off?"

"I don't know . . . I expect they will be here any minute."

"My love . . . hide yourself . . . Hey, who's there? You wretched girl, come in; what are you afraid of, you fool? The officers will be here in a minute: you say that your master is not at home, say that he won't be home at all, that he went out early in the morning . . . Do you hear? and tell all the servants the same; make haste!" Saying this, he hurriedly snatched up his dressing gown and ran to hide in the carriage house, supposing that there he would be in a position of complete security, but, standing in the corner of the carriage house, he saw that even there he might be seen. "Ah, this will be better," flashed through his mind, and in one minute he flung down the steps of the carriage standing near, jumped in, closed the door after him, for greater security covering himself with the leather apron, and lay perfectly still, curled up in his dressing gown.

Meanwhile the carriages drove up to the front steps. The general stepped out and shook himself; after him the colonel, smoothing the plume of his hat with his hands, then the fat major, holding his saber under his arm, jumped out of the chaise, the slim sublieutenants skipped down from the *bon-voyage* with the lieutenant who had been sitting on the others' knees, and, last of all, the officers who had been elegantly riding on horseback alighted from their saddles.

"The master is not at home," said a footman, coming out onto the steps.

"Not at home? He'll be back at dinner, I suppose?"

"No. His Honor has gone out for the whole day. He won't be back until tomorrow about this time, perhaps."

"Well, I'll be damned!" said the general. "What is the meaning of this?"

"What a joke!" said the colonel, laughing.

"No, really . . . how can he behave like this?" the general went on with displeasure. "Whew! . . . Damn it! . . . why, if he can't receive people, why does he ask them?"

"I can't understand how anyone could do it, your Excellency," a young officer observed.

"What, what?" said the general, who had the habit of always uttering this interrogative monosyllable when he was talking to an officer.

"I said, your Excellency, that it is not the way to behave!"

"Naturally . . . why, if anything has happened, he might let us know at any rate, or else not have asked us."

"Well, your Excellency, there's nothing we can do, we shall have to go back," said the colonel.

"Of course, there is nothing else to do. We can look at the carriage, though, without him; it is not likely he has taken it with him. Hey, you there! Come here, my man!"

"What is your pleasure?"

"Are you the stableboy?"

"Yes, your Excellency."

"Show us the new carriage your master got lately."

"This way, sir; come to the carriage house."

The general went to the carriage house with the officers.

"Shall I push it out a little? It is rather dark in here."

"That's enough, that's enough, that's right!"

The general and the officers stood around the carriage and carefully examined the wheels and the springs.

"Well, there is nothing special about it," said the general. "It is a most ordinary carriage."

"A very ugly one," said the colonel; "there is nothing good about it at all."

"I think, your Excellency, it is not worth four thousand," said the young officer.

"What?"

"I say, your Excellency, that I think it is not worth four thousand."

"Four thousand, indeed! why, it is not worth two, there is nothing in it at all. Perhaps there is something special about the inside . . . Unbutton the apron, my dear fellow, please."

And what met the officers' eyes was Chertokutsky sitting in his dressing gown, curled up in an extraordinary way. "Ah, you are here!" . . . said the astonished general.

Saying this he slammed the carriage door at once, covered Chertokutsky with the leather apron again, and drove away with the officers.

THE PORTRAIT[1]

PART I

Nowhere were so many people standing as before the little picture shop in Shchukin Court.[2] The shop did indeed contain the most varied collection of curiosities: the pictures were for the most part painted in oils, covered with dark green varnish, in dark-yellow gilt frames. A winter scene with white trees, an absolutely red sunset that looked like the glow of a conflagration, a Flemish peasant with a pipe and a broken arm, more like a turkey cock in frills than a human being—such were usually their subjects. To these must be added some engravings: a portrait of Khozrev-Mirza[3] in a sheepskin cap, and portraits of generals with crooked noses in three-cornered hats.

---

[1] This is the final (1842) version of the story. Because Mrs. Garnett translated only the earlier version (which appeared in 1835, as one of the pieces in *Arabesques*), this is an almost completely new translation—only about one hundred lines of the original having survived. The 1842 version is profoundly different from the earlier one; not even the artist's original name (Chertkov) being retained (it becomes Chartkov). The final version, for the most part, is less blatantly fantastic; it is infused with realistic elements (e.g., the portrait no longer simply disappears, but the word "stolen" is added and seriously alters the tone); the emphasis is shifted (from the fantastic and mysterious to the concepts of religion, retribution, and expiation—things with which Gogol was becoming more and more obsessed). Gogol knew of an Indian money-lender who catered to the actors in St. Petersburg, and one of the actors described his "bronze face" and singular eyes. (ed.)

[2] One of the numerous open-air markets in St. Petersburg. (ed.)

[3] A Persian prince (see p. 494, n. 2, for fuller comment). (ed.)

The doors of such shops are usually hung with bundles of pictures[4] which bear witness to the native talent of the Russian. On one of them was the Czarina Miliktrisa Kirbityevna,[5] on another the city of Jerusalem, over the houses and churches of which a flood of red color was flung without stint, covering half the earth, and two Russian peasants in big gloves kneeling in prayer. The purchasers of these creations were commonly few in number, but there was always a crowd looking at them. Some dissipated footman would usually be gaping at them with dishes from the restaurant in his hand for the dinner of his master, whose soup would certainly not be too hot. A soldier in a greatcoat, a cavalier of the flea market, with two penknives to sell, and a peddler woman from Okhta with a box filled with slippers would be sure to be standing before them. Each one would show his enthusiasm in his own way: the peasants usually point with their fingers; the soldiers examine them seriously; the footboys and the apprentices laugh and tease each other over the colored caricatures; old footmen in frieze overcoats stare at them simply because they offer somewhere to stop and gape; and the peddler women, young women from the villages, hasten there by instinct, eager to hear what people are gossiping about and to see what people are looking at.

At this time, Chartkov, a young artist who was passing by, paused involuntarily before the shop. His old overcoat and unfashionable clothes indicated that he was a man who devoted himself to his work with self-denying zeal and had not time to worry himself about clothes, which usually have a mysterious attraction for young people. He stopped before the shop, at first inwardly laughing at the grotesque pictures; at last he sank unconsciously into meditation: he began wondering to whom these productions were of use. That the Russian people should gaze at the Eruslan Lazereviches, at the Gluttons and Imbibers, on Foma and Erioma,[6] did not strike him as surprising: the subjects depicted were well within the grasp and comprehension of the people; but where were the purchasers of these gaudy, dirty oil paintings? Who wanted these Flemish peasants, these red and blue landscapes which bespoke pre-

---

[4] *Lubok,* cheap tricolored work dealing with popular subjects, e.g., a wistful girl, a forlorn soldier, a battle scene, comic figures. (ed.)
[5] Fairy princess of "Bova-Korolevich" ("Prince Bova"), a popular folktale. (ed.)
[6] Comic figures which were often the subject of the *Lubok.* (ed.)

tension to a rather high level of art, though its most profound degradation was displayed in them? If only they had been the works
of a precocious child obeying an unconscious impulse; in that event,
in spite of the intentional caricature of the design, one would have
perceived in them a certain intensity of feeling; but all that could
be found in them was a total lack of talent, the feeble, faltering,
dull incompetence of a born failure that impudently pushes himself among the arts, while his true place is among the lowest crafts,
a failure which is true, nevertheless, to its vocation, and drags its
trade into art. The same colors, the same manner, the same practiced, accustomed hand which seemed to belong to a crudely
fashioned automaton rather than to a man. He stood for a long time
before these grimy pictures without even thinking of them any
more; but meanwhile, the proprietor of the shop, a little drab man
in a frieze overcoat and with a beard which had not been shaved
since Sunday, had been nudging him for some time, bargaining
and discussing prices, without even knowing what pleased him or
what he was likely to buy.

"I'll take a white note[7] for these peasants, and for this little landscape. What art! It almost makes your eyes pop out! I just received
them from the factory; the varnish is not yet quite dry. Or here is
a winter scene—take the winter scene. It's only fifteen rubles!
The frame alone is worth more than that. What a winter scene!"
Here the art merchant tapped the canvas lightly with his finger as
if to demonstrate the fine merits of the winter landscape. "Shall I
tie them all up and take them to your place? Where do you live?
Hey, boy, give me some string!"

"Wait, brother, not so fast!" said the artist, recovering with a jolt
as he saw the enterprising dealer beginning in earnest to tie up the
pictures. He was a little ashamed not to take anything after being
in the shop for so long, and he said, "Wait a minute, I'll see if
there's anything I want here," and bending over, he began picking
up from the floor, from where they had been thrown in a heap,
worn, dusty old paintings, which evidently no longer were considered to be of value. Among these there were old family portraits,
whose descendants, probably, could no longer be found on earth,
totally unknown pictures on torn canvases, frames which had lost
their gilding; in short, all sorts of trash. But the painter began his

---

[7] Colloquial for twenty rubles. (ed.)

search, thinking to himself, "Perhaps I will find something." He had heard stories about pictures of the great masters having been found among the rubbish of popular print shops.

The dealer, perceiving that he was likely to be busy for some time, ceased his importunities, and, assuming his usual attitude and the proper expression which is its concomitant, once more took his position at the door of his shop, hailing the passers-by, and pointing to his store with one hand.

"Come in, friends, look at my pictures. Come in, come in! Just received them from the factory!" He shouted till he was hoarse, and generally in vain, had a long conversation with a rag merchant who was standing opposite him at the door of his shop, and finally, remembering that he had a customer in his shop, he turned his back on the public and again went inside. "Well, friend, have you selected anything?" The artist, however, had been standing motionless for some time before a portrait in a very large and once-magnificent frame, a frame which retained only a trace of its original gilt. The portrait was of an old man with a face of a bronze hue, thin and with high cheekbones; it seemed as if the features of his face were caught in a moment of convulsive agitation, and there was a puissance about the face which bespoke the fact that it was not of the north. The torrid south was imprinted upon the features. About his shoulders a voluminous Asiatic costume was draped. The portrait was dusty and had suffered damage, but Chartkov, after removing the dust which covered the face, could see undeniable evidence of a great artist. The portrait had apparently never been finished, but the strength of the artist's hand was amazing. The eyes were the most singular of all the features; it was apparent that the artist had used the full power of his brush and that all his care had been lavished on them. They seemed to glare, glare out of the portrait, destroying its harmony with their unnatural liveliness. When he carried the portrait to the door, the eyes glared with even more penetration, and the people before the shop were impressed almost the same way. A woman who was standing behind him cried, "He looks at you, he looks!" and she drew back. Chartkov experienced a discomforting feeling, a feeling that was inexplicable, and he put the portrait down on the floor.

"Well? You going to take the portrait?" said the dealer.

"How much?" asked the artist.

"Why quibble about it? I'll take seventy-five kopeks."

"No."

"How much will you give me?"

"Twenty kopeks," said the artist preparing to leave.

"What a price! Why, even the frame couldn't be bought for that! Perhaps you will return and buy it tomorrow. Sir, sir, come back! Add another ten kopeks. All right, take it! Take it for twenty kopeks. The only reason I sell it to you at that price is that, to be honest, you are my first customer today." Then the dealer gestured as if to say, "Ah well, so be it!"

Thus it was that Chartkov quite unexpectedly bought the old portrait, and at once he wondered, "Why did I buy it! Why do I need it?" But there was nothing Chartkov could do about it. He took the twenty-kopek note and gave it to the dealer, and carried home the portrait, under his arm. On the way home, he recalled that the note he had spent for it was his last. He grew depressed. Anger and a certain listlessness took possession of him at the same time. "Damn it! What a miserable world!" he said with the emotion of a man whose affairs have completely collapsed. And he walked toward home almost mechanically, faster than before, totally indifferent to everything. The red glow of sunset still lingered over half the sky; the houses which faced the sunset were faintly illuminated by its warm light, while the cold blue light of the moon grew more powerful. Light, half-transparent shadows were cast by houses and people, fell like long bars on the earth. More and more the artist began to glance at the sky, which was shimmering in a faint, translucent, uncertain light, and almost at the same moment there burst from his mouth the words, "What a delicate tone!" and the words, "Damn it! How upsetting!" He repositioned the portrait which was forever slipping from under his arm, and walked more quickly.

Exhausted, bathed in perspiration, he dragged himself to his home on the fifteenth row of Vasilievsky Island. He climbed the stairs, which were soaked with wash water and decorated with the footprints of dogs and cats. He knocked on the door. There was no answer. There was no one at home. He leaned against the window and determined to wait patiently, until, finally, the steps of a boy in a blue shirt sounded behind him. This was his servant, model, paint grinder, and scrubber of floors, and the one who dirtied the floors with his boots. The boy was called Nikita, and he spent all his free time in the streets. Nikita tried to position the key in the lock for a long time, a task made difficult by the darkness. Finally the door was opened, Chartkov entered his hall which, like the rooms of most artists, was unbearably cold, a circumstance which they hardly ever notice. Without giving his coat to Nikita, he went into his studio, a large, square but low room with frosted windowpanes, filled with all kinds of artistic rubbish: pieces of plaster hands, frames with canvas stretched over them, sketches begun and discarded, draperies thrown over chairs. He was extremely tired. He flung off his coat, absent-mindedly placed the portrait between two other pictures, and threw himself on a narrow sofa, a sofa which could hardly be determined to have been covered with leather, because a row of brass nails which had once fastened the leather to the frame of the sofa had long been standing by themselves, so that Nikita stuffed his dirty socks and shirts and all the dirty linen under it. Having stretched as far as it was possible to stretch on such a narrow sofa, Chartkov finally called for a candle.

"There are no more candles," said Nikita.

"Why not?"

"We didn't have any yesterday either," said Nikita. The artist remembered that there had indeed been no candles yesterday, and he calmed himself and grew silent. He allowed himself to be undressed, and he put on his old and very warm dressing gown.

"The landlord was here again," said Nikita.

"Well, he came because of money," Chartkov said, waving his hand.

"Well, he was not here alone," said Nikita.

"Who was with him?"

"I don't know who. Some policeman, it looked like."

"But why a policeman?"

"I don't know why," he said. "It's because you still haven't paid your rent."

"What will happen?"

"I don't know what will happen. He said, 'He will have to get out of the apartment if he can't pay.' They're both coming again tomorrow."

"Let them come," said Chartkov with mournful indifference, and melancholy gripped him.

Young Chartkov was an artist possessed of talent which augured a bright future; there were instances when his work bespoke his sharp observation, deep understanding, and a powerful inclination to draw closer to nature. "See here, brother," his professor said to him more than once, "you have talent. It would be shameful if you were to waste it, but you have no patience. If you happen to be attracted to something, you become so engrossed in it that everything else becomes meaningless, everything else becomes trivial, you won't even look at it. Be careful that you do not become a fashionable artist. Even now your colors seem to be gaudy and too blatant; your drawing is no longer strong, and many times it is very weak. The lines disappear; you are already endeavoring to imitate fashionable light effects, because they impress the eye quickly and effectively. Be careful that you do not become merely an imitator of the English school.[8] Take care. The outside world begins to attract you. I have already noticed you sometimes wearing a dandyish scarf or a shiny hat.[9] I know how tempting the prospect is. It is possible to paint portraits for money, to paint fashionable little pictures that sell, but in that event talent is destroyed, not developed. Be patient, devote yourself to every piece of work. Forget about fineries. Let others make money; your own time will not fail to come."

The professor was partially correct. Sometimes our artist wanted to carouse, to show off, in a word, to display in some way the fact that he was still young, but, despite this tendency, he could always control himself. At times, when he took a brush in his hand, he could forget everything, and he could only tear himself away from the brush very reluctantly, as one is reluctant to wake from a beautiful dream. His taste improved perceptibly. He was not yet capable of fathoming all the profundities of Raphael, but he was already attracted to Guido's[10] powerful and swift brush, lingered before the portraits by Titian,[11] was enthralled by the Flemish masters. He was unable to see through the dark veil which hid the works of the old masters, but he already saw something in them, though in his

---

[8] Reference is to those who were led by Sir Joshua Reynolds (1723-92), an eminent portrait painter and first president of the Royal Academy. The works of the English school were especially noted for their dignity and expressiveness, and for the beauty of their coloring. (ed.)
[9] I.e., a new one. (ed.)
[10] Guido Reni (1575-1642), Italian artist famous for the voluptuous sentimentality of his baroque paintings. (ed.)
[11] Tiziano Vecellio (1477-1576), celebrated Venetian painter renowned for his sumptuous, coloristic style. (ed.)

heart he disagreed with the view of his professor that the pinnacle reached by the old masters was unattainable for the modern painter. It seemed to him that the nineteenth century had in many ways already surpassed their accomplishment, that the presentation of nature had somehow become more vivid, clearer, more intimate. In a word, he was reasoning as young people always reason who have already accomplished some understanding and recognize it with conscious pride. He was sometimes angered when he noticed that a foreign artist, a Frenchman or a German, sometimes not even a professional painter but only a skilled dauber, was able to cause a general commotion and to amass a fortune almost immediately. This did not concern him when he was completely absorbed in his work, for on those occasions he quite forgot food and drink and the whole world, but when dire need occurred, when he was devoid of funds with which to buy brushes and paints, and when his relentless landlord came to his apartment ten times a day to demand rent, then it was that the good fortune of wealthy painters appealed to his hungry imagination so strongly; it was then that the thought which so often passes through the mind of a Russian flashed through his: to totally surrender to grief, to devote himself to drink. And now he was almost in such a mood.

"Yes, be patient, be patient!" he repeated angrily. "But even patience has its limits. Be patient! But what am I to use for dinner tomorrow? No one will lend me any money, and even if I were to take all my drawings and sketches to a dealer, he wouldn't give me more than twenty kopeks for the lot of them. They have been of some use to me. I am convinced that not one of them was a waste of time. Each one taught me something. But what use is it? Sketches, drafts. It's an endless process. And without knowing my name who would buy my pictures? Who wants drawings from the antique or from life? Or my unfinished Psyche, or my nature studies, or my portrait of Nikita, though it is, in truth, damned superior to the portraits of the fashionable artists? And what's it all for? Why do I trouble myself and burden myself like a student learning his ABC's when I might be no less famous than the rest of them and make as much money as they do?"

At these words, the artist suddenly shuddered and grew pale; a terribly distorted face stared at him from behind the canvas. Two horrible eyes fixed themselves on him as if getting ready to devour him; a menacing expression was on the lips. Terrified, he wanted to scream and call Nikita who was already loudly snoring in his room. Suddenly, however, he stopped and laughed. The feeling of fear left him in an instant; it was the portrait he had bought and completely forgotten. The light of the moon, illuminating the room, fell upon it and invested it with a singular lifelike quality. He began examining and wiping the portrait. Moistening a sponge with water, he wiped the portrait with it, washing off almost all the accumulated and encrusted dust and dirt, hung it on the wall before him and, more than ever, wondered at the quite remarkable quality of the painting. Almost the whole face seemed to have come alive, and the eyes looked at him in a way that made him shudder, and jumping back, he exclaimed in a voice full of astonishment, "It looks, it looks at you with human eyes!" Suddenly he remembered he had long ago heard from his professor a story of a portrait by Leonardo da Vinci.[12] The great master regarded it as unfinished though he had labored on it for several years, but, despite that, Vasari[13] considered it the most complete and finished example of his art. The most finished thing about it was the eyes, which amazed Leonardo's contemporaries; the most minute, almost invisible veins were not neglected and were committed to the canvas. But here in the portrait now before him there was something strange. This was no longer art. The eyes actually destroyed the harmony of the portrait. They were alive, human! It was as if they had been cut from a living man and inserted in the canvas. Here was none of that sublime feeling of enjoyment which imbued the spirit at the sight of an artist's endeavors, regardless of how terrible the subject he may have put on canvas. There was a painful, joyless sense of anxiety instead. "What's wrong?" the artist had to ask himself. "After all, this is only an imitation of something from life. Where does this strange and discomforting feeling come from? Or is a literal depiction of nature a crime which must affect one like a shrill discordant shriek? Or if you paint objectively and without feeling on some pathetic subject, must it confront you in all its fearful reality, unillumined by the light of some intangible, hidden

---

[12] The reference is very probably to the Mona Lisa. There are also two sketches in which the eyes are singular: his study of the head of St. James (1496), in which the eyes are dominant, and his study of the head of St. Philip (done the same year), a profile, in which both the eyes and the mouth are prominent, but it is unlikely that Gogol knew these. (ed.)

[13] Giorgio Vasari (1511-74), Italian art historian and critic. (ed.)

thought? Will it appear to you with the realism which is displayed when, searching to understand the secrets of the beauty in man, you arm yourself with a scalpel and dissect a man's insides only to discover the man? Why is it that in the work of one artist, simple, lowly nature appears so illumined that there is no sense of degradation? On the contrary! It is very pleasurable for some reason, and later everything flows more quietly and smoothly around you. And yet, in the hands of another artist, the same subject seems low and sordid, though he was true to nature, too. Actually, there is nothing illuminating in it. Something is lacking in it, regardless of how beautiful it is. It is like a landscape in nature; if the sun is not in the sky, regardless of how magnificent it may be, there is something lacking."

He once again approached the portrait to examine those wonderful eyes, and again noticed with horror that they were once more staring at him. This was no imitation of nature. It was a strange kind of life that might have lit up the face of a corpse arisen from the grave. Was it the effect of moonlight which brought with it fantastic thoughts and dreams, transformed everything into strange shapes so different from what they appeared like in absolute daylight? Or was there some other cause? He suddenly became—and he himself didn't know why—fearful of remaining in the room by himself. He walked softly away from the portrait, trying not to look at it, but his effort was wasted; involuntarily his eyes glanced at it furtively. He finally became frightened of walking in the room. He had a strange feeling that someone would be walking up behind him at any moment, and, apprehensively, he kept glancing over his shoulder. He was not a coward, but his imagination and his nerves were sensitive, and he could not have explained to himself of what he was so afraid that evening. He sat down in a corner, but even there he had the feeling that someone would any minute be peering over his shoulder and into his face. Even Nikita's snoring, which resounded from the hall, did not mitigate his fear. Finally he got up timidly, without raising his eyes, went behind the screen, undressed, went to bed. Through the chinks in the screen he could see the illumination of the moon in the room, and he saw the portrait immediately in front of him, hanging on the wall. The eyes were fixed upon him, more terribly and meaningfully than ever, and it seemed as if they would look at nothing but him. Overpowered by a feeling of restlessness, he determined to get up from his bed, seized a sheet and, walking up to the portrait, covered it up completely.

This accomplished, he once more lay down on his bed, and began to think of the poverty and the miserable fate of the artist, of the thorny path that awaits him in this world. Meanwhile his eyes looked involuntarily through the chinks in the screen, at the portrait covered by the sheet. The glow of the moon accented the whiteness of the sheet, and it seemed to Chartkov that the terrible eyes were glaring through the cloth. Terror-stricken, he stared at it as if he wished to convince himself that it was all nonsense. But . . . in fact . . . the sheet had disappeared and . . . the portrait was completely uncovered and, ignoring everything else, it stared straight at him; stared right into his heart . . . His heart grew cold, and suddenly he saw that the old man began moving and, presently, supporting himself on the frame with both arms, he raised himself on his hands and, thrusting out his legs, he leaped out of the frame. . . . Through the chink in the screen only the empty frame was visible. There were footsteps in the room, and they were drawing ever closer to the screen. The poor artist's heart pounded more and more violently. Panting, almost breathless from fear, he awaited the appearance of the old man who would look around the screen at him. Behold! He did indeed look behind the screen, his bronze face no different from before, and his big eyes staring about. Chartkov tried to scream, but his voice failed him; he tried to move, to make some gesture, but his limbs were as if paralyzed. With gaping mouth and failing breath, he gazed at this terrible phantom of great height, wearing some kind of voluminous Asiatic robe, and waited to see what it would do next. The old man sat down almost on his very feet, and pulled something out from between the folds of his wide robe. A bag. The old man untied it, seized it at both ends, and shook it. Heavy rolls of money like large rolls of coins fell on the floor with a dull thud; blue paper was wrapped about each roll, and each was marked: *1,000 gold coins.* The old man stretched forth his long, bony hands from his wide sleeves, and began unwrapping the rolls. The gold glittered, but however great the artist's fear and depression had been, he could not keep from looking greedily at the gold, staring motionless at it as it appeared, gleaming and ringing lightly or dully in the bony hands, and as it was again wrapped up. Then he noticed that one roll had rolled farther than the rest and was near the leg of his bed, near his pillow. He grasped it almost convulsively and, in terror, glanced at the old man to see whether he had seen it. But the old man was too occupied to notice anything. He collected all his rolls, put them back in the bag, and went around the screen without even looking at Chartkov. Chartkov's heart beat wildly as he heard the sound of the retreating footsteps. He clasped the roll more firmly in his hand, every limb quivering, and suddenly he heard the footsteps approaching the screen again. The old man apparently had remembered that one of the rolls was missing. And behold! Again he looked around the screen at him. In despair, the artist grasped the roll in his hand with all his possible strength, exerted all his power to make a movement, shrieked, and . . . he awoke.

He was drenched in cold perspiration. His heart beat as violently as a heart could beat. His chest was constricted as though his last breath was about to leave it. "Was it only a dream?" he said, holding his head with both hands, but the incredibly lifelike appearance of the apparition was not at all like a dream. After he awoke, he saw the old man step inside the frame, and he even saw the skirts of his wide robe, and his hand could still feel that but a moment before there was something heavy in it. Moonlight bathed the room, and from out of the dark corners of the room it illuminated a canvas in one spot, in another the mold of a hand, in another a piece of drapery thrown over a chair, trousers and unclean boots. Then he saw that he was not lying in bed any longer, but that he was standing immediately before the portrait. How he had gotten there he had absolutely no idea, and he was even more surprised to find that the portrait was completely uncovered and the sheet was not to be seen. Frozen with terror, he stared at it and he saw that the human eyes were riveted upon him. Once more a cold sweat broke out on his face. He wanted to run away, but his feet were as if rooted to the earth, and he could see that this was not a dream. The old man's face moved and his lips began to project toward him, as though they wished to suck him in. . . . With a loud shriek of despair, Chartkov jumped back—and woke up.

"Was it a dream?" His heart was beating so that it was about to burst. He groped about him with his hands. Yes, he was lying in bed, and in exactly the same position in which he had fallen asleep. The screen was before him. Moonlight flooded the room. Through the chink of the screen the portrait, covered just as he had covered it, was visible. So this too was a dream? But his clenched fist still felt as though something had been in it. His heart beat violently, terrifyingly. The weight on his chest was unendurable. He set his eyes on the chink and stared steadily at the sheet. Behold! He saw clearly that the sheet began to unfold as though hands were pushing from beneath it and trying to throw it off. "Good God, what is this!" he screamed, crossing himself in despair—and woke up.

Was this also a dream? He sprang from his bed, frantic, half insane, and could not understand what was happening to him: was it the after-effects of a nightmare, or an evil spirit,[14] the raving born of fever, or a real apparition? Attempting to calm himself, to calm his overwrought nerves and the wildly flowing blood which pulsated through his veins, he went to the window and opened the pane. The cool fragrant breeze revived him. Moonlight was on the roofs and on the white walls of the houses, though small clouds passed often across the sky. Everything was quiet. From the distance, he could occasionally hear the sound of a carriage whose driver must have fallen asleep on his box in some obscure alley, lulled to sleep by his lazy nag while he waited for a belated passenger. He put his head out of the window and gazed for a long time. Already the approaching dawn was visible in the sky. At last he felt drowsy, shut the window, went back to his bed, and, like one truly exhausted, he fell into a sound sleep.

He awoke late, with the unpleasant feeling of a man who was stricken with coal-gas poisoning. He had a terrible headache. The room was dim; moisture imbued the air and was coming into the room through the cracks of the windows which were covered up with pictures and primed canvases. Depressed and sullen as a wet rooster, he sat down on his dilapidated sofa without any idea of what to do, what to plan, and finally he remembered his dream. The dream, as he remembered it, became so alarmingly real that he was not sure that it had only been a dream or the result of delirium, and whether there was not indeed something else involved, perhaps an apparition. He removed the sheet and examined the portrait by the light of day. The eyes, truthfully, were peculiarly striking and alive, but there was nothing in them that was singularly terrible, and yet an indescribable feeling of uneasiness persisted.

---

[14] *Domovoi*, either a good or evil spirit that lives in the house. A demon, goblin. (ed.)

He could not be certain that it had all been a dream. He could not
keep from feeling that there must have been some terrible fragment of reality within the dream. In the old man's look and in the
expression on his face, there was something which bespoke his
having been with the artist during the night. Chartkov's hand still
felt the weight which had so recently been in it, as if someone had
only a minute before snatched it away from him. He had a peculiar
sensation that if he had managed to grasp the roll more firmly in
his hand it would have remained there even after he awoke.

"Good God, if only I had part of that money!" he said, sighing
deeply, and in his imagination he could see all those rolls again,
each fascinatingly inscribed: *1,000 gold coins*, pouring out of the
bag. The rolls opened up, there was a gleam of gold, and they were
wrapped up again. He sat without moving, his eyes staring at nothing, as if he was unable to tear his thoughts away from such a vision, like a child who sits in front of a plate of candy and, with
watering mouth, watches other people eating it.

Soon there was a knock on his door which brought him back to
reality with unpleasant swiftness. The landlord and a policeman
of the district came in, and it is well known that the policeman's
appearance is more disturbing to the poor than the presence of a
petitioner is to the wealthy. The landlord of the small house in
which Chartkov lived resembled the other people who owned
houses somewhere in the fifteenth row in Vasilievsky Island, on the
Petersburg side, or in some remote corner of Kolomna—people
who are very numerous in Russia and whose character is as difficult
to describe as the color of a threadbare frock coat. He had been a
captain in his youth, and a bully, and a master in the art of flogging.
He had served in the civil service. He was stupid and rather foppish, but not without some efficiency; but in his old age he combined all of these different peculiarities of his character into a kind
of uniform obtuseness. He was a widower for some time, and he
had long been retired. There was no longer anything of the dandy
about him, and his temperament was no longer cantankerous. Now
he cared only for drinking tea and gossiping as he did so. He
walked around his room snuffing the ends of his candles, calling
punctually on his tenants for the rent at the end of each month,
and he went out into the street, key in hand, to look at the roof of
his house, and sometimes he chased the caretaker out of his den
where he had hidden himself to take a nap; in brief, he was a retired

army officer who after the turmoils and dissoluteness of his life, was left with nothing more than a few trivial habits.

"Please see for yourself, Varukh Kuzmich," the landlord said, gesturing with his hands as he turned to the policeman. "He simply doesn't pay his rent; he does not pay!"

"How do you expect me to pay when I have no money? Be patient and I will pay you."

"I can't wait, my friend," said the landlord angrily, gesturing with the key in his hand. "Lieutenant Colonel Potogonkin has been here seven years; Anna Petrovna Bukhmisterova rents the coach house and stable, except for two stalls, and has three servants. . . . That's the sort of tenants I have. I say to you honestly that this is not a place where I have difficulty collecting rent. Will you please pay your rent immediately or leave."

"Well," said the policeman with a slight shake of the head as he put his finger on one of the buttons of his uniform, "if you've rented the rooms, you have to pay."

"What am I to pay with? That's the question. I haven't got a copper right now."

"Then, in that case, you'd better satisfy the demands of Ivan Ivanovich by giving him some of your pictures," said the policeman. "Maybe he will agree to take the pictures."

"No thank you, my dear fellow, no pictures. If there were some pictures of holy subjects that one could hang on a wall, that wouldn't be so bad, or if there was a picture of a general with a star, or Prince Kutuzov's portrait,[15] but this fellow has painted the peasant, the peasant in a shirt, the peasant who grinds his paint! The idea of painting the portrait of that pig! I'll give it to him! He's been removing all the nails from the bolts, the rogue! Just look at these subjects! Here's a picture of his room. It would not be bad if he had at least chosen a clean and well-furnished room, but he has painted this one with all the filth and rubbish which he has collected. Look at how he has messed up my room! Look! And some of my tenants have been in my house for more than seven years! The Lieutenant Colonel, Anna Petrovna Bukhmisterova. . . . No, I tell you that there is nothing in the world that is a worse tenant than an artist. He lives like a pig!"

---

[15] (1745-1813), Russian field marshal who distinguished himself against the Turks and against Napoleon. (ed.)

And the poor artist had to listen to all of this patiently. The policeman meanwhile amused himself by examining the pictures and the sketches, indicating at once that he was more sensitive than the landlord and that he was not insensible to artistic impressions.

"Aha!" he said, tapping a canvas on which there was a picture of a nude. "This one is—lively. But why does she have that black mark under her nose? Did she use snuff?"

"Shadow," Chartkov said angrily, without looking at him.

"You should have put it in another place. It's too conspicuous under the nose," said the policeman. "And whose portrait is this?" he went on, approaching the portrait of the old man. "It's terrible, too terrible. Was he really so terrifying? Why, he actually sees through you! What a Gromoboy! [16] Who modeled for this?"

"Ah! It is . . ." said Chartkov and did not finish his sentence. He heard a loud crack. The policeman had held the frame too tightly in his policeman's hands, and the molding on the side broke and fell with a loud noise, and with it fell a roll wrapped in blue paper. Chartkov's eyes fastened on the inscription: *1,000 gold coins,* and like a madman he flew to it to pick it up, seized the roll, and clasped it convulsively in his hand, which sank from the weight.

"Wasn't that the sound of money?" the policeman asked, having heard the noise of something falling on the floor, but not being fast enough to see what it was because of the rapidity with which Chartkov had picked it up.

"What concern is it of yours whether I have anything or not?"

"It's my concern because you should pay your landlord the rent you owe him at once. You have money but you won't pay."

"I'll pay him today."

"Why didn't you pay him before? Why do you make all this trouble for your landlord? And why are you bothering the police?"

"I didn't want to touch that money. I'll pay him all I owe this evening and then I'll leave this apartment tomorrow. I will not stay with this kind of a landlord."

"So, Ivan Ivanovich, he will pay you," the policeman said, turning to the landlord. "But if you are not fully satisfied this evening, then I will be very sorry, Mr. Painter." Having said this, he put

---

[16] Hero of a ballad who sold his soul to the devil, by V. A. Zhukovsky (1783-1852). (ed.)

on his three-cornered hat and walked out into the hall followed by the landlord, whose head was bowed as though he were engaged in meditation.

"Thank God the devil has taken him away!" said Chartkov when he heard the hall door shut. He looked out into the hall and, because he wanted to be alone, he sent Nikita off on some errand. Then he locked the door behind him and began, with a wildly beating heart, to unwrap the roll of coins when he got back to his room.

The roll consisted of coins which were all new and glistening like fire. Almost beside himself, he sank down before the pile of gold, asking himself, "Isn't this all a dream?" There were precisely one thousand coins in the roll, which looked exactly as he had seen it in his dream. He turned them over in his hand and looked at them closely for some time without regaining his composure. In his imagination all sorts of tales were conjured up, of hidden treasures, cabinets with secret drawers left by ancestors to their spendthrift descendants in the firm belief that the money would restore their fortune. He began to think that perhaps some grandfather might have wanted to leave a present for his grandchild, and had hidden it in the frame of the family portrait. Filled with such romantic ideas he began to wonder whether this did not have some mysterious connection with his fate. Wasn't the existence of the portrait tied in with his own existence, and wasn't its very acquisition by him due to some kind of predestination? He began to examine the frame with great curiosity. There was a cavity on one side, so skillfully and neatly hidden by a little board that, if the heavy hand of the policeman had not smashed through it, the gold coins might have remained hidden forever. Examining the portrait again, he was once more struck by the remarkable workmanship and the extraordinary treatment of the eyes; they no longer seemed frightening, but each time he looked at them he experienced unpleasant feelings. "No," he said to himself, "regardless of whose grandfather you are, I will put you behind glass and I'll get you a gilt frame." And then he put his hand on the heap of gold piled before him, and his heart raced at the feel of it. "What will I do with them?" he said, staring at the coins. "Now I am free of worry for at least three years. I can shut myself up in my room and work. I have enough money for paints now, for dinner, and for tea, and for rent—no one will trouble me or disturb me now. I'll buy myself an excellent mannequin. I'll order a plaster torso. I'll model feet. I will set up a Venus. I will buy copies of the best pictures. And if I work for three years without hurrying, without being concerned about selling my pictures, I will be better than them all, and I may become a first-rate artist."

That was what he said to himself at the prompting of his good judgment, but within him another voice, growing ever louder, was making itself heard. And when he glanced at the gold again, it was something quite different that was said by his twenty-two years and ardent youth. Everything which he had before looked at with envious eyes was now within his reach. That which he had from afar looked at longingly could now be his. How his heart beat when he merely thought of it! To be able to wear a stylish coat, to be able to eat well after so long a fast, to be able to rent a fine apartment, to be able, at any time, to go to the theater, to the confectioners, or to other places, and seizing his money he suddenly found himself in the street. The very first thing he did was to go to a tailor and clothe himself in fresh attire from head to foot and, like a child, he admired himself incessantly. He bought perfumes and pomades, and then he rented the first elegant apartment, one with mirrors and plate-glass windows, which he came across on Nevsky Prospekt, and without bickering over the price. On an impulse he bought an expensive *lorgnette* and a huge quantity of neckties of every kind, many more than he could possibly need. Then he went to a hairdresser's, and he had his hair waved; he rode twice through the city without any object in mind; he ate an enormous amount of candy at the confectioner's; and he went to a French restaurant in town about which he had heard rumors that were as vague as the rumors concerning the Chinese Empire. And there he dined in majestic style, with his arms akimbo, looking disdainfully at the other diners, and continually fixing his hair in the mirror. He drank a bottle of champagne which had, up to this time, been known to him only through hearsay. The wine went to his head, and he went into the street, alacritous, pugnacious, as though he were the devil's best friend, according to the Russian expression. He strutted along the sidewalk ogling everyone through his *lorgnette*. He caught sight of his old professor on the bridge, and he dashed past him as if he did not see him, leaving the astounded professor quite flabbergasted, rooted to the spot, his face looking like a question mark.

That very same evening everything Chartkov owned—easels, canvas, pictures—was moved to his new elegant apartment. He arranged the best of them in conspicuous places, and threw the worst of them into a corner, and he promenaded up and down the handsome rooms, constantly looking at himself in the mirrors. An inexorable desire to become immediately famous and show the world how great he was took hold of him. He could already hear the shouts. "Chartkov! Chartkov! Have you seen Chartkov's picture? How well he paints! How much talent he has!" He paced the rooms in a state of exaltation, unconscious of where he walked. The next day, taking ten gold coins with him, he went to see the publisher of a popular daily whom he wanted to ask for assistance. The journalist received him with great cordiality, and at once called him "Most respected sir," squeezed both his hands, made careful inquiries as to his name, birthplace, and address, and on the very next day, there appeared in the paper, below a notice of some newly invented tallow candles, an article under the following heading:

CHARTKOV'S ENORMOUS TALENT

We are honored to inform the cultured readers of the capital of a discovery which is highly desirable in every respect. All are agreed that there are very many physiognomies and faces among us, but up till this time there was no way of immortalizing them on canvas. This need has now been satisfied. An artist has been found who combines all desirable qualities. The beauty can now feel assured of being depicted with all the grace of her spiritual charms, bewitchingly as a butterfly fluttering among spring flowers. The respectable father of a family can now behold himself as he is surrounded by all the members of his family. The merchant, the warrior, citizens, statesmen—hurry, hurry from your journey, from your visits to your friends, to your cousins, to the glittering bazaar; hurry to him, to this great artist, from wherever you may be. The magnificent establishment of the artist, Nevsky Prospekt . . . contains portraits from his brush which are worthy of Van Dyck or Titian. One does not know which one to admire most, the reality and likeness to the originals or the extraordinary artistry and freshness of the coloring. Hail to you, my artist, you have drawn a winning number in the lottery. Long live Andrei Petrovich! (The journalist liked familiarity). Glorify yourself and us. We know how to value you, and we are certain that great popularity and wealth—though some of our fellow journalists seem to despise the latter—will be your reward. . . .

The artist read this notice with absolute delight. His face
beamed. He was being discussed in print. It was a novelty to him,
and he reread the notice several times. He was extremely flattered
by the comparison to Van Dyck and Titian, and very pleased by
the phrase, "Long live Andrei Petrovich." To be called in print by
both his Christian name and patronymic was an honor that he had
never known before. He paced up and down the room quickly,
running his fingers through his hair, and sat down in a chair for a
moment, only to get up and then to seat himself on the sofa, each
moment anticipating how he would receive ladies and gentlemen.
He walked up to a canvas and swept his brush grandly over it with
a graceful movement of his hand.

The next day his doorbell rang and he ran to open the door. A
lady, accompanied by a footman in a livery that was fur-lined,
entered, and her daughter, a young girl of eighteen, followed her in.

"Are you Monsieur Chartkov?" the lady asked. The artist bowed.

"So much is being written about you. Your portraits are considered to be absolutely wonderful." After these introductory words
the lady raised her *lorgnette* to her eyes and glanced quickly over
the walls which were bare. "Where are your portraits?"

"I've had them taken away," said the artist, somewhat embarrassed, "I just recently moved into this apartment and that's why
it is that they are still on the way . . . they have still not arrived."

"Were you in Italy?" asked the woman, looking at him through
the *lorgnette* because there was no other object she could point it
at.

"No, I have not been there, but I have always had the desire
. . . I have put it off for a while . . . Please, here is an armchair.
Aren't you tired?"

"Thank you. I have been sitting in my carriage for some time.
Aha, finally I see one of your works," said the woman running to
the opposite wall and looking through her glass at his sketches,
studies, perspectives, and portraits which were standing on the
floor. "*C'est charmant, Lise, venez-ici!*[17] Look, a room in the style
of Teniers.[18] Do you see, everything is in disorder! A table, a bust
on it, a hand, a palette. Do you see the dust here? Do you see how
the dust is painted? *C'est charmant!* And here on the other canvas

[17] "That's charming, Lise, come here!" (ed.)
[18] David Teniers (1582-1649), Flemish painter who usually selected homely
tavern scenes, rustic games, etc., for subjects. (ed.)

there is a woman who is washing her face. *Quelle jolie figure*.[19] Ah,
a little peasant, a muzhik in a Russian shirt! See, a little muzhik!
So you don't confine yourself exclusively to portraits?"

"Oh, that is only trash, just experiments, just studies."

"Tell me please, what is your opinion of our contemporary
painters? Isn't it really true that there are none like Titian? The
strength of colors is lacking, that . . . that . . . I'm sorry that I
can't express it in Russian." (The lady was a great admirer of
painting, and she had, armed with her *lorgnette*, wandered through
all of the Italian galleries.) "But Monsieur Nohl,[20] ah, what a remarkable painter! What extraordinary talent! I find that there is
even more expression in his faces than in Titian's. Do you know
Monsieur Nohl?"

"Who is this Nohl?" asked the artist.

"Monsieur Nohl? Ah, that is talent! He did my daughter's portrait when she was only twelve years old. You must absolutely
come and see it. Lise, you will show him your album. You know,
we came here specifically so that you might begin her portrait
immediately."

"With pleasure. I am ready right now." He immediately pulled
out the easel and a piece of canvas which was already on it, and,
his palette in hand, he gazed on the pale little face of the daughter.
If he had been an authority on human nature he might at once have
seen in it the first traces of a childish passion for balls, the dawning
of unhappiness and misery during the long waiting periods before
and after dinner, of a desire to promenade new clothes, the heavy
traces of uninspired application to various arts which her mother
insisted upon so that her soul and her sensitivity could be uplifted.
But the only thing the artist saw was this tender face, so alluring
a subject for his brush; a body of porcelain transparency, a charming, barely visible languor, a delicate white neck, and an aristocrati-
cally slender figure. And he prepared himself beforehand to tri-
umph, to display the brilliance of his brush, because, before this
time, he had dealt with only the harsh features of coarse models,
the severe lines of classic masters. In his mind he already envisioned
how this delicate face would turn out.

"You know," said the lady with a very rapturous expression on

19 "That's a lovely face." (ed.)
20 Almost certainly intended satirically. The name means "zero" in Russian.
(ed.)

her face, "I would like . . . she has on this dress which I don't think is very flattering. I'd like her to be dressed quite simply, and to have her sit under the shade of a tree with fields in the background or just the woods. I don't, you see, want anything in the picture that might indicate that she goes to balls or fashionable parties. Our balls, you know, so murder the spirit, and murder the last trace of feeling. Simplicity, more simplicity!" Alas, it could be clearly seen from the faces of the mother and daughter that they had so exerted themselves dancing at balls that they were now like wax figures.

Chartkov began working. He seated the model, thought a minute, waved his brush through the air, screwed up his eyes a little, stepped back a little, studied the young girl from a distance, and finished the sketching in an hour. Feeling content with his work, he began to paint. The work so fascinated him that he forgot everything else. He even forgot the presence of the aristocratic ladies and began to display some artistic mannerisms, uttering strange sounds, occasionally humming, as is common with an artist who is totally immersed in what he is doing. Without the slightest ceremony, with one movement of his brush, he made the sitter raise her moving head which, because she was fatigued, was beginning to express obvious signs of absolute weariness.

"Enough, that's enough for the first time!" said the lady.

"No, please, just a little more," said the artist, forgetting himself.

"No, it is time to stop! Lise, it is already three o'clock!" said the lady, taking out a watch that hung from her waist on a gold chain. "Ah, how late it is," she said.

"Just a moment," said Chartkov with the innocence and pleading voice of a child. Despite this, the lady did not seem amenable to this proposition. She promised instead to stay for a greater length of time at the next sitting.

"That is irritating," said Chartkov to himself. "My hand had just got involved with it," and he recalled how no one interrupted or stopped him when he worked in his studio on Vasilievsky Island. Nikita used to sit without moving in one spot; you could paint him as long as you desired to. Yes, he even slept in the position which you had him take. Unsatisfied, Chartkov laid his brush and palette on the chair and, in irritation, paused before the portrait.

A compliment which the society woman paid him roused him from his reverie. He ran quickly to the door to show them out. On the stairs he received an invitation to dine with them the next week, and he returned to his room with a happy face. The aristocratic lady had totally charmed him. Before this time he had conceived of such people as being completely unapproachable, as people who were born only to ride in wondrous carriages with footmen dressed in livery and stylish coachmen, and to be disinterested in the poor man with the cheap coat trudging along on foot, and now, suddenly, one of those beings had been in his room, he was painting her portrait, he had received an invitation to dine in an aristocratic house. He was absolutely drunk from happiness, and he rewarded himself with a first-rate dinner and a visit to the theater, and afterwards, for no reason in particular, he rode through the city in a carriage.

During all these days, his ordinary work never occurred to him at all. He prepared only for the next visit, and waited for the moment when the bell would ring. Finally the lady and her pale daughter appeared again. He seated them, pulled the canvas forward with a certain bravado, and began to paint after some show of affectation. The sunny day and the bright light were very helpful. In his dainty sitter he saw a great deal which, if he could capture it and put it on canvas, would make the portrait very valuable. He perceived that he might create something rare if only he could accurately reproduce everything which was now before his eyes. His heart throbbed faster when he anticipated capturing something which others had not yet seen. He was completely engrossed in his work, again totally absorbed in his painting, and once more he forgot that the sitter was an aristocrat. With heaving chest, he saw how he had achieved the presentation of those delicate features and the almost transparent body of the seventeen-year-old girl.[21] He captured every shade, the slight sallowness, the almost imperceptible blueness under the eyes, and he was making ready to paint in a little pimple on her forehead when he suddenly heard the mother's voice.

"Ah, are you going to paint that? It's really unnecessary, and in several spots it's quite yellow, and here there are dark spots." The artist tried to explain that the spots and the yellow brought out the muted and pleasing tones of her face. He was told that they did not bring out the tones at all and that this was merely his impression.

[21] Another example of Gogol's not infrequent inconsistency. The girl's age was given as eighteen several pages earlier. (ed.)

"But," said the good-natured artist, "permit me to add a bit of yellow to this spot." But he was not allowed to do this. He was told that Lise was not quite well that day, that she was ordinarily never sallow and that, in fact, her face was always remarkably distinguished for its fresh color. With heavy heart, Chartkov began erasing what he had painted on the canvas. Many almost imperceptible traits disappeared, and with them a part of the resemblance disappeared as well. Apathetically, he added to the canvas that prosaic coloring which is put on mechanically and which gives to a face drawn from life something coldly ideal, something resembling that which is found in paintings in art schools. But the lady was satisfied when the colors she had objected to were removed. She merely expressed surprise that the artist was taking so long, and added that she had been told that he finished a portrait in two sittings. Chartkov could not think of an answer for this. The ladies got up and prepared to leave. Chartkov put his brush aside, walked them to the door, and then, for a long while, stood dejectedly before the portrait.

Chartkov stared stupidly at the portrait, his head full of those soft feminine features, those shades, the ethereal tints which he had copied and which his brush had now destroyed.

Imbued with these thoughts, he put the portrait to one side and searched for the head of Psyche which he had sketched on canvas a long time before. It was a pretty, girlish face, cleverly painted, but entirely idealized, with the cold, prosaic features which belonged to no living being. Because he had nothing to do, he began retouching it, putting into it all that he had observed in his aristocratic sitter. Those features, shadows, and tones which he had noted, appeared on it in the refined form in which they appear when the artist, after closely studying nature, surrenders to her and produces a work of art which is comparable to her own.

Psyche began to come alive, and the faintly dawning idea began gradually to be clothed in a visible form. The type of face of the aristocratic young lady was unconsciously transferred to Psyche, and because she had a unique expression, it could be considered as truly original. He seemed to make use of certain singular features of his sitter and of the total impression that the original suggested to him, and he devoted himself entirely to his own work. It was the only thing that occupied his thoughts for the next few days, and while working on this picture, the ladies surprised him. The picture

was still on its easel because he had not had time to remove it. Both
ladies uttered a cry of joy and clasped their hands in amazement.

"Lise, Lise, ah, how like you! *Superbe! Superbe!* What a wonderful idea to dress her in a Greek costume. Oh, what a surprise!"

Chartkov did not know how to disillusion the ladies of their
pleasant error. Shamefacedly, with drooping head, he muttered,
"This is Psyche."

"As Psyche? *C'est charmant!*" The mother said with a smile,
and her daughter smiled too. "Admit it, Lise. Doesn't it make
you happy to be painted as Psyche rather than in any other way?
Quelle idée délicieuse! [22] What art! It's a Correggio! [23] I must admit
that although I had of course read and heard of you, I never
thought you had so much talent. You absolutely have to paint me
too." Obviously, the mother also wanted to be painted as some sort
of Psyche.

What am I to with them? thought the artist. If they insist
that it is so, let it be so. And he said aloud, "Would you mind
posing for a few minutes? I'd like to touch it up here and there."

"Ah, I'm afraid you will . . . it is so much like her now!"

But the artist realized that the mother was fearful lest he add
yellow tones to the face, and he reassured them by saying that
he wished only to add to the brilliance and expression of the
eyes. In truth, however, he was quite ashamed, and he wanted to
impart a little more likeness to the original so that he might not
be accused of barefaced fraud and, indeed, at length the features
of the pale young girl did appear more clearly in Psyche's face.
"Enough," said the mother, becoming anxious that the resemblance
might be too clearly expressed. The artist was paid in every possible way: smiles, money, flattery, gentle pressure of the hands,
invitations to dinner—in a word, he was overwhelmed with a
thousand flattering words.

The portrait created a sensation in the city. It was exhibited
by the lady to all her friends. Everyone admired the ability of
the artist to depict the likeness and, at the very same time, to be-
stow additional beauty on the original. It should be understood,
of course, that this latter remark was motivated by a slight tinge
of envy. And suddenly Chartkov was overwhelmed with work.

---

[22] "What a delicious idea!" (ed.)
[23] Antonio Allegri da Correggio (1494-1534), great Italian painter of mytholog-
ical frescoes. (ed.)

It was as if everyone in the city wanted a portrait done by him. The doorbell rang continuously, and from a particular point of view this might even be considered beneficial because it offered him continuous practice with numbers of different faces. Unfortunately, however, they consisted of people who were difficult to please, busy, harassed people, or people who belonged to the world of society and who were consequently more occupied than others and, therefore, extremely impatient. From all quarters of the city the demand arose that the portrait should be done quickly and be done well. Chartkov knew that it was totally impossible to complete his work, that, indeed, it had become necessary to modify his technique so that he could capture only that which was obvious and general and not expend effort painting delicate details. In short, to faithfully represent complete nature was wholly out of the question. It should also be added that most of those who sat for him made many conditions on different points. The ladies insisted that mind and character should be the chief qualities represented in their portraits, and that nothing else was important; that all angles should be rounded and that everything uneven should be smoothed away and, if possible, even completely removed. In a word, they demanded that their face should cause viewers to stare and should provoke admiration, indeed, if not cause them to fall in love with it immediately. Because of this those who sat for him sometimes assumed expressions which completely amazed Chartkov: one made an effort to express melancholy; another, meditation; another desired to make her mouth appear small regardless of the cost, and she so puckered it up that it finally looked like a dot about as large as a pinhead. Despite it all, they demanded that the portraits bear strong resemblance to the original and be completely natural. As for the men, they were no better than the ladies: one insisted upon being painted with an energetic, masculine turn to his head; another on being painted with upturned and inspired eyes; a lieutenant of the guard insisted absolutely that Mars be visible in his eyes; an official in the civil service posed in his full height so that he might express honesty and nobility in his face, and so that his hand might rest on a book in which the following words, plainly printed, stood out: "He always stood for truth." At first, demands such as these threw the artist into cold perspiration: he felt that he had to think it over, to consider it, and yet there was terribly

little time for that. Finally he acquired the knack of it and no
longer concerned himself with such questions. A word was sufficient to indicate to him how someone wanted a portrait painted.
If a man insisted that Mars was to appear in his face, Mars appeared;
those who wanted to look like Lord Byron, he painted in Byronic
pose and attitude. If the ladies wanted to be shown as Corinne,[24]
Undine,[25] Aspasia,[26] he avidly agreed and imaginatively supplied
an adequate measure of good looks, which as everyone knows can
do no harm, and for the sake of which an artist may even be forgiven for any lack of resemblance. Soon he began to amaze himself with the rapidity and verve of his brush, and of course, those
who sat for him were ecstatic, and they proclaimed him a genius.
Chartkov, in every sense of the word, became a fashionable painter.
He dined out, escorted ladies to the art galleries, and even began
to walk and to dress as a fop, and he was heard to express the opinion that an artist must belong to society, that he must uphold the
honor of his profession, that artists usually dress like shoemakers,
that they do not conduct themselves properly, that they lack good
taste, and that they are devoid of sophistication. At home in his
studio everything was exceedingly tidy and clean. He employed
two marvelous footmen, tutored dandyish pupils, changed his costume several times a day, allowed his hair to be waved, concerned
himself greatly with improving his manners, devoted a great deal
of time to adorning his appearance in every possible way so that
he would produce a pleasurable impression on the ladies. In a
word, it would have been quite impossible for anyone to now recognize that this was the once-modest artist who had previously
toiled in obscurity in his squalid quarters in Vasilievsky Island.
He was opinionated about art and artists. He declared that too
much credit had been bestowed upon the old masters and that
all that the artists could paint before Raphael was herrings, not
figures; that the idea that there was anything holy about them
existed only in the imagination of those who viewed them, and
that not even Raphael himself always painted well, and that tradition was responsible for the fame attached to many of his works;

---

[24] Heroine of a novel by Mme Germaine de Staël (1776-1817). *Corinne,*
published in 1807, was eminently successful. (ed.)
[25] Heroine of a popular fairy tale, *Undine,* published in 1811, by Friedrich
de La Motte-Fouqué (1777-1843). (ed.)
[26] The beautiful and learned Greek mistress of Pericles (5th century B.C.)
(ed.)

that Michaelangelo was a braggart because he chose merely to display his knowledge of anatomy, and that there was not any grace about him, and that, in fact, for real brilliance and power of drawing and splendor of colors, you only had to look at the last century. And here, quite naturally, the question involved him personally. "No, I can't understand why other artists slave and work with such difficulty. In my opinion, a man who labors over a picture for months is not an artist at all, he's a hack. He's devoid of talent. Genius works boldly, rapidly." Turning to his visitors he said, "This is a portrait which took me only two days to paint, I did this head in one day, I did this in a few hours, and this only took little more than an hour. No, I confess that I do not recognize as art anything which adds one line to another laboriously. That is hardly art; that is a trade." And in this manner, he lectured those who came to see him, and the visitors marveled at the strength and power of his works, and uttered exclamations of surprise upon hearing how quickly he produced his pictures and said to each other, "That's talent, real talent. Look how he speaks, see how his eyes flash. *Il y a quelque chose d'extraordinaire dans toute sa figure!*" [27]

The artist was flattered to listen to such comments. When the papers contained a notice praising his work he was as delighted as a child, even though his money had bought the praise. Everywhere he went he carried the press clippings with him, showed them to his friends and acquaintances with a practiced air of casualness, and this, in a good-natured, naïve way, pleased him. His words and orders increased as his fame did. He was growing weary of always painting the same portraits over and over again in the same attitudes and poses which he knew quite by heart. Now he painted with no interest in what he was doing, drawing a rough likeness of a head and giving it to his pupils for the finishing touches. In the beginning he had tried to find a new pose for everyone who sat for him, to startle and surprise everyone by the power of his work and the effect achieved. Now even this was devoid of pleasure. His brain was exhausted from planning and thinking. He soon could do it no longer; he did not have the time. The irregular mode of living and society, in which he played the role of a man of the world, estranged him from thought and work.

---

[27] "There is something extraordinary written on his face." (ed.)

His work grew dim and indifferent and, without feeling, he began to paint monotonous, well-defined, exhausted forms. The uniform, lifeless, forever immaculate and, as it were, buttoned-up faces of the government officials, soldiers, and statesmen did not offer his brush adequate scope. The brush forgot how to represent magnificent draperies and strong emotion and passion, and as for composition, dramatic effect and its elevated purpose, there was nothing to be said. The only thing he saw before him was a uniform, a corsage, or a dress coat before which the artist is unmoved, and before which all imagination withers and dies. Even his own peculiar merits vanished from his work; and yet he continued to enjoy fame, this despite the fact that experts and artists merely shrugged their shoulders when they saw his latest paintings. Some who had known Chartkov before could not understand how the talent which was so clearly visible before had now been dissipated, and they tried in vain to solve the enigma of how a man at the peak of his power could suddenly find himself without his gift.

But the intoxicated artist did not hear this criticism. He was already approaching the age of dignity, in mind and in years. He began to grow heavier. He saw adjectives in the papers: "Our honored Andrei Petrovich; our distinguished Andrei Petrovich." And he began to receive offers for important positions in the civil service; he was invited to serve on boards of examiners and on committees. He began, as is usual in maturity, to defend Raphael and the old masters, not really because he had become absolutely convinced of their transcendent merits, but in order to snub the younger artists. He began, as all those who have attained maturity always begin, to indiscriminately accuse all young people of immorality and vicious thoughts, and began to believe that everything in the world is commonplace and simple, that there is no such thing as revelation from on high, and that everything essential can be brought under the stern principles of correctness and uniformity. Already he was reaching that time of life when everything inspired by impulse contracts in a man, when the strains of the mighty violin rouse feebler echoes in the soul and its pure notes no longer thrill the heart, when the touch of beauty no longer turns its virgin forces into fire and flame, but all the burnt-out feelings grow more responsive to the jingle of gold, listen more attentively to its alluring music, and, little by little, imperceptibly permit it to absorb them. Fame cannot satisfy and give pleasure to one who has stolen and not deserved it; it produces a permanent thrill only in those worthy of it. And therefore all his feelings and his impulses turned to gold. Gold became his passion, his ideal, his terror, his pleasure, his goal. Piles of notes grew in his boxes and, like everyone to whom this terrible privilege is vouchsafed, he began to grow tedious, inaccessible to everything, indifferent to everything. It seemed as though he were on the point of being transformed into one of those strange beings, sometimes to be found in the world, at whom a man full of energy and passion looks with horror, seeing in them living corpses. But one circumstance made a violent impression upon him and gave a different turn to his life.

One day he saw on his table a note in which the Academy of Arts invited him as an honored member to come and give his criticism on the work of a Russian painter, who had sent it from Italy where he was studying. This artist was one of his old fellow students, who had from his earliest years cherished a passion for art, had devoted himself to it with the ardent soul of a patient worker, and, tearing himself away from friends, from relations, from cherished habits, had hastened without means to a strange land; he had endured poverty, humiliation, even hunger; but with rare self-sacrifice had remained, regardless of everything, insensible to all but his cherished art.

When Chartkov went into the hall, he found a crowd of visitors already gathered about the picture. A profound silence prevailed such as is rare in a large assembly of critics. He hastened to assume the important air of a connoisseur as he advanced to the picture, but, good heavens! What did he see!

Pure, stainless, lovely as a bride, the painter's work stood before him. There was not the faintest sign of desire to dazzle, of pardonable vanity. No thought of showing off to the crowd could be seen in it! It excelled with modesty. It was simple, innocent, divine as talent, as genius. The amazingly lovely figures were grouped unconstrainedly, freely, as if they were not touching the canvas, and they seemed to be modestly casting down their lovely eyelashes in amazement at so many eyes fixed upon them. The features of these godlike faces seemed to be breathing with the mysteries which the soul has no power, no means, to convey to another: the inexpressible found serene expression in them; and all this was put on to the canvas so lightly, with such modest freedom, that it might have seemed the fruit of a moment's inspiration dawning upon the artist's mind. The whole picture was a moment, but it was a moment for which all human life had been but preparation. Involuntary tears were ready to start to the eyes of the visitors who stood around the picture. It seemed as though all tastes, all sorts of diversities of taste, were blended into a silent hymn of praise. Chartkov stood motionless, open-mouthed before the picture, and as the onlookers and connoisseurs gradually began to break the silence and discuss the qualities of the work and finally turned to him asking for his opinion, he came to himself; he tried to regain his ordinary air of indifference, tried to utter the commonplace vulgar criticisms of blasé artists: to observe that the picture was good and that the artist had talent, but it was to be regretted that the idea was not perfectly carried out in certain details—but the words died on his lips, confused tears and sobs broke from him in response, and he ran out of the hall like one possessed.

For a minute he stood senseless and motionless in the middle of his magnificent studio. His whole being, his whole life had been awakened in one instant, as though his youth had come back to him, as though the smoldering sparks of talent had burst into flame again. Good God! To have ruined so ruthlessly all the best years of his youth, to have destroyed, to have quenched, the spark of fire that glowed perhaps in his breast, that would perhaps by now have developed into greatness and beauty, that would perhaps in the same way have wrung tears of amazement and gratitude from the eyes of beholders! And to have ruined it all, to have ruined it without mercy! It seemed as though at that moment the impulses and strivings that had once been familiar revived in his soul. He snatched up a brush and approached a canvas. The sweat of effort came out on his brow; he was all absorbed in one desire and might be said to be glowing with one thought: he longed to paint a fallen angel. No idea could have been more in harmony with his present frame of mind. But, alas! his figures, his attitudes, his groupings, his thoughts were artificial and disconnected. His painting and his imagination had been too long confined to one pattern; and a feeble impulse to escape from the limits and fetters he had laid upon himself ended in inaccuracy and failure. He had disdained the wearisome, long ladder of steady work and the first fundamental laws of future greatness. In vexation he took out of the room all his fashionable and lifeless pictures, all those portraits of hussars and ladies and state councilors, locked the door, ordered no food, and absorbed himself in his work with the ardor of youth. But alas! at every step he was stopped by ignorance of the most fundamental elements; the humble, insignificant mechanism of his art cooled all his ardor and stood an impassable barrier before his imagination. His brush involuntarily returned to hackneyed forms, his hands went back to his stereotyped manner. The heads dared not take an original attitude, the very folds of the garments insisted on being commonplace and refused to drape and hang on unfamiliar poses of the body. And he felt it, he felt it and saw it himself!

"Did I ever really have any talent?" he finally said. "Didn't I deceive myself?" And having uttered these words he turned to his old paintings which he had once produced so purely and altruistically in his wretched apartment far off in lonely Vasilievsky Island, so far removed from crowds, luxury, and cravings. He turned to them now, and with great care began to examine them all, and all the details of the misery of his former existence came back to him. "Yes," he cried in despair, "I had talent. The traces of it and the signs of it are everywhere. . . ."

He stopped suddenly and trembled all over. His eyes encountered eyes which were staring at him. It was that remarkable portrait he had bought in Shchukin Court. All this time the portrait had been covered up, hidden by other pictures, and he had completely forgotten about it. And now, as if by plan, when all the fashionable portraits and paintings had been taken from the studio, it emerged together with the productions of his youth. As he recalled all of that strange incident, as he remembered that this strange portrait had been responsible for his errors, that, indeed, it was the hoard of money which he so miraculously obtained from it which had awakened in him all those wild desires which had destroyed his talent, he became almost mad. Immediately he ordered that the hateful portrait be removed, but his mental agitation was not mitigated by its removal. His emotions, his entire being, were shaken to their foundation, and he suffered that terrible torture which sometimes appears in nature when a man with feeble talent tries to display it on a scale which is too large for it and fails miserably —the kind of torture which in youth may lead to greatness, but which is converted into unquenchable thirst in a man who should have long ago removed himself from reverie, that horrible torture which renders a man capable of the most terrible things. A horrible envy obsessed him, an envy which bordered upon madness. When he beheld a work which bore the stamp of genius, hatred distorted his features. He ground his teeth and devoured it with the eyes of a basilisk. At last the most hellish design which the heart of man has ever cherished sprang up within him, and with frenzied violence he flew to carry it out. He began buying up all the finest works of art. After buying a picture at a high price he carried it home carefully to his room and with the fury of a tiger he fell upon it, tore it, rent it, cut it up into little scraps, and stamped on it, accompanying this with a horrid laugh of fiendish glee. The enormous wealth which he had amassed enabled him to gratify this fiendish desire. He opened his bags of gold, and he unlocked his chests. No ignorant monster ever destroyed so many marvelous works of art as this raving avenger. Whenever he appeared at an auction everyone despaired of buying any work of art. It was as if a wrathful heaven had sent this terrible scourge into the world specifically to deprive it of its harmony. A horrible color created by this passion suffused his face. On his features were expressed scorn for the world, and blame. It was as if that terrible demon which Pushkin had described[28] had been reincarnated in him. From his tongue, there poured forth nothing but bitter and caustic words. He swooped through the streets like a Harpy, and all his acquaintances, seeing him from a distance, tried to avoid meeting him, noting that it poisoned the whole day for them.

Fortunately for the world and for art, such an overstrained and unnatural life could not last long; its passions were too abnormal and colossal for his feeble strength. Fits of frenzy and madness began to be frequent, and at last it ended in a terrible illness. Acute fever, combined with galloping consumption, took such a violent hold on him that in three days he was only a shadow of his former self. And to this was added all the symptoms of hopeless insanity. Sometimes it needed several men to hold him. He began to be haunted by the long-forgotten, living eyes of the strange portrait, and then his frenzy was terrible. All the people who stood around his bed seemed to him like dreadful portraits. The portrait was

[28] In his poem "The Demon." (ed.)

doubled, quadrupled before his eyes, and at last he imagined that all the walls were hung with these awful portraits, all fastening upon him their unmoving, living eyes. Terrible portraits looked at him from the ceiling, from the floor, and to crown it all he saw the room grow larger and extend into space to provide more room for these staring eyes. The doctor who had undertaken to treat him, and who had heard something of his strange story, did all he could to discover the mysterious connection between the hallucinations that haunted him and the incidents of his life, but could not arrive at any conclusion. The patient understood nothing and felt nothing but his sufferings, and in a piercing, indescribable, heart-rending voice screamed incoherently. At last he died in a final paroxysm of speechless agony. His corpse was dreadful to behold. Nor could they find any trace of his vast wealth, but, seeing the torn-up shreds of the great masterpieces of art, the price of which reached millions, they understood the terrible uses to which it had been put.

PART II

Masses of carriages, chaises, and coaches were standing round the entrance of the house in which an auction was taking place. It was a sale of all the belongings of one of those wealthy art connoisseurs who sweetly slumber away their lives plunged in zephyrs and amours, who are naïvely reputed to be Maecenases,[29] and good-naturedly spend on keeping up that reputation the millions accumulated by their businesslike fathers, and often, indeed, by their own earlier labors. As is well known, there are no longer such Maecenases, for the nineteenth century long ago acquired the aspect of a stingy banker who delights himself only with the figures written in ledgers. The long drawing room was filled with the most motley crowd of visitors who had come swooping down like birds of prey on an abandoned body. Here was a regular flotilla of Russian merchants from the bazaar, and even from the old-clothes market, in dark blue coats of German cut. They had here a harder and more free-and-easy air and appearance, and were not marked by the obsequiousness which is so prominent a feature of the Russian merchant. They did not stand on ceremony, in spite of the

---

[29] I.e., patrons of art. Maecenas was the patron of Horace and Vergil. (ed.)

fact that there were in the room many distinguished aristocrats, before whom in any other place they would have been ready to bow down to the ground till they swept away the dust brought in by their own boots. Here they were completely at ease and they fingered books and pictures without ceremony, trying to feel the quality of the goods, and boldly outbid aristocratic connoisseurs. Here were many of those persons who are invariably seen at auctions, who make it a rule to attend one every day as regularly as they have their breakfast; distinguished connoisseurs who look upon it as a duty not to miss a chance of increasing their collections, and have nothing else to do between twelve and one o'clock; and finally there were those excellent gentlemen whose coats and pockets are not well lined but who turn up every day at such functions with no mercenary motives, solely to see how things will go: who would give more and who less, who would outbid whom, and to whom the goods would be sold. Many of the pictures had been flung down here and there without any system; they were mixed up with the furniture and books, which all bore the monogram of their owner, though he probably had not had the laudable curiosity to look into them. Chinese vases, marble tabletops, furniture both modern and antique with curved lines adorned with the paws of griffins, sphinxes, and lions, chandeliers gilt and not gilt, and knickknacks of all sorts were heaped together, not arranged in order as in shops. It was a chaos of works of art. Generally the impression made by an auction is strange. There is something in it suggestive of a funeral procession. The room in which it takes place is always rather gloomy, the windows are blocked up with furniture and pictures, the light filters in sparingly; there is silent attention on all the faces, and the effect of a funeral procession is enhanced by the voice of the auctioneer, as he taps with his hammer and recites the requiem over the poor works of art so strangely gathered together. All this further accents the singular unpleasantness of the impression.

The auction was at its height. A throng of respectable people were gathered in a group and were excitedly discussing something. From all sides resounded the words, "Rubles, rubles," allowing the auctioneer no opportunity to repeat the last bid which had already mounted to a sum quadruple the original price announced. The surging crowd was bidding for a portrait which could not fail but attract the attention of anyone who had any knowledge of art. The gifted hand of a master was easily discernible in it. Apparently the portrait had been restored and refinished several times, and it showed the dark features of an Asiatic in a wide robe who wore a peculiar expression on his face. But it was the remarkable liveliness of the eyes that struck the buyers most of all. The longer the people looked at them, the more did they seem to bore right into every man's heart. This peculiarity, this mysterious illusion created by the artist, forced the attention of almost all upon it. Many of those who had bid for the picture finally withdrew from the bidding when the price rose to an incredible sum. Only two well-known, art-collecting aristocrats remained, both absolutely determined not to forgo such a purchase. In the heat of excitement they would probably have continued out-bidding each other until the price had finally assumed incredible proportions if one of those in attendance had not suddenly said, "Allow me to interrupt your competition for a while. I, perhaps, have more right to his picture than anyone else." Immediately these words drew the attention of everyone upon him. He was a tall man of thirty-five, with long black hair. His pleasant face, full of a kind of gay nonchalance, showed a soul devoid of all mundane concerns. His clothes made no pretense to be fashionable. Everything about him indicated the artist. In fact, he was the artist B., well known personally to many of those present.

"Regardless of how strange my words may seem to you," he continued, noticing that all attention was focused on him, "you will see, if you agree to listen to a little story, that I was right to speak them. Everything convinces me that this is the portrait for which I have been looking."

A very natural curiosity took hold of nearly everyone, and even the auctioneer, with an open mouth and a raised hammer, paused and prepared to listen. At the beginning of the story many people involuntarily looked at the portrait, but later all attention was fixed on the narrator as what he said grew more and more interesting.

"You all know that part of the city which is called Kolomna," he began. "Everything there is different from any other part of Petersburg. There we have neither capital nor provinces. It seems, indeed, that when you walk through the streets of Kolomna, all the youthful desires and passions are drained from you. There the future never comes; all is still and desolate. Everything suggests

withdrawal from the life of the capital. Retired officials move
there to live, and widows and poor people who are familiar with
the senate and therefore sentence themselves to this district for
nearly all of their lives; cooks who have retired and spend the
whole day haggling in the market, gossiping with the peasants in
the milkshop, buying five kopeks' worth of coffee and four kopeks'
worth of sugar every day; and that class of people whom I call
ashen, whose clothes and faces and hair all have a dingy appearance
like ashes. They are like a gray day when the sun does not dazzle
with its brilliance, nor the storm whistle with thunder, rain, and
hail, but when the sky is neither one thing nor the other: there is a
veil of mist that blurs the outline of every object. And to these
must be added retired people who were ushers in the theater, titular councilors, retired disciples of Mars with swollen lips and eyes
poked out. These people are quite without passions. Nothing matters to them; they go about without taking the slightest notice of
anything, and remain quite silent thinking of nothing at all. In their
room they have nothing but a bed and a bottle of pure Russian
vodka, which they imbibe with equal regularity every day, without any of the rush of ardor to the head that is provoked by a
strong dose, such as the young German artisan, that bully of
Meshchansky Street, who has undisputed possession of the pavement after twelve o'clock at night, loves to give himself on Sundays.

"Life in Kolomna is dull: rarely does a carriage rumble through
its quiet streets, unless it be one full of actors, which disturbs the
general stillness with its bells, its creaking and rattling. Here almost
everyone goes on foot. Only at rare intervals a cab crawls along
lazily, almost always without a fare, taking a load of hay for its
humble nag. An apartment can be rented for five rubles a month,
morning coffee included. The widows of government clerks, in
receipt of a pension, are the most substantial inhabitants of the
quarter. They behave with great propriety, keep their rooms fairly
clean, and talk to their female neighbors and friends of the high
price of beef and cabbages. They not infrequently have a young
daughter, a silent creature who has nothing to say for herself,
though sometimes rather nice-looking; they have also a disgusting
little dog and an old-fashioned clock with a dismally ticking pen-
dulum. Next to them in precedence come the actors, whose salaries
don't allow of their leaving Kolomna. They are rather a free and

easy group, like all artists, and live for their own pleasure. Sitting
in their dressing gowns they either clean a pistol or glue pieces of
cardboard together to make something of use in the house, or play
checkers or cards with a friend, and so they spend their mornings; they follow the same pursuits in the evening, mingling them
with punch. Below these swells, these aristocrats of Kolomna,
come the smaller fry, and it is as hard for the observer to reckon up
all the people occupying the different corners and nooks in one
room as it is to enumerate all the creatures that breed in stale
vinegar. What people does one not meet there! Old women who
say their prayers, old women who get drunk, old women who
both get drunk and say their prayers; old women who live from
hand to mouth by means that pass all understanding, who like ants
drag old rags and linen from Kalinkin Bridge to the flea market,
to sell them there for fifteen kopeks—in fact all the pitiful and
luckless dregs of humanity whose lot not even a benevolent econo-
mist could improve. I have listed them so that you will understand how often people like this are driven by need to seek immediate temporary help by borrowing. And among these people a
certain kind of moneylender settles, and he lends them small loans
on little security and charges exorbitant interest. These petty
usurers often are more heartless than the major moneylenders because they live in the midst of poverty among people dressed in
rags that the rich usurer who deals only with the carriage trade
never sees, and every humane feeling in them is soon extinguished.
Among these usurers there was one . . . but I must not forget to
mention that the events which I have begun to relate refer to the
last century in the reign of our late Empress Catherine II.[30] You
will realize that since then the very appearance of Kolomna and its
life has altered significantly. Now, among these usurers there was a
certain person, a remarkable being in every respect, who had long
before settled in that part of the city. He went about in a voluminous Asiatic robe. His dark complexion bespoke his southern origin, but as to his nationality, whether he belonged to India, or
Greece, or Persia, no one was certain. He was tall and of enormous
height, and had a dark, haggard, scorched face, and in his large

---

[30] Catherine the Great (1729-96) was of German birth, but she became thoroughly Russian and was extremely popular. Greatly influenced by the En-
lightenment, she planned vast reforms which were never carried out because
of the Pugachev rebellion and the French Revolution. (ed.)

eyes there was the blaze of strange fire, and he had heavy protrud-
ing eyebrows which made him so different from all the ash-colored
inhabitants of the capital. Even his house was different from the
other small wooden houses. It was made of stone, of a style which
Genoese merchants had once preferred. It had irregular windows
of various sizes and iron shutters and bars. This usurer was different from other usurers because he was willing to lend anyone any
required amount, from that needed by a penurious beggarwoman
to that required by a profligate courtier. And in front of his house
there were often to be seen splendid carriages, and sometimes, out
of their windows, there would appear the head of an elegant lady
of society. It was rumored, as usual, that his iron chests were
brimming with gold, treasures, diamonds, and all sorts of pledged
articles, but nevertheless, that he was not so enslaved by greed as
other usurers were. He lent money avidly and the terms of payment were fairly stipulated, but by some devious method of figur-
ing, he made the payments amount to an enormous rate of interest.
At least, that's how rumor had it. But what was most striking of all,
and that which could not fail to arouse the attention of many, was
the strange fate of all those who had borrowed money from him:
all came to a miserable end. Whether all this was merely the kind of
thing that people said about him or some superstition-born talk or
reports spread for the purpose of harming him, is not known,
but several things which happened within a short time of each
other, and before everybody's eyes, were remarkable and striking.

"Among the aristocracy of that day there was one young man of
a fine family who quickly attracted the attention of all. While
still young he had distinguished himself in court circles. He was
an ardent admirer of all that was true and noble. He was a patron
of all which art or the mind of man produced, and a man who gave
promise of becoming a Maecenas. Soon, deservedly, he was rewarded by the Empress; she appointed him to an important office
which was exactly what he wished for, and in which he could ac-
complish much for science and the general good. The youthful
statesman surrounded himself with artists, poets, and men of learning. He desired to give work to everyone, to encourage everyone
and, at his own expense, he undertook very many useful publications, placed many orders, and offered many prizes to encourage
the different arts. He spent a great deal of money and finally ruined
himself financially. Full of noble impulses, however, he did not

want to stop his work, and he looked for a loan wherever he could find it, and finally he came to the well-known moneylender. After obtaining a loan of considerable size from him, the man changed completely in a short time. He became a persecutor and oppressor of young artists and intellectuals. He saw only the bad side in everything published, and every word he spoke perverted the truth. Unfortunately, at this time, the French Revolution took place, and this supplied him with an excuse for every sort of suspicion.[31] He began discovering a revolutionary tendency in everything; everything hinted of subversion, and he finally became so suspicious that he began even to suspect himself. He began to fabricate terrible and unjust accusations and he made scores of people miserable. Obviously, news of this behavior finally reached the throne of the Empress. The kindhearted Empress, full of the noble spirit which adorns crowned heads, was shocked. She uttered words which, despite their failure to have been preserved, have yet had the memory of their meaning impressed upon many hearts. The Empress observed that it was not under a monarchy that the high and noble impulses of souls were persecuted, not under such a government were the finest achievements of the intellect, of poetry, and of the arts condemned and persecuted; that on the contrary, the monarchs alone were their protectors, and that Shakespeare and Molière flourished under their gracious protection,[32] while Dante could not even find a spot for himself in his republican birthplace,[33] that true geniuses arose at the time when emperors and empires were at the zenith of their brilliance and power, and not at the time of monstrous political unrest and republican terror which had, up to that time, never given the world a single poet;[34] that poets must be marked for favor, for they brought peace and divine contentment, and not excitement and discontent; that learned men and poets and all producers and all those who work in the arts were, indeed, the pearls and diamonds in the imperial

---

[31] During the French Revolution the Czarist regime became more reactionary than ever. **(ed.)**

[32] Shakespeare flourished under the reign of the brilliant Elizabeth I. Jean Baptiste Molière found Louis XIV a generous patron and a protector against his many enemies. (ed.)

[33] Dante Alighieri went into exile with the White Guelphs (a political faction) in 1302 and died in exile in Ravenna. (ed.)

[34] Gogol's strongly conservative point of view finds clear expression here. (ed.)

crown, for they glorified and immortalized the epic which the great ruler adorned, and made it more brilliant. In short, the Empress, speaking these words, was divinely beautiful for the moment. I recall old men who could not speak of it without tears. Everyone was interested in that affair. It must be noted, to the honor of our national pride, that in the Russian's heart there is always an impulse to aid the persecuted. The statesman who had betrayed his trust was punished in an exemplary manner and degraded from his post. But a much worse punishment could be read in the faces of his countrymen: sharp and universal scorn. Nothing could describe the sufferings of this vainglorious soul: pride, frustrated ambitions, destroyed aspirations, all joined together, and he died in a horrible attack of raving madness.

"Another striking example also occurred in the sight of all. Among the beauties in which our northern capital is decidedly not poor, one completely surpassed all the others. Her beauty was a blend of our northern charm with the charm of the south, a diamond only rarely seen in the world. My father told me that during his whole life he had never seen any woman like her. Everything seemed combined in her—wealth, intelligence, and spiritual charm. Throngs of admirers surrounded her, and the most distinguished of them all was Prince R., the most noble and best of all young men, the handsomest of face, and in chivalrous character, the great ideal of novels and women, a Grandison[35] in every respect. Prince R. was passionately, desperately in love, and his love was returned. But the girl's parents did not approve of the match. The Prince's ancestral estates had long before gone out of his hands and his family was in disfavor. Everyone knew of the sad state of his affairs. The prince suddenly left the capital, leaving the impression that he was bent upon improving his affairs, and he reappeared not long afterward surrounded with luxury and remarkable splendor. Those at court came to know him because of his brilliant balls and parties. The father of the beauty removed his objection, and the town soon witnessed one of the most fashionable weddings. What the real reason was for this change in fortune, and what the source was for this enormous wealth, no one fully knew, but it was whispered that he had made a deal with the mysterious usurer, and that he had borrowed money from him. Be that as it may, the

---

35 Hero of *Sir Charles Grandison*, third novel of Samuel Richardson (1689-1761), who was designed to portray the perfect gentleman. (ed.)

wedding occupied the whole town, and the bride and the bride-groom were the objects of general envy. Everyone knew of their warm and devoted love, how long they had endured persecution from every quarter, the great virtue of both. Romantic women already spoke of the heavenly happiness which the young couple would enjoy. But it turned out very differently.

"In one year a frightful change took place in the husband. His character, which until that time had been so fine and noble, was poisoned with jealous suspicions, intolerance, and inexorable ca-price. He became a tyrant and torturer of his wife, which no one could have foreseen, and he indulged in the most abominable acts, even beating her. In only a year no one recognized the woman who only so recently had been so radiant and who had drawn around her crowds of submissive admirers. Finally, finding it impossible to endure her misery, she suggested a divorce, but at the mere sug-gestion of such a thing her husband flew into a rage. In the first outpouring of emotion he stormed into her room, and had he not been seized and restrained, he would undoubtedly have murdered her then and there. In a fit of madness and despair he turned the knife against himself, and he ended his life in the most horrible suf-fering.

"In addition to these two instances which occurred before the eyes of the whole world, there were many stories told of such happenings among the lower classes, nearly all of which ended tragically. An honest, sober man became a drunkard; a shopkeep-er's assistant stole from his employer; an honest cabby cut the throat of his passenger for a few kopeks. Naturally such inci-dents, often told with embellishment, inspired horror in the simple hearts of Kolomna's inhabitants. No one at all doubted that the devil resided in this man. They said that he imposed conditions on a man which made the hair rise on one's head and which the poor wretch never dared to repeat to anyone else; that his money had the power to attract, possessed the power of becoming incandes-cent, and that it bore strange symbols. In short, there were many fantastic tales which circulated about him. It is worth noting that the entire population of Kolomna, the entire world of poor old women, petty officials, petty artists, and all those insignificant peo-ple we earlier mentioned, agreed that they would endure any-thing and suffer any misery rather than go to the terrible usurer. There were even old women who had died of hunger, preferring to starve to death rather than lose their souls. Anyone who met him in the street felt an involuntary fear. Pedestrians were careful to move away from him as he walked, and for a long time they gazed at the receding tall figure. Even in his face there was so much that was strange that they could not help but ascribe to him supernatural powers. The powerful features, so deeply chiseled that they were unlike those in any other man; the glowing bronze of his complexion; the incredible thickness of his eyebrows; those intolerable, terrible eyes; even the wide folds of his Asiatic robe—everything seemed to note that all the passions within other men paled when compared to the passions which raged within him. Whenever my father met him he stopped short, and he could not help but say, 'A devil, a real devil!' But I must, as speedily as possible, introduce you to my father, who is the true hero of this story.

"In many respects my father was a remarkable man. He was an artist of unusual ability, a self-taught artist who without teachers or schools discovered in his own soul the rules and laws of art, and, for reasons he did not understand, motivated only by his passion for perfection, he walked on the path which his spirit pointed out to him. He was one of those natural geniuses whom their contemporaries so often honor with the contemptuous word 'ignorant' and who are not disheartened by sneers or their own lack of success, who gain fresh strength and are, constantly, in their own minds, far beyond those works because of which they had earned the title 'ignorant.' Through some lofty and basic instinct, he perceived the presence of a soul in every object. He grasped, with his untutored mind, the true significance of the words 'historical painting.' He understood why a simple head, a simple portrait by Raphael, Leonardo da Vinci, Titian, or Correggio could be appreciated as an historical painting, while a huge picture of historical subjects remained, nevertheless, nothing more than a genre picture, despite all the artist's pretensions to historical painting. And this inherent instinct and personal conviction turned his brush to Christian subjects, the highest and loftiest degree of the sublime. He was devoid of vanity and irritability, which are so much a part of the character of many artists. His character was strong. He was honorable, frank, even a man with rough manners, covered with a hard shell, but not lacking in pride, and he always expressed himself about people both gently and scornfully. "What are they looking at?' he usually said. 'I am not working for them. I don't take my pictures to the tavern! He who understands me will thank me. The worldly man cannot be held at fault because he comprehends nothing of painting; he understands cards, and he knows wine and horses—what more need a gentleman know? If he tries one thing and then another, he becomes too much to endure. Let every man concern himself with his own business. So far as I am concerned, I much prefer a man who honestly admits that he does not understand a thing to one who pretends to know something he really does not know and is simply base and intolerable.' He worked for very little pay, that is to say, for just enough with which to keep his family and to buy the tools necessary for his work. Further, under no circumstances did he ever refuse to help anyone or to offer assistance to a destitute artist. He believed with the simple, reverent faith of his ancestors, and, because of that, a lofty expression appeared in all the faces he painted, an expression which even the most brilliant artists could not reproduce. Finally, by dedicated labor and perseverance in the path he had marked out for himself, he began to win the respect of those who had before derided his amateur status and his self-taught talent. They constantly commissioned him to do churches, and he was never without employment. In particular, one of his paintings interested him very strongly. What its precise subject was I can't recall; I know only that he had to represent the Prince of Darkness in it. For a long time, he pondered over what kind of form to present him in because he wanted to represent in that face all that weighs down and oppresses man. And while involved with these thoughts, there suddenly raced through his mind the image of the mysterious moneylender, and he could not help but say, 'That's who ought to be the model for the devil!' Imagine his surprise when, while at work in his studio one day, he heard a knock at the door and immediately the same terrible usurer entered the room. My father could not repress a cold chill which ran through every limb.

" 'Are you an artist?' he asked my father quickly.

" 'I am,' answered my surprised father, wondering what was to come next.

" 'Good. Paint my portrait. It is possible that I may be dead soon. I have no children, and I don't want to die completely. I wish to live. Can you do a portrait that will look as though it were alive?'

"My father thought, 'What could be better? He offers himself

as the devil I'm painting in my picture.' So he agreed. They came
to terms about time and price, and on the very next day, my
father took his palette and his brushes and went to his house.
The high walls encircling the courtyard, dogs, iron doors and locks,
arched windows, chests draped with strange rugs, and finally, the
singular owner himself who was seated motionless before him: all
this produced a strange impression upon him. The lower half of
the windows were covered so that only from the top of the windows was the light admitted. 'Damn it. How remarkably well his
face is lighted up!' he said to himself, and he began to paint feverishly, as though he were afraid that the favorable light would
somehow disappear. 'What power!' he said to himself. 'If I even
capture half of how he appears now, all my other works will be
surpassed. He'll just leap from the canvas even if I capture only a
little of his nature. What remarkable features!' he kept repeating to
himself, redoubling his energy, and soon he himself began to see
how certain traits were already appearing on the canvas. But the
closer he approached them the more he became aware of an op-
pressive uneasiness which was beyond his explanation. Despite
this, he began to reproduce them exactly as they were. But he
made up his mind, at any price, to discover their most minute characteristics and shades and to penetrate their secret. . . . But as
soon as he painted them with redoubled efforts, there arose in him
such a terrible revulsion, such a feeling of inexplicable oppression,
that he was forced to put aside his brush for a while and then to begin afresh. At last he could endure it no longer. He felt as though
those eyes pierced into his very soul and filled it with intolerable
alarm. On the second and third days this feeling became stronger.
He became frightened. He threw down his brush and bluntly announced that he could paint no longer. You should have seen how
the sinister usurer's face changed at these words. He fell at his feet,
begged him to finish the portrait, pleading that his fate and his very
existence in the world depended on it, that he had already captured his prominent features, and if he would accurately reproduce
them his life would be preserved in some supernatural manner in
the portrait, and then he would not die completely, for it was necessary for him to remain in the world.

"These words terrified my father; they seemed so strange and
so terrible that he discarded his brushes and his palette and dashed
out of the room.

"All day and all night he was vexed by what had happened, but on the next morning he received the portrait from the money-lender. It was brought by a woman who was the only human being the usurer employed, and she declared that her master did not want the portrait, that he would not pay for it, and that he had, therefore, sent it back. He learned that the usurer had died on the evening of the very same day, and that preparations were being made for him to be buried according to the rites of his religion. This seemed inexplicably strange, but from that day on there was a decided change in my father's character. An uneasy and restless feeling which he could not explain possessed him and, soon after, he did something which no one would have expected of him. For some time the paintings of one of his pupils had attracted the attention of a small group of connoisseurs and art lovers. My father appreciated his talent and because of that had always been very helpful. Suddenly, however, he became jealous of him. The general interest expressed about his work and the conversations which centered about it became unbearable to my father. Finally, to heighten his annoyance, he learned that a rich church which had recently been rebuilt had commissioned him to do a picture. He was enraged. 'No, this youngster must not be permitted to defeat me!' he said. 'It's too soon for you, my friend, to think of relegating the old men to the gutters. Thank God I am not without strength! We will see who will defeat whom!' And this straightforward and honorable man planned intrigues and schemes which he had hitherto detested. Finally, he succeeded in arranging a competition for the commission so that other artists were offered the opportunity of entering their own works. And then he shut himself up in his room and began painting feverishly. It was as if he wanted to use all his strength for this one occasion, and, indeed, it turned out to be one of his best works. No one doubted that he would win. The pictures were exhibited, and all the others were as night to day compared to his. Then suddenly one of the members present (If I am not mistaken, a person in holy orders) said something which surprised everyone: 'Certainly there is much talent in the picture of this artist,' he said, 'but there is nothing holy in the faces; on the contrary, in fact, there is even something demoniacal in the eyes, as though some evil feeling had guided the artist's hand.' And everyone looked at the picture and could not help admitting that these words were true. My father rushed up to his

picture to see for himself whether this offensive remark was jus-
tified, and with horror he saw that the usurer's eyes were contained
in nearly all the figures. They gazed with such a devastatingly
diabolical gaze that he could not help but shudder. The picture
was rejected and, to his great vexation, he was forced to hear that
his pupil had won the competition. It is impossible to describe the
degree of fury in him when he returned home. He almost murdered my mother, he drove all the children away, he smashed his
brushes and his easels; and he ripped the usurer's portrait from its
place on the wall, demanded a knife, and ordered a fire to be built
in the fireplace, intending to slash it to pieces and to burn it. An
artist friend caught him in the act upon entering the room. He was
a jovial fellow, like my father, who was content, aspired to nothing unobtainable, did anything that came to hand happily, and was
especially gay at dinner or at parties.

" 'What are you doing? What are you going to burn?' he asked,
walking up to the portrait. 'Why, this is one of your best works.
It's the usurer who recently died. It's a very fine painting. You
didn't cease your efforts until you captured his very eyes. Even in
life eyes never look like that.'

" 'Well, I'll see how they look in the fire!' said my father, seizing
the portrait to fling it into the flames.

" 'For God's sake, stop!' shouted his friend, restraining him. 'If it
offends you so much, give it to me.' My father began to insist on
his way at first, but at length he gave in, and his jovial friend,
pleased with his new acquisition, carried the portrait home with
him.

"My father was calmer after he had left; it was as if that which
oppressed him was removed with the portrait. He was himself
surprised at his previous evil feelings, his jealousy, and the apparent change in his character. Reviewing what he had done, he grew
sad and, not without inward sorrow, he said, 'It was God who
punished me! My picture deserved disgrace. It was intended to
ruin a fellow man. A fiendish feeling of envy controlled my brush
and the fiendish feeling was reflected in what it produced!' Immediately he went out to find his former pupil, and he embraced him
warmly and begged his forgiveness and, as far as possible, he did all
he could to assuage the wrongs he had committed. His work continued as undisturbed as it had once been, but his face was more
frequently thoughtful. He prayed more often, he became more

taciturn, he spoke less negatively about people, and even the coarse exterior of his character was somehow changed. But something soon happened which disturbed him more than ever. For some time he had seen nothing of the friend who had begged him for the portrait. He had been contemplating looking him up when he suddenly appeared in my father's room, and, after the usual words exchanged between friends, he said, 'Well, friend, there was a reason why you wished to burn that portrait. Damn it, there's something strange about it! . . . I don't believe in sorcery, but, and I beg your pardon, there's something evil in it . . .'

" 'What is it?' asked my father.

" 'Well, from the instant I hung it up in my room, I've been so depressed, as if I was thinking of murdering someone. Never before did I know what insomnia was, but now I suffer not only insomnia, but from terrible dreams! . . . I hardly know whether they can be called dreams or something else. It's as if a *domovoi* was strangling me, and the old man appears to me in my sleep. In short, I simply can't describe my state of mind to you. Nothing of the sort ever happened to me before. I have been wandering about in misery all this time—obsessed with fear, expecting something awful. I felt as if I couldn't say a friendly word, a sincere word, to anyone. It's as if a spy were watching over me. And only after I had given that portrait to my nephew who asked for it did I feel as if a stone had been rolled from my shoulders. Immediately I felt as happy as you see me now. Well, brother, you made the devil!'

"My father listened to this story with absolute attention, and he finally asked, 'Does your nephew now have the portrait?'

" 'My nephew, no! He couldn't stand it!' said the jovial fellow. 'Do you know that the soul of that usurer is in that portrait? He leaps out of the frame and walks about the room, and the story my nephew tells of him is beyond comprehension. I would have thought him a lunatic if I myself had not experienced some of it. He sold it to an art collector who couldn't stand it either and who finally got rid of it by getting someone else to take it.'

"The story produced a deep impression on my father, and now he was seriously worried, oppressed with melancholy, and finally he became convinced that his brush had been a tool of the devil and that a part of the usurer's life had somehow or other really passed into the portrait and was now plaguing people, inspiring diabolical ideas, beguiling artists from the righteous path, inflicting the horrible torments of jealousy, and so forth. Three catastrophes which happened afterwards, the sudden deaths of his wife and his daughter and his infant son, he regarded as divine punishment, and he firmly resolved to remove himself from the world. As soon as I reached nine years of age he placed me in an art academy and, paying his debts, he retired to a lonely monastery where he soon took the vows. There he amazed everyone with the austerity of his life and his absolute observance of all the monastic rules. The prior of the monastery ordered him to paint the principal icon in the church after hearing of his skill as an artist, but the humble brother bluntly refused, noting that he was unworthy of touching a brush, that it had been contaminated, that he must first purify his spirit with hard work and great sacrifice before he would deem himself worthy of undertaking such a task. They did not want to force the issue. He increased the rigors of monastic life as much as possible until even this life no longer satisfied him because it did not demand sufficient austerity. With the approval of the prior, he retired into the wilderness so that he could be absolutely alone. And there he built a hut of tree branches, and he ate only uncooked roots, and he dragged a large stone from place to place, and he stood on the same spot with his hands lifted to heaven from the time the sun went up till the time it went down, and, without stop, he recited his prayers. In brief, he experienced, it seems, every possible degree of suffering and pitiless self-abnegation, examples of which can only be found in some Lives of the Saints. In this manner, he long—for several years—exhausted his body and strengthened it at the same time only through fervent prayer. At last, one day he returned to the monastery and firmly said to the prior, 'I am ready now. If God wills, I shall do my task.' And he selected for his subject the birth of Christ. And he worked on it for a whole year without ever leaving his cell, barely sustaining himself with coarse food and praying incessantly. The picture was finished at the end of the year. It was a remarkable achievement. It should be understood that neither the prior nor the monks knew much about painting, but they were all struck by the wonderful holiness of the figures. The expression of divine humility and gentleness on the face of the Holy Mother as she bent over the Child; the profound intelligence in the eyes of the Holy Child, as though they perceived something from afar; the triumphant silence of the Magi, amazed by the Divine Miracle as they prostrated themselves at His feet, and finally, the ineffable tranquillity which pervaded the entire picture—all this was presented with such harmonious strength and great beauty that the impression it created was magical. All of the brethren fell on their knees before the new icon, and the deeply moved prior said, 'No, it is impossible for any artist to produce such a picture solely with the aid of human art alone: your brush was guided by a holy and divine power, and heaven's blessing rested upon your labors!'

"At that time, I had just finished my education at the Academy and had been awarded a gold medal, and with it the joyful hope of going to Italy—the greatest dream of a twenty-year-old artist. I had only to say goodbye to my father whom I had not seen for twelve years. I admit that I had quite forgotten even what he looked like. I had heard some comment about his austerity, and I expected to meet a recluse of rough exterior, a man who had become estranged from everything in the world but his cell and his prayers, a man who was worn out and shriveled from eternal fasting and penance. How great was my surprise when I beheld before me a handsome, almost inspired old man! And on his face there was no trace of exhaustion. It shone with the light of heavenly joy. His beard was white as snow, and his thin, almost transparent hair, of the same silvery hue, fell picturesquely over his breast, and on the folds of his black frock, to the rope which encircled his humble, monastic garb. But still more surprising to me was to hear such words and thoughts about art which, I confess, I will long keep in my mind, and I sincerely wish that all of my friends would do the same.

" 'I awaited you, my son,' he said as I approached him for his blessing. 'The path in which, henceforth, your life is to flow awaits you. It is clear. Do not desert it. You have talent; do not destroy it, for it is the most priceless of God's gifts. Search, study everything you see, master everything, but in everything try to discover the hidden meaning and, above all else, endeavor to attain comprehension of the great mystery of creation. Blessed is he who masters that! For him there is nothing low in nature. A creative artist is as great in lowly things as he is in great ones; in the despicable there is nothing for him to despise, for the glorious spirit of the Creator imbues it, and what is despicable receives glory because it has passed through the purifying fire of His spirit. An intimation of God's heavenly paradise is found in art, and it is for this reason that art is higher than all else. As life spent in triumphant contemplation of God is nobler than a life involved with earthly turmoil, so is the lofty creation of art higher than anything else on earth. As much as the angel is by the purity and innocence of its bright spirit above all invisible powers and the proud passions of Satan, by exactly that much is the great creation of art higher than anything on earth. Sacrifice everything to it and love it with great passion, not with the passion born of earthly lust, but with a gentle and heavenly passion. Without it a man is powerless to raise himself above the earth, and he cannot produce the wonderful sounds which bespeak contentment. For the great creations of art come into the world in order to soothe and reconcile everything. It cannot sow discord in the soul, but it aspires, like a resounding prayer, to God. But there are moments, dark moments . . .' He paused, and I saw a darkness on his face as though some cloud had for a moment passed before him. 'There is one incident in my life,' he said. 'To this very moment, I cannot grasp what that terrible being was whose portrait I painted. It was surely some manifestation of something diabolical. I am aware that the world denies the existence of the devil, and because of that, I will not speak of him. I will only note that it was with revulsion that I painted him. Even at that time I felt no love for my work. I tried to force myself to be true to nature, and I stifled every emotion in me. It was not a work of art, and, therefore, the feelings which are aroused in everyone who looks at it are feelings of revulsion, disturbing feelings, not the feelings of an artist, for an artist puts peace into turmoil. I have been told that this portrait passes from hand to hand and sows dissatisfaction and creates jealousy and black hatred in artists toward their fellow artists, and evil desires to persecute and oppress. May God keep you from such passions. Nothing is more terrible. Better to endure the anguish of the most horrible persecution than to inflict anyone with even a hint of persecution. Keep your mind pure. He who is talented must be purer than all others. Much must be forgiven him. A man who goes forth from his house dressed in brilliant holiday garments has only to be spattered with a single spot of mud from a wheel and people encircle him and point a finger at him and talk of his lack of cleanliness, while the same people do not notice the very many spots on the ordinary garments of other passers-by, for spots on ordinary clothes are never seen.'

"He blessed me and he embraced me. Never in my life was I so deeply moved. I leaned upon his breast reverently rather than with the feeling of a son, and I kissed his flowing silver hair.

"Tears glistened in his eyes. 'Fulfill one request, dear son,' said he at the moment of parting. 'You may one day come across the portrait I have mentioned. You will recognize it at once by its strange eyes and unnatural expression. If you find it, I beg you, destroy it at any cost.'

"You may yourselves judge whether I could refuse to promise to fulfill this request. For fifteen years I have never come across anything which even slightly corresponded to the description of the portrait which my father had given me, until suddenly, at this auction . . ."

The artist did not finish the sentence; he turned his eyes to the wall to look at the portrait once more. And everyone who had listened to him instinctively did the same thing. To their amazement, however, it was no longer on the wall. A soft murmur ran through the crowd, followed suddenly by the word "stolen" which was distinctly heard. Someone had succeeded in taking it away, taking advantage of the fact that the attention of the listeners was distracted by the story. And for a long time those who were present were bewildered, wondering whether they had really seen those remarkable eyes or whether it was merely a dream which had flashed before their eyes, strained from long examination of old pictures.

THE OVERCOAT[1]

In the department of . . . but I had better not mention which department. There is nothing in the world more touchy than a department, a regiment, a government office, and, in fact, any sort of official body. Nowadays every private individual considers all so-

[1] It is usually agreed that the theme of this story was suggested to Gogol by a tale about an indigent clerk who loved to hunt but had no money to buy a gun. After enormous privation, the tale continued, the clerk finally saved enough to buy one. On his first hunting trip, however, he dropped it into the water and it was lost forever. Grief-stricken, the moribund clerk was saved from death by the generosity of his fellow workers, who bought him a new gun. Despite very important differences, there is obviously a strong thematic thread which ties this to *The Overcoat*. Professor Stilman ("Afterword," *The Diary of a Madman and Other Stories* [New York, 1960], pp. 229-32) notes three possible sources. The first, the story of the indigent clerk. The second, "to facts, or anecdotes, recorded in the diary of Pushkin . . ." (and the entry in Pushkin's diary which Professor Stilman quotes notes that strange occurrences had made the streets unsafe—such occurrences consisting mainly of furniture jumping around, thieves very active in the streets). And third, a possible source which was uncovered by F. C. Driessen, a Dutch scholar: namely, a legend of a sixteenth-century saint of the Orthodox Church, Saint Akaky, who died after being abused for nine years by his elder. The elder, the legend continues, was stricken with guilt and, obsessed with the thought that Akaky was still alive, he visited his grave where he heard his voice saying, " 'I am not dead, for a man who lived in obedience may not die.' " We consider this last possible source highly unlikely. Rather, we would suggest, Akaky is "Akaky" (as was his father) because the name is so suggestive, something of which the language-conscious Gogol could not conceivably have been unaware; indeed, to a native Russian who has never read or heard of the story, the name is provocative, the resemblance to *kaka* (defecator) being quite impossible to miss. And Gogol's fondness for the word is evident from a reading of the Russian text. (ed.)

ciety insulted in his person. I have been told that very lately a complaint was lodged by a police inspector of which town I don't remember, and that in this complaint he set forth clearly that the institutions of the State were in danger and that his sacred name was being taken in vain; and, in proof thereof, he appended to his complaint an enormously long volume of some romantic work in which a police inspector appeared on every tenth page, occasionally, indeed, in an intoxicated condition. And so, to avoid any unpleasantness, we had better call the department of which we are speaking "a certain department."

And so, in a *certain department* there was a *certain clerk;* a clerk of whom it cannot be said that he was very remarkable; he was short, somewhat pock-marked, with rather reddish hair and rather dim, bleary eyes, with a small bald patch on the top of his head, with wrinkles on both sides of his cheeks and the sort of complexion which is usually described as hemorrhoidal . . . nothing can be done about that, it is the Petersburg climate. As for his grade in the civil service (for among us a man's rank is what must be established first) he was what is called a perpetual titular councilor, a class at which, as we all know, various writers who indulge in the praiseworthy habit of attacking those who cannot defend themselves jeer and jibe to their hearts' content. This clerk's surname was Bashmachkin. From the very name it is clear that it must have been derived from a shoe (*bashmak*); but when and under what circumstances it was derived from a shoe, it is impossible to say. Both his father and his grandfather and even his brother-in-law, and all the Bashmachkins without exception wore boots, which they simply resoled two or three times a year. His name was Akaky Akakievich. Perhaps it may strike the reader as a rather strange and contrived name, but I can assure him that it was not contrived at all, that the circumstances were such that it was quite out of the question to give him any other name. Akaky Akakievich was born toward nightfall, if my memory does not deceive me, on the twenty-third of March. His mother, the wife of a government clerk, a very good woman, made arrangements in due course to christen the child. She was still lying in bed, facing the door, while on her right hand stood the godfather, an excellent man called Ivan Ivanovich Yeroshkin, one of the head clerks in the Senate, and the godmother, the wife of a police official and a woman of rare qualities, Arina Semeonovna Belobriushkova. Three names were

offered to the happy mother for selection—Mokky, Sossy, or the
name of the martyr Khozdazat. "No," thought the poor lady,
"they are all such names!" To satisfy her, they opened the calendar
at another page, and the names which turned up were: Trifily,
Dula, Varakhasy. "What an infliction!" said the mother. "What
names they all are! I really never heard such names. Varadat or
Varukh would be bad enough, but Trifily and Varakhasy!" They
turned over another page and the names were: Pavsikakhy and
Vakhisy. "Well, I see," said the mother, "it is clear that it is his
fate. Since that is how it is, he had better be named after his father;
his father is Akaky; let the son be Akaky, too." This was how he
came to be Akaky Akakievich. The baby was christened and cried
and made sour faces during the ceremony, as though he foresaw
that he would be a titular councilor. So that was how it all came to
pass. We have reported it here so that the reader may see for himself that it happened quite inevitably and that to give him any other
name was out of the question.

No one has been able to remember when and how long ago he
entered the department, nor who gave him the job. Regardless of
how many directors and higher officials of all sorts came and went,
he was always seen in the same place, in the same position, at the
very same duty, precisely the same copying clerk, so that they used
to declare that he must have been born a copying clerk, uniform,
bald patch, and all. No respect at all was shown him in the department. The porters, far from getting up from their seats when he
came in, took no more notice of him than if a simple fly had flown
across the reception room. His superiors treated him with a sort of
despotic aloofness. The head clerk's assistant used to throw papers
under his nose without even saying "Copy this" or "Here is an interesting, nice little case" or some agreeable remark of the sort, as
is usually done in well-bred offices. And he would take it, gazing
only at the paper without looking to see who had put it there and
whether he had the right to do so; he would take it and at once begin copying it. The young clerks jeered and made jokes at him
to the best of their clerkly wit, and told before his face all sorts of
stories of their own invention about him; they would say of his
landlady, an old woman of seventy, that she beat him, would ask
when the wedding was to take place, and would scatter bits of
paper on his head, calling them snow. Akaky Akakievich never
answered a word, however, but behaved as though there were no

one there. It had no influence on his work; in the midst of all this teasing, he never made a single mistake in his copying. It was only when the jokes became too unbearable, when they jolted his arm, and prevented him from going on with his work, that he would say: "Leave me alone! Why do you insult me?" and there was something touching in the words and in the voice in which they were uttered. There was a note in it of something that aroused compassion, so that one young man, new to the office, who, following the example of the rest, had allowed himself to tease him, suddenly stopped as though cut to the heart, and from that time on, everything was, as it were, changed and appeared in a different light to him. Some unseen force seemed to repel him from the companions with whom he had become acquainted because he thought they were well-bred and decent men. And long afterward, during moments of the greatest gaiety, the figure of the humble little clerk with a bald patch on his head appeared before him with his heart-rending words: "Leave me alone! Why do you insult me?" and within those moving words he heard others: "I am your brother." And the poor young man hid his face in his hands, and many times afterward in his life he shuddered, seeing how much inhumanity there is in man, how much savage brutality lies hidden under refined, cultured politeness, and, my God! even in a man whom the world accepts as a gentleman and a man of honor. . . .

It would be hard to find a man who lived for his work as did Akaky Akakievich. To say that he was zealous in his work is not enough; no, he loved his work. In it, in that copying, he found an interesting and pleasant world of his own. There was a look of enjoyment on his face; certain letters were favorites with him, and when he came to them he was delighted; he chuckled to himself and winked and moved his lips, so that it seemed as though every letter his pen was forming could be read in his face. If rewards had been given according to the measure of zeal in the service, he might to his amazement have even found himself a civil councilor; but all he gained in the service, as the wits, his fellow clerks, expressed it, was a button in his buttonhole[2] and hemorrhoids where he sat. It cannot be said, however, that no notice had ever been taken of him. One director, being a good-natured man and anxious to reward him for his long service, sent him something a little

---

[2] Whereas most clerks of long service wore a medal of achievement. (ed.)

more important than his ordinary copying; he was instructed to make some sort of report from a finished document for another office; the work consisted only of altering the headings and in places changing the first person into the third. This cost him so much effort that he was covered with perspiration: he mopped his brow and said at last, "No, I'd rather copy something."

From that time on they left him to his copying forever. It seemed as though nothing in the world existed for him except his copying. He gave no thought at all to his clothes; his uniform was—well, not green but some sort of rusty, muddy color. His collar was very low and narrow, so that, although his neck was not particularly long, yet, standing out of the collar, it looked as immensely long as those of the dozens of plaster kittens with nodding heads which foreigners carry about on their heads and peddle in Russia. And there were always things sticking to his uniform, either bits of hay or threads; moreover, he had a special knack of passing under a window at the very moment when various garbage was being flung out into the street, and so was continually carrying off bits of melon rind and similar litter on his hat. He had never once in his life noticed what was being done and what was going on in the street, all those things at which, as we all know, his colleagues, the young clerks, always stare, utilizing their keen sight so well that they notice anyone on the other side of the street with a trouser strap hanging loose—an observation which always calls forth a sly grin. Whatever Akaky Akakievich looked at, he saw nothing but his clear, evenly written lines, and it was only perhaps when a horse suddenly appeared from nowhere and placed its head on his shoulder, and with its nostrils blew a real gale upon his cheek, that he would notice that he was not in the middle of his writing, but rather in the middle of the street.

On reaching home, he would sit down at once at the table, hurriedly eat his soup and a piece of beef with an onion; he did not notice the taste at all but ate it all with the flies and anything else that Providence happened to send him. When he felt that his stomach was beginning to be full, he would get up from the table, take out a bottle of ink and begin copying the papers he had brought home with him. When he had none to do, he would make a copy especially for his own pleasure, particularly if the document were remarkable not for the beauty of its style but because it was addressed to some new or distinguished person.

Even at those hours when the gray Petersburg sky is completely
overcast and the whole population of clerks have dined and eaten
their fill, each as best he can, according to the salary he receives
and his personal tastes; when they are all resting after the scratching of pens and bustle of the office, their own necessary work and
other people's, and all the tasks that an overzealous man voluntarily
sets himself even beyond what is necessary; when the clerks are
hastening to devote what is left of their time to pleasure; some
more enterprising are flying to the theater, others to the street to
spend their leisure staring at women's hats, some to spend the
evening paying compliments to some attractive girl, the star of a
little official circle, while some—and this is the most frequent of
all—go simply to a fellow clerk's apartment on the third or fourth
story, two little rooms with a hall or a kitchen, with some pretensions to style, with a lamp or some such article that has cost many
sacrifices of dinners and excursions—at the time when all the
clerks are scattered about the apartments of their friends, playing a
stormy game of whist, sipping tea out of glasses, eating cheap biscuits, sucking in smoke from long pipes, telling, as the cards are
dealt, some scandal that has floated down from higher circles, a
pleasure which the Russian can never by any possibility deny himself, or, when there is nothing better to talk about, repeating the
everlasting anecdote of the commanding officer who was told that
the tail had been cut off the horse on the Falconet monument[3]—in
short, even when everyone was eagerly seeking entertainment,
Akaky Akakievich did not indulge in any amusement. No one
could say that they had ever seen him at an evening party. After
working to his heart's content, he would go to bed, smiling at
the thought of the next day and wondering what God would send
him to copy. So flowed on the peaceful life of a man who knew
how to be content with his fate on a salary of four hundred rubles,[4]
and so perhaps it would have flowed on to extreme old age, had it
not been for the various disasters strewn along the road of life, not
only of titular, but even of privy, actual court, and all other councilors, even those who neither give counsel to others nor accept it
themselves.

There is in Petersburg a mighty foe of all who receive a salary

[3] Famous statue of Peter the First. (ed.)
[4] See Vol. 1, p. 232, n. 12. (ed.)

of about four hundred rubles. That foe is none other than our
northern frost, although it is said to be very good for the health.
Between eight and nine in the morning, precisely at the hour when
the streets are filled with clerks going to their departments, the
frost begins indiscriminately giving such sharp and stinging nips at
all their noses that the poor fellows don't know what to do with
them. At that time, when even those in the higher grade have a
pain in their brows and tears in their eyes from the frost, the poor
titular councilors are sometimes almost defenseless. Their only
protection lies in running as fast as they can through five or six
streets in a wretched, thin little overcoat and then warming their
feet thoroughly in the porter's room, till all their faculties and tal-
ents for their various duties thaw out again after having been
frozen on the way. Akaky Akakievich had for some time been
feeling that his back and shoulders were particularly nipped by
the cold, although he did try to run the regular distance as fast as
he could. He wondered at last whether there were any defects
in his overcoat. After examining it thoroughly in the privacy of
his home, he discovered that in two or three places, on the back
and the shoulders, it had become a regular sieve; the cloth was so
worn that you could see through it and the lining was coming out.
I must note that Akaky Akakievich's overcoat had also served as a
butt for the jokes of the clerks. It had even been deprived of the
honorable name of overcoat and had been referred to as the "dressing gown." [5] It was indeed of rather a peculiar make. Its collar had
been growing smaller year by year as it served to patch the other
parts. The patches were not good specimens of the tailor's art, and
they certainly looked clumsy and ugly. On seeing what was wrong,
Akaky Akakievich decided that he would have to take the overcoat
to Petrovich, a tailor who lived on the fourth floor up a back staircase, and, in spite of having only one eye and being pockmarked
all over his face, was rather successful in repairing the trousers
and coats of clerks and others—that is, when he was sober, be it
understood, and had no other enterprise in his mind. Of this tailor
I ought not, of course, say much, but since it is now the rule that
the character of every person in a novel must be completely described, well, there's nothing I can do but describe Petrovich too.
At first he was called simply Grigory, and was a serf belonging

---

[5] *Kapot*, usually a woman's garment. (ed.)

to some gentleman or other. He began to be called Petrovich[6] from the time that he got his freedom and began to drink rather heavily on every holiday, at first only on the main holidays, but afterward, on all church holidays indiscriminately, wherever there was a cross in the calendar. In this he was true to the customs of his forefathers, and when he quarreled with his wife he used to call her a worldly woman and a German. Since we have now mentioned the wife, it will be necessary to say a few words about her, too, but unfortunately not much is known about her, except indeed that Petrovich had a wife and that she wore a cap and not a kerchief, but apparently she could not boast of beauty; anyway, none but soldiers of the guard peered under her cap when they met her, and they twitched their mustaches and gave vent to a rather peculiar sound.

As he climbed the stairs leading to Petrovich's—which, to do them justice, were all soaked with water and slops and saturated through and through with that smell of ammonia which makes the eyes smart, and is, as we all know, inseparable from the backstairs of Petersburg houses—Akaky Akakievich was already wondering how much Petrovich would ask for the job, and inwardly resolving not to give more than two rubles. The door was open, because Petrovich's wife was frying some fish and had so filled the kitchen with smoke that you could not even see the cockroaches. Akaky Akakievich crossed the kitchen unnoticed by the good woman, and walked at last into a room where he saw Petrovich sitting on a big, wooden, unpainted table with his legs tucked under him like a Turkish pasha. The feet, as is usual with tailors when they sit at work, were bare; and the first object that caught Akaky Akakievich's eye was the big toe, with which he was already familiar, with a misshapen nail as thick and strong as the shell of a tortoise. Around Petrovich's neck hung a skein of silk and another of thread and on his knees was a rag of some sort. He had for the last three minutes been trying to thread his needle, but could not get the thread into the eye and so was very angry with the darkness and indeed with the thread itself, muttering in an undertone: "She won't go in, the savage! You wear me out, you bitch." Akaky Akakievich was unhappy that he had come just at the minute when Petrovich was in a bad humor; he liked to give him an order when

---

[6] Customarily, serfs were addressed by first name only, while free men were addressed either by first name and patronymic or just the patronymic. (ed.)

he was a little "elevated," or, as his wife expressed it, "had fortified himself with vodka, the one-eyed devil." In such circumstances Petrovich was as a rule very ready to give way and agree, and invariably bowed and thanked him. Afterward, it is true, his wife would come wailing that her husband had been drunk and so had asked too little, but adding a single ten-kopek piece would settle that. But on this occasion Petrovich was apparently sober and consequently curt, unwilling to bargain, and the devil knows what price he would be ready to demand. Akaky Akakievich realized this, and was, as the saying is, beating a retreat, but things had gone too far, for Petrovich was screwing up his solitary eye very attentively at him and Akaky Akakievich involuntarily said: "Good day, Petrovich!"

"I wish you a good day, sir," said Petrovich, and squinted at Akaky Akakievich's hands, trying to discover what sort of goods he had brought.

"Here I have come to you, Petrovich, do you see . . . !"

It must be noticed that Akaky Akakievich for the most part explained himself by apologies, vague phrases, and meaningless parts of speech which have absolutely no significance whatever. If the subject were a very difficult one, it was his habit indeed to leave his sentences quite unfinished, so that very often after a sentence had begun with the words, "It really is, don't you know . . ." nothing at all would follow and he himself would be quite oblivious to the fact that he had not finished his thought, supposing he had said all that was necessary.

"What is it?" said Petrovich, and at the same time with his solitary eye he scrutinized his whole uniform from the collar to the sleeves, the back, the skirts, the buttonholes—with all of which he was very familiar since they were all his own work. Such scrutiny is habitual with tailors; it is the first thing they do on meeting one.

"It's like this, Petrovich . . . the overcoat, the cloth . . . you see everywhere else it is quite strong; it's a little dusty and looks as though it were old, but it is new and it is only in one place just a little . . . on the back, and just a little worn on one shoulder and on this shoulder, too, a little . . . do you see? that's all, and it's not much work . . ."

Petrovich took the "dressing gown," first spread it out over the table, examined it for a long time, shook his head, and put his hand out to the window sill for a round snuffbox with a portrait on the lid of some general—which general I can't exactly say, for a finger had been thrust through the spot where a face should have been, and the hole had been pasted over with a square piece of paper. After taking a pinch of snuff, Petrovich held the "dressing gown" up in his hands and looked at it against the light, and again he shook his head; then he turned it with the lining upward and once more shook his head; again he took off the lid with the general pasted up with paper and stuffed a pinch into his nose, shut the box, put it away, and at last said: "No, it can't be repaired; a wretched garment!" Akaky Akakievich's heart sank at those words.

"Why can't it, Petrovich?" he said, almost in the imploring voice of a child. "Why, the only thing is, it is a bit worn on the shoulders; why, you have got some little pieces . . ."

"Yes, the pieces will be found all right," said Petrovich, "but it can't be patched, the stuff is rotten; if you put a needle in it, it would give way."

"Let it give way, but you just put a patch on it."

"There is nothing to put a patch on. There is nothing for it to hold on to; there is a great strain on it; it is not worth calling cloth; it would fly away at a breath of wind."

"Well, then, strengthen it with something—I'm sure, really, this is . . . !"

"No," said Petrovich resolutely, "there is nothing that can be done, the thing is no good at all. You had far better, when the cold winter weather comes, make yourself leg wrappings out of it, for there is no warmth in stockings; the Germans invented them just to make money." (Petrovich enjoyed a dig at the Germans occasionally.) "And as for the overcoat, it is obvious that you will have to have a new one."

At the word "new" there was a mist before Akaky Akakievich's eyes, and everything in the room seemed blurred. He could see nothing clearly but the general with the piece of paper over his face on the lid of Petrovich's snuffbox.

"A new one?" he said, still feeling as though he were in a dream; "why, I haven't the money for it."

"Yes, a new one," Petrovich repeated with barbarous composure.

"Well, and if I did have a new one, how much would it . . . ?"

"You mean what will it cost?"

"Yes."

"Well, at least one hundred and fifty rubles," said Petrovich, and he compressed his lips meaningfully. He was very fond of making an effect; he was fond of suddenly disconcerting a man completely and then squinting sideways to see what sort of a face he made.

"A hundred and fifty rubles for an overcoat!" screamed poor Akaky Akakievich—it was perhaps the first time he had screamed in his life, for he was always distinguished by the softness of his voice.

"Yes," said Petrovich, "and even then it depends on the coat. If I were to put marten on the collar, and add a hood with silk linings, it would come to two hundred."

"Petrovich, please," said Akaky Akakievich in an imploring voice, not hearing and not trying to hear what Petrovich said, and missing all his effects, "repair it somehow, so that it will serve a little longer."

"No, that would be wasting work and spending money for nothing," said Petrovich, and after that Akaky Akakievich went away completely crushed, and when he had gone Petrovich remained standing for a long time with his lips pursed up meaningfully before he began his work again, feeling pleased that he had not demeaned himself or lowered the dignity of the tailor's art.

When he got into the street, Akaky Akakievich felt as though he was in a dream. "So that is how it is," he said to himself. "I really did not think it would be this way . . ." and then after a pause he added, "So that's it! So that's how it is at last! and I really could never have supposed it would be this way. And there . . ." There followed another long silence, after which he said: "So that's it! well, it really is so utterly unexpected . . . who would have thought . . . what a circumstance . . ." Saying this, instead of going home he walked off in quite the opposite direction without suspecting what he was doing. On the way a clumsy chimney sweep brushed the whole of his sooty side against him and blackened his entire shoulder; a whole hatful of plaster scattered upon him from the top of a house that was being built. He noticed nothing of this, and only after he had jostled against a policeman who had set his halberd down beside him and was shaking some snuff out of his horn into his rough fist, he came to himself a little and then only because the policeman said: "Why are you poking yourself right in one's face, haven't you enough room on the street?" This made him look around and turn homeward;

only there he began to collect his thoughts, to see his position in a clear and true light, and began talking to himself no longer incoherently but reasonably and openly as with a sensible friend with whom one can discuss the most intimate and vital matters. "No," said Akaky Akakievich, "it is no use talking to Petrovich now; just now he really is . . . his wife must have been giving it to him. I had better go to him on Sunday morning; after Saturday night he will have a crossed eye and be sleepy, so he'll want a little drink and his wife won't give him a kopek. I'll slip ten kopeks into his hand and then he will be more accommodating and maybe take the overcoat . . ."

So reasoning with himself, Akaky Akakievich cheered up and waited until the next Sunday; then, seeing from a distance Petrovich's wife leaving the house, he went straight in. Petrovich certainly had a crossed eye after Saturday. He could hardly hold his head up and was very drowsy; but, despite all that, as soon as he heard what Akaky Akakievich was speaking about, it seemed as though the devil had nudged him. "I can't," he said, "you must order a new one." Akaky Akakievich at once slipped a ten-kopek piece into his hand. "I thank you, sir, I will have just a drop to your health, but don't trouble yourself about the overcoat; it is no good for anything. I'll make you a fine new coat; you can have faith in me for that."

Akaky Akakievich would have said more about repairs, but Petrovich, without listening, said: "A new one I'll make you without fail; you can rely on that; I'll do my best. It could even be like the fashion that is popular, with the collar to fasten with silver-plated hooks under a flap."

Then Akaky Akakievich saw that there was no escape from a new overcoat and he was utterly depressed. How indeed, for what, with what money could he get it? Of course he could to some extent rely on the bonus for the coming holiday, but that money had long ago been appropriated and its use determined beforehand. It was needed for new trousers and to pay the cobbler an old debt for putting some new tops on some old boots, and he had to order three shirts from a seamstress as well as two items of undergarments which it is indecent to mention in print; in short, all that money absolutely must be spent, and even if the director were to be so gracious as to give him a holiday bonus of forty-five or even fifty, instead of forty rubles, there would be still left a mere trifle, which would be but a drop in the ocean compared to the fortune needed for an overcoat. Though, of course, he knew that Petrovich had a strange craze for suddenly demanding the devil knows what enormous price, so that at times his own wife could not help crying out: "Why, you are out of your wits, you idiot! Another time he'll undertake a job for nothing, and here the devil has bewitched him to ask more than he is worth himself." Though, of course, he knew that Petrovich would undertake to make it for eighty rubles, still where would he get those eighty rubles? He might manage half of that sum; half of it could be found, perhaps even a little more; but where could he get the other half? . . . But, first of all, the reader ought to know where that first half was to be found. Akaky Akakievich had the habit every time he spent a ruble of putting aside two kopeks in a little box which he kept locked, with a slit in the lid for dropping in the money. At the end of every six months he would inspect the pile of coppers there and change them for small silver. He had done this for a long time, and in the course of many years the sum had mounted up to forty rubles and so he had half the money in his hands, but where was he to get the other half; where was he to get another forty rubles? Akaky Akakievich thought and thought and decided at last that he would have to diminish his ordinary expenses, at least for a year; give up burning candles in the evening, and if he had to do any work he must go into the landlady's room and work by her candle; that as he walked along the streets he must walk as lightly and carefully as possible, almost on tiptoe, on the cobbles and flagstones, so that his soles might last a little longer than usual; that he must send his linen to the wash less frequently, and that, to preserve it from being worn, he must take it off every day when he came home and sit in a thin cotton dressing gown, a very ancient garment which Time itself had spared. To tell the truth, he found it at first rather difficult to get used to these privations, but after a while it became a habit and went smoothly enough—he even became quite accustomed to being hungry in the evening; on the other hand, he had spiritual nourishment, for he carried ever in his thoughts the idea of his future overcoat. His whole existence had in a sense become fuller, as though he had married, as though some other person were present with him, as though he were no longer alone but an agreeable companion had consented to walk the path of life hand in hand with him, and that companion was none other than the new overcoat with its thick padding and its strong, durable lining. He became, as it were, more alive, even more strong-willed, like a man who has set before himself a definite goal. Uncertainty, indecision, in fact all the hesitating and vague characteristics, vanished from his face and his manners. At times there was a gleam in his eyes; indeed, the most bold and audacious ideas flashed through his mind. Why not really have marten on the collar? Meditation on the subject always made him absent-minded. On one occasion when he was copying a document, he very nearly made a mistake, so that he almost cried out "ough" aloud and crossed himself. At least once every month he went to Petrovich to talk about the overcoat: where it would be best to buy the cloth, and what color it should be, and what price; and, though he returned home a little anxious, he was always pleased at the thought that at last the time was at hand when everything would be bought and the overcoat would be made. Things moved even faster than he had anticipated. Contrary to all expectations, the director bestowed on Akaky Akakievich a bonus of no less than sixty rubles. Whether it was that he had an inkling that Akaky Akakievich needed a coat, or whether it happened by luck, owing to this he found he had twenty rubles extra. This circumstance hastened the course of affairs. Another two or three months of partial starvation and Akaky Akakievich had actually saved up nearly eighty rubles. His heart, as a rule very tranquil, began to throb.

The very first day he set out with Petrovich for the shops. They bought some very good cloth, and no wonder, since they had been thinking of it for more than six months, and scarcely a month had passed without their going out to the shop to compare prices; now Petrovich himself declared that there was no better cloth to be had. For the lining they chose calico, but of such good quality, that in Petrovich's words it was even better than silk, and actually as strong and handsome to look at. Marten they did not buy, because it was too expensive, but instead they chose cat fur, the best to be found in the shop—cat which in the distance might almost be taken for marten. Petrovich was busy making the coat for two weeks, because there was a great deal of quilting; otherwise it would have been ready sooner. Petrovich charged twelve rubles for the work; less than that it hardly could have been; everything was sewn with silk, with fine double seams, and Petrovich went over every seam afterwards with his own teeth, imprinting various patterns with them. It was . . . it is hard to say precisely on what day, but probably on the most triumphant day in the life of Akaky Akakievich, that Petrovich at last brought the overcoat. He brought it in the morning, just before it was time to set off for the department. The overcoat could not have arrived at a more opportune time, because severe frosts were just beginning and seemed threatening to become even harsher. Petrovich brought the coat himself as a good tailor should. There was an expression of importance on his face, such as Akaky Akakievich had never seen there before. He seemed fully conscious of having completed a work of no little importance and of having shown by his own example the gulf that separates tailors who only put in linings and do repairs from those who make new coats. He took the coat out of the huge handkerchief in which he had brought it (the handkerchief had just come home from the wash); he then folded it up and put it in his pocket for future use. After taking out the overcoat, he looked at it with much pride and holding it in both hands, threw it very deftly over Akaky Akakievich's shoulders, then pulled it down and smoothed it out behind with his hands; then draped it about Akaky Akakievich somewhat jauntily. Akaky Akakievich, a practical man, wanted to try it with his arms in the sleeves. Petrovich helped him to put it on, and it looked splendid with his arms in the sleeves, too. In fact, it turned out that the overcoat was completely and entirely successful. Petrovich did not let slip the occasion for observing that it was only because he lived in a small street and had no signboard, and because he had known Akaky Akakievich so long, that he had done it so cheaply, and that on Nevsky Prospekt they would have asked him seventy-five rubles for the tailoring alone. Akaky Akakievich had no inclination to discuss this with Petrovich; besides he was frightened of the big sums that Petrovich was fond of flinging airily about in conversation. He paid him, thanked him, and went off, with his new overcoat on, to the department. Petrovich followed him out and stopped in the street, staring for a long time at the coat from a distance and then purposely turned off and, taking a short cut through a side street, came back into the street, and got another view of the coat from the other side, that is, from the front.

Meanwhile Akaky Akakievich walked along in a gay holiday mood. Every second he was conscious that he had a new overcoat on his shoulders, and several times he actually laughed from inward satisfaction. Indeed, it had two advantages: one that it was warm and the other that it was good. He did not notice how far he had walked at all and he suddenly found himself in the department; in the porter's room he took off the overcoat, looked it over, and entrusted it to the porter's special care. I cannot tell how it happened, but all at once everyone in the department learned that Akaky Akakievich had a new overcoat and that the "dressing gown" no longer existed. They all ran out at once into the cloakroom to look at Akaky Akakievich's new overcoat; they began welcoming him and congratulating him so that at first he could do nothing but smile and then felt positively embarrassed. When, coming up to him, they all began saying that he must "sprinkle" the new overcoat and that he ought at least to buy them all a supper, Akaky Akakievich lost his head completely and did not know what to do, how to get out of it, nor what to answer. A few minutes later, flushing crimson, he even began assuring them with great simplicity that it was not a new overcoat at all, that it wasn't much, that it was an old overcoat. At last one of the clerks, indeed the assistant of the head clerk of the room, probably in order to show that he wasn't too proud to mingle with those beneath him, said: "So be it, I'll give a party instead of Akaky Akakievich and invite you all to tea with me this evening; as luck would have it, it is my birthday." The clerks naturally congratulated the assistant head clerk and eagerly accepted the invitation. Akaky Akakievich was beginning to make excuses, but they all declared that it was uncivil of him, that it would be simply a shame and a disgrace and that he could not possibly refuse. So, he finally relented, and later felt pleased about it when he remembered that through this he would have the opportunity of going out in the evening, too, in his new overcoat. That whole day was for Akaky Akakievich the most triumphant and festive day in his life. He returned home in the happiest frame of mind, took off the overcoat, and hung it carefully on the wall, admiring the cloth and lining once more, and then pulled out his old "dressing gown," now completely falling apart, and put it next to his new overcoat to compare the two. He glanced at it and laughed: the difference was enormous! And long afterwards he went on laughing at dinner, as the position in which the "dressing gown" was placed recurred to his mind. He dined in excellent spirits and after dinner wrote nothing, no papers at all, but just relaxed for a little while on his bed, till it got dark; then, without putting things off, he dressed, put on his overcoat, and went out into the street. Where precisely the clerk who had invited him lived we regret to say we cannot tell; our memory is beginning to fail sadly, and everything there in Petersburg, all the streets and houses, are so blurred and muddled in our head that it is a very difficult business to put anything in orderly fashion. Regardless of that, there is no doubt that the clerk lived in the better part of the town and consequently a very long distance from Akaky Akakievich. At first Akaky Akakievich had to walk through deserted streets, scantily lighted, but as he approached his destination the streets became more lively, more full of people, and more brightly lighted; passers-by began to be more frequent, ladies began to appear, here and there beautifully dressed, and beaver collars were to be seen on the men. Cabmen with wooden, railed sledges, studded with brass-topped nails, were less frequently seen; on the other hand, jaunty drivers in raspberry-colored velvet caps, with lacquered sledges and bearskin rugs, appeared and carriages with decorated boxes dashed along the streets, their wheels crunching through the snow.

Akaky Akakievich looked at all this as a novelty; for several years he had not gone out into the streets in the evening. He stopped with curiosity before a lighted shop window to look at a picture in which a beautiful woman was represented in the act of taking off her shoe and displaying as she did so the whole of a very shapely leg, while behind her back a gentleman with whiskers and a handsome imperial on his chin was sticking his head in at the door. Akaky Akakievich shook his head and smiled and then went on his way. Why did he smile? Was it because he had come across something quite unfamiliar to him, though every man retains some instinctive feeling on the subject, or was it that he reflected, like many other clerks, as follows: "Well, those Frenchmen! It's beyond anything! If they go in for anything of the sort, it really is . . . !" Though possibly he did not even think that; there is no creeping into a man's soul and finding out all that he thinks. At last he reached the house in which the assistant head clerk lived in fine style; there was a lamp burning on the stairs, and the apartment was on the second floor. As he went into the hall Akaky Akakievich saw rows of galoshes. Among them in the middle of the room stood a hissing samovar puffing clouds of steam. On the walls hung coats and cloaks among which some actually had beaver collars or velvet lapels. From the other side of the wall there came noise and talk, which suddenly became clear and loud when the door opened and the footman came out with a tray full of empty glasses, a jug of cream, and a basket of biscuits. It was evident that the clerks had arrived long before and had already drunk their first glass of tea. Akaky Akakievich, after hanging up his coat with his own hands, went into the room, and at the same moment there flashed before his eyes a vision of candles, clerks, pipes and card tables, together with the confused sounds of conversation rising up on all sides and the noise of moving chairs. He stopped very awkwardly in the middle of the room, looking about and trying to think of what to do, but he was noticed and received with a shout and they all went at once into the hall and again took a look at his overcoat. Though Akaky Akakievich was somewhat embarrassed, yet, being a simplehearted man, he could not help being pleased at seeing how they all admired his coat. Then of course they all abandoned him and his coat, and turned their attention as usual to the tables set for whist. All this—the noise, the talk, and the crowd of people—was strange and wonderful to Akaky Akakievich. He simply did not know how to behave, what to do with his arms and legs and his whole body; at last he sat down beside the players, looked at the cards, stared first at one and then at another of the faces, and in a little while, feeling bored, began to yawn—especially since it was long past the time at which he usually went to bed. He tried to say goodbye to his hosts, but they would not let him go, saying that he absolutely must have a glass of champagne in honor of the new coat. An hour later supper was served, consisting of salad, cold veal, pastry and pies from the bakery, and champagne. They made Akaky Akakievich drink two glasses, after which he felt that things were much more cheerful, though he could not forget that it was twelve o'clock, and that he ought to have been home long ago. That his host might not take it into his head to detain him, he slipped out of the room, hunted in the hall for his coat, which he found, not without regret, lying on the floor, shook it, removed some fluff from it, put it on, and went down the stairs into the street. It was still light in the streets. Some little grocery shops, those perpetual clubs for servants and all sorts of people, were open; others which were closed showed, however, a long streak of light

at every crack of the door, proving that they were not yet
deserted, and probably maids and menservants were still finishing their conversation and discussion, driving their masters to utter perplexity as to their whereabouts. Akaky Akakievich walked
along in a cheerful state of mind; he was even on the point of
running, goodness knows why, after a lady of some sort who
passed by like lightning with every part of her frame in violent
motion. He checked himself at once, however, and again walked
along very gently, feeling positively surprised at the inexplicable
impulse that had seized him. Soon the deserted streets, which
are not particularly cheerful by day and even less so in the evening, stretched before him. Now they were still more dead and
deserted; the light of street lamps was scantier, the oil evidently
running low; then came wooden houses and fences; not a soul anywhere; only the snow gleamed on the streets and the low-pitched
slumbering hovels looked black and gloomy with their closed shutters. He approached the spot where the street was intersected by an
endless square, which looked like a fearful desert with its houses
scarcely visible on the far side.

In the distance, goodness knows where, there was a gleam of
light from some sentry box which seemed to be at the end of the
world. Akaky Akakievich's lightheartedness faded. He stepped
into the square, not without uneasiness, as though his heart had a
premonition of evil. He looked behind him and to both sides—it
was as though the sea were all around him. "No, better not look,"
he thought, and walked on, shutting his eyes, and when he opened
them to see whether the end of the square was near, he suddenly
saw standing before him, almost under his very nose, some men
with mustaches; just what they were like he could not even distinguish. There was a mist before his eyes, and a throbbing in
his chest. "Why, that overcoat is mine!" said one of them in a
voice like a clap of thunder, seizing him by the collar. Akaky
Akakievich was on the point of shouting "Help" when another put
a fist the size of a clerk's head against his lips, saying: "You just
shout now." Akaky Akakievich felt only that they took the overcoat off, and gave him a kick with their knees, and he fell on his
face in the snow and was conscious of nothing more. A few minutes later he recovered consciousness and got up on his feet, but
there was no one there. He felt that it was cold on the ground and
that he had no overcoat, and began screaming, but it seemed as

though his voice would not carry to the end of the square. Overwhelmed with despair and continuing to scream, he ran across the square straight to the sentry box beside which stood a policeman leaning on his halberd and, so it seemed, looking with curiosity to see who the devil the man was who was screaming and running toward him from the distance. As Akaky Akakievich reached him, he began breathlessly shouting that he was asleep and not looking after his duty not to see that a man was being robbed. The policeman answered that he had seen nothing, that he had only seen him stopped in the middle of the square by two men, and supposed that they were his friends, and that, instead of abusing him for nothing, he had better go the next day to the police inspector, who would certainly find out who had taken the overcoat. Akaky Akakievich ran home in a terrible state: his hair, which was still comparatively abundant on his temples and the back of his head, was completely disheveled; his sides and chest and his trousers were all covered with snow. When his old landlady heard a fearful knock at the door, she jumped hurriedly out of bed and, with only one slipper on, ran to open it, modestly holding her chemise over her bosom; but when she opened it she stepped back, seeing in what a state Akaky Akakievich was. When he told her what had happened, she clasped her hands in horror and said that he must go straight to the district commissioner, because the local police inspector would deceive him, make promises and lead him a dance; that it would be best of all to go to the district commissioner, and that she knew him, because Anna, the Finnish girl who was once her cook, was now in service as a nurse at the commissioner's; and that she often saw him himself when he passed by their house, and that he used to be every Sunday at church too, saying his prayers and at the same time looking good-humoredly at everyone, and that therefore by every token he must be a kind-hearted man. After listening to this advice, Akaky Akakievich made his way very gloomily to his room, and how he spent that night I leave to the imagination of those who are in the least able to picture the position of others.

Early in the morning he set off to the police commissioner's but was told that he was asleep. He came at ten o'clock, he was told again that he was asleep; he came at eleven and was told that the commissioner was not at home; he came at dinnertime, but the clerks in the anteroom would not let him in, and insisted on knowing what was the matter and what business had brought him and exactly what had happened; so that at last Akaky Akakievich for the first time in his life tried to show the strength of his character and said curtly that he must see the commissioner himself, that they dare not refuse to admit him, that he had come from the department on government business, and that if he made complaint of them they would see. The clerks dared say nothing to this, and one of them went to summon the commissioner. The latter received his story of being robbed of his overcoat in an extremely peculiar manner. Instead of attending to the main point, he began asking Akaky Akakievich questions: why had he been coming home so late? wasn't he going, or hadn't he been, to some bawdy house? so that Akaky Akakievich was overwhelmed with confusion, and went away without knowing whether or not the proper measures would be taken regarding his overcoat. He was absent from the office all that day (the only time that it had happened in his life). Next day he appeared with a pale face, wearing his old "dressing gown" which had become a still more pitiful sight. The news of the theft of the overcoat—though there were clerks who did not let even this chance slip of jeering at Akaky Akakievich—touched many of them. They decided on the spot to get up a collection for him, but collected only a very trifling sum, because the clerks had already spent a good deal contributing to the director's portrait and on the purchase of a book, at the suggestion of the head of their department, who was a friend of the author, and so the total realized was very insignificant. One of the clerks, moved by compassion, ventured at any rate to assist Akaky Akakievich with good advice, telling him not to go to the local police inspector, because, though it might happen that the latter might succeed in finding his overcoat because he wanted to impress his superiors, it would remain in the possession of the police unless he presented legal proofs that it belonged to him; he urged that by far the best thing would be to appeal to a Person of Consequence; that the Person of Consequence, by writing and getting into communication with the proper authorities, could push the matter through more successfully. There was nothing else to do. Akaky Akakievich made up his mind to go to the Person of Consequence. What precisely was the nature of the functions of the Person of Consequence has remained a matter of uncertainty. It must be noted that this Person of Consequence had only lately become a person of consequence, and until recently had been a person of no consequence. Though, indeed, his position even now was not reckoned of consequence in comparison with others of still greater consequence. But there is always to be found a circle of persons to whom a person of little consequence in the eyes of others is a person of consequence. It is true that he did his utmost to increase the consequence of his position in various ways, for instance by insisting that his subordinates should come out onto the stairs to meet him when he arrived at his office; that no one should venture to approach him directly but all proceedings should follow the strictest chain of command; that a collegiate registrar should report the matter to the governmental secretary; and the governmental secretary to the titular councilor or whomsoever it might be, and that business should only reach him through this channel. Everyone in Holy Russia has a craze for imitation; everyone apes and mimics his superiors. I have actually been told that a titular councilor who was put in charge of a small separate office, immediately partitioned off a special room for himself, calling it the head office, and posted lackeys at the door with red collars and gold braid, who took hold of the handle of the door and opened it for everyone who went in, though the "head office" was so tiny that it was with difficulty that an ordinary writing desk could be put into it. The manners and habits of the Person of Consequence were dignified and majestic, but hardly subtle. The chief foundation of his system was strictness; "strictness, strictness, and—strictness!" he used to say, and at the last word he would look very significantly at the person he was addressing, though, indeed, he had no reason to do so, for the dozen clerks who made up the whole administrative mechanism of his office stood in appropriate awe of him; any clerk who saw him in the distance would leave his work and remain standing at attention till his superior had left the room. His conversation with his subordinates was usually marked by severity and almost confined to three phrases: "How dare you? Do you know to whom you are speaking? Do you understand who I am?" He was, however, at heart a good-natured man, pleasant and obliging with his colleagues; but his advancement to a high rank had completely turned his head. When he received it, he was perplexed, thrown off his balance, and quite at a loss as to how to behave. If he chanced to be with his equals, he was still quite a decent man, a very gentlemanly man, in fact, and in many ways even an intelligent man; but as soon as he was in company with men who were even one grade below him, there was simply no doing anything with him: he sat silent and his position excited compassion, the more so as he himself felt that he might have been spending his time to so much more advantage. At times there could be seen in his eyes an intense desire to join in some interesting conversation, but he was restrained by the doubt whether it would not be too much on his part, whether it would not be too great a familiarity and lowering of his dignity, and in consequence of these reflections he remained everlastingly in the same mute condition, only uttering from time to time monosyllabic sounds, and in this way he gained the reputation of being a terrible bore.

So this was the Person of Consequence to whom our friend Akaky Akakievich appealed, and he appealed to him at a most unpropitious moment, very unfortunate for himself, though fortunate, indeed, for the Person of Consequence. The latter happened to be in his study, talking in the very best of spirits with an old friend of his childhood who had only just arrived and whom he had not seen for several years. It was at this moment that he was informed that a man called Bashmachkin was asking to see him. He asked abruptly, "What sort of man is he?" and received the answer, "A government clerk." "Ah! he can wait. I haven't time now," said the Person of Consequence. Here I must observe that this was a complete lie on the part of the Person of Consequence; he had time; his friend and he had long ago said all they had to say to each other and their conversation had begun to be broken by very long pauses during which they merely slapped each other on the knee, saying, "So that's how things are, Ivan Abramovich!" —"So that's it, Stepan Varlamovich!" but, despite that, he told the clerk to wait in order to show his friend, who had left the civil service some years before and was living at home in the country, how long clerks had to wait for him. At last, after they had talked or rather been silent, to their heart's content and had smoked a cigar in very comfortable armchairs with sloping backs, he seemed suddenly to recollect, and said to the secretary, who was standing at the door with papers for his signature: "Oh, by the way, there is a clerk waiting, isn't there? tell him he can come in." When he saw Akaky Akakievich's meek appearance and old uniform, he turned to him at once and said: "What do you want?" in a firm and abrupt voice, which he had purposely rehearsed in his own room in solitude before the mirror for a week before receiving his present post and the grade of a general. Akaky Akakievich, who was overwhelmed with appropriate awe beforehand, was somewhat confused and, as far as his tongue would allow him, explained to the best of his powers, with even more frequent "ers" than usual, that he had had a perfectly new overcoat and now he had been robbed of it in the most inhuman way, and that now he had come to beg him by his intervention either to correspond with his honor, the head police commissioner, or anybody else, and find the overcoat. This mode of proceeding struck the general for some reason as too familiar. "What next, sir?" he went on abruptly. "Don't you know the way to proceed? To whom are you addressing yourself? Don't you know how things are done? You ought first to have handed in a petition to the office; it would have gone to the head clerk of the room, and to the head clerk of the section; then it would have been handed to the secretary and the secretary would have brought it to me . . ."

"But, your Excellency," said Akaky Akakievich, trying to gather the drop of courage he possessed and feeling at the same time that he was perspiring all over, "I ventured, your Excellency, to trouble you because secretaries . . . er . . . are people you can't depend on . . ."

"What? what? what?" said the Person of Consequence, "where did you get hold of that attitude? where did you pick up such ideas? What insubordination is spreading among young men against their superiors and their chiefs!" The Person of Consequence did not apparently observe that Akaky Akakievich was well over fifty, and therefore if he could have been called a young man it would only have been in comparison with a man of seventy. "Do you know to whom you are speaking? Do you understand who I am? Do you understand that, I ask you?" At this point he stamped, and raised his voice to such a powerful note that Akaky Akakievich was not the only one to be terrified. Akaky Akakievich was positively petrified; he staggered, trembling all over, and could not stand; if the porters had not run up to support him, he would have flopped on the floor; he was led out almost unconscious. The Person of Consequence, pleased that the effect had surpassed his expectations and enchanted at the idea that his words could even deprive a man of consciousness, stole a sideway glance

at his friend to see how he was taking it, and perceived not without satisfaction that his friend was feeling very uncertain and even
beginning to be a little terrified himself.

How he got downstairs, how he went out into the street—of
all that Akaky Akakievich remembered nothing; he had no feeling in his arms or his legs. In all his life he had never been so severely reprimanded by a general, and this was by one of another
department, too. He went out into the snowstorm that was whistling through the streets, with his mouth open, and as he went he
stumbled off the pavement; the wind, as its way is in Petersburg,
blew upon him from all points of the compass and from every side
street. In an instant it had blown a quinsy into his throat, and when
he got home he was not able to utter a word; he went to bed
with a swollen face and throat. That's how violent the effects of
an appropriate reprimand can be!

Next day he was in a high fever. Thanks to the gracious assistance of the Petersburg climate, the disease made more rapid
progress than could have been expected, and when the doctor
came, after feeling his pulse he could find nothing to do but pre-
scribe a poultice, and that simply so that the patient might not be
left without the benefit of medical assistance; however, two days
later he informed him that his end was at hand, after which he
turned to Akaky Akakievich's landlady and said: "And you had
better lose no time, my good woman, but order him now a pine
coffin, for an oak one will be too expensive for him." Whether
Akaky Akakievich heard these fateful words or not, whether they
produced a shattering effect upon him, and whether he regretted
his pitiful life, no one can tell, for he was constantly in delirium
and fever. Apparitions, each stranger than the one before, were
continually haunting him: first he saw Petrovich and was ordering
him to make an overcoat trimmed with some sort of traps for
robbers, who were, he believed, continually under the bed, and he
was calling his landlady every minute to pull out a thief who had
even got under the quilt; then he kept asking why his old "dressing
gown" was hanging before him when he had a new overcoat; then
he thought he was standing before the general listening to the
appropriate reprimand and saying, "I am sorry, your Excellency";
then finally he became abusive, uttering the most awful language,
so that his old landlady positively crossed herself, having never

heard anything of the kind from him before, and the more horrified because these dreadful words followed immediately upon the phrase "your Excellency." Later on, his talk was merely a medley of nonsense, so that it was quite unintelligible; all that was evident was that his incoherent words and thoughts were concerned with nothing but the overcoat. At last poor Akaky Akakievich gave up the ghost. No seal was put upon his room nor upon his things, because, in the first place, he had no heirs and, in the second, the property left was very small, to wit, a bundle of quills, a quire of white government paper, three pairs of socks, two or three buttons that had come off his trousers, and the "dressing gown" with which the reader is already familiar. Who came into all this wealth God only knows; even I who tell the tale must admit that I have not bothered to inquire. And Petersburg carried on without Akaky Akakievich, as though, indeed, he had never been in the city. A creature had vanished and departed whose cause no one had championed, who was dear to no one, of interest to no one, who never attracted the attention of a naturalist, though the latter does not disdain to fix a common fly upon a pin and look at him under the microscope—a creature who bore patiently the jeers of the office and for no particular reason went to his grave, though even he at the very end of his life was visited by an exalted guest in the form of an overcoat that for one instant brought color into his poor, drab life—a creature on whom disease fell as it falls upon the heads of the mighty ones of this world . . . !

Several days after his death, a messenger from the department was sent to his lodgings with instructions that he should go at once to the office, for his chief was asking for him; but the messenger was obliged to return without him, explaining that he could not come, and to the inquiry "Why?" he added, "Well, you see, the fact is he is dead; he was buried three days ago." This was how they learned at the office of the death of Akaky Akakievich, and the next day there was sitting in his seat a new clerk who was very much taller and who wrote not in the same straight handwriting but made his letters more slanting and crooked.

But who could have imagined that this was not all there was to tell about Akaky Akakievich, that he was destined for a few days to make his presence felt in the world after his death, as though to make up for his life having been unnoticed by anyone? But so it happened, and our little story unexpectedly finishes with a fantastic ending.

Rumors were suddenly floating about Petersburg that in the neighborhood of the Kalinkin Bridge and for a little distance beyond, a corpse[7] had begun appearing at night in the form of a clerk looking for a stolen overcoat, and stripping from the shoulders of all passers-by, regardless of grade and calling, overcoats of all descriptions—trimmed with cat fur or beaver or padded, lined with raccoon, fox, and bear—made, in fact of all sorts of skin which men have adapted for the covering of their own. One of the clerks of the department saw the corpse with his own eyes and at once recognized it as Akaky Akakievich; but it excited in him such terror that he ran away as fast as his legs could carry him and so could not get a very clear view of him, and only saw him hold up his finger threateningly in the distance.

From all sides complaints were continually coming that backs and shoulders, not of mere titular councilors, but even of upper court councilors, had been exposed to catching cold, as a result of being stripped of their overcoats. Orders were given to the police to catch the corpse regardless of trouble or expense, dead or alive, and to punish him severely, as an example to others, and, indeed, they very nearly succeeded in doing so. The policeman of one district in Kiryushkin Alley snatched a corpse by the collar on the spot of the crime in the very act of attempting to snatch a frieze overcoat from a retired musician, who used, in his day, to play the flute. Having caught him by the collar, he shouted until he had brought two other policemen whom he ordered to hold the corpse while he felt just a minute in his boot to get out a snuff-box in order to revive his nose which had six times in his life been frostbitten, but the snuff was probably so strong that not even a dead man could stand it. The policeman had hardly had time to put his finger over his right nostril and draw up some snuff in the left when the corpse sneezed violently right into the eyes of all three. While they were putting their fists up to wipe their eyes,

[7] Mrs. Garnett excepted, this is often translated "ghost," but there is no doubt of Gogol's intention. He uses the word *mertverts* (corpse) and not *prividenye* (ghost). To confuse the two is damaging to Gogol's delight in the fantastic, and seriously alters the tone of the story. (ed.)

the corpse completely vanished, so that they were not even sure whether he had actually been in their hands. From that time forward, the policemen had such a horror of the dead that they were even afraid to seize the living and confined themselves to shouting from the distance: "Hey, you! Move on!" and the clerk's body began to appear even on the other side of the Kalinkin Bridge, terrorizing all timid people.

We have, however, quite neglected the Person of Consequence, who may in reality almost be said to be the cause of the fantastic ending of this perfectly true story. To begin with, my duty requires me to do justice to the Person of Consequence by recording that soon after poor Akaky Akakievich had gone away crushed to powder, he felt something not unlike regret. Sympathy was a feeling not unknown to him; his heart was open to many kindly impulses, although his exalted grade very often prevented them from being shown. As soon as his friend had gone out of his study, he even began brooding over poor Akaky Akakievich, and from that time forward, he was almost every day haunted by the image of the poor clerk who had been unable to survive the official reprimand. The thought of the man so worried him that a week later he actually decided to send a clerk to find out how he was and whether he really could help him in any way. And when they brought him word that Akaky Akakievich had died suddenly in delirium and fever, it made a great impression on him; his conscience reproached him and he was depressed all day. Anxious to distract his mind and to forget the unpleasant incident, he went to spend the evening with one of his friends, where he found respectable company, and what was best of all, almost everyone was of the same grade so that he was able to be quite uninhibited. This had a wonderful effect on his spirits. He let himself go, became affable and genial—in short, spent a very agreeable evening. At supper he drank a couple of glasses of champagne—a proceeding which we all know is not a bad recipe for cheerfulness. The champagne made him inclined to do something unusual, and he decided not to go home yet but to visit a lady of his acquaintance, a certain Karolina Ivanovna—a lady apparently of German extraction, for whom he entertained extremely friendly feelings. It must be noted that the Person of Consequence was a man no longer young. He was an excellent husband, and the respectable father of a family.

He had two sons, one already serving in an office, and a nice-looking
daughter of sixteen with a rather turned-up, pretty little nose, who
used to come every morning to kiss his hand, saying: *"Bon jour,
Papa."* His wife, who was still blooming and decidedly good-
looking, indeed, used first to give him her hand to kiss and then
turning his hand over would kiss it. But though the Person of Consequence was perfectly satisfied with the pleasant amenities of his
domestic life, he thought it proper to have a lady friend in another
quarter of the town. This lady friend was not a bit better looking
nor younger than his wife, but these puzzling things exist in the
world and it is not our business to criticize them. And so the Person
of Consequence went downstairs, got into his sledge, and said to
his coachman, "To Karolina Ivanovna." While luxuriously wrapped
in his warm fur coat he remained in that agreeable frame of
mind sweeter to a Russian than anything that could be invented,
that is, when one thinks of nothing while thoughts come into the
mind by themselves, one pleasanter than the other, without your
having to bother following them or looking for them. Full of satisfaction, he recalled all the amusing moments of the evening he
had spent, all the phrases that had started the intimate circle of
friends laughing; many of them he repeated in an undertone and
found them as amusing as before, and so, very naturally, laughed
very heartily at them again. From time to time, however, he was
disturbed by a gust of wind which, blowing suddenly, God knows
why or where from, cut him in the face, pelting him with flakes
of snow, puffing out his coat collar like a sail, or suddenly flinging it with unnatural force over his head and giving him endless
trouble to extricate himself from it. All at once, the Person of Consequence felt that someone had clutched him very tightly by the
collar. Turning around he saw a short man in a shabby old uniform, and not without horror recognized him as Akaky Akakievich. The clerk's face was white as snow and looked like that of a
corpse, but the horror of the Person of Consequence was beyond
all bounds when he saw the mouth of the corpse distorted into
speech, and breathing upon him the chill of the grave, it uttered
the following words: "Ah, so here you are at last! At last I've
. . . er . . . caught you by the collar. It's your overcoat I want;
you refused to help me and abused me into the bargain! So now
give me yours!" The poor Person of Consequence very nearly

dropped dead. Resolute and determined as he was in his office and before subordinates in general, and though anyone looking at his manly air and figure would have said: "Oh, what a man of character!" yet in this situation he felt, like very many persons of heroic appearance, such terror that not without reason he began to be afraid he would have some sort of fit. He actually flung his overcoat off his shoulders as far as he could and shouted to his coachman in an unnatural voice: "Drive home! Let's get out of here!" The coachman, hearing the tone which he had only heard in critical moments and then accompanied by something even more tangible, hunched his shoulders up to his ears in case of worse following, swung his whip, and flew on like an arrow. In a little over six minutes, the Person of Consequence was at the entrance of his own house. Pale, panic-stricken, and without his overcoat, he arrived home instead of at Karolina Ivanovna's, dragged himself to his own room, and spent the night in great distress, so that next morning his daughter said to him at breakfast, "You look very pale today, Papa"; but her papa remained mute and said not a word to anyone of what had happened to him, where he had been, and where he had been going. The incident made a great impression upon him. Indeed, it happened far more rarely that he said to his subordinates, "How dare you? Do you understand who I am?" and he never uttered those words at all until he had first heard all the facts of the case.

What was even more remarkable is that from that time on the apparition of the dead clerk ceased entirely; apparently the general's overcoat had fitted him perfectly; anyway nothing more was heard of overcoats being snatched from anyone. Many restless and anxious people refused, however, to be pacified, and still maintained that in remote parts of the town the dead clerk went on appearing. One policeman, in Kolomna, for instance, saw with his own eyes an apparition appear from behind a house; but, being by natural constitution somewhat frail—so much so that on one occasion an ordinary grown-up suckling pig, making a sudden dash out of some private building, knocked him off his feet to the great amusement of the cabmen standing around, whom he fined two kopeks each for snuff for such disrespect—he did not dare to stop it, and so followed it in the dark until the apparition suddenly looked around and, stopping, asked him: "What do you want?" displaying a huge fist such as you never see among the living. The policeman said: "Nothing," and turned back on the spot. This apparition, however, was considerably taller and adorned with immense mustaches, and, directing its steps apparently toward Obukhov Bridge, vanished into the darkness of the night.

CHRONOLOGICAL LIST
OF GOGOL'S WORKS

1824-28 Done while Gogol was at school in Nyezhin, some of these pieces appeared in the school magazine to which he was an avid contributor: "The Brothers Tverdoslavich" (a story on an historical theme—the first piece burned by Gogol); "Something about Nyezhin, or a Fool Is His Own Law" (a satire); "Two Little Fishes" (a ballad); "The Robbers" (a tragedy in verse); "Russia under the Yoke of the Tartar" (a poem in the epic style).

1829 *Hans Küchelgarten* (published anonymously, at Gogol's expense, as *Hanz [sic] Küchelgarten*); his only published poem. He burned all the copies he could get his hands on after its disastrous reception.

1830 *Woman* (an essay important for understanding Gogol's highly romanticized "alabaster-breasted" women); *St. John's Eve* (printed anonymously in *Annals of the Fatherland*).

1831 *Hetman* (a chapter from an historical novel, never completed, which Gogol signed OOOO); *The Teacher* and *The Successful Mission* (both stories from the never-completed *The Terrible Boar*). *Hetman* appeared in *Northern Flowers*, an almanac, the other two in *The Literary Journal*.

Evenings on a Farm near Dikanka (*Vechera na Khutore Bliz Dikanki*), Volume I, which consists of: *The Fair at Sorochintsy, St. John's Eve, A May Night, or The Drowned Maiden, The Lost Letter*.

1832 *Evenings on a Farm near Dikanka*, Volume II, which consists of *Christmas Eve, A Terrible Vengeance, Ivan Fiodorovich Shponka and His Aunt, A Bewitched Place*.

Completed a play, *The Order of Vladimir of the Third Class*, of which only four scenes survive; the first, "An Official's

Morning," was published in Pushkin's magazine, *The Contemporary*, in 1836. The other three scenes, published in the 1842 edition of Gogol's collected works, are "A Lawsuit," "The Servant's Hall," "A Fragment." Completed *The Suitor* (to become *The Marriage* in 1842).

1834   *On Ukrainian Folksongs* (first published by the Ministry of Public Education, in April. Republished in the second part of *Arabesques*).

1835   *Arabesques*, a collection of essays and stories in two parts. The first part consists of *The Portrait; A Chapter from an Historical Novel* (both fiction); *Sculpture; Painting and Music; About the Middle Ages; On the Teaching of World History; A Peek at the Composition of the Ukraine; A Few Words on Pushkin; On Modern Architecture; Al Mamun* (an historical portrait). The second part consists of *Nevsky Prospekt, The Prisoner* (a fragment), *Diary of a Madman* (all three fiction); *Life; Schlözer, Müller, and Herder; On Ukrainian Folksongs; Thoughts on Geography* (for children); *The Last Days of Pompeii* (a painting by Briulov); *On the Migrations of Peoples at the End of the Fifth Century*.

King Alfred (fragment of an historical play).

Mirgorod, which consists of two parts, the first containing *Old-World Landowners* and *Taras Bulba* (which is seriously revised for the 1842 edition of his works), and the second containing *Viy* and *The Tale of How Ivan Ivanovich Quarreled with Ivan Nikiforovich*.

1836   *The Nose; The Coach* (both published in *The Contemporary*); *The Inspector General* (performed for the first time on the first of May); *Development of our Journalistic Literature in 1834, 1835*.

1837   *Petersburg Notes for 1836* (published in *The Contemporary*).

1842   *The Portrait* (totally revised, published in *The Contemporary*).

Dead Souls (the first part only, on the second of June).

Late in the year, the first collection of Gogol's works appeared in four volumes, and included *Evenings on a Farm near Dikanka; Mirgorod* (with the revised version of *Taras Bulba*); *The Portrait* (the revised version); *Nevsky Prospekt; Diary of a Madman; Rome* (a long fragment containing interesting impressions); *The Nose; The Coach; The Overcoat; The Marriage; The Gamblers; The Inspector General* (partially revised); *A Lawsuit, The Servant's Hall, A Fragment* (the three dramatic fragments begun in 1832, in revised form); *Home-going from the Theater.*

1846   *The Dénouement of The Inspector General.*

1847   *Addition to The Dénouement of The Inspector General.*

     Selected Passages from Correspondence with Friends.

——   The second part of *Dead Souls* (he burned almost all of it), *An Author's Confession* (invaluable psychological material), *Meditations on the Divine Liturgy* (the voice from above), and several less important pieces which were published posthumously.

SELECTED BIBLIOGRAPHY

Works frequently cited have been identified by the following abbreviations:

ASEER: American Slavic and East European Review
PMLA: Publications of the Modern Language Association of America
SEEJ: Slavic and East European Journal
SEER: Slavic and East European Review
ZsP: Zeitschrift für slavische Philologie

IN ENGLISH

Annenkov, Pavel Vasilevich. *The Extraordinary Decade*. Ed. Arthur P. Mendel; trans. Irwin R. Titunik. Ann Arbor, 1968. [First published as *Literaturnye vospominanija (Literary Reminiscences)*, ed. Boris Eichenbaum, Leningrad, 1928.]

Annenskii, Innokentii. "The Esthetics of Gogol's *Dead Souls* and its Legacy." Trans. Victor Erlich. In Victor Erlich, ed., *Twentieth-Century Russian Criticism*. New Haven, 1975, 51–60.

Baring, Maurice. *An Outline of Russian Literature*. New York, 1914.

———. *Landmarks in Russian Literature*. London, 1910.

Belinsky, Vissarion. "Letter to N. V. Gogol." In Ralph E. Matlaw, ed., *Belinsky, Chernyshevsky, and Dobrolyubuv*. New York, 1962.

Bely, Andrey. "Gogol." Trans. Elizabeth Trahan and John Fred Beebe. In Victor Erlich, ed., *Twentieth-Century Russian Criticism*. New Haven, 1975, 33–50.

Bernheimer, Charles C. "Cloaking the Self: The Literary Space of Gogol's 'Overcoat.'" *PMLA* 90, no. 1 (1975): 53–61.

Besoushko, Volodymyr. "Nicholas Gogol and Ukrainian Literature." *Ukrainian Quarterly* 16, no. 3 (1960): 263–68.

Birkhead, A. "Russian Pickwick." *Living Age* 287 (1915): 312–15.

Bogojavlensky, M. "On the Development and Concept of Gogol's

Religious Thought." Ph.D. diss., University of Pennsylvania, 1959.

Bowen, C. M. "*Dead Souls* and *Pickwick Papers*." *Living Age* 280 (1916): 369–73.

Bowman, N. E. " 'The Nose.' " *SEER* 31, no. 76 (1952): 204–11.

Brasol, Boris L. *The Mighty Three: Poushkin, Gogol, Dostoevski.* New York, 1934.

Brodiansky, Nina. "Gogol and his Characters." *SEER* 31, no. 76 (December 1952): 36–57.

Brückner, A. *A Literary History of Russia.* London, 1908. [A translation of his *Geschichte der russischen Literatur.* Leipzig, 1905.]

Bryner, Cyril. "Gogol, Dickens and the Realistic Novel." *Etudes slaves et est-européennes* 8 (1963): 17–42.

———. "Gogol's *The Overcoat* in World Literature." *SEER* 32, no. 79 (1954): 499–509.

Campbell, D. J., trans. *Government Inspector.* London, 1981.

Charquee, R. D. "Nikolay Gogol." *Fortnightly Review* (New York) 130 (1931): 230–42.

Čiževskij, Dmitry. "Gogol: Artist and Thinker." *Annals of the Ukrainian Academy of Arts and Sciences in the U.S.* 4 (1952): 261–78.

———. *History of Nineteenth-Century Russian Literature.* Trans. Richard Noel Porter; ed. Serge A. Zenkovsky. Nashville, 1974.

Čiževskij, Dmitry, and Hofre, P. "An Illustrated Manuscript of Gogol." *Harvard Library Bulletin* 6 (1952): 397–400.

———. "The Unknown Gogol." *SEER* 30 (1952): 476–93.

"The Cloak," *Lippincott's Monthly Magazine.* 92 (1913): 249–62.

Coleman, Arthur P. *Humour in the Russian Comedy from Catherine to Gogol.* New York, 1925.

Cook, A. S. "Reflexive Attitudes: Sterne, Gogol, Gide." *Criticism* 2 (1960): 164–74.

Costello, Bella, trans. *Marriage.* New York, 1969.

Debreczeny, Paul. *Nikolai Gogol and His Contemporary Critics.* Transactions of the American Philosophical Society, 56, pt. 3. Philadelphia, 1966.

Dupuy, Ernest. *The Great Masters of Russian Literature.* New York, 1886. [A translation of his *Les grands maîtres de la littérature russe au XIX^c siècle.* Paris, 1885.]

Driessen, F. *Gogol as a Short Story Writer: A Study of his Technique of Composition.* The Hague, 1965.

Ehre, Milton, ed. *The Theater of Nikolay Gogol.* Trans. Milton Ehre and

Fruma Gottschalk, with an introduction by Milton Ehre. Chicago, 1980.

Eichenbaum, Boris. "The Structure of Gogol's *The Overcoat*." *Russian Review*, 22 (1918): 377–99.

Erlich, Victor. *Gogol.* New Haven, 1969.

———. "Gogol and Kafka: a Note on 'Realism' and 'Surrealism.' " *For Roman Jakobson.* The Hague, 1956, 100–108.

———. *Russian Formalism.* New York, 1955.

Fanger, Donald. *The Creation of Nikolai Gogol.* Cambridge, Mass., 1979.

———. "Dickens and Gogol: Energies of the Word." In Harry Levin, ed., *Veins of Humor*, Cambridge, Mass., 1972.

———. *Dostoevsky and Romantic Realism: A Study of Dostoevsky in Relation to Balzac, Dickens, and Gogol.* Cambridge, Mass., 1965.

———. "The Gogol Problem: Perspectives from Absence." In Michael S. Flier, ed., *Slavic Forum: Essays in Linguistics and Literature.* The Hague, 1974.

Finch, Chauncey. "Classical Influence on N. V. Gogol." *The Classical Journal* 48, No. 8 (May 1953): 291–96.

Friedman, Peter. "The Nose." *The American Imago* No. 8 (December 1951): 337–50.

Futrell, M. "Dickens and Three Russian Novelists: Gogol, Dostoevsky, Tolstoy." School of Slavonic and East European Studies, London, 1954.

———. "Gogol and Dickens." *SEER* 34 (1956): 443–59.

Garnett, Constance, trans. *Dead Souls.* New York, 1923.

———. *Evenings on a Farm Near Dikanka.* New York, 1926.

———. *The Government Inspector and Other Plays.* New York, 1926.

———. *Mirgorod.* New York, 1929.

———. *The Overcoat and Other Stories.* New York, 1923.

Gerrard, John G. "Some Thoughts on Gogol's '*Kolyaska*' [*The Coach*]." *PMLA* 90 (October 1975): 848–60.

Gorchakov, Ovid, trans. *Evenings Near the Village of Dikanka.* New York, 1960.

Guerney, Bernard G., trans. *Dead Souls.* New York, 1965.

———. "Great Grotesque." *New Republic* (September 25, 1944): 376–78.

———. "Introduction." *The Portable Russian Reader.* New York, 1947.

Gustafson, R. F. "The Suffering Usurper: Gogol's *Diary of a Madman.*" *SEEJ* 9, no. 3 (1965): 268–81.

Hare, Richard. *Russian Literature.* London, 1947.

Harkins, William E. "Gogol." In *Dictionary of Russian Literature*. New York, 1956.

Hasenclever, Nora. "Gogol and Dostoyevsky." Ph.D. diss., Bennington College, 1951.

Hippisley, Anthony. "Gogol's 'The Overcoat': A Further Interpretation." *SEEJ* 20 (Summer 1976): 121–129.

Hogarth, C. J., trans. *Dead Souls*. With an introduction by John Cournas. London, 1948

———, trans. *"Taras Bulba" and other Tales*. London 1962. [Contains B. G. Guerney's translation of *The Inspector General*.]

Holquist, James M. "The Devil in Mufti: The *Märchenwelt* in Gogol's Short Stories." *PMLA* 82, no. 5 (October 1967): 352–62.

Hughes, Olga Raevsky. "The Apparent and the Real in Gogol's 'Nevskij Prospekt.' *California Slavic Studies* 8, no. 8 (1975): 77–91.

Juran, Sylvia. "*Zapiski sumassedsego* [*Diary of a Madman*]: Some Insights into Gogol's World." *SEEJ* 5 (1961): 331–33.

Kanevsky, A., and E. Krivanskaya, trans. *Mirgorod*. Moscow, 1960.

Kanzer, M. "Gogol: A Study in Wit and Paranoia." *Journal of the American Psychoanalytic Association* 3, no. 1 (January 1955): 110–25.

Karlinsky, Simon. "Portrait of Gogol as a Word Glutton, with Rabelais, Sterne, and Gertrude Stein as Background Figures." *California Slavic Studies* 5 (1970): 169–86.

———. *The Sexual Labyrinth of Nikolai Gogol*. Cambridge, Mass., 1976.

Kaun, A. "Poe and Gogol: A Comparison." *SEER* 15, no. 44 (1937): 389–99.

Kent, Leonard J., ed. *The Collected Tales and Plays of Nikolai Gogol*. Edited, with an introduction and notes by Leonard J. Kent. New York, 1964, New York, 1969. [The Constance Garnett translation is revised throughout by the editor.]

———. *The Subconscious in Gogol' and Dostoevskij, and its Antecedents*. The Hague, 1969.

Kropotkin, P. *Russian Literature*. London, 1945.

Landolfi, Tommaso. *"Gogol's Wife" and Other Stories*. Trans. Wayland Young. New York, 1963.

Landry, Hilton, "Gogol's *The Overcoat*." *Explicator* 19, no. 8 (1961): 54.

Lavrin, Janko. *Gogol*. New York, 1926.

———. Introduction to *Studies from St. Petersburg*. London, 1945.

———. Introduction to *Tales from Gogol*. London, 1945.

———. *Introduction to the Russian Novel*. London, 1942.

———. *Nikolai Gogol (1809–1852). A Centenary Survey*. London, 1951.

Lefevre, Carl. "Gogol and Anglo-Russian Literary Relations during the Crimean War." *ASEER* (April 1949): 106–25.

———. "Gogol's First Century in England and America (1841–1941)." Ph.D. diss., University of Minnesota. 1944.

Lindstrom, Thais. *Nikolay Gogol.* New York, 1974.

Littell, R. "Gogol." *The New Republic* 48 (1926): 218–219.

MacAndrew, Andrew, trans. *Dead Souls.* New York, 1961.

———, trans. *"The Diary of a Madman" and Other Stories.* New York, 1960.

Magarshack, David, trans. *Dead Souls.* With an introduction. London, 1978.

———. *Gogol.* New York, 1957.

———, trans. *Tales of Good and Evil.* With an introduction. New York, 1957.

Maguire, Robert A., ed. and trans. *Gogol from the Twentieth Century: Eleven Essays.* Princeton, 1974. [Includes his introduction, "The Legacy of Criticism."]

Malkiel, Yakov. "Cervantes in Nineteenth-Century Russia." *Comparative Literature* 3, no. 4 (1951): 310–29.

Manning, Clarence. "Gogol and Ukraine." *Ukrainian Quarterly* 7: 323–30.

———. "Nicolas Gogol." *SEER* 4 (1926): 573–87.

Markov, Vladimir. "The Poetry of Russian Prose Writers." *California Slavic Studies* 1 (1960): 77–82.

Martin, Mildred A. "The Last Shall Be First: A Study of Three Russian Short Stories." *Bucknell Review* 6, no. 1 (1956): 13–23.

Masson, E. "Russia's Gogol: A Centenary." *Pacific Spectator* 7, no. 3 (1953): 322–31.

Maurois, André. "Nicolas Gogol." In *The Art of Writing.* New York, 1960, 265–95.

McLean, Hugh. "Gogol's Retreat from Love: Towards an Interpretation of *Mirgorod*," *American Contributions to the Fourth International Congress of Slavicists.* The Hague, 1958, 225–45.

———. "Gogol and the Whirling Telescope." In L. H. Legters, ed., *Russia: Essays in History and Literature.* Leyden, 1972, 79–99.

Meyer, Priscilla and Stephen Rudy, ed. and trans. *Dostoevsky and Gogol.* Ann Arbor, 1979.

Michailoff, Helen, trans. *Dead Souls.* With an introduction. New York, 1964.

Miliukov, Paul. *Literature in Russia.* New York, 1943.

Mirsky, D. S. *A History of Russian Literature*, ed. F. J. Whitfield. New York, 1959. [This volume contains almost all of the next entry.]

———. *The History of Russian Literature from Earliest Times to the Death of Dostoevsky*. London, 1927.

Muchnic, Helen. *An Introduction to Russian Literature*. New York, 1947.

———. "A Long Nose Argued with its Owner." *The New York Times Book Review* (December 23, 1973).

———. *The Unhappy Consciousness: Gogol, Poe, Baudelaire*. Smith College, 1967. [A 22-page lecture]

Nabokov, Vladimir. *Gogol*. Norfolk, Connecticut, 1944.

Noyes, G. R. "Gogol, a precursor of Modern Realists in Russia." *The Nation* 101 (1915): 592–94.

Obolensky, Alexander P. *Food-Notes on Gogol*. Winnipeg, 1972.

Passage, Charles. *The Russian Hoffmannists*. The Hague, 1963.

Peace, Richard Arthur. *The Enigma of Gogol: An Examination of the Writings of N. V. Gogol and their Place in the Russian Literary Tradition*. Cambridge, 1981.

Pedrotti, Louis, "The Architecture of Love in Gogol's 'Rome.' " *California Slavic Studies* 6 (1971): 17–27.

Perry, Idris. "Kafka, Gogol and Nathanael West." In Ronald Gray, ed., *Kafka*. Englewood Cliffs, New Jersey, 1962.

Phelps, William L. *Essays on Russian Novelists*. New York, 1911.

Poggioli, Renato. "Gogol's 'Old-fashioned Landowners': An Inverted Eclogue." *Indiana Slavic Studies* 3 (1963): 54–72.

———. "Realism in Russia." *Comparative Literature* 3, no. 3 (1951): 253–67.

Proffer, Carl R. "*Dead Souls* in Translation." *SEEJ* 8, no. 4 (1964): 420–33.

———. "Gogol's Definition of Romanticism." *Studies in Romanticism* 6, no. 2 (1967): 120–127.

———, ed. and trans, in collaboration with Vera Krivoshein. *Letters of Nikolai Gogol*. Ann Arbor, 1967.

———. "Gogol's *Taras Bulba* and the *Iliad*." *Comparative Literature* 17, no. 2 (1965): 142–50.

———. *The Simile and Gogol's "Dead Souls"*. The Hague, 1967.

Rabkin, Leslie. *Psychopathology and Literature*. Rochester, 1966.

Rahv, Philip. "Gogol as a Modern Instance." In Donald Davie, ed., *Russian Literature and Modern English Fiction*. Chicago, 1965.

Reavey, George, trans. *Dead Souls*. With an introduction by George Gibian. New York, 1971.

Reeve, F. D. "Dead Souls." *The Russian Novel*. New York, 1966.

Rowe, William Woodin. *Through Gogol's Looking Glass: Reverse Vision, False Focus and Precarious Logic*. New York, 1976.

Schillinger, John. "Gogol's 'The Overcoat' as a Travesty of Hagiography." *SEEJ* 16 (Spring 1972): 36–41.

Selig, Karl. "Concerning Gogol's *Dead Souls* and *Lazarillo de Tormes*." *Symposium* 8 (1954): 34–40.

Setchkarev, Vsevolod. *Gogol—His Life and Works*. Trans. Robert Kramer. New York, 1965. [A translation of *N. V. Gogol. Leben und Schafen*. Berlin, 1953.]

Shepard, Elizabeth C. "Pavlov's 'Demon' and Gogol's 'Overcoat.' " *Slavic Review* 33, no. 2 (June 1974): 288–301.

Simmons, E. J. "Gogol and English Literature." *Modern Language Review* 26 (1931): 445–50.

Slonim, Mark. *An Outline of Russian Literature*. New York, 1958.

———. *The Epic of Russian Literature: From its Origins through Tolstoy*. New York, 1950.

Spilka, Mark. "Kafka's Sources for *The Metamorphosis*." *Comparative Literature* 11, no. 4 (1959): 289–308.

Spycher, Peter. "N. V. Gogol's 'The Nose': A Satirical Comic Fantasy Born of an Impotence Complex." *SEEJ* 7, no. 4 (1963): 361–75.

Stilman, Leon. "Gogol's 'Overcoat,' Thematic Pattern and Origins." *ASEER* 11, no. 1 (February 1952): 138–48.

———. "Nikolai Gogol: Historical and Biographical Elements of his Creative Personality." Ph.D. diss., Columbia University, 1953.

Strakhovsky, L. I. "Historianism of Gogol." *ASEER* 12, no. 3 (1953): 360–70.

Strong, Robert L. "The Soviet Interpretation of Gogol." *ASEER* 14:528–39.

Tertz, Abram [Andrei Sinyavsky]. *In the Shadow of Gogol*. London, 1975.

Tilley, A. "Gogol, the Father of Russian Realism." *Living Age* 202 (1894): 489–97.

Todd, William Mills. "Gogol's Epistolary Writing." *Columbia Essays in International Affairs*. New York, 1970, 51–76.

Trahan, Elizabeth W., ed. *Gogol's "Overcoat": An Anthology of Critical Essays*. Ann Arbor, 1982.

Troyart, Henri. *Divided Soul: The Life of Gogol*. Trans. Nancy Amphoux. New York, 1972.

Tsanoff, Radoslav. "The Russian Soil and Nikolai Gogol." *Rice Institute Pamphlet*, 4, no. 2 (Houston, 1917): 119–26.

Turner, Charles E. *Studies in Russian Literature*. London, 1882.

Vlach, Robert. "Gogol and Hasck: Two Masters of 'Poshlost'." *Etudes slaves et est-européennes* 7:239–42.

Vogel, Lucy. "Gogol's *Rome*." *SEEJ* 2, no. 2 (1967): 145–158.

deVogüé, E. M. *The Russian Novelists*. New York, 1900. [A translation of *Le roman russe*. Paris, 1886.]

Waliszewski, K. *A History of Russian Literature*. New York, 1900.

Weathers, Winston. "Gogol's *Dead Souls*: The Degrees of Reality." *College English* 17 (1956): 159–64.

Wellek, René. Introduction to *Dead Souls*. Trans. B. G. Guerney. New York, 1948.

Wilks, Ronald, trans. *"The Diary of a Madman" and Other Stories*. London, 1972.

Wilson, Edmund. "Gogol: the demon in the overgrown garden." *The Nation* 175 (1952): 520–24.

———. "Nikolai Gogol." *The New Yorker*, 20 (1944): 72–73.

Wittlin, Jozef. "Gogol's Inferno." *Polish Review* 7(4):5–20.

Yurieff, Zoya. "Gogol and the Russian Symbolists." Ph.D. diss., Harvard University, 1954.

Zeldin, Jesse. *Nikolai Gogol's Quest for Beauty*. Lawrence, Kan., 1978.

———, trans. *Selected Passages from Correspondence with Friends*. Nashville, 1969.

IN GERMAN

Adams, V. "Gogols Erstlingswerk 'Hans Küchelgarten' im Lichte seines Natur- und Welterlebens." *ZsP* (1931): 323–68.

Anderson, W. "Gogols *Porträt* als Posener Volkssage." *ZsP* 20 (1950): 234–36.

Annenkow, P. "Meine Erlebnisse mit Gogol." *Corona* (June 1933): 584–610.

Berdjajew, Nikolai. "Gogol in der russischen Revolution." *Wort und Wahrheit* 15 (1960): 611–16.

Blagoi, D., W. I. Strashew, K. Gudzi. *Drei russische Dichter: Leben und Werk von Puschkin, Gogol und L. Tolstoi*. Trans. J. Kiescritzky. Weimar, 1952.

Braun, M. "Gogol als Satiriker." *Die Welt der Slaven* 4 (1959): 129–147.

Braun, M. *N. W. Gogol; eine literarische Biographie*. Munich, 1973.

Čiževskij, D. "Nachwort." *Die Toten Seelen*. Munich, 1949.

———. "Zur komposition von Gogols 'Mantel'." *ZsP* 14 (1937): 63–94.

Dauenhauer, A. "Gogols 'Schreckliche Rache' und 'Pietro von Abano' von L. Tieck." *ZsP* 13 (1936): 315–18.

Emmer, H. "Neuere Gogol-Literatur." *Wiener slawistisches Jahrbuch* 3 (1953): 79–114.

Emmer, Karl. "Vergleichende Studien zu Gogols *Porträt*." Vienna, 1948. (Dissertation)

Fischer, Ernst. "Nikolai Gogol—Roman des Burgerkriegs." *Dichtung und Deutung; Beitrage zur Literaturbetrachtung*. Vienna, 1953.

———. "Nikolaj Gogol—Festrede zu seinem 100. Todestag gehalten am 11, März, 1952." Vienna, 1952.

Gerhardt, Dietrich. *Gogol' und Dostoewskij in ihrem kunstlerischen Verhältnis, Versuch einer Zusammenfassenden Darstellung*. Leipzig, 1941.

Gesemann, Gerhardt. "Grundlagen einer Charakterologic Gogols." *Jahrbuch der Charakterologie* 1 (Berlin, 1924): 49–88.

Gorlin, M. *N. V. Gogol und E. Th. A. Hoffmann*. Leipzig, 1935.

Günther, Hans. *Das Groteske bei N. V. Gogol; Formen under Funktionen*. Munich, 1968.

Harder, Johannes. *Der Mensch im russischen Roman. Deutungen: Gogol, Dostojewski, Leskov, Tolstoi*. Wuppertal-Barmen, 1961.

Haertel, Emma. "N. V. Gogol als Maler," *Jahrbuch für Kultur und Geschichte der Slaven* 5 (Breslau, 1929): 145–68.

Hippius, W. "Die Gogol Forschung 1914–24." *ZsP* 2 (1925): 530–39.

Iwanow, Wjatscheslaw. "Gogol und Aristophanes." *Corona* 3 (1933): 611–12.

Jilck, Heinrich. "Das Weltbild N. W. Gogols." *Zeitschrift für deutsche Geisteswissenschaft* 1 (1938): 162–76.

Kasack, Wolfgang. *Die Technik der Personendarstellung bei Nikolaj Vasilevič Gogol*. Wiesbaden, 1957.

Kassner, R. "Stil u. Gesicht: Swift, Gogol, Kafka." *Merkur* 7, no. 8 (1955): 737–52.

Kessel, Martin. "Gogol und die Satire." *Romantische Liebhabereien*. Braunschweig, 1938.

———. "Satiriker der Weltliterature: Gogol." *Neue Rundschau* (August 1937): 128–49.

Klempt, Heinrich. "Nikolay Gogol: *Das Porträt*—Ein beitrag zu Behandlung des Problemkreises 'Kunst und Leben' auf der Oberstufe." *Wirkendes Wort* 15 (1965): 50–57.

Kraus, Otto. *Der Fall Gogol*. Munich, 1912.

348   *Selected Bibliography*

Leiste, H. W. *Gogol und Molière.* Nuremberg, 1958.

Luther, A. *Geschichte der russischen Literatur.* Leipzig, 1924.

Merezhkovskii, D. S. *Gogol und der Teufel.* Trans. Alexander Eliasberg, with an introductory essay by Juri Semjonow. Hamburg, 1963.

Nilsson, Nils Åke. "Zur Entstehungsgeschichte des Gogolschen *Mantels.*" *Scando-Slavica* 2 (1956): 116–33.

Pakosch, Hyacinth. "Der Humor N. V. Gogols." Munich, 1944. (Dissertation)

Pietsch, Eva-Maria. "Gogol in der Publizistik Thomas Mann." In Günther Rienäcker, ed., *Zum 90. Geburtstag Thomas Manns. Spektrum* 11 (1965): 187–91.

Pollok, Karl-Heinz. "Zur dramatischen Form von Gogols 'Spielern.' " *Die Welt der Slaven* 4 (1959): 169–80.

Propper, Maximillian von. "Nikolai Gogols theatralische Sendung." *Dramaturgische Blätter* 2, no. 2 (Berlin, 1948): 67–73.

Pypin, A. "Die Bedeutung Gogols für die heutige internationale Stellung der russischen Literatur." *Archiv für slavische Philologie* 15 (1903): 290–306.

Richter, Sigrid, *Rom und Gogol': Gogol's Romerlebnis und sein Fragment "Rim."* Hamburg, 1964.

Roch, Herbert. *Richter ihrer Zeit: Grimmelshausen, Swift, Gogol.* Berlin, 1956.

Rost, P. "Gogol." In F. K. Mann, *Russland.* Königsberg, 1926.

Schreiber, Hildegund. *Gogol's religiöses Weltbild und sein literavisches Werk.* Munich, 1977.

———. "Zur Interpretation von Gogols *Nase.*" *ZsP* 21 (1952): 118–21.

Stender-Petersen, A. *Geschichte der russischen Literatur.* Munich, 1957.

———. "Gogol und die deutsche Romantik." *Euphorion* 24 (1922).

———. "Gogol und Kotzebue. Zur thematischen Entstehung Gogols 'Revizor.' " *ZsP* 12 (1935): 16–35.

———. "Der groteske Stil Gogols." *Welt und Wort* 15 (1960): 71–73.

———. "Johann Heinrich Voss und der junge Gogol." *Edda* 15 (1921): 98–128.

———. "Der Ursprung des Gogolschen Teufels." Göteborgs Noskolas Arsskrift. Bd. 26 (1920).

Stolze, Helmut. *Die Französische Gogol rezeption.* Cologne, 1974.

Thiess, F. *Gogol und seine Bühnenwerke.* Berlin, 1922.

Triomphe, Robert. "Gogol und die russische Kritik über den *Revisor.*" *Vorträge* (1957): 140–61.

Tschizewskij, D. "Zur Komposition von Gogols 'Mantel.' " *ZsP* 14 (1937).

Winkel, Hans-Jurgen. "Unbekannte Briefe von Gogol', Turgenev, Gor'kij und Sienkiewicz." *ZsP* 31 (1964): 261–64.

Wissemann, Heinz. "Struktur und Ideengehalt von Gogols 'Mantel.' " *Stil- und Formprobleme in der Literatur.* Heidelberg, 1959, 389–96.

———. "Zum Ideengehalt von Gogols 'Mantel'." *ZsP* 26:391–415.

Wytrzens, G. "Vjazemskij und Gogol." *Wiener Slavistisches Jahrbuch.* Graz-Köln, 1955, 83–97.

Zabel, E. *Russische Literaturbilder.* Berlin, 1899.

Zelm, E. "Ein Brief Gogols and V. O. Balabina." *ZsP* 14 (1937): 54–59.

Zenkovskij, V. "Die ästhetische Utopie Gogols." *ZsP* 13 (1936): 1–34.

———. "Gogol als Denker." *ZsP* 9 (1932): 104–30.

IN FRENCH

Cabanes, B. A. "Nicolas Gogol." *Grands Névropathes* 3 (Paris, 1935), 239–77.

Chaplenko, Vasyl'. "Les Ukrainismes dans le langue de M. Hohol." Augsbrug: Ed. de les Soc. des amis de l'Academie ukrainienne libre des sciences, 1948. [Essay in Ukrainian with a French summary.]

Charrière, Ernest. Preface to his translation of *Dead Souls.* Paris, 1859.

Clavel, Bernard. "La Politique dans l'oeuvre de Gogol." *Revue politique et parlementaire* (July-August 1965): 65–76.

Eng, J. van der. "Le personage de Basmackin: Un assemblage d'éléments comiques, grotesques, tragi-comiques et tragiques." *Dutch Contributions to the Fourth International Congress of Slavicists.* The Hague, 1958, 87–103.

Evdokimoff, Paul. *Gogol et Dostoievsky, ou La Descente aux enfers.* Bruges, 1961.

Gorlin, Michel, "Hoffmann en Russie." *Etudes littéraires et historiques.* Paris, 1957, 189–206.

Gourfinkel, Nina. "Gogol et le théâtre." *Revue d'histoire du theatre* 4, no. 3 (Paris, 1952): 189–219.

———. *Nicolas Gogol dramaturge.* Paris, 1956.

Hill, Elizabeth. "Une Lettre de Nicholas Gogol." *Revue des études slaves* 38:105–9.

Hofman, M. *Gogol. Sa vie, son oeuvre.* Paris, 1946.

Juin, Hubert. "De Tarass Boulba à Tchitchikov." *Esprit* 7–8 (1957): 144–55.

Landolfi, Tommaso. "La femme de Gogol." *Nouvelle Nouvelle Revue Française* (1957): 673–88.

Leger, Louis. *Nicolas Gogol.* Paris, 1914.

Lourié, Osip. *La psychologie des romanciers russes du XIXe siècle.* Paris, 1905.

Marthe, Robert. "L'imitation souveraine." *Temps Modernes* 16 (1961): 1124–49.

Merejkovsky, D. S. *Gogol et le diable.* Paris, 1939.

Mérimée, Prosper. "La littérature en Russie." *Revue des Deux Mondes* (November, 1851).

Mongault, H. "Gogol et Mérimée." *Revue de littérature Comparée* (1930).

Nilsson, Nils Åke. *Gogol et St. Petersbourg. Recherches sur les antécédents des contes Petersbourgeois.* Stockholm, 1954.

Radoyce, Lubomir. "La conception du 'Poète national' chez Gogol." *Langue et littérature* (1962): 343–44.

Rudnyčki, Jaroslav. "Gogol et Chevtchenko: deux hommes—deux symboles." *Etudes slaves et est-européennes* (1956): 158–63.

Sainte-Beuve, C. *Premiers lundis.* Vol. 3. Paris, 1875.

Schloezer, Boris F. *Gogol.* Paris, 1932.

Shick, A. *Nicolas Gogol—une vie de torments.* Sceaux, 1949.

Smirnova, O. N. "Etudes et Souvenirs." *La Nouvelle Revue.* Paris, 1885.

Troyat, Henri. *Sainte Russie. Souvenirs et reflexions.* Paris, 1956.

de Vogüé, E. M., and Louis Leger. *Inauguration du monument élévé à la mémoire de Nicolas Gogol à Moscou le neuf mai 1909.* Paris, 1909.

Webber, Jean-Paul. "Les transpositions du nez dans l'oeuvre de Gogol," *Nouvelle Nouvelle Revue Française* (1959), 108–20.

OTHER LANGUAGES

Borghese, Daria. *Gogol a Roma.* Florence, 1957.

Ferrer, Olga Prijevalinsky. "*Las Almas muertas* de Gogol y *Don Quijote.*" *Cuadernos de literatura* 7 (July-December 1950): 201–14.

Giaconi, Claudio. "Gogol y Thomas Wolfe." *Cuadernos americanos* 21(123):214–28.

———. *Un Hombre en la trampa* (Gogol). Santiago, Chile, 1960.

Lo Gatto, Ettore. *Storia della letteratura Russa.* 5:3–137. Rome, 1935.

Milano, Paolo. *Il Lettore di professione.* Milan, 1960.

Pacini Savoj, Leone. "La Povest' o Kapitana Kopejkine." Rome, 1958.

————. "Il 'Revisore' e la 'Follia mistica' gogoliana." *Ricerche slavistiche* 1 (Rome, 1952): 3–21.

Pappacena, Enrico. *Gogol.* Milan, 1930.

Steffensen, Eigil. *Idé og vikkelighed i Gogol's kunst.* Copenhagen, 1967.

Vito, Mosca. "Il poema di Gogol." *Rassegna nazionale* Ser. 3., no. 18 (Rome, 1933): 317–22.

ABOUT THE AUTHOR

Nikolai Gogol was born in the province of Poltava, in southern Russia, on April 1, 1809. He was educated at the gymnasium at Niezhin, where he began writing as an adolescent. In 1828 he went to St. Petersburg, where he made an unsuccessful attempt at a career on the stage. In 1830 he published the first of the stories which subsequently appeared under the title of *Evenings on a Farm near Dikanka*. This work immediately obtained a great success. Gogol was appointed to a professorship in the University of St. Petersburg, where he taught history with no distinction and for a very short time. In 1835 he resigned and subsequently traveled to Western Europe, where he resided, especially in Rome, while working on essays, stories, and novellas. The first part of his novel *Dead Souls* appeared in 1842. In 1848 he made a pilgrimage to Jerusalem, and on his return, settled at Moscow, where he died on March 4, 1852.

ABOUT THE EDITOR

LEONARD J. KENT was born in Brooklyn, New York, in 1930. He took a bachelor's degree from Long Island University, a master's degree from New York University, and a doctorate in comparative literature from Yale University. He has taught on all levels in public and private institutions, was a professor of English and Dean of the Graduate School at California State University, in Chico, and is currently professor of English at Quinnipiac College, Hamden, Connecticut, where he also served as President from 1971 to 1977. Among other works, he has edited and revised (with Nina Berberova) the translation of *Anna Karenina*, edited and translated (with Elizabeth C. Knight) *The Selected Writings of E. T. A. Hoffmann*, written *The Subconscious in Gogol and Dostoevskij, and its Antecedents*, and authored some two dozen articles and reviews.